SUPERNATURAL
SHERLOCKS

Other Books by Nick Rennison

Pocket Essentials
Sigmund Freud
Peter Mark Roget: The Man Who Became a Book
Robin Hood: Myth, History & Culture
A Short History of Polar Exploration

No Exit Press
The Rivals of Sherlock
The Rivals of Dracula

SUPERNATURAL SHERLOCKS

STORIES FROM
The GOLDEN AGE of the OCCULT DETECTIVE

EDITED AND INTRODUCED BY
NICK RENNISON

NO EXIT PRESS

First published in 2017 by No Exit Press,
an imprint of Oldcastle Books Ltd,
PO Box 394, Harpenden,
Herts, AL5 1XJ
noexit.co.uk

A CIP catalogue record for this book is available from the British Library.

ISBN
978-1-84344-975-1 (print)
978-1-84344-976-8 (epub)
978-1-84344-977-5 (kindle)
978-1-84344-978-2 (pdf)

2 4 6 8 10 9 7 5 3 1

Typeset by Avocet Typeset, Somerton, Somerset, TA11 6RT
in 11.25pt Bembo
Printed and bound in Denmark by Nørhaven

CONTENTS

INTRODUCTION

What exactly *is* an occult detective? In the most basic definition, an occult detective is a fictional character who investigates mysteries of the supernatural rather than the natural world. Such psychic sleuths have been familiar figures in popular literature since the nineteenth century. The origins of what I have chosen to call 'Supernatural Sherlocks' lie outside the time parameters of this anthology. Before the 1880s there were characters who can retrospectively be described as occult detectives. As early as the 1830s, the Welsh lawyer, MP and novelist Samuel Warren published a series of tales in *Blackwoods Magazine* narrated by a doctor whose case files involve most of the standard themes of Gothic literature from lunacy and alcoholism to ghosts and grave robbing. The best of Warren's stories mix the occult and the macabre into a satisfyingly lurid brew. They were very popular in the middle decades of the nineteenth century, both in Britain and in America, where Edgar Allan Poe read them, although he did dismiss them as 'shamefully ill-written'. Fitz-James O'Brien, an Irish writer who emigrated from his native land to the United States in the 1850s and was killed in the American Civil War, wrote a large number of fantastical and weird stories in his short literary career. Two of them ('The Pot of Tulips' and 'What Was It? A Mystery') feature a character named Harry Escott who uses the skills of a detective to unravel supernatural mysteries. Dr Martin Hesselius, who appears in Sheridan Le Fanu's novella 'Green Tea' and acts as a framing narrator for the other stories in the 1872 volume *In a Glass Darkly*, is another pioneering supernatural investigator.

However, it was at the end of the nineteenth century, that the occult detective really came into his (or her) own. These were the years in which Conan Doyle's Sherlock Holmes short stories were first published and became so astonishingly successful that they inspired innumerable imitators. They were also years which saw a flourishing interest in the supernatural. Mediums such as Daniel Douglas Home, renowned for his supposed ability to levitate and to communicate with the dead, were famous figures, celebrated in newspapers and magazines, and lionised by high society. The Society for Psychical Research, the first organisation of its kind in the world, was founded in London in 1882. It was not some grouping from the lunatic fringe, populated exclusively by eccentrics and the barely sane. Its founders included leading scientists and academics of the day. Its first president was the Cambridge philosopher and economist Henry Sidgwick and early members included the chemist William Crookes, the physicist Oliver Lodge and the American psychologist William James, older brother of the novelist Henry James.

The growth in interest in the scientific investigation of the supernatural and paranormal was matched by an increasing fascination for ghost stories. Tales of ghosts and hauntings have, of course, been around as long as men, women and children have gathered around a fireside to cheer their spirits and keep the darkness at bay. All cultures have examples of them. Spirits of the dead can be found in the Bible and in the works of Homer. They exist in Japanese literature, in the mediaeval Arabic stories of the *One Thousand and One Nights* and in the drama of Renaissance Europe. Ghouls and ghosts flourished in the Gothic fiction of the late eighteenth and early nineteenth centuries. Edgar Allan Poe and Sheridan Le Fanu picked up themes from Gothic fiction and developed them in their stories. Dickens spotted the commercial potential in ghost stories and began to produce his own examples, most famously *A Christmas Carol*. However, the 'Golden Age' of the ghost story began in the last decades of the nineteenth century when writers began to fill the pages of the periodical press with tales of haunted houses and spectral visitors from another world.

In the 1890s a new sub-genre emerged from the mass of fiction that was produced for this magazine market. It mingled elements of the detective story, as newly popularised by Conan Doyle, and the ghost story. The occult detective – in the sense of someone who was a specialised investigator of supernatural mysteries – was born. Arabella Kenealy's character Lord Syfret, who first appeared in stories published in *Ludgate Magazine* in 1896, had some of the characteristics of an occult detective but it is generally agreed that the first fully-fledged occult detective was Flaxman Low. Low was created by the mother-and-son writing team of Kate and Hesketh Prichard, working under the pseudonyms of E and H Heron, and made his bow in a series of stories published in *Pearson's Magazine* in 1898. These were then collected the following year in a volume entitled *Ghosts: Being the Experiences of Flaxman Low*. The Prichards' character, like so many others of the period, owed much to Sherlock Holmes but he had his own originality. Many more followed in his footsteps.

Over the next two decades, a regiment of occult detectives lined up to do battle with the forces of darkness. John Silence, 'physician extraordinary' as the subtitle of a 1908 collection of stories described him, was the creation of Algernon Blackwood, one of the twentieth century's most gifted authors of supernatural fiction. (Blackwood had earlier created a character named Jim Shorthouse who appeared in four short stories and had some of the attributes of an occult detective.) LT Meade and Robert Eustace's Diana Marburg was a clairvoyant who investigated crimes and mysteries. The prolific pulp fiction writer Victor Rousseau, using the pseudonym HM Egbert, published a dozen short stories in various American newspapers in 1910 (reprinted in the 1920s in the legendary pulp magazine *Weird Tales*) which featured an investigator of supernatural mysteries named Dr Ivan Brodsky.

Many of these occult detectives, like their counterparts in standard detective fiction, had particular gifts or qualities which contributed to their investigative successes. Harold Begbie's Andrew Latter, who appeared in six short stories published in *London Magazine* in 1904, had the ability to enter a dream-world, moving through it to access information hidden from others. Alice and Claude Askew's Aylmer Vance, with his Dr Watson-like sidekick Dexter, who appeared in stories published in a magazine called *The Weekly Tale-Teller* in 1914, was the most obviously Sherlockian of the occult detectives. Perhaps the most famous of these pre-First World War psychic sleuths was Carnacki the Ghost Finder, hero of stories by William Hope Hodgson which were published mostly in *The Idler* in 1910 and collected into book form three years later. More than any other occult detective of the period, Carnacki has become a recurring figure in popular culture. Contemporary writers have written new Carnacki stories and the ghost finder is a member of the 'League of Extraordinary Gentlemen' in Alan Moore's graphic novel of that name.

Writers who have proved much more famous for other work also wrote occult detective stories. Under his pen-name of Sax Rohmer, Arthur Ward invented the oriental criminal mastermind Fu Manchu but he was also the creator in 1913 of Moris Klaw, a clairvoyant detective who dreamt the solutions to weird mysteries. During the First World War, Aleister Crowley, the occultist and practising magician who was later dubbed the 'Wickedest Man in the World', was forced by poverty to turn his hand to writing fiction. His stories of a philosopher-cum-mystic-cum-psychic detective named Simon Iff were first published in a magazine in 1917 and have recently been collected in book form.

The First World War, with its appalling toll of young lives, stimulated interest in ideas of life beyond the grave. So many men had died and those who had loved them sought reasons for their losses. Many looked for reassurance that the souls of the dead lived on. Traditional religions could not always provide the comfort required and spiritualism and other alternative belief systems flourished. In this context, stories of the supernatural

INTRODUCTION

in general – and of supernatural investigators in particular –
continued to find a wide readership. Many of the new writers
of occult detective stories in the 1920s were women. The actress
and author Ella Scrymsour published a series of tales about
Shiela Crerar, a young Scotswoman with psychic abilities. The
impressively named Rose Champion de Crespigny created an
occult detective called Norton Vyse and Jessie Douglas Kerruish
published a still readable novel entitled *The Undying Monster*, made
into a Hollywood horror movie in the 1940s, which featured
Luna Bartendale, a woman of many psychic abilities, and her
investigations into an outbreak of werewolfism. However, the
best known of these female writers was Dion Fortune. Fortune is
still a familiar name on the New Age shelves of British bookshops
and her works of occult and magical philosophy, with titles like
The Cosmic Doctrine and *Moon Magic*, still find a readership seventy
years after her death. In the 1920s, she also published a series of
enjoyable stories about a multi-talented psychic sleuth and healer
called Dr John Taverner.

Fortune was able to find a place for her Taverner stories in the
traditional periodical press (they appeared in *Royal Magazine*) but
this market for writers of the supernatural, so flourishing in the
late Victorian and Edwardian eras, now began its slow decline.
In contrast, the pulp magazine grew in popularity, particularly in
America. From the 1920s onward, the occult detective was more
likely to be found in the pages of *Weird Tales* than in, say, *Pearson's
Magazine* or *The Strand Magazine*. An ideal example is Henry S
Whitehead's Gerald Canevin, one of whose adventures I have
included in this anthology. In many ways, Whitehead was quite
a sophisticated writer and his prose would not have seemed out
of place in the more upmarket magazines. Perhaps, had he been
publishing twenty years earlier, that is where it would have been
found. As it was, his Canevin stories all appeared in the pulps,
mostly in *Weird Tales*.

In the decades since 1930, the year which I have chosen as
the cut-off point for this anthology of stories from the 'Golden

11

Age' of the occult detective, the psychic sleuth has continued to thrive. The American pulp writer Seabury Quinn created Jules de Grandin, an expert on the supernatural and former member of the French Sûreté, in 1925. Over the next quarter of a century, de Grandin appeared in more than ninety stories, mostly published in *Weird Tales*, in which he confronted a wide variety of ghosts, ghouls and things that go bump in the night. *Weird Tales* was also the first home of Manly Wade Wellman's creation John Thunstone, a wealthy scholar and occultist who battles assorted supernatural creatures.

Thunstone appeared in stories throughout the 1940s and, late in his career, Wade Wellman published two novels featuring the character. In the sixties, Joseph Payne Brennan introduced readers of the *Alfred Hitchcock's Mystery Magazine* to his occult detective Lucius Leffing who went on to appear in more than forty stories, many of them collected into hardback volumes.

Throughout the twentieth century, the occult detective has appeared not only in the traditional print media but in other media as well. In the 1930s and 1940s, radio had 'The Shadow' (briefly voiced by Orson Welles) and 'The Mysterious Traveller', both enigmatic narrators of often supernatural tales. TV has had its share of psychic investigators from 'Kolchak the Night Stalker' to Sam and Dean Winchester in *Supernatural*. What else are Mulder and Scully in *The X-Files* but occult detectives? Films such as Alan Parker's *Angel Heart* (based on a novel by William Hjörstberg) owe something to the tradition. And *Ghostbusters*, both in its 1980s and its 2016 incarnations, basically follows the activities of a gang of occult investigators, although ones with more sophisticated technology to call upon than Carnacki the Ghost Finder ever had. The occult detective has become a familiar figure in comics and graphic novels from *The Occult Files of Dr. Spektor* to *Hellblazer*. In the twenty-first century, although practitioners in print like Jim Butcher's Harry Dresden continue to flourish, it may well be in films, TV shows and games that the occult detective's future mostly lies.

INTRODUCTION

It should always be remembered, however, that the figure has a long history. In this volume, I have covered fifty years of that history. I have tried to bring together all kinds of stories from the 'Golden Age' of the occult detective. The anthology begins with tales (including ones by Rudyard Kipling and Sir Arthur Conan Doyle) which feature amateur investigators drawn by curiosity to look into paranormal phenomena. It moves on to include examples of the adventures of those like Flaxman Low, Thomas Carnacki and Aylmer Vance who were created as professional or semi-professional investigators of the supernatural. I have also chosen stories about intrepid souls who undertake one-off inquiries into haunted houses. They too deserve to be called 'Supernatural Sherlocks'. The result, I hope, is a collection of classic tales which can still raise the hair and chill the spines of modern readers.

THE MARK OF THE BEAST (1890)

Rudyard Kipling (1865–1936)

When, in 1907, Kipling became the first English-language writer to win the Nobel Prize for Literature, the Swedish Academy which awarded the prize called him 'the greatest genius in the realm of narrative that his country has produced in our times'. This genius showed itself as much, if not more, in short stories as in longer works of fiction like Kim. *In common with other writers of the late Victorian era, Kipling was fascinated by the weird and the supernatural, and a number of his stories demonstrate that. In two of these, this one and 'The Return of Imray', his character Strickland (who also appears in other non-supernatural tales) investigates occult mysteries. 'The Mark of the Beast' first appeared in* The Pioneer, *the English language newspaper in India for which Kipling had worked until leaving for London in 1889. It was later included in his collection of short stories entitled* Life's Handicap. *Its power lies as much in what is left unsaid as in what is bluntly stated. Kipling deliberately withholds information about exactly what happens. Partly this is because of the sensitivities of the age ('Several other things happened also, but they cannot be put down here') but mostly it is a deliberate strategy designed to leave a space in which the reader's imagination can go to work. When it was first published, 'The Mark of the Beast' was severely criticised. A reviewer in* The Spectator *called it 'curious but… loathsome'. Today we might be more concerned about its depiction of the Indian leper and his treatment than anything else but it remains a striking story.*

Your Gods and my Gods – do you or I know which are the stronger?
                                                        Native Proverb

EAST of Suez, some hold, the direct control of Providence ceases; Man being there handed over to the power of the Gods

14

and Devils of Asia, and the Church of England Providence only exercising an occasional and modified supervision in the case of Englishmen.

This theory accounts for some of the more unnecessary horrors of life in India: it may be stretched to explain my story.

My friend Strickland of the Police, who knows as much of natives of India as is good for any man, can bear witness to the facts of the case. Dumoise, our doctor, also saw what Strickland and I saw. The inference which he drew from the evidence was entirely incorrect. He is dead now; he died, in a rather curious manner, which has been elsewhere described.

When Fleete came to India he owned a little money and some land in the Himalayas, near a place called Dharmsala. Both properties had been left him by an uncle, and he came out to finance them. He was a big, heavy, genial, and inoffensive man. His knowledge of natives was, of course, limited, and he complained of the difficulties of the language.

He rode in from his place in the hills to spend New Year in the station, and he stayed with Strickland. On New Year's Eve there was a big dinner at the club, and the night was excusably wet. When men foregather from the uttermost ends of the Empire, they have a right to be riotous. The Frontier had sent down a contingent o' Catch-'em-Alive-O's who had not seen twenty white faces for a year, and were used to ride fifteen miles to dinner at the next Fort at the risk of a Khyberee bullet where their drinks should lie. They profited by their new security, for they tried to play pool with a curled-up hedgehog found in the garden, and one of them carried the marker round the room in his teeth. Half a dozen planters had come in from the south and were talking 'horse' to the Biggest Liar in Asia, who was trying to cap all their stories at once. Everybody was there, and there was a general closing up of ranks and taking stock of our losses in dead or disabled that had fallen during the past year. It was a very wet night, and I remember that we sang 'Auld Lang Syne' with our feet in the Polo Championship Cup, and our heads among the stars, and swore that we were all dear friends. Then some of us went away and annexed Burma, and some tried to open up the Soudan and were opened up by Fuzzies in that cruel scrub outside Suakim, and some found stars and medals, and some were married, which was bad, and some did other things which were worse, and the others of us stayed in our chains and strove to make money on insufficient experiences.

Fleete began the night with sherry and bitters, drank champagne steadily up to dessert, then raw, rasping Capri with all the strength of whisky, took Benedictine with his coffee, four or five whiskies and sodas to improve his pool strokes, beer and bones at half-past two, winding up with old brandy. Consequently, when he came out, at half-past three in the morning, into fourteen degrees of frost, he was very angry with his horse for coughing, and tried to leapfrog into the saddle. The horse broke away and went to his stables; so Strickland and I formed a Guard of Dishonour to take Fleete home.

Our road lay through the bazaar, close to a little temple of Hanuman, the Monkey-god, who is a leading divinity worthy of respect. All gods have good points, just as have all priests. Personally, I attach much importance to Hanuman, and am kind to his people – the great grey apes of the hills. One never knows when one may want a friend.

There was a light in the temple, and as we passed, we could hear voices of men chanting hymns. In a native temple, the priests rise at all hours of the night to do honour to their god. Before we could stop him, Fleete dashed up the steps, patted two priests on the back, and was gravely grinding the ashes of his cigar-butt into the forehead of the red stone image of Hanuman. Strickland tried to drag him out, but he sat down and said solemnly:

'Shee that? Mark of the B-beasht! *I* made it. Ishn't it fine?'

In half a minute the temple was alive and noisy, and Strickland, who knew what came of polluting gods, said that things might occur. He, by virtue of his official position, long residence in the country, and weakness for going among the natives, was known to the priests and he felt unhappy. Fleete sat on the ground and refused to move. He said that 'good old Hanuman' made a very soft pillow.

Then, without any warning, a Silver Man came out of a recess behind the image of the god. He was perfectly naked in that bitter, bitter cold, and his body shone like frosted silver, for he was what the Bible calls 'a leper as white as snow.' Also he had no face, because he was a leper of some years' standing and his disease was heavy upon him. We two stooped to haul Fleete up, and the temple was filling and filling with folk who seemed to spring from the earth, when the Silver Man ran in under our arms, making a noise exactly like the mewing of an otter, caught Fleete round the body and dropped his head on Fleete's breast before we could wrench him away. Then he retired to a corner and sat mewing while the crowd blocked all the doors.

The priests were very angry until the Silver Man touched Fleete. That nuzzling seemed to sober them.

At the end of a few minutes' silence one of the priests came to Strickland and said, in perfect English, 'Take your friend away. He has done with Hanuman, but Hanuman has not done with him.' The crowd gave room and we carried Fleete into the road.

Strickland was very angry. He said that we might all three have been knifed, and that Fleete should thank his stars that he had escaped without injury.

Fleete thanked no one. He said that he wanted to go to bed. He was gorgeously drunk.

We moved on, Strickland silent and wrathful, until Fleete was taken with violent shivering fits and sweating. He said that the smells of the bazaar were overpowering, and he wondered why slaughter-houses were permitted so near English residences. 'Can't you smell the blood?' said Fleete.

We put him to bed at last, just as the dawn was breaking, and Strickland invited me to have another whisky and soda. While we were drinking he talked of the trouble in the temple, and admitted that it baffled him completely. Strickland hates being mystified by natives, because his business in life is to overmatch them with their own weapons. He has not yet succeeded in doing this, but in fifteen or twenty years he will have made some small progress.

'They should have mauled us,' he said, 'instead of mewing at us. I wonder what they meant. I don't like it one little bit.'

I said that the Managing Committee of the temple would in all probability bring a criminal action against us for insulting their religion. There was a section of the Indian Penal Code which exactly met Fleete's offence. Strickland said he only hoped and prayed that they would do this. Before I left I looked into Fleete's room, and saw him lying on his right side, scratching his left breast. Then I went to bed cold, depressed, and unhappy, at seven o'clock in the morning.

At one o'clock I rode over to Strickland's house to inquire after Fleete's head. I imagined that it would be a sore one. Fleete was breakfasting and seemed unwell. His temper was gone, for he was abusing the cook for not supplying him with an underdone chop. A man who can eat raw meat after a wet night is a curiosity. I told Fleete this and he laughed.

'You breed queer mosquitoes in these parts,' he said. 'I've been bitten to pieces, but only in one place.'

'Let's have a look at the bite,' said Strickland. 'It may have gone down since this morning.'

While the chops were being cooked, Fleete opened his shirt and showed us, just over his left breast, a mark, the perfect double of the black rosettes – the five or six irregular blotches arranged in a circle – on a leopard's hide. Strickland looked and said, 'It was only pink this morning. It's grown black now.'

Fleete ran to a glass.

'By Jove!' he said, 'this is nasty. What is it?'

We could not answer. Here the chops came in, all red and juicy, and Fleete bolted three in a most offensive manner. He ate on his right grinders only, and threw his head over his right shoulder as he snapped the meat. When he had finished, it struck him that he had been behaving strangely, for he said apologetically, 'I don't think I ever felt so hungry in my life. I've bolted like an ostrich.'

After breakfast Strickland said to me, 'Don't go. Stay here, and stay for the night.'

Seeing that my house was not three miles from Strickland's, this request was absurd. But Strickland insisted, and was going to say something when Fleete interrupted by declaring in a shamefaced way that he felt hungry again. Strickland sent a man to my house to fetch over my bedding and a horse, and we three went down to Strickland's stables to pass the hours until it was time to go out for a ride. The man who has a weakness for horses never wearies of inspecting them; and when two men are killing time in this way they gather knowledge and lies the one from the other.

There were five horses in the stables, and I shall never forget the scene as we tried to look them over. They seemed to have gone mad. They reared and screamed and nearly tore up their pickets; they sweated and shivered and lathered and were distraught with fear. Strickland's horses used to know him as well as his dogs; which made the matter more curious. We left the stable for fear of the brutes throwing themselves in their panic. Then Strickland turned back and called me. The horses were still frightened, but they let us 'gentle' and make much of them, and put their heads in our bosoms.

'They aren't afraid of *us*,' said Strickland. 'D'you know, I'd give three months' pay if *Outrage* here could talk.'

But *Outrage* was dumb, and could only cuddle up to his master and blow out his nostrils, as is the custom of horses when they wish to explain things but can't. Fleete came up when we were in the stalls, and as soon as the horses saw him, their fright broke out afresh. It was all that we could do to escape from the place unkicked. Strickland said, 'They don't seem to love you, Fleete.'

'Nonsense,' said Fleete; 'my mare will follow me like a dog.' He went to her; she was in a loose-box; but as he slipped the bars she plunged, knocked him down, and broke away into the garden. I laughed, but Strickland was not amused. He took his moustache in both fists and pulled at it till it nearly came out. Fleete, instead of going off to chase his property, yawned, saying that he felt sleepy. He went to the house to lie down, which was a foolish way of spending New Year's Day.

Strickland sat with me in the stables and asked if I had noticed anything peculiar in Fleete's manner. I said that he ate his food like a beast; but that this might have been the result of living alone in the hills out of the reach of society as refined and elevating as ours for instance. Strickland was not amused. I do not think that he listened to me, for his next sentence referred to the mark on Fleete's breast, and I said that it might have been caused by blister-flies, or that it was possibly a birth-mark newly born and now visible for the first time. We both agreed that it was unpleasant to look at, and Strickland found occasion to say that I was a fool.

'I can't tell you what I think now,' said he, 'because you would call me a madman; but you must stay with me for the next few days, if you can. I want you to watch Fleete, but don't tell me what you think till I have made up my mind.'

'But I am dining out to-night,' I said.

'So am I,' said Strickland, 'and so is Fleete. At least if he doesn't change his mind.'

We walked about the garden smoking, but saying nothing – because we were friends, and talking spoils good tobacco – till our pipes were out. Then we went to wake up Fleete. He was wide awake and fidgeting about his room.

'I say, I want some more chops,' he said. 'Can I get them?'

We laughed and said, 'Go and change. The ponies will be round in a minute.'

'All right,' said Fleete. 'I'll go when I get the chops – underdone ones, mind.'

He seemed to be quite in earnest. It was four o'clock, and we had had breakfast at one; still, for a long time, he demanded those underdone chops. Then he changed into riding clothes and went out into the verandah. His pony – the mare had not been caught – would not let him come near. All three horses were unmanageable – mad with fear – and finally Fleete said that he would stay at home and get something to eat. Strickland and I rode out wondering. As we passed the temple of Hanuman, the Silver Man came out and mewed at us.

'He is not one of the regular priests of the temple,' said Strickland. 'I think I should peculiarly like to lay my hands on him.'

There was no spring in our gallop on the racecourse that evening. The horses were stale, and moved as though they had been ridden out.

'The fright after breakfast has been too much for them,' said Strickland.

That was the only remark he made through the remainder of the ride. Once or twice I think he swore to himself; but that did not count.

We came back in the dark at seven o'clock, and saw that there were no lights in the bungalow. 'Careless ruffians my servants are!' said Strickland.

My horse reared at something on the carriage drive, and Fleete stood up under its nose.

'What are you doing, grovelling about the garden?' said Strickland.

But both horses bolted and nearly threw us. We dismounted by the stables and returned to Fleete, who was on his hands and knees under the orange-bushes.

'What the devil's wrong with you?' said Strickland.

'Nothing, nothing in the world,' said Fleete, speaking very quickly and thickly. 'I've been gardening – botanising you know. The smell of the earth is delightful. I think I'm going for a walk – a long walk – all night.'

Then I saw that there was something excessively out of order somewhere, and I said to Strickland, 'I am not dining out.'

'Bless you!' said Strickland. 'Here, Fleete, get up. You'll catch fever there. Come in to dinner and let's have the lamps lit. We'll all dine at home.'

Fleete stood up unwillingly, and said, 'No lamps – no lamps. It's much nicer here. Let's dine outside and have some more chops – lots of 'em and underdone – bloody ones with gristle.'

Now a December evening in Northern India is bitterly cold, and Fleete's suggestion was that of a maniac.

'Come in,' said Strickland sternly. 'Come in at once.'

Fleete came, and when the lamps were brought, we saw that he was literally plastered with dirt from head to foot. He must have been rolling in the garden. He shrank from the light and went to his room. His eyes were horrible to look at. There was a green light behind them, not in them, if you understand, and the man's lower lip hung down.

Strickland said, 'There is going to be trouble – big trouble – to-night. Don't you change your riding-things.'

We waited and waited for Fleete's reappearance, and ordered dinner in the meantime. We could hear him moving about his own room, but there was no light there. Presently from the room came the long-drawn howl of a wolf.

People write and talk lightly of blood running cold and hair standing up and things of that kind. Both sensations are too horrible to be trifled with. My heart stopped as though a knife had been driven through it, and Strickland turned as white as the tablecloth.

The howl was repeated, and was answered by another howl far across the fields.

That set the gilded roof on the horror. Strickland dashed into Fleete's room. I followed, and we saw Fleete getting out of the window. He made beast-noises in the back of his throat. He could not answer us when we shouted at him. He spat.

I don't quite remember what followed, but I think that Strickland must have stunned him with the long boot-jack or else I should never have been able to sit on his chest. Fleete could not speak, he could only snarl, and his snarls were those of a wolf, not of a man. The human spirit must have been giving way all day and have died out with the twilight. We were dealing with a beast that had once been Fleete.

The affair was beyond any human and rational experience. I tried to say 'Hydrophobia', but the word wouldn't come, because I knew that I was lying.

We bound this beast with leather thongs of the punkah-rope, and tied its thumbs and big toes together, and gagged it with a shoe-horn, which makes a very efficient gag if you know how to arrange it. Then we carried it into the dining-room, and sent a man to Dumoise, the doctor, telling him to come over at once. After we had despatched the messenger and were drawing breath, Strickland said, 'It's no good. This isn't any doctor's work.' I, also, knew that he spoke the truth.

The beast's head was free, and it threw it about from side to side. Anyone entering the room would have believed that we were curing a wolf's pelt. That was the most loathsome accessory of all.

Strickland sat with his chin in the heel of his fist, watching the beast as it wriggled on the ground, but saying nothing. The shirt had been torn open in the scuffle and showed the black rosette mark on the left breast. It stood out like a blister.

In the silence of the watching we heard something without mewing like a she-otter. We both rose to our feet, and, I answer for myself, not Strickland, felt sick – actually and physically sick. We told each other, as did the men in *Pinafore*, that it was the cat.

Dumoise arrived, and I never saw a little man so unprofessionally shocked. He said that it was a heart-rending case of hydrophobia, and that nothing could be done. At least any palliative measures would only prolong the agony. The beast was foaming at the mouth. Fleete, as we told Dumoise, had been bitten by dogs once or twice. Any man who keeps half a dozen terriers must expect a nip now and again. Dumoise could offer no help. He could only certify that Fleete was dying of hydrophobia. The beast was then howling, for it had managed to spit out the shoe-horn. Dumoise said that he would be ready to certify to the cause of death, and that the end was certain. He was a good little man, and he offered to remain with us; but Strickland refused the kindness. He did not wish to poison Dumoise's New Year. He would only ask him not to give the real cause of Fleete's death to the public.

So Dumoise left, deeply agitated; and as soon as the noise of the cart-wheels had died away, Strickland told me, in a whisper, his suspicions. They were so wildly improbable that he dared not say them out aloud; and I, who entertained all Strickland's beliefs, was so ashamed of owning to them that I pretended to disbelieve.

'Even if the Silver Man had bewitched Fleete for polluting the image of Hanuman, the punishment could not have fallen so quickly.'

As I was whispering this the cry outside the house rose again, and the beast fell into a fresh paroxysm of struggling till we were afraid that the thongs that held it would give way.

'Watch!' said Strickland. 'If this happens six times I shall take the law into my own hands. I order you to help me.'

He went into his room and came out in a few minutes with the barrels of an old shot-gun, a piece of fishing-line, some thick cord, and his heavy wooden bedstead. I reported that the convulsions had followed the cry by two seconds in each case, and the beast seemed perceptibly weaker.

Strickland muttered, 'But he can't take away the life! He can't take away the life!'

I said, though I knew that I was arguing against myself, 'It may be a cat. It must be a cat. If the Silver Man is responsible, why does he dare to come here?'

Strickland arranged the wood on the hearth, put the gun-barrels into the glow of the fire, spread the twine on the table and broke a walking stick in two. There was one yard of fishing line, gut, lapped with wire, such as is used for *mahseer*-fishing, and he tied the two ends together in a loop.

Then he said, 'How can we catch him? He must be taken alive and unhurt.'

I said that we must trust in Providence, and go out softly with polo-sticks into the shrubbery at the front of the house. The man or animal that made the cry was evidently moving round the house as regularly as a night-watchman. We could wait in the bushes till he came by and knock him over.

Strickland accepted this suggestion, and we slipped out from a bath-room window into the front verandah and then across the carriage drive into the bushes.

In the moonlight we could see the leper coming round the corner of the house. He was perfectly naked, and from time to time he mewed and stopped to dance with his shadow. It was an unattractive sight, and thinking of poor Fleete, brought to such degradation by so foul a creature, I put away all my doubts and resolved to help Strickland from the heated gun-barrels to the loop of twine – from the loins to the head and back again – with all tortures that might be needful.

The leper halted in the front porch for a moment and we jumped out on him with the sticks. He was wonderfully strong, and we were afraid that he might escape or be fatally injured before we caught him. We had an idea that lepers were frail creatures, but this proved to be incorrect. Strickland knocked his legs from under him and I put my foot on his neck. He mewed hideously, and even through my riding-boots I could feel that his flesh was not the flesh of a clean man.

He struck at us with his hand and feet-stumps. We looped the lash of a dog-whip round him, under the armpits, and dragged him backwards into the hall and so into the dining-room where the beast lay. There we tied him with trunk-straps. He made no attempt to escape, but mewed.

When we confronted him with the beast the scene was beyond description. The beast doubled backwards into a bow as though he had been poisoned with strychnine, and moaned in the most pitiable fashion. Several other things happened also, but they cannot be put down here.

'I think I was right,' said Strickland. 'Now we will ask him to cure this case.'

But the leper only mewed. Strickland wrapped a towel round his hand and took the gun-barrels out of the fire. I put the half of the broken walking stick through the loop of fishing-line and buckled the leper comfortably to Strickland's bedstead. I understood then how men and women and little children can endure to see a witch burnt alive; for the beast was moaning on the floor, and though the Silver Man had no face, you could see horrible feelings passing through the slab that took its place, exactly as waves of heat play across red-hot iron – gun-barrels for instance.

Strickland shaded his eyes with his hands for a moment and we got to work. This part is not to be printed.

* * * * *

The dawn was beginning to break when the leper spoke. His mewings had not been satisfactory up to that point. The beast had fainted from exhaustion and the house was very still. We unstrapped the leper and told him to take away the evil spirit. He crawled to the beast and laid his hand upon the left breast. That was all. Then he fell face down and whined, drawing in his breath as he did so.

We watched the face of the beast, and saw the soul of Fleete coming back into the eyes. Then a sweat broke out on the forehead and the eyes – they were human eyes – closed. We waited for an hour but Fleete still slept. We carried him to his room and bade the leper go, giving him the bedstead, and the sheet on the bedstead to cover his nakedness, the gloves and the towels with which we had touched him, and the whip that had been hooked round his body. He put the sheet about him and went out into the early morning without speaking or mewing.

Strickland wiped his face and sat down. A night-gong, far away in the city, made seven o'clock.

'Exactly four-and-twenty hours!' said Strickland. 'And I've done enough to ensure my dismissal from the service, besides permanent quarters in a lunatic asylum. Do you believe that we are awake?'

The red-hot gun-barrel had fallen on the floor and was singeing the carpet. The smell was entirely real.

That morning at eleven we two together went to wake up Fleete. We looked and saw that the black leopard-rosette on his chest had disappeared. He was very drowsy and tired, but as soon as he saw us, he said, 'Oh! Confound you fellows. Happy New Year to you. Never mix your liquors. I'm nearly dead.'

'Thanks for your kindness, but you're over time,' said Strickland. 'To-day is the morning of the second. You've slept the clock round with a vengeance.'

The door opened, and little Dumoise put his head in. He had come on foot, and fancied that we were laying out Fleete.

'I've brought a nurse,' said Dumoise. 'I suppose that she can come in for... what is necessary.'

'By all means,' said Fleete cheerily, sitting up in bed. 'Bring on your nurses.'

Dumoise was dumb. Strickland led him out and explained that there must have been a mistake in the diagnosis. Dumoise remained dumb and left the house hastily. He considered that his professional reputation had been injured, and was inclined to make a personal matter of the recovery. Strickland went out too. When he came back, he said that he had been to call on the Temple of Hanuman to offer redress for the pollution of the god, and had been solemnly assured that no white man had ever touched the idol and that he was an incarnation of all the virtues labouring under a delusion.

'What do you think?' said Strickland.

I said, 'There are more things...'

But Strickland hates that quotation. He says that I have worn it threadbare.

One other curious thing happened which frightened me as much as anything in all the night's work. When Fleete was dressed he came into the dining-room and sniffed. He had a quaint trick of moving his nose when he sniffed. 'Horrid doggy smell, here,' said he. 'You should really keep those terriers of

27

yours in better order. Try sulphur, Strick.'

But Strickland did not answer. He caught hold of the back of a chair, and, without warning, went into an amazing fit of hysterics. It is terrible to see a strong man overtaken with hysteria. Then it struck me that we had fought for Fleete's soul with the Silver Man in that room, and had disgraced ourselves as Englishmen for ever, and I laughed and gasped and gurgled just as shamefully as Strickland, while Fleete thought that we had both gone mad. We never told him what we had done.

Some years later, when Strickland had married and was a church-going member of society for his wife's sake, we reviewed the incident dispassionately, and Strickland suggested that I should put it before the public.

I cannot myself see that this step is likely to clear up the mystery; because, in the first place, no one will believe a rather unpleasant story, and, in the second, it is well known to every right-minded man that the gods of the heathen are stone and brass, and any attempt to deal with them otherwise is justly condemned.

IN KROPFSBERG KEEP (1895)

Ralph Adams Cram (1863–1942)

Ralph Adams Cram's main claim to fame is as an architect. Born in New Hampshire, he became one of America's leading designers of buildings in the Gothic Revival style. His churches can be found all over the USA from New York and Boston to Denver and Houston. Most of his published writings were on the subject of architecture but, as a young man, he wrote some fiction. Black Spirits and White, *first published in 1895, was a collection of ghost stories, many of which drew on his memories of travelling in Europe to study architecture. 'The Dead Valley', one of the stories in this volume, is about two twelve-year-old boys in rural Sweden who journey to the next village from theirs and blunder into the terrifying landscape which provides the tale with its title. It is a minor classic of supernatural fiction and was described by H. P. Lovecraft as achieving 'a memorably potent degree of vague regional horror'. Most of the other stories describe the experiences of the narrator and his friend Tom Rendel (clearly based on Cram himself and his friend Thomas Randall) as they traipse around Europe in search of the Gothic. 'In Kropfsberg Keep' purports to be a story they heard in the Tyrol and features two other young men who, with fatal consequences, take it upon themselves to investigate the ghosts reputed to haunt a ruined castle.*

To the traveller from Innsbrück to Munich, up the lovely valley of the silver Inn, many castles appear, one after another, each on its beetling cliff or gentle hill – appear and disappear, melting into the dark fir trees that grow so thickly on every side – Laneck, Lichtwer, Ratholtz, Tratzberg, Matzen, Kropfsberg, gathering close around the entrance to the dark and wonderful Zillerthal.

But to us – Tom Rendel and myself – there are two castles only: not the gorgeous and princely Ambras, nor the noble old

Tratzberg, with its crowded treasures of solemn and splendid mediævalism; but little Matzen, where eager hospitality forms the new life of a never-dead chivalry, and Kropfsberg, ruined, tottering, blasted by fire and smitten with grievous years – a dead thing, and haunted – full of strange legends, and eloquent of mystery and tragedy.

We were visiting the von C—s at Matzen, and gaining our first wondering knowledge of the courtly, cordial castle life in the Tyrol – of the gentle and delicate hospitality of noble Austrians. Brixleg had ceased to be but a mark on a map, and had become a place of rest and delight, a home for homeless wanderers on the face of Europe, while Schloss Matzen was a synonym for all that was gracious and kindly and beautiful in life. The days moved on in a golden round of riding and driving and shooting: down to Landl and Thiersee for chamois, across the river to the magic Achensee, up the Zillerthal, across the Schmerner Joch, even to the railway station at Steinach. And in the evenings after the late dinners in the upper hall where the sleepy hounds leaned against our chairs looking at us with suppliant eyes, in the evenings when the fire was dying away in the hooded fireplace in the library, stories. Stories, and legends, and fairy tales, while the stiff old portraits changed countenance constantly under the flickering firelight, and the sound of the drifting Inn came softly across the meadows far below.

If ever I tell the story of Schloss Matzen, then will be the time to paint the too inadequate picture of this fair oasis in the desert of travel and tourists and hotels; but just now it is Kropfsberg the Silent that is of greater importance, for it was only in Matzen that the story was told by Fräulein E— the gold-haired niece of Frau von C— one hot evening in July, when we were sitting in the great west window of the drawing-room after a long ride up the Stallenthal. All the windows were open to catch the faint wind, and we had sat for a long time watching the Otzethaler Alps turn rose-colour over distant Innsbrück, then deepen to violet as the sun went down and the white mists rose slowly until Lichtwer and Laneck and Kropfsberg rose like craggy islands in a silver sea.

And this is the story as Fräulein E— told it to us – the Story of Kropfsberg Keep.

★ ★ ★ ★ ★

A great many years ago, soon after my grandfather died, and Matzen came to us, when I was a little girl, and so young that I remember nothing of the affair except as something dreadful that frightened me very much, two young men who had studied painting with my grandfather came down to Brixleg from Munich, partly to paint, and partly to amuse themselves – 'ghost-hunting' as they said, for they were very sensible young men and prided themselves on it, laughing at all kinds of 'superstition', and particularly at that form which believed in ghosts and feared them. They had never seen a real ghost, you know, and they belonged to a certain set of people who believed nothing they had not seen themselves – which always seemed to me *very* conceited. Well, they knew that we had lots of beautiful castles here in the 'lower valley', and they assumed, and rightly, that every castle has at least *one* ghost story connected with it, so they chose this as their hunting ground, only the game they sought was ghosts, not chamois. Their plan was to visit every place that was supposed to be haunted, and to meet every reputed ghost, and prove that it really was no ghost at all.

There was a little inn down in the village then, kept by an old man named Peter Rosskopf, and the two young men made this their headquarters. The very first night they began to draw from the old innkeeper all that he knew of legends and ghost stories connected with Brixleg and its castles, and as he was a most garrulous old gentleman he filled them with the wildest delight by his stories of the ghosts of the castles about the mouth of the Zillerthal. Of course the old man believed every word he said, and you can imagine his horror and amazement when, after telling his guests the particularly blood-curdling story of Kropfsberg and its haunted keep, the elder of the two boys, whose surname I have forgotten, but whose Christian name was Rupert, calmly said, 'Your story is most satisfactory: we will sleep in Kropfsberg Keep to-morrow night, and you must provide us with all that we may need to make ourselves comfortable.'

The old man nearly fell into the fire. 'What for a blockhead are you?' he cried, with big eyes. 'The keep is haunted by Count Albert's ghost, I tell you!'

'That is why we are going there to-morrow night; we wish to make the acquaintance of Count Albert.'

'But there was a man stayed there once, and in the morning he was dead.'

'Very silly of him; there are two of us, and we carry revolvers.'

'But it's a *ghost*, I tell you,' almost screamed the innkeeper; 'are ghosts afraid of firearms?'

'Whether they are or not, we are *not* afraid of *them*.'

Here the younger boy broke in – he was named Otto von Kleist. I remember the name, for I had a music teacher once by that name. He abused the poor old man shamefully; told him that they were going to spend the night in Kropfsberg in spite of Count Albert and Peter Rosskopf, and that he might as well make the most of it and earn his money with cheerfulness.

In a word, they finally bullied the old fellow into submission, and when the morning came he set about preparing for the suicide, as he considered it, with sighs and mutterings and ominous shakings of the head.

You know the condition of the castle now – nothing but scorched walls and crumbling piles of fallen masonry. Well, at the time I tell you of, the keep was still partially preserved. It was finally burned out only a few years ago by some wicked boys who came over from Jenbach to have a good time. But when the ghost hunters came, though the two lower floors had fallen into the crypt, the third floor remained. The peasants said it *could* not fall, but that it would stay until the Day of Judgment, because it was in the room above that the wicked Count Albert sat watching the flames destroy the great castle and his imprisoned guests, and where he finally hung himself in a suit of armour that had belonged to his mediæval ancestor, the first Count Kropfsberg.

No one dared touch him, and so he hung there for twelve years, and all the time venturesome boys and daring men used to creep up the turret steps and stare awfully through the chinks in the door at that ghostly mass of steel that held within itself the body of a murderer and suicide, slowly returning to the dust from which it was made. Finally it disappeared, none knew whither, and for another dozen years the room stood empty but for the old furniture and the rotting hangings.

So, when the two men climbed the stairway to the haunted room, they found a very different state of things from what exists now. The room was absolutely as it was left the night Count Albert burned the castle, except that all trace of the suspended suit of armour and its ghastly contents had vanished.

No one had dared to cross the threshold, and I suppose that for forty years no living thing had entered that dreadful room.

On one side stood a vast canopied bed of black wood, the damask hangings of which were covered with mould and mildew. All the clothing of the bed was in perfect order, and on it lay a book, open, and face downward. The only other furniture in the room consisted of several old chairs, a carved oak chest, and a big inlaid table covered with books and papers, and on one corner two or three bottles with dark solid sediment at the bottom, and a glass, also dark with the dregs of wine that had been poured out almost half a century before. The tapestry on the walls was green with mould, but hardly torn or otherwise defaced, for although the heavy dust of forty years lay on everything the room had been preserved from further harm. No spider web was to be seen, no trace of nibbling mice, not even a dead moth or fly on the sills of the diamond-paned windows; life seemed to have shunned the room utterly and finally.

The men looked at the room curiously, and, I am sure, not without some feelings of awe and unacknowledged fear; but, whatever they may have felt of instinctive shrinking, they said nothing, and quickly set to work to make the room passably inhabitable. They decided to touch nothing that had not absolutely to be changed, and therefore they made for themselves a bed in one corner with the mattress and linen from the inn. In the great fireplace they piled a lot of wood on the caked ashes of a fire dead for forty years, turned the old chest into a table, and laid out on it all their arrangements for the evening's amusement: food, two or three bottles of wine, pipes and tobacco, and the chess-board that was their inseparable travelling companion.

All this they did themselves: the innkeeper would not even come within the walls of the outer court; he insisted that he had washed his hands of the whole affair, the silly dunderheads might go to their death their own way. *He* would not aid and abet them. One of the stable boys brought the basket of food and the wood and the bed up the winding stone stairs, to be sure, but neither money nor prayers nor threats would bring him within the walls of the accursed place, and he stared fearfully at the hare-brained boys as they worked around the dead old room preparing for the night that was coming so fast.

At length everything was in readiness, and after a final visit to the inn for dinner Rupert and Otto started at sunset for the Keep. Half the village went with them, for Peter Rosskopf had babbled the whole story to an open-mouthed crowd of wondering men and women, and as to an execution the awe-struck crowd followed the two boys dumbly, curious to see if they surely would put their plan into execution. But none went farther than the outer doorway of the stairs, for it was already growing twilight. In absolute silence they watched the two foolhardy youths with their lives in their hands enter the terrible Keep, standing like a tower in the midst of the piles of stones that had once formed walls joining it with the mass of the castle beyond. When a moment later a light showed itself in the high windows above, they sighed resignedly and went their ways, to wait stolidly until morning should come and prove the truth of their fears and warnings.

In the meantime the ghost hunters built a huge fire, lighted their many candles, and sat down to await developments. Rupert afterwards told my uncle that they really felt no fear whatever, only a contemptuous curiosity, and they ate their supper with good appetite and an unusual relish. It was a long evening. They played many games of chess, waiting for midnight. Hour passed after hour, and nothing occurred to interrupt the monotony of the evening. Ten, eleven, came and went – it was almost midnight. They piled more wood in the fireplace, lighted new candles, looked to their pistols – and waited. The clocks in the village struck twelve; the sound coming muffled through the high, deep-embrasured windows. Nothing happened, nothing to break the heavy silence; and with a feeling of disappointed relief they looked at each other and acknowledged that they had met another rebuff.

Finally they decided that there was no use in sitting up and boring themselves any longer, they had much better rest; so Otto threw himself down on the mattress, falling almost immediately asleep. Rupert sat a little longer, smoking, and watching the stars creep along behind the shattered glass and the bent leads of the lofty windows; watching the fire fall together, and the strange shadows move mysteriously on the mouldering walls. The iron hook in the oak beam, that crossed the ceiling midway, fascinated him, not with fear, but morbidly. So, it was from that hook that for twelve years, twelve long years of changing summer and winter, the body of Count Albert, murderer and suicide, hung in its strange casing of mediæval steel; moving a little at first, and turning gently while the fire died out on the hearth, while the ruins of the castle grew cold, and horrified peasants sought for the bodies of the score of gay, reckless, wicked guests whom Count Albert had gathered in Kropfsberg for a last debauch, gathered to their terrible and untimely death. What a strange and fiendish idea it was, the young, handsome noble who had ruined himself and his family in the society of the splendid debauchees, gathering them all together, men and women who had known only love and pleasure, for a glorious and awful riot of luxury, and then, when they were all dancing in the great ballroom, locking the doors and burning the whole castle about them, the while he sat in the great keep listening to their screams of agonised fear, watching the fire sweep from wing to wing until the whole mighty mass was one enormous and awful pyre, and then, clothing himself in his great-great-grandfather's armour, hanging himself in the midst of the ruins of what had been a proud and noble castle. So ended a great family, a great house.

But that was forty years ago.

He was growing drowsy; the light flickered and flared in the fireplace; one by one the candles went out; the shadows grew thick in the room. Why did that great iron hook stand out so plainly? Why did that dark shadow dance and quiver so mockingly behind it? – why – but he ceased to wonder at anything. He was asleep.

It seemed to him that he woke almost immediately; the fire still burned, though low and fitfully on the hearth. Otto was sleeping, breathing quietly and regularly; the shadows had gathered close around him, thick and murky; with every passing moment the light died in the fireplace; he felt stiff with cold. In the utter silence he heard the clock in the village strike two. He shivered with a sudden and irresistible feeling of fear, and abruptly turned and looked towards the hook in the ceiling.

Yes, It was there. He knew that It would be. It seemed quite natural, he would have been disappointed had he seen nothing; but now he knew that the story was true, knew that he was wrong, and that the dead *do* sometimes return to earth, for there, in the fast-deepening shadow, hung the black mass of wrought steel, turning a little now and then, with the light flickering on the tarnished and rusty metal. He watched it quietly; he hardly felt afraid; it was rather a sentiment of sadness and fatality that filled him, of gloomy forebodings of something unknown, unimaginable. He sat and watched the thing disappear in the gathering dark, his hand on his pistol as it lay by him on the great chest. There was no sound but the regular breathing of the sleeping boy on the mattress.

It had grown absolutely dark; a bat fluttered against the broken glass of the window. He wondered if he was growing mad, for – he hesitated to acknowledge it to himself – he heard music; far, curious music, a strange and luxurious dance, very faint, very vague, but unmistakable.

Like a flash of lightning came a jagged line of fire down the blank wall opposite him, a line that remained, that grew wider, that let a pale cold light into the room, showing him now all its details – the empty fireplace, where a thin smoke rose in a spiral from a bit of charred wood, the mass of the great bed, and, in the very middle, black against the curious brightness, the armoured man, or ghost, or devil, standing, not suspended, beneath the rusty hook. And with the rending of the wall the music grew more distinct, though sounding still very, very far away.

Count Albert raised his mailed hand and beckoned to him; then turned, and stood in the riven wall.

Without a word, Rupert rose and followed him, his pistol in hand. Count Albert passed through the mighty wall and disappeared in the unearthly light. Rupert followed mechanically. He felt the crushing of the mortar beneath his feet, the roughness of the jagged wall where he rested his hand to steady himself.

The keep rose absolutely isolated among the ruins, yet on passing through the wall Rupert found himself in a long, uneven corridor, the floor of which was warped and sagging, while the walls were covered on one side with big faded portraits of an inferior quality, like those in the corridor that connects the Pitti and Uffizi in Florence. Before him moved the figure of Count Albert – a black silhouette in the ever-increasing light. And always the music grew stronger and stranger, a mad, evil, seductive dance that bewitched even while it disgusted.

In a final blaze of vivid, intolerable light, in a burst of hellish music that might have come from Bedlam, Rupert stepped from the corridor into a vast and curious room where at first he saw nothing, distinguished nothing but a mad, seething whirl of sweeping figures, white, in a white room, under white light, Count Albert standing before him, the only dark object to be seen. As his eyes grew accustomed to the fearful brightness, he knew that he was looking on a dance such as the damned might see in hell, but such as no living man had ever seen before.

Around the long, narrow hall, under the fearful light that came from nowhere, but was omnipresent, swept a rushing stream of unspeakable horrors, dancing insanely, laughing, gibbering hideously; the dead of forty years. White, polished skeletons, bare of flesh and vesture, skeletons clothed in the dreadful rags of dried and rattling sinews, the tags of tattering grave-clothes flaunting behind them. These were the dead of many years ago. Then the dead of more recent times, with yellow bones showing only here and there, the long and insecure hair of their hideous heads writhing in the beating air. Then green and grey horrors, bloated and shapeless, stained with earth or dripping with spattering water; and here and there white, beautiful things, like chiselled ivory, the dead of yesterday, locked it may be, in the mummy arms of rattling skeletons.

Round and round the cursed room, a swaying, swirling maelstrom of death, while the air grew thick with miasma, the floor foul with shreds of shrouds, and yellow parchment, clattering bones, and wisps of tangled hair.

And in the very midst of this ring of death, a sight not for words nor for thought, a sight to blast forever the mind of the man who looked upon it: a leaping, writhing dance of Count Albert's victims, the score of beautiful women and reckless men who danced to their awful death while the castle burned around them, charred and shapeless now, a living charnel-house of nameless horror.

Count Albert, who had stood silent and gloomy, watching the dance of the damned, turned to Rupert, and for the first time spoke.

'We are ready for you now; dance!'

A prancing horror, dead some dozen years, perhaps, flaunted from the rushing river of the dead, and leered at Rupert with eyeless skull.

'Dance!'

Rupert stood frozen, motionless.

'Dance!'

His hard lips moved. 'Not if the devil came from hell to make me.'

Count Albert swept his vast two-handed sword into the fœtid air while the tide of corruption paused in its swirling, and swept down on Rupert with gibbering grins.

The room, and the howling dead, and the black portent before him circled dizzily around, as with a last effort of departing consciousness he drew his pistol and fired full in the face of Count Albert.

★ ★ ★ ★ ★

Perfect silence, perfect darkness; not a breath, not a sound: the dead stillness of a long-sealed tomb. Rupert lay on his back, stunned, helpless, his pistol clenched in his frozen hand, a smell of powder in the black air. Where was he? Dead? In hell? He reached his hand out cautiously; it fell on dusty boards. Outside, far away, a clock struck three. Had he dreamed? Of course; but how ghastly a dream! With chattering teeth he called softly –

'Otto!'

There was no reply, and none when he called again and again. He staggered weakly to his feet, groping for matches and candles. A panic of abject terror came on him; the matches were gone! He turned towards the fireplace: a single coal glowed in the white ashes. He swept a mass of papers and dusty books from the table, and with trembling hands cowered over the embers, until he succeeded in lighting the dry tinder. Then he piled the old books on the blaze, and looked fearfully around.

No: It was gone – thank God for that; the hook was empty.

But why did Otto sleep so soundly; why did he not awake?

He stepped unsteadily across the room in the flaring light of the burning books, and knelt by the mattress.

★ ★ ★ ★ ★

So they found him in the morning, when no one came to the inn from Kropfsberg Keep, and the quaking Peter Rosskopf arranged a relief party – found him kneeling beside the mattress where Otto lay, shot in the throat and quite dead.

NUMBER NINETY (1895)

BM Croker (1848–1920)

Bithia Mary Sheppard was born, the daughter of a country clergyman, in County Roscommon, Ireland. In her early twenties, she married John Stokes Croker, an officer in the Royal Munster Fusiliers, and followed him to India when he was posted there in 1877. Her first novels were written in India and many of the dozens that followed were set on the sub-continent. Village Tales and Jungle Tragedies, *published in 1895, was a collection of short stories, much praised at the time, which showed her sympathies with ordinary Indians and their lives. Like so many other writers of her time, Croker was also interested in the supernatural and the Gothic tradition in literature. This interest is reflected in* To Let, *a volume of short stories, mostly set in India, which was published in 1893. The title story is probably Croker's best known work today and has appeared in several modern anthologies, including* The Oxford Book of Victorian Ghost Stories. *'Number Ninety' was first published in the UK in* Pearson's Magazine. *A variant version of it, in which the setting is moved from London to Charleston, was later published in the USA. It is a prime example of a particularly popular type of late Victorian ghost story in which an intrepid disbeliever in the supernatural chooses to spend a night in an allegedly haunted house and pays a terrible price for his scepticism.*

'To let furnished, for a term of years, at a very low rental, a large old-fashioned family residence, comprising eleven bed-rooms, four reception-rooms, dressing-rooms, two staircases, complete servants' offices, ample accommodation for a Gentleman's establishment, including six-stall stable, coach-house, etc.'

The above advertisement referred to number ninety.

For a period extending over some years this notice appeared

spasmodically in various daily papers. Occasionally you saw it running for a week or a fortnight at a stretch, as if it were resolved to force itself into consideration by sheer persistency. Sometimes for months I looked for it in vain. Other ignorant folk might possibly fancy that the effort of the house agent had been crowned at last with success – that it was let, and no longer in the market.

I knew better. I knew that it would never, never find a tenant as long as oak and ash endured. I knew that it was passed on as a hopeless case, from house-agent to house-agent. I knew that it would never be occupied, save by rats – and, more than this, I knew the reason why!

I will not say in what square, street, or road number ninety may be found, nor will I divulge to any human being its precise and exact locality, but this I'm prepared to state, that it is positively in existence, is in London, and is still empty.

Twenty years ago, this very Christmas, my friend John Hollyoak (civil engineer) and I were guests at a bachelor's party; partaking, in company with eight other celibates, of a very recherché little dinner, in the neighbourhood of Piccadilly. Conversation became very brisk, as the champagne circulated, and many topics were started, discussed, and dismissed.

They (I say *they* advisedly, as I myself am a man of few words) talked on an extraordinary variety of subjects.

I distinctly recollect a long argument on mushrooms – mushrooms, murders, racing, cholera; from cholera we came to sudden death, from sudden death to churchyards, and from churchyards, it was naturally but a step to ghosts.

On this last topic the arguments became fast and furious, for the company was divided into two camps. The larger, 'the opposition', who scoffed, sneered, and snapped their fingers, and laughed with irritating contempt at the very name of ghosts, was headed by John Hollyoak; the smaller party, who were dogged, angry, and prepared to back their opinions to any extent, had for their leader our host, a baldheaded man of business, whom I certainly would have credited (as I mentally remarked) with more sense.

The believers in the supernatural obtained a hearing, so far as to relate one or two blood-curdling, first- or second-hand experiences, which, when concluded, instead of being received with an awe-struck and respectful silence, were pooh-poohed, with shouts of laughter, and taunting suggestions that were by no means complimentary to the intelligence, or sobriety, of the victims of superstition. Argument and counter-argument waxed louder and hotter, and there was every prospect of a very stormy conclusion to the evening's entertainment.

John Hollyoak, who was the most vehement, the most incredulous, the most jocular, and the most derisive of the anti-ghost faction, brought matters to a climax by declaring that nothing would give him greater pleasure than to pass a night in a haunted house – and the worse its character, the better he would be pleased!

His challenge was instantly taken up by our somewhat ruffled host, who warmly assured him that his wishes could be easily satisfied, and that he would be accommodated with a night's lodging in a haunted house within twenty-four hours – in fact, in a house of such a desperate reputation, that even the adjoining mansions stood vacant.

He then proceeded to give a brief outline of the history of number ninety. It had once been the residence of a well-known country family, but what evil events had happened therein tradition did not relate.

On the death of the last owner – a diabolical-looking aged person, much resembling the typical wizard – it had passed into the hands of a kinsman, resident abroad, who had no wish to return to England, and who desired his agents to let it, if they could – a most significant proviso!

Year by year went by, and still this 'highly desirable family mansion' could find no tenant, although the rent was reduced, and reduced, and again reduced, to almost zero!

The most ghastly whispers were afloat – the most terrible experiences were actually proclaimed on the housetops!

No tenant would remain, even gratis; and for the last ten years, this, 'handsome, desirable town family residence' had been the abode of rats by day, and something else by night – so said the neighbours.

Of course it was the very thing for John, and he snatched up the gauntlet on the spot. He scoffed at its evil repute, and solemnly promised to rehabilitate its character within a week.

It was in vain that he was solemnly warned – that one of his fellow guests gravely assured him 'that he would not pass a night in number ninety for ninety thousand pounds – it would be the price of his reason.'

'You value your reason at a very high figure,' replied John, with an indulgent smile. 'I will venture mine for nothing.'

'Those laugh who win,' put in our host sharply. 'You have not been through the wood yet though your name is Hollyoak! I invite all present to dine with me in three days from this; and then, if our friend here has proved that he has got the better of the spirits, we will all laugh together. Is that a bargain?'

This invitation was promptly accepted by the whole company; and then they fell to making practical arrangements for John's lodgings for the next night.

I had no actual hand – or, more properly speaking, tongue – in this discussion, which carried us on till a late hour; but nevertheless, the next night at ten o'clock – for no ghost with any self-respect would think of appearing before that time – I found myself standing, as John's second, on the steps of the notorious abode; but I was not going to remain; the hansom that brought us was to take me back to my respectable chambers.

This ill-fated house was large, solemn-looking, and gloomy. A heavy portico frowned down on neighbouring bare-faced hall-doors. The caretaker (an army pensioner, bravest of the brave in daylight) was prudently awaiting us outside with a key, which said key he turned in the lock, and admitted us into a great echoing hall, black as Erebus, saying as he did so: 'My missus has haired the bed, and made up a good fire in the first front, sir. Your things is all laid hout, and (dubiously to John) I hope you'll have a comfortable night, sir.'

'No, sir! Thank you, sir! Excuse me, I'll not come in! Goodnight!' and with the words still on his lips, he clattered down the steps with most indecent haste, and – vanished.

'And of course you will not come in either?' said John. 'It is not in the bond, and I prefer to face them alone!' and he laughed contemptuously, a laugh that had a curious echo, it struck me at the time. A laugh strangely repeated, with an unpleasant mocking emphasis. 'Call for me, alive or dead, at eight o'clock to-morrow morning!' he added, pushing me forcibly out into the porch, and closing the door with a heavy, reverberating clang, that sounded half-way down the street.

I did call for him the next morning as desired, with the army pensioner, who stared at his common-place, self-possessed appearance, with an expression of respectful astonishment.

'So it was all humbug, of course,' I said, as he took my arm, and we set off for our club.

'You shall have the whole story whenever we have had something to eat,' he replied somewhat impatiently. 'It will keep till after breakfast – I'm famishing!'

I remarked that he looked unusually grave as we chatted over our broiled fish and omelette, and that occasionally his attention seemed wandering, to say the least of it. The moment he had brought out his cigar-case and lit up he turned to me and said:

'I see you are just quivering to know my experience, and I won't keep you on tenterhooks any longer. In four words – I have seen them!'

I am (as before hinted) a silent man. I merely looked at him with widely-parted mouth and staring interrogative eyes.

I believe I had best endeavour to give the narrative without comment, and in John Hollyoak's own way. This is, as well as I can recollect, his experience word for word: –

'I proceeded upstairs, after I had shut you out, lighting my way by a match, and found the front room easily, as the door was ajar, and it was lit up by a roaring and most cheerful-looking fire, and two wax candles. It was a comfortable apartment, furnished with old-fashioned chairs and tables, and the traditional four-poster. There were numerous doors, which proved to be cupboards; and when I had executed a rigorous search in each of these closets and locked them, and investigated the bed above and beneath, sounded the walls, and bolted the door, I sat down before the fire, lit a cigar, opened a book, and felt that I was going to be master of the situation, and most thoroughly and comfortably "at home". My novel proved absorbing. I read on greedily, chapter after chapter, and so interested was I, and amused – for it was a lively book – that I positively lost sight of my whereabouts, and fancied myself reading in my own chamber! There was not a sound – not even a mouse in wainscot. The coals dropping from the grate occasionally broke the silence, till a neighbouring church-clock slowly boomed twelve! "The Hour!" I said to myself, with a laugh, as I gave the fire a rousing poke, and commenced a fresh chapter; but ere I had read three pages I had occasion to pause and listen. What was that distinct sound now coming nearer and nearer? "Rats, of course," said Common-sense – "it was just the house for vermin." Then a longish silence. Again a stir, sounds approaching, as if apparently caused by many feet passing down the corridor – high heeled shoes, the sweeping switch of silken trains! Of course it was all imagination, I assured myself – or rats! Rats were capable of making such curiously improbable noises!

'Then another silence. No sound but cinders and the ticking of my watch, which I had laid upon the table.

'I resumed my book, rather ashamed, and a little indignant with myself for having neglected it, and calmly dismissed my late interruption as "rats – nothing but rats".

'I had been reading and smoking for some time in a placid and highly incredulous frame of mind, when I was somewhat rudely startled by a loud single knock at my room door. I took no notice of it, but merely laid down my novel and sat tight. Another knock more imperious this time. After a moment's mental deliberation I arose, armed myself with a poker, prepared to brain any number of rats, and threw the door open with a violent swing that strained its very hinges, and beheld, to my amazement, a tall powdered footman in a laced scarlet livery, who, making a formal inclination of his head, astonished me still further by saying:

'"Dinner is ready!"

'"I'm not coming!" I replied, without a moment's hesitation, and thereupon I slammed the door in his face, locked it, and resumed my seat, also my book; but reading was a farce; my ears were aching for the next sound.

'It came soon – rapid steps running up the stairs, and again a single knock. I went over to the door, and once more discovered the tall footman, who repeated, with a studied courtesy:

'"Dinner is ready, and the company are waiting."

'"I told you I was not coming. Be off, and be hanged to you!" I cried again, shutting the door violently.

'This time I did not make even a pretence at reading, I merely sat and waited for the next move.

'I had not long to sit. In ten minutes I heard a third loud summons. I rose, went to the door, and tore it open. There, as I expected, was the servant again, with his parrot speech:

'"Dinner is ready, the company are waiting, and the master says you must come!"

'"All right, then, I'll come," I replied, wearied by reason of his importunity, and feeling suddenly fired with a desire to see the end of the adventure.

'He accordingly led the way downstairs, and I followed him, noting as I went the gilt buttons on his coat, and his splendidly turned calves, also that the hall and passages were now brilliantly illuminated, and that several liveried servants were passing to and fro, and that from – presumably – the dining room, there issued a buzz of tongues, loud volleys of laughter, many hilarious voices, and a clatter of knives and forks. I was not left much time for speculation, as in another second I found myself inside the door, and my escort announced me in a stentorian voice as "Mr Hollyoak".

'I could hardly credit my senses, as I looked round and saw about two dozen people, dressed in a fashion of the last century, seated at the table, which was loaded with gold and silver plate, and lighted up by a blaze of wax candles in a massive candelabra.

'A swarthy elderly gentleman, who presided at the head of the board, rose deliberately as I entered. He was dressed in a crimson coat, braided with silver. He wore a peruke, had the most piercing black eyes I ever encountered, made me the finest bow I ever received in all my life, and with a polite wave of a taper hand, indicated my seat – a vacant chair between two powdered and patched beauties, with overflowing white shoulders and necks sparkling with diamonds.

'At first I was fully convinced that the whole affair was a superbly-matured practical joke. Everything looked so real, so truly flesh and blood, so complete in every detail; but I gazed around in vain for one familiar face.

'I saw young, old, and elderly; handsome and the reverse. On all faces there was a similar expression – reckless, hardened defiance, and something else that made me shudder, but that I could not classify or define.

'Were they a secret community? Burglars or coiners? But no; in one rapid glance I noticed that they belonged exclusively to the upper stratum of society – bygone society. The jabber of talking had momentarily ceased, and the host, imperiously hammering the table with a knife-handle, said in a singularly harsh grating voice:

'"Ladies and gentlemen, permit me to give you a toast! Our guest!" looking straight at me with his glittering coal-black eyes.

'Every glass was immediately raised. Twenty faces were turned towards mine, when, happily, a sudden impulse seized me. I sprang to my feet and said:

'"Ladies and gentlemen, I beg to thank you for your kind hospitality, but before I accept it, allow me to say grace!"

'I did not wait for permission, but hurriedly repeated a Latin benediction. Ere the last syllable was uttered, in an instant there was a violent crash, an uproar, a sound of running, of screams, groans and curses, and then utter darkness.

'I found myself standing alone by a big mahogany table which I could just dimly discern by the aid of a street-lamp that threw its meagre rays into the great empty dining-room from the other side of the area.

'I must confess that I felt my nerves a little shaken by the instantaneous change from light to darkness – from a crowd of gay and noisy companions, to utter solitude and silence. I stood for a moment trying to recover my mental balance. I rubbed my eyes hard to assure myself that I was wide awake, and then I placed this very cigar-case in the middle of the table, as a sign and token that I had been downstairs – which cigar-case I found exactly where I left it this morning – and then went and groped my way into the hall and regained my room.

'I met with no obstacle *en route*. I saw no one, but as I closed and double-locked my door I distinctly heard a low laugh outside the keyhole – a sort of suppressed, malicious titter, that made me furious.

'I opened the door at once. There was nothing to be seen. I waited and listened – dead silence. I then undressed and went to bed, resolved that a whole army of footmen would fail to allure me once more to that festive board. I was determined not to lose my night's rest – ghosts or no ghosts.

'Just as I was dozing off I remember hearing the neighbouring clock chime two. It was the last sound I was aware of; the house was now as silent as a vault. My fire burnt away cheerfully. I was no longer in the least degree inclined for reading, and I fell fast asleep and slept soundly till I heard the cabs and milk-carts beginning their morning career.

'I then rose, dressed at my leisure, and found you, my good, faithful friend, awaiting me, rather anxiously, on the hall-door steps.

'I have not done with that house yet. I'm determined to find out who these people are, and where they come from. I shall sleep there again to-night, and so shall "Crib", my bulldog; and you will see that I shall have news for you to-morrow morning – if I am still alive to tell the tale,' he added with a laugh.

In vain I would have dissuaded him. I protested, argued, and implored. I declared that rashness was not courage; that he had seen enough; that I, who had seen nothing, and only listened to his experiences, was convinced that number ninety was a house to be avoided.

I might just as well have talked to my umbrella! So, once more, I reluctantly accompanied him to his previous night's lodging. Once more I saw him swallowed up inside the gloomy, forbidding-looking, re-echoing hall.

I then went home in an unusually anxious, semi-excited, nervous state of mind; and I, who generally outrival the Seven Sleepers, lay wide awake, tumbling and tossing hour after hour, a prey to the most foolish ideas – ideas I would have laughed to scorn in daylight.

More than once I was certain that I heard John Hollyoak distractedly calling me; and I sat up in bed and listened intently. Of course it was fancy, for the instant I did so, there was no sound.

At the first gleam of winter dawn, I rose, dressed, and swallowed a cup of good strong coffee to clear my brain from the misty notions it had harboured during the night. And then I invested myself in my warmest topcoat and comforter, and set off for number ninety. Early as it was – it was but half-past seven – I found the army pensioner was before me, pacing the pavement with a countenance that would have made a first-rate frontispiece for 'Burton's Anatomy of Melancholy' – a countenance the reverse of cheerful.

I was not disposed to wait for eight o'clock. I was too uneasy, and too impatient for further particulars of the dinner-party. So I rang with all my might, and knocked with all my main.

No sound within – no answer! But John was always a heavy sleeper. I was resolved to arouse him all the same, and knocked and rang, and rang and knocked, incessantly for fully ten minutes.

I then stooped down and applied my eye to the keyhole; I looked steadily into the aperture, till I became accustomed to the darkness, and then it seemed to me that another eye – a very strange, fiery eye – was glaring into mine from the other side of the door!

I removed my eye and applied my mouth instead, and shouted with all the power of my lungs (I did not care a straw if passers-by took me for an escaped lunatic):

'John! John! Hollyoak!'

How his name echoed and re-echoed up through that great empty house! 'He must hear that,' I said to myself as I pressed my ear closely against the lock, and listened with throbbing suspense.

The echo of 'Hollyoak' had hardly died away when I swear that I distinctly heard a low, sniggering, mocking laugh – that was my only answer – that and a vast unresponsive silence.

I was now quite desperate. I shook the door frantically, with all my strength. I broke the bell; in short, my behaviour was such that it excited the curiosity of a policeman, who crossed the road to know 'What was up?'

'I want to get in!' I panted, breathless with my exertions.

'You'd better stay where you are!' said Bobby; 'the outside of this house is the best of it! There are terrible stories –'

'But there is a gentleman inside it!' I interrupted impatiently. 'He slept there last night, and I can't wake him. He has the key!'

'Oh, you can't wake him!' returned the policeman gravely. 'Then we must get a locksmith!'

But already the thoughtful pensioner had procured one; and already a considerable and curious crowd surrounded the steps.

After five minutes of (to me) maddening delay, the great heavy door was opened and swung slowly back, and I instantly rushed in, followed less precipitately by the policeman and the pensioner.

I had not far to seek John Hollyoak! He and his dog were lying at the foot of the stairs, both stone dead!

AN EXPIATION (1896)

Arabella Kenealy (1859–1938)

Arabella Kenealy was the daughter of one of the most notorious lawyers of the Victorian era. Edward Kenealy came to the public's attention because of his wildly eccentric behaviour as defence counsel during the trial of the so-called Tichborne Claimant, a man who said he was a long-lost English aristocrat but turned out to be a butcher from Australia. Arabella was in her teens during the years of her father's greatest notoriety. She went on to study at the London School of Medicine for Women and was a doctor for six years before her own ill-health obliged her to retire. She became a prolific writer on feminism, medicine and evolutionary ideas. She also wrote a number of novels, beginning with Dr Janet of Harley Street *(1893), and was a regular contributor to the magazine press of the late Victorian and Edwardian period. Her character Lord Syfret appeared in a series of short stories published in* Ludgate Magazine *in 1896 which were collected the following year in a volume entitled* Belinda's Beaux and Other Stories. *Most of the apparently supernatural cases that the arrogantly upper-class Syfret investigates prove to have entirely natural (if wildly far-fetched) explanations. 'An Expiation' is an exception in that the events it describes fall clearly into the category of the paranormal. Like all of Kenealy's Syfret stories, it reads clumsily today and yet the image of the doomed child forever drawn back to the scene of a murder lingers in the memory.*

Only in exceptional cases do I trouble to put the law on the track of murder, though in the course of their activities on my behalf, my agents witness the commission of such a crime. For my part, I prefer the delinquent to escape, that I may find, as I do find, the penalty closing in on him as an indirect consequence of his action, rather than that it shall take the clumsy form we dignify by the title of justice. Far crueller, subtler, and a hundredfold more fitting to a particular crime are the methods whereby time, character, and circumstance enmesh the criminal. Expedient it may be to rid ourselves of the confessedly vicious. But the Powers which are moulding us to ends our finite minds have so far failed to grasp are neither assisted in their ultimate objects nor appeased in their far-reaching wrath – so to put it – by our crude expedients. The long arm of development which encompasses the human family, and places effect in the unerring train of cause, will find the murderer, many years it may be after we have done with him, but find him it will as inevitably as the impulse given to pool by pebble laps the shore.

How can it reach him after death? you ask. Death is but change of identity. Entities in the school of evolution pass through myriad lives in training for eternity, and the ill acts of one existence may not find expiation until a later one. A theory, you say! A theory, I admit. But I ask you for another which shall equally explain the inexplicabilities of human life.

I have a story illustrative of my theory. Read into it any other interpretation that you will, and judge if it apply as mine does.

In a cottage on one of my estates a gamekeeper lived, some ten years since, with his young and pretty wife. He was middle-aged and morose, considering, as does many another, that the one cardinal virtue he practised – in his case that of honesty – absolved him from the obligation of practising any of the minor amenities and amiabilities of life. Nobody could imagine by what sorcery or fortuitous concomitance of accidents he had persuaded pretty Polly Penrose to mate with him. He had saved a certain sum of money, for to the other unlovable qualities he added that of screw. Polly had swains better circumstanced than he, however, so that this offered no solution of the problem. The village wondered, chattered, and finally decided that 'you could nivver calculate on what gells do, for they're chock full o' whimsies'; and so they let the matter drop. Cooper was but one of Polly's whimsies.

It is probable I should never have concerned myself with Polly's affairs had I not one day come upon her crying her eyes out in a wood. On seeing me, she blushed and stole away. Matters just then were dull. I had no other case on hand; and, without anticipating much result, idly determined to trace the cause of Polly's tears. I had, among my agents, a girl of about her age and temperament, who soon made Polly's acquaintance. It came out then that Polly had married for pique. There was a certain stalwart sweetheart of hers – another of my keepers – of whom she was fond, but he rousing her jealousy, in a fit of temper she accepted Cooper. To make a long story short – for this is but a preface – Polly and her lover made it up again too late, for Polly was then Mrs Cooper.

Polly was a good girl, and I do not believe Cooper had any substantial reason for complaint, as she saw Dell but rarely. But she grew pallid and depressed. Occasionally she was seen with Dell. The circumstances reaching Cooper's ears, with doubtless some embellishment, there was trouble in the cottage. Cooper even went so far as to strike her. In her fear and agitation – the poor girl was soon to be a mother – she fled to Dell.

Cooper, following, found her in a shed near the latter's cottage. From words the men passed to blows, and eventually Dell struck Cooper over the head with the butt-end of his gun. Whether he meant murder or not, who can say? But a long acquaintance with the poor fellow makes me confident the impulse was momentary and uncontrollable. But murder it turned out. Cooper's skull was fractured and he died in a few hours.

Dell made no effect to escape. His one fear seems to have been for Polly. He remained with her in the cottage, soothing and reassuring her till he was handcuffed and taken to gaol. I did all I could on his behalf. I even had the gaol-lock tampered with. I had an instinct of what would happen should his case come to trial, and hanging was the last death for the fine young fellow he was.

I was a magistrate and could easily have contrived his escape. But the blockhead would not take his liberty. He could not now marry Polly, he said, and he did not care for life.

A thick-skulled jury, directed by a judge who on the Bench was as keen a stickler for the proprieties as off the Bench he was obtuse about them, put the worst – and I believe, the false – construction on Dell's and Polly's fondness. He was convicted of murder, and sentenced to death. Under the circumstances it was a monstrous sentence. There had assuredly been no premeditation, and his provocation was great. We petitioned the Home Secretary; we petitioned Parliament. We might have spared our signatures and ink. When Dell's time came he was hanged. And now comes the gist of my story.

I filled up the places left vacant by Dell and his victim, putting in two keepers from a distance. There was a strong local feeling against the occupation of either of the cottages. For it was rumoured that the shed wherein the murder had occurred was haunted. But the new keepers, unaffected by the tragedy which to them was merely hearsay, pooh-poohed the rumour.

Curiously enough, the wife of one turned out to be a distant cousin of Dell's. She was a buxom person, strong nerved, and braced with common sense. She scoffed at ghost-talk.

'Depend on it, your lordship,' she said once to me, 'there's a deal more to be afeard on in the livin' than the dead; and as long as it's nobody comin' to meddle wi' Johnson's belongins, why, let the poor things, if things there be, come an' go as it pleases 'em.'

I mention this to free my story from an implication to which it may presently seem open. Mrs Johnson was as unimpressionable a woman as could be, and was as little affected by the talk of ghosts as she would have been by their apparition.

Now the ghost which was said to walk and to have been seen by more than one person, was not, as I have gathered is the way of ghosts, the shade of the murdered man, but that of his murderer. All who had caught a fleeting glimpse which is as much as the ghost-seer generally permits himself, agreed that this apparition haunting the wood-shed was Dell's. Round and round in a restricted circle, skirting the space whereon a ghastly form had stretched, the ghost was seen to pass. Its head was bent, its face leaned down. Its eyes stared, frozen with horror. Moans and sighs of the direst distress were heard to issue from the shed. But the man from whom I had a description, a tramp who, unwitting of its reputation had stolen there one rainy evening for the purpose of a night's lodging, described the thing he saw as mute and noiseless, making a dumb and ceaseless circuit of the floor. To him the circuit taken by the apparition was but a stretch of dusty boards, but the stark horror in the shadow's eyes told of some ghastly visibility.

The man was green with fright. He had lain there staring nearly all night, afraid to move, afraid almost to breathe, lest he should turn the horror of the eyes upon himself. He painted in the vivid speech of panic the curious effect of morning: how as the light grew, it left less and still less of the apparition visible, how from being something luminous against the darkness it passed into a thin translucent shade against the light: how the outlines slowly faded and the form was lost, yet he could see it whirling like a grey smoke round and round six feet of floor. When the sun came up it slipped away as mist slips into the air. In the morning when the man was brought to me he was piebald. The hair and beard of one side had gone white in the night.

A time came when the ghost was seen no more. The sighs and moanings ceased. Still the shed lost no whit of its evil reputation.

A year after the Johnsons' advent to the cottage, a child was born to them. They had already several children – buxom, cherry-cheeked youngsters, after the type of their mother. This child was different. The difference did not show at first. The infant was as other infants – a mere homogenous mass of red-pink flesh, with the slate-grey eyes of its kind; eyes which deluded mothers call dark or light according to their fancy, for the rest of the world perceives that not until long after seeing the light do babies' eyes take on the shade they eventually keep. But this infant, though like enough to others, differed from them in one particular – it had a large blood-red spot in the palm of its right hand. The doctor pronounced the spot accidental and ephemeral; it would disappear before the week was out. Subsequently, he modified his opinion. It was a variety of naevus, but he considered that it did not call for operation. The child would outgrow it. But the doctor was wrong. As the palm grew the blood-spot grew, and its colour did not wane. Presently, when the child assumed with age the waxen whiteness afterwards characterising it, the spot had a curious effect of focusing all the blood in its body.

As the babe slowly evolved an individuality out of its pink homogeneousness, it was seen to differ singularly from the rest of the Johnson children. In the place of their fair chubbiness, it was pallid and dark. Its brows were strongly and sombrely marked, and its eyes gathered slowly a weird look of horror. It cried rarely or never. Nor did it smile. It sat staring before it with a fixed expression and a blood-red palm upturned.

A child is born with its hands knotted into fists, fists which for weeks are opened with difficulty. It is an instinctive action of grasping the life before it. A man or woman dies with the palms extended. The life has been wrought and is rendered up. The Johnson baby never curled its fists as normal babies do. It held its palms limply open with the blood-red spot for all to see. The villagers talked as villagers talk of something out of the common. They drew conclusions – the short-sighted conclusions of their kind. They pronounced the child's uncanniness a judgment on the mother for her scoffing.

'It don't do to make light o' they things,' they croaked. They predicted the baby's early death. The child attracted my attention from the first. I got a curious impression about it. Its face had a familiar look. The horror in its eyes reminded me of something. It was not until later that I knew of what.

I had a vacant cottage near. In it I installed an elderly woman of observant faculty. She made friends with the mother, and having leisure took the infant frequently off her hands. By her means I am able to relate that which happened. So soon as it showed signs of intelligence – signs such as those used to children interpret, while to others they are still meaningless – the Johnson baby developed interest in the haunted shed – now, it must be remembered, no longer haunted.

The moment it was taken out of doors its eyes turned in the direction of the building, which stood but a short distance from the cottage. It was restless and wayward out of sight of it, and would weary and fret with inarticulate demands until carried whence it could see it. So soon as it was able, it would drag itself along the floor and out at the door to sit there with its hands on its tiny knees, staring with fascinated looks.

Before it was ten months old it was found, having crept across the patch of ground between the house and shed, tired with its efforts, lying extended on the grass, its waxen face turned solemnly upon the building. Later it managed to escape attention long enough to reach the shed, shuffling along as infants do on hands and knees. It was discovered huddling at the open door, its head dropt till its chin rested almost in its lap, its pupils wide upon some portion of the floor. An illness followed. For some weeks the child's life was in danger. It had taken a chill, the doctor said. Even then, though weakened with fever, the poor little creature, left for a moment, would struggle feebly to the foot of the bed, whence through a window a corner of the shed was visible. There it would be found staring with wide, frightened eyes.

When strong enough to be up again it made always for the window, to stand there with its face pressed close against the glass. The doctor diagnosed the child as weak-minded, but I cannot say the term at all described the terrible intelligence looking out of its eyes. The women shook their heads.

'It knows too much, poor little dear,' they said. 'There isn't nothing that's said it don't know. If anybody could find out what it's always askin' in its eyes, per'aps it ud be able to die quiet, for anybody can see it isn't long for this world.'

Mrs Johnson paid but little heed to the talk.

'I don't see anything much different in the child from other children,' she said impatiently, 'only it don't thrive. I expect it'll be stronger on its legs when it's got its teeth and can take a bit o' meat wi' the rest of us.'

But the child grew no stronger on its legs, nor did it grow the least bit less unlike the chubby-cheeked Johnson brood. It seemed to have no wish to walk. It was a patient little thing, and when planted by a chair would stand there; but so soon as attention was drawn from it, it would drop on its hands and knees again, and creep to the door.

Johnson made a little fence, to keep it from straying; but it developed a weird sagacity for evading this, wriggling through or clambering over, or escaping by a back door. Then, if not intercepted, it would work its way across the ground till it reached the doorway of the shed. There it would sit for hours together, straining its eyes upon some portion of the floor – always the same portion. Rain, snow or wind, it minded not. Frequently it was found squatted in the entrance, wet to the skin, with a heavy rain beating on it, to all appearance unconscious of its wet and chilled condition – its gaze and powers magnetised. It took but little food, and was a puny, miserable morsel. Such food as it took it took mechanically and in obedience to its mother. It never seemed hungry, or interested, as babies are interested, in the sweet and edible.

It did not play, nor did it seem to have a notion of the use of toys. A doll or painted ball it would turn seriously over in its fingers, then lay aside with a quaint solemnity as though it had weightier matters on hand. Its only comfort was its thumb, which it sucked gravely, with a thoughtful sobriety as of an old man smoking a pipe. It had no fear of darkness. It had been found in the shed at midnight, having scrambled from its cot, down the cottage stairs, and out at the door. Sometimes it sat at a distance, gazing spell-bound. Generally its time was spent in shuffling round and round a certain area of floor, dragging itself laboriously on hands and knees, as one doing penance.

The villagers grew scared, and whispered that it had the evil eye. They would turn back to avoid passing it on the road. I have had boys thrashed for stoning it. Even its matter-of-fact mother came to have a horror of it, with its weird ways and terrible eyes. Yet it was patient, and gave no trouble, so long as it were permitted to be in the shed. Its limbs, they told me, were raw and red, from the continuous rub of the boards against its baby skin. And the nails of its toes and fingers were worn to the quick with ceaseless clambering.

That the child suffered mentally, I cannot say. Possibly not. It seemed to gather satisfaction from its treadmill labours, though there was always that dread in its eyes.

'Perhaps your lordship would be pleased to come and see it,' my agent suggested one day, when I chanced to pass the Johnson cottage. 'Mrs Johnson has gone into the village. The baby was shut in, but it has got out somehow and crept to the shed.'

I followed her. We went quietly; but I doubt if the child would have heard in any case, so absorbed was it. We watched it through the window. Its frock and feet were stained with the soil over which it had dragged itself. The day was damp, and mud clung about its hands. But it minded nothing. In the half-sitting, half-kneeling posture of creeping children it dragged itself sideways round and round a circle encompassing some six feet of floor – six feet in length, and from three to four in breadth. Dust lay thick on the boards, so that its circuit was clearly traced. It went always over the same ground, marking a curious zigzagged shape. Round and round, now up, now down, tracing the same inexplicable course it plodded, a thick dust rising on either side to the infantile flop of its skirts.

Its face was bent toward the centre of the trail it followed, its eyes rivetted. Sweat stood moist on its skin, and in the moisture dust clung, giving it a dark, unearthly look. It sighed and panted at its task. Every now and again it would cease from utter weariness, and, sitting up, would lift a dusty frock and wipe its lips. After a minute it resumed that treadmill round. I went in. It lifted its awed and grimy countenance and looked at me with its terrible intelligence. Then it resumed its dusty way.

I took it up and sat it on a pile of wood. It whined and fretted, stretching its arms to the shape on the floor. I crossed the shed, and stood looking down upon the figure traced. I could make nothing of it. It was an irregular oblong of indefinite form, wider to one end, narrowing to the other. A grim thought struck me that it resembled a coffin. I was interested. What was the meaning of it? What, if anything, did those weird eyes see? I bade the woman bring some cake or sweets. She came back with an orange.

'He'll do anything for an orange,' she said.

I made her take the child and set him on the floor to one side of the figure. I placed myself on the other. The oblong was between us at its widest part. I held the orange up, and beckoned him.

'Go, get it!' the woman urged.

He gazed at me questioningly, as though probing my intention. His eyes rested on the orange; then something which in another child would have been a smile floated over his face. He set out, creeping toward me. I watched him intently. Would he cross that circle? He came on, shuffling slowly, raising a cloud of dust. But when he reached the further limit of the oblong, he stopped short. He turned his face down, and bent his looks on something he seemed to see within the circle – something about the level of his eyes.

I stamped my foot and called to him. He looked up curiously, but did not move. I held the orange toward him. He stretched a hand out, raising it carefully as though to prevent it coming into contact with the something there.

'Come,' I said.

His eyes again levelled. They travelled slowly over that I could not see. Then he looked up, dully reproachful.

'Come,' I called again, tossing the orange.

He shook his head with a grave, old-man solemnity. I stamped my foot once more.

'Come,' I insisted.

His lips quivered feebly. Tears came into his eyes. Suddenly his features quickened with a new sagacity. He swerved aside and

61

came creeping to me round the outer edge of the figure, bending his looks with an awed avoidance upon that which he saw there. I tried a dozen times. But he would not cross the line. He scanned me plaintively. Why did I so torment him?

I took him in my arms. I carried him toward the charmed circle. Looking back, I can see that the act was a brutal one, such a brutal one as the curiosity we dignify by the term intellectual or scientific is frequently guilty of. But the woman stopped me. She caught him out of my arms.

'For Heaven's sake, don't, my lord,' she gasped; 'I did it once. I thought he would have died.'

I looked into his face. Poor little wretch! There was all the dumb agony of a ripe intelligence frozen there. He clung to me strenuously, turning his rigid looks from that over which we stood. I gave him to her.

'Take him away. Get the poor little wretch out into the air. Give him the orange. Give him anything – only drive that look from his face.' She took him out. He turned a shuddering head over her shoulder, seeking that spot. It was the spot where Cooper had lain. I knew it now. He had lain there full length, and over him Dell had stood with stricken eyes. Heavens! Why had the child those eyes? And why had it been cursed with this terrible vision? Had re-birth come so soon? Were the retributive forces of murder expiating in a little child?

I stood looking down at the figure traced in dust. I thrust my stick into it. Did I really feel dull resistance? I lowered my hand to within some inches of the floor. Was the air truly chilled? Pshaw! The babe had infected me. It was but a draught from the door. As I stood my stick slipped from my hold, and sliding, stopped between the curves composing the lower end of the oblong. The branch of a tree, stirred by the wind, shot its shadow through the doorway immediately across the tracery. In a moment, as a few strokes put to outlines which had had no meanings gather the lines into life, so now the unmeaning tracery took shape. The stick formed a line of demarcation between the extended legs, a limb of the shadow tree lay like an outstretched arm and hand. Even for a moment convulsing features were given to a curve which might have been a face, as a flicker of twigs and fluttering leaves hurried like vanishing pencil-marks across the outline. In that moment the murdered body of Cooper was reproduced as I had seen it. I am sufficiently strong-nerved. Yet I admit I turned sick. I picked up my stick and went out.

I knew now what had been momentarily visible to me was ever before the doomed baby, that to its eyes the murdered man was always there. I felt my hair lift as though an ice-wind swept under my hat.

I had the shed pulled down. I had the ground sown with flowers. But the spot kept its old fascination for the poor little creature. He could not now drag round it, the way being barred. But he sat for hours tracing with a waxen finger something that for him lay there, something which to us was but space between flower-stalks.

I sent him to the sea, a hundred miles away. In three days his life was despaired of. His impulse in living was gone. He fell into a state of stupor. When brought back he revived. He dragged himself out to the flower-bed, and sat there crooning with a kind of plaintive content, tracing that outline with his pallid hands.

One morning they found him dead there. He had crept from his cot at some time during the night, and had scrambled in the darkness – he never learned to walk – to the old spot. Rain was falling, and he lay on his back with face upturned and wet, his fair hair limp about him. His brows were unbent and tranquil, through his half-closed lids peace at last looked. The flowers stood round him like gentle sentinels, their flower cups full of rain as eyes with tears. For the first time in his life the smile of a child lay over his lips. And the blood-spot on his palm was white as wool.

THE BLUE ROOM (1897)

Lettice Galbraith (fl. 1893–97)

Lettice Galbraith was one of a number of late Victorian women writers who produced some fine ghost stories. (Others include Louisa Baldwin, mother of the later Prime Minister Stanley Baldwin, Alice Perrin and Dora Havers, who wrote children's stories, some in collaboration with the more famous Edith Nesbit and produced ghostly fiction under the male pseudonym of Theo Gift.) Galbraith is probably the most mysterious figure in the history of supernatural literature. The date of her birth is unknown; so too is the date of her death. She surfaced in the 1890s as a writer of expertly crafted stories such as 'The Trainer's Ghost', 'The Ghost in the Chair' and 'A Ghost's Revenge'. Her collection entitled New Ghost Stories *was published in 1893. 'The Blue Room', in which an intrepid 'New Woman' of the period joins forces with a clever Oxford undergraduate to hunt down the ghost in a country house, appeared in* Macmillan's Magazine *in 1897. After that no fiction was published under her name and Lettice Galbraith disappears from the records.*

It happened twice in my time. It will never happen again, they say, since Miss Erristoun (Mrs Arthur, that is now) and Mr Calder-Maxwell between them found out the secret of the haunted room, and laid the ghost; for ghost it was, though at the time Mr Maxwell gave it another name, Latin, I fancy, but all I can remember about it now is that it somehow reminded me of poultry-rearing. I am the housekeeper at Mertoun Towers, as my aunt was before me, and her aunt before her, and first of all, my great-grandmother, who was a distant cousin of the Laird, and had married the chaplain, but being penniless at her husband's death, was thankful to accept the post which has ever since been occupied by one of her descendants. It gives us a sort of standing with the servants, being, as it were, related to the family; and Sir Archibald and my Lady have always acknowledged the connection, and treated us with more freedom than would be accorded to ordinary dependants.

Mertoun has been my home from the time I was eighteen. Something occurred then of which, since it has nothing to do with this story, I need only say that it wiped out for ever any idea of marriage on my part, and I came to the Towers to be trained under my aunt's ever vigilant eye for the duties in which I was one day to succeed her.

Of course I knew there was a story about the blue tapestry room. Everyone knew that, though the old Laird had given strict orders that the subject should not be discussed among the servants, and always discouraged any allusion to it on the part of his family and guests. But there is a strange fascination about everything connected with the supernatural, and orders or no orders, people, whether gentle or simple, will try to gratify their curiosity; so a good deal of surreptitious talk went on, both in the drawing-room and the servants' hall, and hardly a guest came to the house but would pay a visit to the Blue Room and ask all manner of questions about the ghost. The odd part of the business was that no-one knew what the ghost was supposed to be, or even if there were any ghost at all. I tried hard to get my aunt to tell me some details of the legend, but she always reminded me of Sir Archibald's orders, and added that the tale most likely started with the superstitious fancy of people who lived long ago and were very ignorant, because a certain Lady Barbara Mertoun had died in that room.

I reminded her that people must have died, at some time or another, in pretty nearly every room in the house, and no-one had thought of calling them haunted, or hinting that it was unsafe to sleep there.

She answered that Sir Archibald himself had used the Blue Room, and one or two other gentlemen, who had passed the night there for a wager, and they had neither seen nor heard anything unusual. For her part, she added, she did not hold with people wasting their time thinking of such folly, when they had much better be giving their minds to their proper business.

Somehow her professions of incredulity did not ring true, and I wasn't satisfied, although I gave up asking questions. But if I said nothing, I thought the more, and often when my duties took me to the Blue Room I would wonder why, if nothing had happened there, and there was no real mystery, the room was never used; it had not even a mattress on the fine carved bedstead, which was only covered by a sheet to keep it from the dust. And then I would steal into the portrait gallery to look at the great picture of the Lady Barbara, who had died in the full bloom of her youth, no-one knew why, for she was just found one morning stiff and cold, stretched across that fine bed under the blue tapestried canopy.

She must have been a beautiful woman, with her great black eyes and splendid auburn hair, though I doubt her beauty was all on the outside, for she belonged to the gayest set of the Court, which was none too respectable in those days, if half the tales one hears of it are true; and indeed, a modest lady would hardly have been painted in such a dress, all slipping off her shoulders and so thin that one can see right through the stuff. There must have been something queer about her too, for they do say that her father-in-law, who was known as the wicked Lord Mertoun, would not have her buried with the rest of the family; but that might have been his spite, because he was angry that she had had no child, and her husband, who was but a sickly sort of man, dying of consumption but a month later, there was no direct heir; so that with the old Lord the title became extinct, and the estates passed to the Protestant branch of the family, of which the present Sir Archibald Mertoun is the head. Be that as it may, Lady Barbara lies by herself in the churchyard, near the lychgate, under a grand marble tomb indeed, but all alone, while her husband's coffin has its place besides those of his brothers who died before him, among their ancestors and descendants in the great vault under the chancel.

I often used to think about her, and wonder why she died, and how; and then It happened and the mystery grew deeper than ever.

There was a family-gathering that Christmas, I remember, the first Christmas for many years that had been kept at Mertoun, and we had been very busy arranging the rooms for the different guests, for on New Year's Eve there was a ball in the neighbourhood, to which Lady Mertoun was taking a large party, and for that night, at least, the house was as full as it would hold.

I was in the linen-room, helping to sort the sheets and pillow-covers for the different beds, when my Lady came in with an open letter in her hand.

She began to talk to my aunt in a low voice, explaining something which seemed to have put her out, for when I returned from carrying a pile of linen to the head-housemaid, I heard her say: 'It is too annoying to upset all one's arrangements at the last moment. Why couldn't she have left the girl at home and brought another maid, who could be squeezed in somewhere without any trouble?'

I gathered that one of the visitors, Lady Grayburn, had written that she was bringing her companion, and as she had left her maid, who was ill, at home, she wanted the young lady to have a bedroom adjoining hers, so that she might be at hand to give any help that was required. The request seemed a trifling matter enough in itself, but it just so happened that there really was no room at liberty. Every bedroom on the first floor corridor was occupied, with the exception of the Blue Room, which, as ill-luck would have it, chanced to be next to that arranged for Lady Grayburn.

My aunt made several suggestions but none of them seemed quite practicable, and at last my Lady broke out: 'Well, it cannot be helped; you must put Miss Wood in the Blue Room. It is only for one night, and she won't know anything about that silly story.'

'Oh, my Lady!' my aunt cried, and I knew by her tone that she had not spoken the truth when she professed to think so lightly of the ghost.

'I can't help it,' her Ladyship answered, 'besides I don't believe there is anything really wrong with the room. Sir Archibald has slept there, and he found no cause for complaint.'

'But a woman, a young woman,' my aunt urged; 'indeed I wouldn't run such a risk, my Lady; let me put one of the gentlemen in there, and Miss Wood can have the first room in the west corridor.'

'And what use would she be to Lady Grayburn out there?' said her Ladyship. 'Don't be foolish, my good Marris. Unlock the door between the two rooms; Miss Wood can leave it open if she feels nervous; but I shall not say a word about that foolish superstition, and I shall be very much annoyed if anyone else does so.'

She spoke as if that settled the question but my aunt wasn't easy. 'The Laird,' she murmured; 'what will he say to a lady being put to sleep there?'

'Sir Archibald does not interfere in the household arrangements. Have the Blue Room made ready for Miss Wood at once. *I* will take the responsibility – if there is any.'

On that her Ladyship went away and there was nothing for it but to carry out her orders. The Blue Room was prepared, a great fire lighted, and when I went round last thing to see all was in order for the visitor's arrival, I couldn't but think how handsome and comfortable it looked. There were candles burning brightly on the toilet-table and the chimney-piece, and a fine blaze of logs on the wide hearth. I saw nothing had been overlooked, and was closing the door when my eyes fell on the bed. It was crumpled just as if someone had thrown themselves across it, and I was vexed that the housemaids should have been so careless, especially with the smart new quilt. I went round, and patted up the feathers, and smoothed the counterpane, just as the carriages drove under the window.

By-and-by Lady Grayburn and Miss Wood came upstairs, and knowing they had brought no maid, I went to assist in the unpacking. I was a long time in her Ladyship's room, and when

I'd settled her, I tapped at the next door and offered to help Miss Wood. Lady Grayburn followed me almost immediately to enquire the whereabouts of some keys. She spoke very sharply, I thought, to her companion, who seemed a timid, delicate slip of a girl, with nothing noticeable about her except her hair, which was lovely, pale golden, and heaped in thick coils around her small head.

'You will certainly be late,' Lady Grayburn said. 'What an age you have been, and you have not half finished unpacking yet.' The young lady murmured something about there being so little time. 'You have had time to sprawl on the bed instead of getting ready,' was the retort, and as Miss Wood meekly denied the imputation, I looked over my shoulder at the bed, and saw there the same strange indentation I had noticed before. It made my heart beat faster, for without any reason at all I felt certain that the crease must have something to do with Lady Barbara.

Miss Wood didn't go to the ball. She had supper in the school-room with the young ladies' governess, and as I heard from one of the maids that she was to sit up for Lady Grayburn, I took her some wine and sandwiches about twelve o'clock. She stayed in the school-room, with a book, till the first party came home soon after two. I'd been round the rooms with the housemaid to see the fires were kept up, and I wasn't surprised to find that queer crease back on the bed again; indeed, I sort of expected it. I said nothing to the maid, who didn't seem to have noticed anything out of the way, but I told my aunt, and though she answered sharply that I was talking nonsense, she turned quite pale, and I heard her mutter something under her breath that sounded like 'God help her!'

I slept badly that night, for, do what I would, the thought of that poor young lady alone in the Blue Room kept me awake and restless. I was nervous, I suppose, and once, just as I was dropping off, I started up, fancying I had heard a scream. I opened my door and listened, but there wasn't a sound, and after waiting a bit I crept back to bed, and lay there shivering till I fell asleep.

The household wasn't astir as early as usual. Everyone was tired after the late night, and tea wasn't to be sent in to the ladies until half-past nine. My aunt said nothing about the ghost, but I noticed she was fidgety, and asked almost first thing if anyone had been to Miss Wood's room. I was telling her that Martha, one of the housemaids, had just taken up the tray, when the girl came running in with a scared, white face. 'For pity's sake, Mrs Marris,' she cried, 'come to the Blue Room; something awful has happened!'

My aunt stopped to ask no questions. She ran straight upstairs, and as I followed I heard her muttering to herself, 'I knew it. I knew it. Oh Lord! What will my Lady feel like now?'

If I live to be a hundred, I shall never forget that poor girl's face. It was just as if she'd been frozen with terror. Her eyes were wide open and fixed, and her little hands clenched in the coverlet on each side of her as she lay across the bed in the very place where that crease had been.

Of course, the whole house was aroused. Sir Archibald sent one of the grooms post-haste for the doctor but he could do nothing when he came; Miss Wood had been dead for at least five hours.

It was a sad business. All the visitors went away as soon as possible, except Lady Grayburn, who was obliged to stay for the inquest.

In his evidence, the doctor stated that death was due to failure of heart-action, occasioned possibly by some sudden shock; and though the jury did not say so in their verdict, it was an open secret that they blamed her Ladyship for permitting Miss Wood to sleep in the haunted room. No-one could have reproached her more bitterly than she did herself, poor lady; and if she had done wrong she certainly suffered for it, for she never recovered from the shock of that dreadful morning, and became more or less of an invalid till her death five years later.

All this happened in 184–. It was fifty years before another woman slept in the Blue Room, and fifty years had brought with them many changes. The old Laird was gathered to his fathers, and his son, the present Sir Archibald, reigned in his stead; his sons were grown men, and Mr Charles, the eldest, married, with a fine little boy of his own. My aunt had been dead many a year, and I was an old woman, though active and able as ever to keep the maids up to their work. They take more looking after now, I think, than in the old days before there was so much talk of education, and when young women who took service thought less of dress and more of dusting. Not but what education is a fine thing in its proper place, that is, for gentlefolk. If Miss Erristoun, now, hadn't been the clever, strong-minded young lady she is, she'd never have cleared the Blue Room of its terrible secret, and lived to make Mr Arthur the happiest man alive.

He'd taken a great deal of notice of her when she first came in the summer to visit Mrs Charles, and I wasn't surprised to find she was one of the guests for the opening of the shooting season. It wasn't a regular house-party (for Sir Archibald and Lady Mertoun were away) but just half-a-dozen young ladies, friends of Mrs Charles, who was but a girl herself, and as many gentlemen that Mr Charles and Mr Arthur had invited. And very gay they were, what with lunches at the covert-side, and tennis-parties, and little dances got up at a few hours' notice, and sometimes of an evening they'd play hide-and-seek all over the house just as if they'd been so many children.

It surprised me at first to see Miss Erristoun, who was said to be so learned and had held her own with all the gentlemen at Cambridge, playing with the rest like any ordinary young lady; but she seemed to enjoy the fun as much as anyone, and was always first in any amusement that was planned. I didn't wonder at Mr Arthur's fancying her, for she was a handsome girl, tall and finely made, and carried herself like a princess. She had a wonderful head of hair, too, so long, her maid told me, it touched the ground as she sat on a chair to have it brushed. Everybody seemed to take to her, but I soon noticed it was Mr Arthur or Mr Calder-Maxwell she liked best to be with.

Mr Maxwell is a professor now, and a great man at Oxford; but then he was just an undergraduate the same as Mr Arthur, though more studious, for he'd spend hours in the library poring over those old books full of queer black characters, that they say the wicked Lord Mertoun collected in the time of King Charles the Second. Now and then Miss Erristoun would stay indoors to help him, and it was something they found out in their studies that gave them the clue to the secret of the Blue Room.

For a long time after Miss Wood's death all mention of the ghost was strictly forbidden. Neither the Laird nor her Ladyship could bear the slightest allusion to the subject, and the Blue Room was kept locked, except when it had to be cleaned and aired. But as the years went by, the edge of the tragedy wore off, and by degrees it grew to be just a story that people talked about in much the same way as they had done when I first came to the Towers; and if many believed and speculated as to what the ghost could be, there were others who didn't hesitate to declare Miss Wood's dying in that room was a mere coincidence and had nothing to do with supernatural agency. Miss Erristoun was one of those who held most strongly to this theory. She didn't believe a bit in ghosts, and said straight out that there wasn't any of the tales told of haunted houses which could not be traced to natural causes, if people had courage and science enough to investigate them thoroughly.

It had been very wet all that day, and the gentlemen had stayed indoors, and nothing would serve Mrs Charles but they should all have an old-fashioned tea in my room and 'talk ghosts' as she called it. They made me tell them all I knew about the Blue Room, and it was then, when everyone was discussing the story and speculating as to what the ghost could be, that Miss Erristoun spoke up. 'The poor girl had heart-complaint,' she finished by saying, 'and she would have died the same way in any other room.'

'But what about the other people who have slept there?' someone objected.

'They did not die. Old Sir Archibald came to no harm, neither

72

did Mr Hawksworth, nor the other man. They were healthy, and had plenty of pluck, so they saw nothing.'

'They were not women,' put in Mrs Charles, 'you see the ghost only appears to the weaker sex.'

'That proves the story to be a mere legend,' Miss Erristoun said with decision. 'First it was reported that everyone who slept in the room died. Then one or two men did sleep there, and remained alive; so the tale had to be modified, and since one woman could be proved to have died suddenly there, the fatality was represented as attaching to women only. If a girl with a sound constitution and a good nerve were once to spend the night there in that room, your charming family-spectre would be discredited forever.'

There was a perfect chorus of dissent. None of the ladies could agree, and most of the gentlemen doubted whether any woman's nerve would stand the ordeal. The more they argued the more Miss Erristoun persisted in her view, till at last Mrs Charles got vexed, and cried, 'Well, it is one thing to talk about it, and another to do it. Confess now, Edith, you daren't sleep in that room yourself.'

'I dare, and I will,' she answered directly, 'I don't believe in ghosts, and I am ready to stand the test. I will sleep in the Blue Room tonight, if you like, and tomorrow morning you will have to confess that whatever there may be against the haunted chamber, it is not a ghost.'

I think Mrs Charles was sorry she'd spoken then, for they all took Miss Erristoun up, and the gentlemen were for laying wagers as to whether she'd see anything or not. When it was too late she tried to laugh aside her challenge as absurd, but Miss Erristoun wouldn't be put off. She said she meant to see the thing through, and if she wasn't allowed to have a bed made up, she'd carry in her blankets and pillows, and camp out on the floor.

The others were all laughing and disputing together, but I saw Mr Maxwell look at her very curiously. Then he drew Mr Arthur aside and began to talk in an undertone. I couldn't hear what he said, but Mr Arthur answered quite short: 'It's the maddest thing I ever heard of, and I won't allow it for a moment.'

'She will not ask your permission perhaps,' Mr Maxwell retorted. Then he turned to Mrs Charles, and inquired how long it was since the Blue Room had been used, and if it was kept aired. I could speak to that, and when he'd heard that there was no bedding there, but that fires were kept up regularly, he said he meant to have the first refusal of the ghost, and if he saw nothing it would be time enough for Miss Erristoun to take her turn.

Mr Maxwell had a kind of knack of settling things, and somehow with his quiet manner always seemed to get his own way. Just before dinner, he came to me with Mrs Charles, and said it was all right, I was to get the room made ready quietly, not for all the servants to know, and he was going to sleep there.

I heard next morning he came down to breakfast as usual. He'd had an excellent night, he said, and never slept better.

It was wet again in the morning, raining 'cats and dogs', but Mr Arthur went out in it all. He'd almost quarrelled with Miss Erristoun, and was furious with Mr Maxwell for encouraging her in her idea of testing the ghost-theory, as they called it. Those two were together in the library for most of the day, and Mrs Charles was chaffing Miss Erristoun as they went upstairs to dress, and asking her if she found demons interesting. Yes, she said, but there was a page missing from the most interesting part of the book. They could not make head or tail of the context for some time, and then Mr Maxwell discovered that a leaf had been cut out. They talked of nothing else all through dinner, the butler told me, and Miss Erristoun seemed so taken up with her studies, I hoped she'd forgotten about the haunted room. But she wasn't one of the sort to forget. Later in the evening I came across her standing with Mr Arthur in the corridor. He was talking very earnestly, and I saw her shrug her shoulders and just look up at him and smile, in a sort of way that meant she wasn't going to give in. I was slipping quietly by, for I didn't want to disturb them, when Mr Maxwell came out of the billiard-room. 'It's our game,' he said, 'won't you come and play the tie?'

'I'm quite ready,' Miss Erristoun answered, and was turning away, when Mr Arthur laid his hand on her arm. 'Promise me first,' he urged, 'promise me that much at least.'

'How tiresome you are!' she said quite pettishly. 'Very well then, I promise; and now please, don't worry me any more.'

Mr Arthur watched her go back to the billiard-room with his friend, and he gave a sort of groan. Then he caught sight of me and came along the passage. 'She won't give it up,' he said, and his face was quite white. 'I've done all I can; I'd have telegraphed to my father, but I don't know where they'll stay in Paris, and anyway there'd be no time to get an answer. Mrs Marris, she's going to sleep in that damned room, and if anything happens to her, I –' he broke off short, and threw himself on the window-seat, hiding his face on his folded arms.

I could have cried for sympathy with his trouble. Mr Arthur has always been a favourite of mine, and I felt downright angry with Miss Erristoun for making him so miserable just out of a bit of bravado.

'I think they are all mad,' he went on presently. 'Charley ought to have stopped the whole thing at once, but Kate and the others have talked him round. He professes to believe there's no danger, and Maxwell has got his head full of some rubbish he has found in those beastly books on Demonology, and he's backing her up. She won't listen to a word I say. She told me point-blank she'd never speak to me again if I interfered. She doesn't care a hang for me; I know that now, but I can't help it; I – I'd give my life for her.'

I did my best to comfort him, saying that Miss Erristoun wouldn't come to any harm; but it wasn't a bit of use, for I didn't believe in my own assurances. I felt nothing but ill could come of such tempting of Providence, and I seemed to see that other poor girl's terrible face as it had looked when we found her dead in that wicked room. However, it is a true saying that 'a wilful woman will have her way', and we could do nothing to prevent Miss

Erristoun's risking her life; but I made up my mind to one thing, whatever other people might do, *I* wasn't going to bed that night.

I'd been getting the winter-hangings into order, and the upholstress had used the little boudoir at the end of the long corridor for her work. I made up the fire, brought in a fresh lamp, and when the house was quiet, I crept down and settled myself there to watch. It wasn't ten yards from the door of the Blue Room, and over the thick carpet I could pass without making a sound, and listen at the keyhole. Miss Erristoun had promised Mr Arthur she would not lock her door; it was the one concession he'd been able to obtain from her. The ladies went to their rooms about eleven, but Miss Erristoun stayed talking to Mrs Charles for nearly an hour while her maid was brushing her hair. I saw her go into the Blue Room, and by-and-by Louise left her, and all was quiet.

It must have been half-past one before I thought I heard something moving outside. I opened the door and looked out, and there was Mr Arthur standing in the passage. He gave a start when he saw me. 'You're sitting up,' he said, coming into the room; 'then you do believe there is evil work on hand tonight? The others have gone to bed, but I can't rest; it's no use my trying to sleep. I meant to stay in the smoking-room, but it is so far away; I couldn't hear there even if she called for help. I've listened at the door; there isn't a sound. Can't you go in and see if it's all right? Oh, Marris, if she should –'

I knew what he meant, but I wasn't going to admit *that* possible – yet. 'I can't go into a young lady's room without any reason,' I said; 'but I've been to the door every few minutes for the last hour and more. It wasn't till half-past twelve that Miss Erristoun stopped moving about, and I don't believe, Mr Arthur, that God will let harm come to her, without giving those that care for her some warning. I mean to keep on listening, and if there's the least hint of anything wrong, why I'll go to her at once, and you are at hand here to help.'

I talked to him a bit more till he seemed more reasonable, and then we sat there waiting, hardly speaking a word except when, from time to time, I went outside to listen. The house was deathly quiet; but there was something terrible, I thought, in the stillness, not a sign of life anywhere save just in the little boudoir, where Mr Arthur paced up and down, or sat with a strained look on his face, watching the door.

As three o'clock struck, I went out again. There is a window in the corridor, angle for angle with the boudoir door. As I passed, someone stepped from behind the curtains and a voice whispered: 'Don't be frightened, Mrs Marris; it is only me, Calder-Maxwell. Mr Arthur is there, isn't he?' He pushed open the boudoir door. 'May I come in?' he said softly. 'I guessed you'd be about, Mertoun. I'm not at all afraid myself, but if there is anything in that little legend, it is as well for some of us to be on hand. It was a good idea of yourself to get Mrs Marris to keep watch with you.'

Mr Arthur looked at him as black as thunder. 'If you didn't *know* there was something in it,' he said, 'you wouldn't be here now; and knowing that, you're nothing less than a blackguard for egging that girl on to risk her life, for the sake of trying to prove your insane theories. You are no friend of mine after this, and I'll never willingly see you or speak to you again.'

I was fairly frightened at his words, and for how Mr Maxwell might take them, but he just smiled, and lighted a cigarette, quite cool and quiet.

'I'm not going to quarrel with you, old chap,' he said. 'You're a bit on the strain tonight, and when a man has nerves he mustn't be held responsible for all his words.' Then he turned to me. 'You're a sensible woman, Mrs Marris, and a brave one too, I fancy. If I stay here with Mr Arthur, will you keep close outside Miss Erristoun's door? She may talk in her sleep quietly; that's of no consequence; but if she should cry out, go in at once, *at once,* you understand; we shall hear you, and follow immediately.'

At that Mr Arthur was on his feet. 'You know more than you pretend,' he cried. 'You slept in that room last night. By Heaven, if you've played any trick on her I'll –'

Mr Maxwell held the door open. 'Will you please go, Mrs Marris?' he said in his quiet way. 'Mertoun, don't be a damn fool.'

I went as he told me, and I give you my word I was all ears, for I felt certain Mr Maxwell knew more than we did, and that he expected something to happen.

It seemed like hours, though I know now it could not have been more than a quarter of that time, before I could be positive someone was moving behind that closed door.

At first I thought it was only my own heart, which was beating against my ribs like a hammer; but soon I could distinguish footsteps and a sort of murmur like someone speaking continuously, but very low. Then a voice (it was Miss Erristoun's this time) said, 'No, it is impossible. I am dreaming, I must be dreaming.' There was a kind of rustling as though she were moving quickly across the floor. I had my fingers on the handle, but I seemed as if I'd lost power to stir; I could only wait for what might come next.

Suddenly she began to say something out loud. I could not make out the words, which didn't sound like English, but almost directly she stopped short. 'I can't remember any more,' she cried in a troubled tone. 'What shall I do? I can't –' There was a pause. Then – 'No, no!' she shrieked, 'Oh, Arthur, Arthur!'

At that my strength came back to me, and I flung open the door.

There was a night-lamp burning on the table, and the room was quite light. Miss Erristoun was standing by the bed; she seemed to have backed up against it; her hands were down at her sides, her fingers clutching at the quilt. Her face was white as a sheet, and her eyes staring wide with terror, as well they might – I know I never had such a shock in my life, for if it was my last word, I swear there was a man standing close in front of her. He turned and looked at me as I opened the door, and I saw his face as plain as I saw hers. He was young and very handsome, and his eyes shone like an animal's when you see them in the dark.

'Arthur!' Miss Erristoun gasped again, and I saw she was

fainting. I sprang forward and caught her by the shoulders just as she was falling back on to the bed.

It was all over in a second. Mr Arthur had her in his arms, and when I looked up there were only us four in the room, for Mr Maxwell had followed on Mr Arthur's heel, and was kneeling beside me with his fingers on Miss Erristoun's pulse. 'It's only a faint,' he said, 'she'll come round directly. Better take her out of this at once; here's a dressing-gown.' He threw the wrapper around her, and would have helped to raise her, but Mr Arthur needed no assistance. He lifted Miss Erristoun as if she'd been a baby, and carried her straight to the boudoir. He laid her on the couch and knelt beside her, chafing her hands. 'Get the brandy out of the smoking-room, Maxwell,' he said. 'Mrs Marris, have you any salts handy?'

I always carry a bottle in my pocket, so I gave it to him, before I ran after Mr Maxwell, who had lighted a candle, and was going for the brandy. 'Shall I wake Mr Charles and the servants?' I cried. 'He'll be hiding somewhere, but he hasn't had time to get out of the house yet.'

He looked as if he thought I was crazed. 'He – who?' he asked.

'The man,' I said. 'There was a man in Miss Erristoun's room. I'll call up Soames and Robert.'

'You'll do nothing of the sort,' he said sharply. 'There was no man in that room.'

'There was,' I retorted, 'for I saw him, and a great powerful man too. Someone ought to go for the police before he has time to get off.'

Mr Maxwell always was an odd sort of gentleman, but I didn't know what to make of the way he behaved then. He just leaned against the wall, and laughed till the tears came into his eyes.

'It is no laughing matter that I can see,' I told him quite short, for I was angry at his treating the matter so lightly; 'and I consider it no more than my duty to let Mr Charles know that there's a burglar on the premises.'

He grew grave at once then. 'I beg your pardon, Mrs Marris,' he said seriously, 'but I couldn't help smiling at the idea of the police. The vicar would be more to the point, all things considered. You really must not think of rousing the household; it might do Miss Erristoun a great injury, and could in no case be of the slightest use. Don't you understand? It was not a man at all you saw, it was an – well, it was what haunts the Blue Room.'

Then he ran downstairs leaving me fairly dazed, for I'd made so sure that what I'd seen was a real man, that I'd clean forgotten all about the ghost.

Miss Erristoun wasn't long in regaining consciousness. She swallowed the brandy we gave her like a lamb, and sat up bravely, though she started at every sound, and kept her hand in Mr Arthur's like a frightened child. It was strange, seeing how independent and stand-off she had been with him before, but she seemed all the sweeter for the change. It was as if they'd come to an understanding without any words; and, indeed, he must have known that she had cared for him all along, when she called out his name in her terror.

As soon as she'd recovered herself a little, Mr Maxwell began asking questions. Mr Arthur would have stopped him, but he insisted it was of the greatest importance to hear everything while the impression was fresh; and when she had got over the first effort, Miss Erristoun seemed to find relief in telling her experience. She sat there with one hand in Mr Arthur's while she spoke, and Mr Maxwell wrote down what she said in his pocket book.

She told us she went to bed quite easy, for she wasn't the least nervous, and being tired she soon dropped off to sleep. Then she had a sort of dream, I suppose, for she thought she was in the same room, only differently furnished, all but the bed. She described exactly how everything was arranged. She had the strangest feeling too, that she was not herself but someone else, and that she was going to do something – something that must be done, though she was frightened to death all the time, and kept stopping to listen at the inner door, expecting someone would hear her moving about and call out for her to go to them. That in itself was queer, for there was nobody sleeping in the adjoining room. In her dream, she went on to say, she saw a curious little silver brazier, one that stands in the cabinet in the picture-gallery (a fine example of *cinque cento* work, I think I've heard my Lady call it), and this she remembered holding in her hands for a long time, before she set it on a little table beside the bed. Now the bed in the Blue Room is very handsome, richly carved on the cornice and frame, and especially the posts, which are a foot square at the base and covered with relief-work, in a design of fruit and flowers. Miss Erristoun said she went to the left-hand post at the foot, and after passing her hand over the carving, she seemed to touch a spring in one of the centre flowers, and the panel fell outwards like a lid, disclosing a secret cupboard out of which she took some papers and a box. She seemed to know what to do with the papers, though she couldn't tell us what was written on them; and she had a distinct recollection of taking a pastille from the box, and lighting it in the silver brazier. The smoke curled up and seemed to fill the whole room with a heavy perfume, and the next thing she remembered was that she awoke to find herself standing in the middle of the floor, and – what I had seen when I opened the door was there.

She turned quite white when she came to this part of the story, and shuddered. 'I couldn't believe it,' she said. 'I tried to think I was still dreaming, but I wasn't, I wasn't. It was real, and it was there, and – oh, it was horrible!'

She hid her face against Mr Arthur's shoulder. Mr Maxwell sat, pen in hand, staring at her. 'I was right then,' he said. 'I felt sure I was but it seemed incredible.'

'It is incredible,' said Miss Erristoun, 'but it is true, frightfully true. When I realised that I was awake, that it was actually real, I tried to remember the charge, you know, out of the office of exorcism, but I couldn't get through it. The words went out of my head; I felt my will-power failing; I was paralysed, as though I could make no effort to help myself and then – then I –' she looked at Mr Arthur and blushed all over her face and neck. 'I thought of you, and I called – I had a feeling that you would save me.'

Mr Arthur made no more ado about us than if we'd been a couple of dummies. He just put his arms around her and kissed her, while Mr Maxwell and I looked the other way.

After a bit, Mr Maxwell said, 'One more question, please; what was it like?'

She answered after thinking for a minute. 'It was like a man, tall and very handsome. I have an impression that its eyes were blue and very bright.' Mr Maxwell looked at me inquiringly, and I nodded. 'And dressed?' he asked. She began to laugh almost hysterically. 'It sounds too insane for words, but I think – I am almost positive it wore ordinary evening dress.'

'It is impossible,' Mr Arthur cried. 'You were dreaming the whole time, that proves it.'

'It doesn't,' Mr Maxwell contradicted. 'They usually appeared in the costume of the day. You'll find that stated particularly both by Scott and Glanvil; Sprenger gives an instance too. Besides, Mrs Marris thought it was a burglar, which argues that the – the manifestation was objective, and presented no striking peculiarity in the way of clothing.'

'What?' Miss Erristoun exclaimed. 'You saw it too?'

I told her exactly what I had seen. My description tallied with hers in everything, but for the white shirt and tie, which from my position at the door, I naturally should not be able to see.

Mr Maxwell snapped the elastic round his note-book. For a long time he sat staring silently at the fire. 'It is almost past belief,' he said at last, speaking half to himself, 'that such a thing could happen at the end of the nineteenth century, in these scientific rationalistic times that we think such a lot about, we, who look down from our superior intellectual height on the benighted superstitions of the Middle Ages.' He gave an odd little laugh. 'I'd like to get to the bottom of this business. I have a theory, and in the interest of psychical research and common humanity, I'd like to work it out. Miss Erristoun, you ought, I know, to have rest and quiet, and it is almost morning; but will you grant me one request? Before you are overwhelmed with questions, before you are made to relate your experience till the impression of tonight's adventure loses edge and clearness, will you go with Mertoun and myself to the Blue Room, and try to find the secret panel?'

'She shall never set foot inside that door again,' Mr Arthur began hotly, but Miss Erristoun laid a restraining hand on his arm.

'Wait a moment, dear,' she said gently; 'let us hear Mr Maxwell's reasons. Do you think,' she went on, 'that my dream had a foundation in fact; that something connected with that dreadful thing is really concealed about the room?'

'I think,' he answered, 'that you hold the clue to the mystery, and I believe, could you repeat the action of your dream, and open the secret panel, you might remove forever the legacy of one woman's reckless folly. Only if it is to be done at all, it must be soon, before the impression has had time to fade.'

'It shall be done now,' she answered; 'I am quite myself again. Feel my pulse; my nerves are perfectly steady.'

Mr Arthur broke out into angry protestations. She had gone through more than enough for one night, he said, and he wouldn't have her health sacrificed to Mr Maxwell's whims.

I have always thought Miss Erristoun handsome, but never, not even on her wedding-day, did she look so beautiful as then when she stood up in her heavy white wrapper, with all her splendid hair loose on her shoulders.

'Listen,' she said, 'if God gives us a plain work to do, we must do it at any cost. Last night, I didn't believe in anything I could not understand. I was so full of pride in my own courage and common sense, that I wasn't afraid to sleep in that room and prove the ghost was all superstitious nonsense. I have learned there are forces of which I know nothing, and against which my strength was utter weakness. God took care of me, and sent help in time; and if He has opened a way by which I may save other women

83

from the danger I escaped, I should be worse than ungrateful were I to shirk the task. Bring the lamp, Mr Maxwell, and let us do what we can.' Then she put both hands on Mr Arthur's shoulders. 'Why are you troubled?' she said sweetly. 'You will be with me, and how can I be afraid?'

It never strikes me as strange now that burglaries and things can go on in a big house at night, and not a soul one whit the wiser. There were five people sleeping in the rooms on that corridor while we tramped up and down without disturbing one of them. Not but what we went as quietly as we could, for Mr Maxwell made it clear that the less was known about the actual facts, the better. He went first, carrying the lamp, and we followed. Miss Erristoun shivered as her eyes fell on the bed, across which that dreadful crease showed plain, and I knew she was thinking of what might have been, had help not been at hand.

Just for a minute she faltered, and then she went bravely on, and began feeling over the carved woodwork for the spring of the secret panel. Mr Maxwell held the lamp close, but there was nothing to show any difference between that bit of carving and the other three posts. For a full ten minutes she tried, and so did the gentlemen, and it seemed as though the dream would turn out a delusion after all, when all at once Miss Erristoun cried, 'I have found it', and with a little jerk, the square of wood fell forward, and there was the cupboard just as she had described it to us.

It was Mr Maxwell who took out the things, for Mr Arthur wouldn't let Miss Erristoun touch them. There were a roll of papers and a little silver box. At the sight of the box, she gave a sort of cry. 'That is it,' she said, and covered her face with her hands.

Mr Maxwell lifted the lid, and emptied out two or three pastilles. Then he unfolded the papers, and before he had fairly glanced at the sheet of parchment covered with queer black characters, he cried, 'I knew it, I knew it! It *is* the missing leaf.' He seemed quite wild with excitement. 'Come along,' he said.

'Bring the light, Mertoun; I always said it was no ghost, and now the whole thing is as clear as daylight. You see,' he went on, as we gathered round the table in the boudoir, 'so much depended on there being an heir. That was the chief cause of the endless quarrels between old Lord Mertoun and Barbara. He never approved of the marriage, and was for ever reproaching the poor woman for having failed in the first duty of an only son's wife. His will shows that he did not leave her a farthing in the event of her husband dying without issue. Then the feud with the Protestant branch of the family was very bitter, and the Sir Archibald of the day had three boys, he having married (about the same time as his cousin) Lady Mary Sarum, who had been Barbara's rival at Court, and whom Barbara very naturally hated. So when the doctors pronounced Dennis Mertoun to be dying of consumption, his wife got desperate and had recourse to black magic. It was well known that the old man's collection of works on Demonology was the most complete in Europe. Lady Barbara must have had access to the books, and it was she who cut out this leaf. Probably Lord Mertoun discovered the theft and drew his own conclusions. That would account for his refusal to admit her body to the family vault. The Mertouns were staunch Romanists, and it is one of the deadly sins, you know, meddling with sorcery. Well, Barbara contrived to procure the pastilles, and she worked the spell according to the directions given here, and then – Good God! Mertoun, what have you done?'

Before anyone could interfere to check him, Mr Arthur had swept papers, box, pastilles, and all off the table and flung them into the fire. The thick parchment curled and shrivelled on the hot coals, and a queer, faint smell like incense spread heavily through the room. Mr Arthur stepped to the window and threw the casement wide open. Day was breaking and a sweet fresh wind swept in from the east which was all rosy with the glow of the rising sun.

'It is a nasty story,' he said; 'and if there be any truth in it, for the credit of the family, and the name of a dead woman, let it rest for ever. We will keep our own counsel about tonight's work. It is enough for others to know that the spell of the Blue Room is broken, since a brave, pure-minded girl has dared to face its unknown mystery and has laid the ghosts.'

Mr Calder-Maxwell considered a moment. 'I believe you are right,' he said presently, with an air of resignation. 'I agree to your proposition, and I surrender my chance of world-wide celebrity among the votaries of Psychical Research; but I *do* wish, Mertoun, you would call things by their proper names. It was not a ghost. It was an –'

But as I said, all I can remember now of the word he used is, that it somehow put me in mind of poultry-rearing.

★ ★ ★ ★ ★

Note – the reader will observe that the worthy Mrs Marris, though no student of Sprenger, unconsciously discerned the root-affinity of the *incubator* of the hen-yard and the *incubus* of the *Malleus Maleficarum*.

THE STORY OF YAND MANOR HOUSE (1898)

E and H Heron

(pseudonyms of Kate Prichard [1851–1935]
and Hesketh Prichard [1876-1922])

Hesketh Prichard led an extraordinarily adventurous life as an explorer and big-game hunter, travelling the world from Patagonia to Newfoundland and from Haiti to Norway. He was also a first-class cricketer and a brilliant marksman. During the First World War he was in charge of training snipers for the Western Front. Somehow, amidst all this other activity, he managed to find time to write fiction, often in collaboration with his mother Kate. Of the fiction Hesketh Prichard wrote on his own, the most interesting features 'November Joe', a Canadian backwoodsman and amateur detective who appears in a number of stories. Working with Kate, he produced tales of a Zorro-like figure named Don Q and, in the 1920s, one of them was turned into a Hollywood film starring Douglas Fairbanks. The Flaxman Low stories, which were the Prichards' first major successes were about an occult detective, and predate William Hope Hodgson's better-known Carnacki stories by almost a decade. They were originally published in Pearson's Magazine *in 1898 and 1899 and were later collected in book form. In the twelve stories, Flaxman Low investigates all kinds of psychic phenomena including a spirit which attacks travellers on a lonely road ('The Story of the Moor Road') and a ghost with a peculiarly unnerving laugh ('The Story of Medhans Lea'). In 'The Story of Yand Manor House' he is accompanied on one of his cases by a sceptical Frenchman named Thierry who is forced, by the end of the tale, to admit that his doubts about ghosts and occult phenomena have been misplaced.*

LOOKING through the notes of Mr Flaxman Low, one sometimes catches through the steel-blue hardness of facts, the pink flush of romance, or more often the black corner of a horror unnameable. The following story may serve as an instance of the latter. Mr Low not only unravelled the mystery at Yand, but at the same time justified his life-work to M. Thierry, the well-known French critic and philosopher.

At the end of a long conversation, M. Thierry, arguing from his own standpoint as a materialist, had said:

'The factor in the human economy which you call "soul" cannot be placed.'

'I admit that,' replied Low. 'Yet, when a man dies, is there not one factor unaccounted for in the change that comes upon him? Yes! For though his body still exists, it rapidly falls to pieces, which proves that that has gone which held it together.'

The Frenchman laughed, and shifted his ground.

'Well, for my part, I don't believe in ghosts! Spirit manifestations, occult phenomena – is not this the ashbin into which a certain clique shoot everything they cannot understand, or for which they fail to account?'

'Then what should you say to me, Monsieur, if I told you that I have passed a good portion of my life in investigating this particular ashbin, and have been lucky enough to sort a small part of its contents with tolerable success?' replied Flaxman Low.

'The subject is doubtless interesting – but I should like to have some personal experience in the matter,' said Thierry dubiously.

'I am at present investigating a most singular case,' said Low. 'Have you a day or two to spare?'

Thierry thought for a minute or more.

'I am grateful,' he replied. 'But, forgive me, is it a convincing ghost?'

'Come with me to Yand and see. I have been there once already, and came away for the purpose of procuring information from MSS to which I have the privilege of access, for I confess that the phenomena at Yand lie altogether outside any former experience of mine.'

Low sank back into his chair with his hands clasped behind his head – a favourite position of his – and the smoke of his long pipe curled up lazily into the golden face of an Isis, which stood behind him on a bracket. Thierry, glancing across, was struck by the strange likeness between the faces of the Egyptian goddess and this scientist of the nineteenth century. On both rested the calm, mysterious abstraction of some unfathomable thought. As he looked, he decided.

'I have three days to place at your disposal.'

'I thank you heartily,' replied Low. 'To be associated with so brilliant a logician as yourself in an inquiry of this nature is more than I could have hoped for! The material with which I have to deal is so elusive, the whole subject is wrapped in such obscurity and hampered by so much prejudice, that I can find few really qualified persons who care to approach these investigations seriously. I go down to Yand this evening, and hope not to leave without clearing up the mystery. You will accompany me?'

'Most certainly. Meanwhile pray tell me something of the affair.'

'Briefly the story is as follows. Some weeks ago I went to Yand Manor House at the request of the owner, Sir George Blackburton, to see what I could make of the events which took place there. All they complain of is the impossibility of remaining in one room – the dining-room.'

'What then is he like, this M. le Spook?' asked the Frenchman, laughing.

'No one has ever seen him, or for that matter heard him.'

'Then how –'

'You can't see him, nor hear him, nor smell him,' went on Low, 'but you can feel him and – taste him!'

'*Mon Dieu!* But this is singular! Is he then of so bad a flavour?'

'You shall taste for yourself,' answered Flaxman Low smiling.

'After a certain hour no one can remain in the room, they are simply crowded out.'

'But who crowds them out?' asked Thierry.

'That is just what I hope we may discover to-night or to-morrow.'

The last train that night dropped Mr Flaxman Low and his companion at a little station near Yand. It was late, but a trap in waiting soon carried them to the Manor House. The big bulk of the building stood up in absolute blackness before them.

'Blackburton was to have met us, but I suppose he has not yet arrived,' said Low. 'Hullo! the door is open,' he added as he stepped into the hall.

Beyond a dividing curtain they now perceived a light. Passing behind this curtain they found themselves at the end of the long hall, the wide staircase opening up in front of them.

'But who is this?' exclaimed Thierry. Swaying and stumbling at every step, there tottered slowly down the stairs the figure of a man. He looked as if he had been drinking, his face was livid, and his eyes sunk into his head.

'Thank Heaven you've come! I heard you outside,' he said in a weak voice.

'It's Sir George Blackburton,' said Low, as the man lurched forward and pitched into his arms.

They laid him down on the rugs and tried to restore consciousness.

'He has the air of being drunk, but it is not so,' remarked Thierry. 'Monsieur has had a bad shock of the nerves. See the pulses drumming in his throat.'

In a few minutes Blackburton opened his eyes and staggered to his feet.

'Come. I could not remain there alone. Come quickly.'

They went rapidly across the hall, Blackburton leading the way down a wide passage to a double-leaved door, which, after a perceptible pause, he threw open, and they all entered together.

On the great table in the centre stood an extinguished lamp, some scattered food, and a big, lighted candle. But the eyes of all three men passed at once to a dark recess beside the heavy, carved chimneypiece, where a rigid shape sat perched on the back of a huge, oak chair.

Flaxman Low snatched up the candle and crossed the room towards it.

On the top of the chair, with his feet upon the arms, sat a powerfully-built young man huddled up. His mouth was open, and his eyes twisted upwards. Nothing further could be seen from below but the ghastly pallor of cheek and throat.

'Who is this?' cried Low. Then he laid his hand gently on the man's knee.

At the touch the figure collapsed in a heap upon the floor, the gaping, set, terrified face turned up to theirs.

'He's dead!' said Low after a hasty examination. 'I should say he's been dead some hours.'

'Oh, Lord! Poor Batty!' groaned Sir George, who was entirely unnerved. 'I'm glad you've come.'

'Who is he?' said Thierry, 'and what was he doing here?'

'He's a gamekeeper of mine. He was always anxious to try conclusions with the ghost, and last night he begged me to lock him in here with food for twenty-four hours. I refused at first, but then I thought if anything happened while he was in here alone, it would interest you. Who could imagine it would end like this?'

'When did you find him?' asked Low.

'I only got here from my mother's half an hour ago. I turned on the light in the hall and came in here with a candle. As I entered the room, the candle went out, and – and – I think I must be going mad.'

'Tell us everything you saw,' urged Low.

'You will think I am beside myself; but as the light went out and I sank almost paralysed into an armchair, I saw two barred eyes looking at me!'

'Barred eyes? What do you mean?'

'Eyes that looked at me through thin vertical bars, like the bars of a cage. What's that?'

With a smothered yell Sir George sprang back. He had approached the dead man and declared something had brushed his face.

'You were standing on this spot under the overmantel. I will remain here. Meantime, my dear Thierry, I feel sure you will help Sir George to carry this poor fellow to some more suitable place,' said Flaxman Low.

When the dead body of the young gamekeeper had been carried out, Low passed slowly round and about the room. At length he stood under the old carved overmantel, which reached to the ceiling and projected bodily forward in quaint heads of satyrs and animals. One of these on the side nearest the recess represented a griffin with a flanged mouth. Sir George had been standing directly below this at the moment when he felt the touch on his face. Now alone in the dim, wide room, Flaxman Low stood on the same spot and waited. The candle threw its dull yellow rays on the shadows which seemed to gather closer and wait also. Presently a distant door banged, and Low, leaning forward to listen, distinctly felt something on the back of his neck!

He swung round. There was nothing! He searched carefully on all sides, then put his hand up to the griffin's head. Again came the same soft touch, this time upon his hand, as if something had floated past on the air.

This was definite. The griffin's head located it. Taking the candle to examine more closely, Low found four long black hairs depending from the jagged fangs. He was detaching them when Thierry reappeared.

'We must get Sir George away as soon as possible,' he said.

'Yes, we must take him away, I fear,' agreed Low. 'Our investigation must be put off till to-morrow.'

On the following day they returned to Yand. It was a large country-house, pretty and old-fashioned, with lattice windows and deep gables, that looked out between tall shrubs and across lawns set with beaupots, where peacocks sunned themselves on the velvet turf. The church spire peered over the trees on one side; and an old wall covered with ivy and creeping plants, and pierced at intervals with arches, alone separated the gardens from the churchyard.

The haunted room lay at the back of the house. It was square and handsome, and furnished in the style of the last century. The oak overmantel reached to the ceiling, and a wide window, which almost filled one side of the room, gave a view of the west door of the church.

Low stood for a moment at the open window looking out at the level sunlight which flooded the lawns and parterres.

'See that door sunk in the church wall to the left?' said Sir George's voice at his elbow. 'That is the door of the family vault. Cheerful outlook, isn't it?'

'I should like to walk across there presently,' remarked Low.

'What! Into the vault?' asked Sir George, with a harsh laugh. 'I'll take you if you like. Anything else I can show you or tell you?'

'Yes. Last night I found this hanging from the griffin's head,' said Low, producing the thin wisp of black hair. 'It must have touched your cheek as you stood below. Do you know to whom it can belong?'

'It's a woman's hair! No, the only woman who has been in this room to my knowledge for months is an old servant with grey hair, who cleans it,' returned Blackburton. 'I'm sure it was not here when I locked Batty in.'

'It is human hair, exceedingly coarse and long uncut,' said Low; 'but it is not necessarily a woman's.'

'It is not mine at any rate, for I'm sandy; and poor Batty was fair. Good-night; I'll come round for you in the morning.'

Presently, when the night closed in, Thierry and Low settled down in the haunted room to await developments. They smoked and talked deep into the night. A big lamp burned brightly on the table, and the surroundings looked homely and desirable.

Thierry made a remark to that effect, adding that perhaps the ghost might see fit to omit his usual visit.

'Experience goes to prove that ghosts have a cunning habit of choosing persons either credulous or excitable to experiment upon,' he added.

To M. Thierry's surprise, Flaxman Low agreed with him.

'They certainly choose suitable persons,' he said, 'that is, not credulous persons, but those whose senses are sufficiently keen to detect the presence of a spirit. In my own investigations, I try to eliminate what you would call the supernatural element. I deal with these mysterious affairs as far as possible on material lines.'

'Then what do you say of Batty's death? He died of fright – simply.'

'I hardly think so. The manner of his death agrees in a peculiar manner with what we know of the terrible history of this room. He died of fright and pressure combined. Did you hear the doctor's remark? It was significant. He said: "The indications are precisely those I have observed in persons who have been crushed and killed in a crowd!"'

'That is sufficiently curious, I allow. I see that it is already past two o'clock. I am thirsty; I will have a little seltzer.' Thierry rose from his chair, and, going to the side-board, drew a tumblerful from the syphon. 'Pah! What an abominable taste!'

'What? The seltzer?'

'Not at all!' returned the Frenchman irritably. 'I have not touched it yet. Some horrible fly has flown into my mouth, I suppose. Pah! Disgusting!'

'What is it like?' asked Flaxman Low, who was at the moment wiping his own mouth with his handkerchief.

'Like? As if some repulsive fungus had burst in the mouth.'

'Exactly. I perceive it also. I hope you are about to be convinced.'

'What?' exclaimed Thierry, turning his big figure round and staring at Low. 'You don't mean –'

As he spoke the lamp suddenly went out.

'Why, then, have you put the lamp out at such a moment?' cried Thierry.

'I have not put it out. Light the candle beside you on the table.'

Low heard the Frenchman's grunt of satisfaction as he found the candle, then the scratch of a match. It sputtered and went out. Another match and another behaved in the same manner, while Thierry swore freely under his breath.

'Let me have your matches, Monsieur Flaxman; mine are, no doubt, damp,' he said at last.

Low rose to feel his way across the room. The darkness was dense.

'It is the darkness of Egypt — it may be felt. Where then are you, my dear friend?' he heard Thierry saying, but the voice seemed a long way off.

'I am coming,' he answered, 'but it's so hard to get along.'

After Low had spoken the words, their meaning struck him. He paused and tried to realise in what part of the room he was. The silence was profound, and the growing sense of oppression seemed like a nightmare. Thierry's voice sounded again, faint and receding.

'I am suffocating, Monsieur Flaxman, where are you? I am near the door. Ach!'

A strangling bellow of pain and fear followed, that scarcely reached Low through the thickening atmosphere.

'Thierry, what is the matter with you?' he shouted, 'Open the door.'

But there was no answer. What had become of Thierry in that hideous, clogging gloom! Was he also dead, crushed in some ghastly fashion against the wall? What was this?

The air had become palpable to the touch, heavy, repulsive, with the sensation of cold humid flesh!

Low pushed out his hands with a mad longing to touch a table, a chair, anything but this clammy, swelling softness that thrust itself upon him from every side, baffling him and filling his grasp. He knew now that he was absolutely alone — struggling against what?

His feet were slipping in his wild efforts to feel the floor – the dank flesh was creeping upon his neck, his cheek – his breath came short and labouring as the pressure swung him gently to and fro, helpless, nauseated!

The clammy flesh crowded upon him like the bulk of some fat, horrible creature; then came a stinging pain on the cheek. Low clutched at something – there was a crash and a rush of air – the next sensation of which Mr Flaxman Low was conscious was one of deathly sickness. He was lying on wet grass, the wind blowing over him, and all the clean, wholesome smells of the open air in his nostrils.

He sat up and looked about him. Dawn was breaking windily in the east, and by its light he saw that he was on the lawn of Yand Manor House. The latticed window of the haunted room above him was open. He tried to remember what had happened. He took stock of himself, in fact, and slowly felt that he still held something clutched in his right hand – something dark-coloured, slender, and twisted. It might have been a long shred of bark or the cast skin of an adder – it was impossible to see in the dim light.

After an interval the recollection of Thierry recurred to him. Scrambling to his feet, he raised himself to the window-sill and looked in. Contrary to his expectation, there was no upsetting of furniture; everything remained in position as when the lamp went out. His own chair and the one Thierry had occupied were just as when they had arisen from them. But there was no sign of Thierry.

Low jumped in by the window. There was the tumbler full of seltzer, and the litter of matches about it. He took up Thierry's box of matches and struck a light. It flared, and he lit the candle with ease. In fact, everything about the room was perfectly normal; all the horrible conditions prevailing but a couple of hours ago had disappeared.

But where was Thierry? Carrying the lighted candle, he passed out of the door, and searched in the adjoining rooms. In one of them, to his relief, he found the Frenchman sleeping profoundly in an armchair.

Low touched his arm. Thierry leapt to his feet, fending off an imaginary blow with his arm. Then he turned his scared face on Low.

'What! You, Monsieur Flaxman! How have you escaped?'

'I should rather ask you how you escaped,' said Low, smiling at the havoc the night's experiences had worked on his friend's looks and spirits.

'I was crowded out of the room against the door. That infernal thing – what was it? – with its damp, swelling flesh, inclosed me!' A shudder of disgust stopped him. 'I was a fly in an aspic. I could not move. I sank into the stifling pulp. The air grew thick. I called to you, but your answers became inaudible. Then I was suddenly thrust against the door by a huge hand – it felt like one, at least. I had a struggle for my life, I was all but crushed, and then, I do not know how, I found myself outside the door. I shouted to you in vain. Therefore, as I could not help you, I came here, and – I will confess it, my dear friend – I locked and bolted the door. After some time I went again into the hall and listened; but, as I heard nothing, I resolved to wait until daylight and the return of Sir George.'

'That's all right,' said Low. 'It was an experience worth having.'

'But, no! Not for me! I do not envy you your researches into mysteries of this abominable description. I now comprehend perfectly that Sir George has lost his nerve if he has had to do with this horror. Besides, it is entirely impossible to explain these things.'

At this moment they heard Sir George's arrival, and went out to meet him.

'I could not sleep all night for thinking of you!' exclaimed Blackburton on seeing them; 'and I came along as soon as it was light. Something has happened.'

'But certainly something has happened,' cried M. Thierry shaking his head solemnly; 'something of the most bizarre, of the most horrible! Monsieur Flaxman, you shall tell Sir George this story. You have been in that accursed room all night, and remain alive to tell the tale!'

As Low came to the conclusion of the story Sir George suddenly exclaimed:

'You have met with some injury to your face, Mr Low.'

Low turned to the mirror. In the now strong light three parallel weals from eye to mouth could be seen.

'I remember a stinging pain like a lash on my cheek. What would you say these marks were caused by, Thierry?' asked Low.

Thierry looked at them and shook his head.

'No one in their senses would venture to offer any explanation of the occurrences of last night,' he replied.

'Something of this sort, do you think?' asked Low again, putting down the object he held in his hand on the table.

Thierry took it up and described it aloud.

'A long and thin object of a brown and yellow colour and twisted like a sabre-bladed corkscrew,' then he started slightly and glanced at Low.

'It's a human nail, I imagine,' suggested Low.

'But no human being has talons of this kind – except, perhaps, a Chinaman of high rank.'

'There are no Chinamen about here, nor ever have been, to my knowledge,' said Blackburton shortly. 'I'm very much afraid that, in spite of all you have so bravely faced, we are no nearer to any rational explanation.'

'On the contrary, I fancy I begin to see my way. I believe, after all, that I may be able to convert you, Thierry,' said Flaxman Low.

'Convert me?'

'To a belief in the definite aim of my work. But you shall judge for yourself. What do you make of it so far? I claim that you know as much of the matter as I do.'

'My dear good friend, I make nothing of it,' returned Thierry, shrugging his shoulders and spreading out his hands. 'Here we have a tissue of unprecedented incidents that can be explained on no theory whatever.'

'But this is definite,' and Flaxman Low held up the blackened nail.

'And how do you propose to connect that nail with the black hairs – with the eyes that looked through the bars of a cage – the fate of Batty, with its symptoms of death by pressure and suffocation – our experience of swelling flesh, that something which filled and filled the room to the exclusion of all else? How are you going to account for these things by any kind of connected hypothesis?' asked Thierry, with a shade of irony.

'I mean to try,' replied Low.

At lunch time Thierry inquired how the theory was getting on.

'It progresses,' answered Low. 'By the way, Sir George, who lived in this house for some time prior to, say, 1840? He was a man – it may have been a woman, but, from the nature of his studies, I am inclined to think it was a man – who was deeply read in ancient necromancy, Eastern magic, mesmerism, and subjects of a kindred nature. And was he not buried in the vault you pointed out?'

'Do you know anything more about him?' asked Sir George in surprise.

'He was, I imagine,' went on Flaxman Low reflectively, 'hirsute and swarthy, probably a recluse, and suffered from a morbid and extravagant fear of death.'

'How do you know all this?'

'I only asked about it. Am I right?'

'You have described my cousin, Sir Gilbert Blackburton, in every particular. I can show you his portrait in another room.'

As they stood looking at the painting of Sir Gilbert Blackburton, with his long, melancholy, olive face and thick, black beard, Sir George went on. 'My grandfather succeeded him at Yand. I have often heard my father speak of Sir Gilbert, and his strange studies and extraordinary fear of death. Oddly enough, in the end he died rather suddenly, while he was still hale and strong. He predicted his own approaching death, and had a doctor in attendance for a week or two before he died. He was placed in a coffin he had had made on some plan of his own and buried in the vault. His death occurred in 1842 or 1843. If you care to see them I can show you some of his papers, which may interest you.'

Mr Flaxman Low spent the afternoon over the papers. When evening came, he rose from his work with a sigh of content, stretched himself, and joined Thierry and Sir George in the garden.

They dined at Lady Blackburton's, and it was late before Sir George found himself alone with Mr Flaxman Low and his friend.

'Have you formed any opinion about the thing which haunts the Manor House?' he asked anxiously.

Thierry elaborated a cigarette, crossed his legs, and added:

'If you have in truth come to any definite conclusion, pray let us hear it, my dear Monsieur Flaxman.'

'I have reached a very definite and satisfactory conclusion,' replied Low. 'The Manor House is haunted by Sir Gilbert Blackburton, who died, or, rather, who seemed to die, on the 15th of August, 1842.'

'Nonsense! The nail fifteen inches long at the least – how do you connect it with Sir Gilbert?' asked Blackburton testily.

'I am convinced that it belonged to Sir Gilbert,' Low answered.

'But the long black hair like a woman's?'

'Dissolution in the case of Sir Gilbert was not complete – not consummated, so to speak – as I hope to show you later. Even in the case of dead persons the hair and nails have been known to grow. By a rough calculation as to the growth of nails in such cases, I was enabled to indicate approximately the date of Sir Gilbert's death. The hair too grew on his head.'

'But the barred eyes? I saw them myself!' exclaimed the young man.

'The eyelashes grow also. You follow me?'

'You have, I presume, some theory in connection with this?' observed Thierry. 'It must be a very curious one.'

'Sir Gilbert in his fear of death appears to have mastered and elaborated a strange and ancient formula by which the grosser factors of the body being eliminated, the more ethereal portions continue to retain the spirit, and the body is thus preserved from absolute disintegration. In this manner true death may be indefinitely deferred. Secure from the ordinary chances and changes of existence, this spiritualised body could retain a modified life practically for ever.'

'This is a most extraordinary idea, my dear fellow,' remarked Thierry.

'But why should Sir Gilbert haunt the Manor House, and one special room?'

'The tendency of spirits to return to the old haunts of bodily life is almost universal. We cannot yet explain the reason of this attraction of environment.'

'But the expansion – the crowding substance which we ourselves felt? You cannot meet that difficulty,' said Thierry persistently.

'Not as fully as I could wish, perhaps. But the power of expanding and contracting to a degree far beyond our comprehension is a well-known attribute of spiritualised matter.'

'Wait one little moment, my dear Monsieur Flaxman,' broke in Thierry's voice after an interval; 'this is very clever and ingenious indeed. As a theory I give it my sincere admiration. But proof – proof is what we now demand.'

Flaxman Low looked steadily at the two incredulous faces.

'This,' he said slowly, 'is the hair of Sir Gilbert Blackburton, and this nail is from the little finger of his left hand. You can prove my assertion by opening the coffin.'

Sir George, who was pacing up and down the room impatiently, drew up.

'I don't like it at all, Mr Low, I tell you frankly. I don't like it at all. I see no object in violating the coffin. I am not concerned to verify this unpleasant theory of yours. I have only one desire; I want to get rid of this haunting presence, whatever it is.'

'If I am right,' replied Low, 'the opening of the coffin and exposure of the remains to strong sunshine for a short time will free you for ever from this presence.'

In the early morning, when the summer sun struck warmly on the lawns of Yand, the three men carried the coffin from the vault to a quiet spot among the shrubs where, secure from observation, they raised the lid.

Within the coffin lay the semblance of Gilbert Blackburton, maned to the ears with long and coarse black hair. Matted eyelashes swept the fallen cheeks, and beside the body stretched the bony hands, each with its dependent sheaf of switch-like nails. Low bent over and raised the left hand gingerly.

The little finger was without a nail!

Two hours later they came back and looked again. The sun had in the meantime done its work; nothing remained but a fleshless skeleton and a few half-rotten shreds of clothing.

The ghost of Yand Manor House has never since been heard of.

When Thierry bade Flaxman Low good-bye, he said:

'In time, my dear Monsieur Flaxman, you will add another to our sciences. You establish your facts too well for my peace of mind.'

THE BROWN HAND (1899)

Sir Arthur Conan Doyle (1859–1930)

Conan Doyle is, of course, best known as the creator of Sherlock Holmes. However, he had many other strings to his bow. He wrote a number of historical novels, including The White Company *and* Micah Clarke; *he created the Napoleonic soldier Brigadier Gerard and the irascible scientist Professor Challenger, hero of* The Lost World; *he was a campaigner against miscarriages of justice and an ardent advocate of spiritualism. He was also a prolific writer of short stories. When Sherlock Holmes looks into what appear to be supernatural mysteries, as he does most famously in* The Hound of the Baskervilles, *they always turn out to have a natural explanation. This is certainly not the case in the many stories Doyle wrote which deal with the weird and the paranormal. They range from the record of a pilot's encounters with bizarre beasts in the upper atmosphere ('The Horror of the Heights') to the tale of a death-defying Ancient Egyptian in search of an antidote to his eternal life ('The Ring of Thoth'). 'The Brown Hand', in which the narrator, Dr Hardacre, investigates a ghost that is driving his uncle to distraction, was first published in* The Strand Magazine *in May 1899. Nine years later it appeared, with 16 others, in the volume* Round the Fire Stories, *a collection which brought together those of Doyle's short stories concerned, in his own words, 'with the grotesque and with the terrible'.*

Everyone knows that Sir Dominick Holden, the famous Indian surgeon, made me his heir, and that his death changed me in an hour from a hard-working and impecunious medical man to a well-to-do landed proprietor. Many know also that there were at least five people between the inheritance and me, and that Sir Dominick's selection appeared to be altogether arbitrary and whimsical. I can assure them, however, that they are quite mistaken, and that, although I only knew Sir Dominick in the closing years of his life, there were none the less very real reasons why he should show his goodwill towards me. As a matter of fact, though I say it myself, no man ever did more for another than I did for my Indian uncle. I cannot expect the story to be believed, but it is so singular that I should feel that it was a breach of duty if I did not put it upon record – so here it is, and your belief or incredulity is your own affair.

Sir Dominick Holden, CB, KCSI, and I don't know what besides, was the most distinguished Indian surgeon of his day. In the Army originally, he afterwards settled down into civil practice in Bombay, and visited as a consultant every part of India. His name is best remembered in connection with the Oriental Hospital, which he founded and supported. The time came, however, when his iron constitution began to show signs of the long strain to which he had subjected it, and his brother practitioners (who were not, perhaps, entirely disinterested upon the point) were unanimous in recommending him to return to England. He held on so long as he could, but at last he developed nervous symptoms of a very pronounced character, and so came back, a broken man, to his native county of Wiltshire. He bought a considerable estate with an ancient manor-house upon the edge of Salisbury Plain, and devoted his old age to the study of Comparative Pathology, which had been his learned hobby all his life, and in which he was a foremost authority.

We of the family were, as may be imagined, much excited by the news of the return of this rich and childless uncle to England. On his part, although by no means exuberant in his hospitality, he showed some sense of his duty to his relations, and each of us in turn had an invitation to visit him. From the accounts of my cousins it appeared to be a melancholy business, and it was with mixed feelings that I at last received my own summons to appear at Rodenhurst. My wife was so carefully excluded in the invitation that my first impulse was to refuse it, but the interests of the children had to be considered, and so, with her consent, I set out one October afternoon upon my visit to Wiltshire, with little thought of what that visit was to entail.

My uncle's estate was situated where the arable land of the plains begins to swell upwards into the rounded chalk hills which are characteristic of the county. As I drove from Dinton Station in the waning light of that autumn day, I was impressed by the weird nature of the scenery. The few scattered cottages of the peasants were so dwarfed by the huge evidences of prehistoric life, that the present appeared to be a dream and the past to be the obtrusive and masterful reality. The road wound through the valleys, formed by a succession of grassy hills, and the summit of each was cut and carved into the most elaborate fortifications, some circular, and some square, but all on a scale which has defied the winds and the rains of many centuries. Some call them Roman and some British, but their true origin and the reasons for this particular tract of country being so interlaced with entrenchments have never been finally made clear. Here and there on the long, smooth, olive-coloured slopes there rose small rounded barrows or tumuli. Beneath them lie the cremated ashes of the race which cut so deeply into the hills, but their graves tell us nothing save that a jar full of dust represents the man who once laboured under the sun.

It was through this weird country that I approached my uncle's residence of Rodenhurst, and the house was, as I found, in due keeping with its surroundings. Two broken and weather-stained pillars, each surmounted by a mutilated heraldic emblem, flanked the entrance to a neglected drive. A cold wind whistled through the elms which lined it, and the air was full of the drifting leaves. At the far end, under the gloomy arch of trees, a single yellow lamp burned steadily. In the dim half-light of the coming night I saw a long, low building stretching out two irregular wings, with deep eaves, a sloping gambrel roof, and walls which were criss-crossed with timber balks in the fashion of the Tudors. The cheery light of a fire flickered in the broad, latticed window to the left of the low-porched door, and this, as it proved, marked the study of my uncle, for it was thither that I was led by his butler in order to make my host's acquaintance.

He was cowering over his fire, for the moist chill of an English autumn had set him shivering. His lamp was unlit, and I only saw the red glow of the embers beating upon a huge, craggy face, with a Red Indian nose and cheek, and deep furrows and seams from eye to chin, the sinister marks of hidden volcanic fires. He sprang up at my entrance with something of an old-world courtesy and welcomed me warmly to Rodenhurst. At the same time I was conscious, as the lamp was carried in, that it was a very critical pair of light-blue eyes which looked out at me from under shaggy eyebrows, like scouts beneath a bush, and that this outlandish uncle of mine was carefully reading off my character with all the ease of a practised observer and an experienced man of the world.

For my part I looked at him, and looked again, for I had never seen a man whose appearance was more fitted to hold one's attention. His figure was the framework of a giant, but he had fallen away until his coat dangled straight down in a shocking fashion from a pair of broad and bony shoulders. All his limbs were huge and yet emaciated, and I could not take my gaze from his knobby wrists, and long, gnarled hands. But his eyes – those peering light-blue eyes – they were the most arrestive of any of his peculiarities. It was not their colour alone, nor was it the ambush of hair in which they lurked; but it was the expression which I read in them. For the appearance and bearing of the man were masterful, and one expected a certain corresponding arrogance in his eyes, but instead of that I read the look which tells of a spirit cowed and crushed, the furtive, expectant look of the dog whose master has taken the whip from the rack. I formed my own medical diagnosis upon one glance at those critical and yet appealing eyes. I believed that he was stricken with some mortal ailment, that he knew himself to be exposed to sudden death, and that he lived in terror of it. Such was my judgment – a false one, as the event showed; but I mention it that it may help you to realise the look which I read in his eyes.

My uncle's welcome was, as I have said, a courteous one, and in an hour or so I found myself seated between him and his wife at a comfortable dinner, with curious pungent delicacies upon the table, and a stealthy, quick-eyed Oriental waiter behind his chair. The old couple had come round to that tragic imitation of the dawn of life when husband and wife, having lost or scattered all those who were their intimates, find themselves face to face and alone once more, their work done, and the end nearing fast. Those who have reached that stage in sweetness and love, who can change their winter into a gentle Indian summer, have come as victors through the ordeal of life. Lady Holden was a small, alert woman with a kindly eye, and her expression as she glanced at him was a certificate of character to her husband. And yet, though I read a mutual love in their glances, I read also mutual horror, and recognised in her face some reflection of that stealthy fear which I had detected in his. Their talk was sometimes merry and sometimes sad, but there was a forced note in their merriment and a naturalness in their sadness which told me that a heavy heart beat upon either side of me.

We were sitting over our first glass of wine, and the servants had left the room, when the conversation took a turn which produced a remarkable effect upon my host and hostess. I cannot recall what it was which started the topic of the supernatural, but it ended in my showing them that the abnormal in psychical experiences was a subject to which I had, like many neurologists, devoted a great deal of attention. I concluded by narrating my experiences when, as a member of the Psychical Research Society, I had formed one of a committee of three who spent the night in a haunted house. Our adventures were neither exciting nor convincing, but, such as it was, the story appeared to interest my auditors in a remarkable degree. They listened with an eager silence, and I caught a look of intelligence between them which I could not understand. Lady Holden immediately afterwards rose and left the room.

Sir Dominick pushed the cigar-box over to me, and we smoked

for some little time in silence. That huge bony hand of his was twitching as he raised it with his cheroot to his lips, and I felt that the man's nerves were vibrating like fiddle-strings. My instincts told me that he was on the verge of some intimate confidence, and I feared to speak lest I should interrupt it. At last he turned towards me with a spasmodic gesture like a man who throws his last scruple to the winds.

'From the little that I have seen of you it appears to me, Dr Hardacre,' said he, 'that you are the very man I have wanted to meet.'

'I am delighted to hear it, sir.'

'Your head seems to be cool and steady. You will acquit me of any desire to flatter you, for the circumstances are too serious to permit of insincerities. You have some special knowledge upon these subjects, and you evidently view them from that philosophical standpoint which robs them of all vulgar terror. I presume that the sight of an apparition would not seriously discompose you?'

'I think not, sir.'

'Would even interest you, perhaps?'

'Most intensely.'

'As a psychical observer, you would probably investigate it in as impersonal a fashion as an astronomer investigates a wandering comet?'

'Precisely.'

He gave a heavy sigh.

'Believe me, Dr Hardacre, there was a time when I could have spoken as you do now. My nerve was a by-word in India. Even the Mutiny never shook it for an instant. And yet you see what I am reduced to – the most timorous man, perhaps, in all this county of Wiltshire. Do not speak too bravely upon this subject, or you may find yourself subjected to as long-drawn a test as I am – a test which can only end in the madhouse or the grave.'

I waited patiently until he should see fit to go farther in his confidence. His preamble had, I need not say, filled me with interest and expectation.

'For some years, Dr Hardacre,' he continued, 'my life and that of my wife have been made miserable by a cause which is so grotesque that it borders upon the ludicrous. And yet familiarity has never made it more easy to bear – on the contrary, as time passes my nerves become more worn and shattered by the constant attrition. If you have no physical fears, Dr Hardacre, I should very much value your opinion upon this phenomenon which troubles us so.'

'For what it is worth my opinion is entirely at your service. May I ask the nature of the phenomenon?'

'I think that your experiences will have a higher evidential value if you are not told in advance what you may expect to encounter. You are yourself aware of the quibbles of unconscious cerebration and subjective impressions with which a scientific sceptic may throw a doubt upon your statement. It would be as well to guard against them in advance.'

'What shall I do, then?'

'I will tell you. Would you mind following me this way?' He led me out of the dining-room and down a long passage until we came to a terminal door. Inside there was a large bare room fitted as a laboratory, with numerous scientific instruments and bottles. A shelf ran along one side, upon which there stood a long line of glass jars containing pathological and anatomical specimens.

'You see that I still dabble in some of my old studies,' said Sir Dominick. 'These jars are the remains of what was once a most excellent collection, but unfortunately I lost the greater part of them when my house was burned down in Bombay in '92. It was a most unfortunate affair for me – in more ways than one. I had examples of many rare conditions, and my splenic collection was probably unique. These are the survivors.'

I glanced over them, and saw that they really were of a very great value and rarity from a pathological point of view: bloated organs, gaping cysts, distorted bones, odious parasites – a singular exhibition of the products of India.

'There is, as you see, a small settee here,' said my host. 'It was far from our intention to offer a guest so meagre an accommodation, but since affairs have taken this turn, it would be a great kindness upon your part if you would consent to spend the night in this apartment. I beg that you will not hesitate to let me know if the idea should be at all repugnant to you.'

'On the contrary,' I said, 'it is most acceptable.'

'My own room is the second on the left, so that if you should feel that you are in need of company a call would always bring me to your side.'

'I trust that I shall not be compelled to disturb you.'

'It is unlikely that I shall be asleep. I do not sleep much. Do not hesitate to summon me.'

And so with this agreement we joined Lady Holden in the drawing-room and talked of lighter things.

It was no affectation upon my part to say that the prospect of my night's adventure was an agreeable one. I had no pretence to greater physical courage than my neighbours, but familiarity with a subject robs it of those vague and undefined terrors which are the most appalling to the imaginative mind. The human brain is capable of only one strong emotion at a time, and if it be filled with curiosity or scientific enthusiasm, there is no room for fear. It is true that I had my uncle's assurance that he had himself originally taken this point of view, but I reflected that the breakdown of his nervous system might be due to his forty years in India as much as to any psychical experiences which had befallen him. I at least was sound in nerve and brain, and it was with something of the pleasurable thrill of anticipation with which the sportsman takes his position beside the haunt of his game that I shut the laboratory door behind me, and partially undressing, lay down upon the rug-covered settee.

It was not an ideal atmosphere for a bedroom. The air was heavy with many chemical odours, that of methylated spirit predominating. Nor were the decorations of my chamber very sedative. The odious line of glass jars with their relics of disease and suffering stretched in front of my very eyes. There was no blind to the window, and a three-quarter moon streamed its white light into the room, tracing a silver square with filigree lattices upon the opposite wall. When I had extinguished my candle this one bright patch in the midst of the general gloom had certainly an eerie and discomposing aspect. A rigid and absolute silence reigned throughout the old house, so that the low swish of the branches in the garden came softly and smoothly to my ears. It may have been the hypnotic lullaby of this gentle susurrus, or it may have been the result of my tiring day, but after many dozings and many efforts to regain my clearness of perception, I fell at last into a deep and dreamless sleep.

I was awakened by some sound in the room, and I instantly raised myself upon my elbow on the couch. Some hours had passed, for the square patch upon the wall had slid downwards and sideways until it lay obliquely at the end of my bed. The rest of the room was in deep shadow. At first I could see nothing; presently, as my eyes became accustomed to the faint light, I was aware, with a thrill which all my scientific absorption could not entirely prevent, that something was moving slowly along the line of the wall. A gentle, shuffling sound, as of soft slippers, came to my ears, and I dimly discerned a human figure walking stealthily from the direction of the door. As it emerged into the patch of moonlight I saw very clearly what it was and how it was employed. It was a man, short and squat, dressed in some sort of dark-grey gown, which hung straight from his shoulders to his feet. The moon shone upon the side of his face, and I saw that it was chocolate-brown in colour, with a ball of black hair like a woman's at the back of his head. He walked slowly, and his eyes were cast upwards towards the line of bottles which contained those gruesome remnants of humanity. He seemed to examine each jar with attention, and then to pass on to the next. When he had come to the end of the line, immediately opposite my bed, he stopped, faced me, threw up his hands with a gesture of despair, and vanished from my sight.

I have said that he threw up his hands, but I should have said his arms, for as he assumed that attitude of despair I observed a singular peculiarity about his appearance. He had only one hand! As the sleeves drooped down from the upflung arms I saw the left plainly, but the right ended in a knobby and unsightly stump. In every other way his appearance was so natural, and I had both seen and heard him so clearly, that I could easily have believed that he was an Indian servant of Sir Dominick's who had come into my room in search of something. It was only his sudden disappearance which suggested anything more sinister to me. As it was I sprang from my couch, lit a candle, and examined the whole room carefully. There were no signs of my visitor, and I was forced to conclude that there had really been something outside the normal laws of Nature in his appearance. I lay awake for the remainder of the night, but nothing else occurred to disturb me.

I am an early riser, but my uncle was an even earlier one, for I found him pacing up and down the lawn at the side of the house. He ran towards me in his eagerness when he saw me come out from the door.

'Well, well!' he cried. 'Did you see him?'

'An Indian with one hand?'

'Precisely.'

'Yes, I saw him' – and I told him all that occurred. When I had finished, he led the way into his study. 'We have a little time before breakfast,' said he. 'It will suffice to give you an explanation of this extraordinary affair – so far as I can explain that which is essentially inexplicable. In the first place, when I tell you that for four years I have never passed one single night, either in Bombay, aboard ship, or here in England without my sleep being broken by this fellow, you will understand why it is that I am a wreck of my former self. His programme is always the same. He appears by my bedside, shakes me roughly by the shoulder, passes from my room into the laboratory, walks slowly along the line of my bottles, and then vanishes. For more than a thousand times he has gone through the same routine.'

'What does he want?'

'He wants his hand.'

'His hand?'

'Yes, it came about in this way. I was summoned to Peshawur for a consultation some ten years ago, and while there I was asked to look at the hand of a native who was passing through with an Afghan caravan. The fellow came from some mountain tribe living away at the back of beyond somewhere on the other side of Kaffiristan. He talked a bastard Pushtoo, and it was all I could do to understand him. He was suffering from a soft sarcomatous swelling of one of the metacarpal joints, and I made him realise that it was only by losing his hand that he could hope to save his life. After much persuasion he consented to the operation, and he asked me, when it was over, what fee I demanded. The poor fellow was almost a beggar, so that the idea of a fee was absurd, but I answered in jest that my fee should be his hand, and that I proposed to add it to my pathological collection.

'To my surprise he demurred very much to the suggestion, and he explained that according to his religion it was an all-important matter that the body should be reunited after death, and so make a perfect dwelling for the spirit. The belief is, of course, an old one, and the mummies of the Egyptians arose from an analogous superstition. I answered him that his hand was already off, and asked him how he intended to preserve it. He replied that he would pickle it in salt and carry it about with him. I suggested that it might be safer in my keeping than his, and that I had better means than salt for preserving it. On realising that I really intended to carefully keep it, his opposition vanished instantly. "But remember, sahib," said he, "I shall want it back when I am dead." I laughed at the remark, and so the matter ended. I returned to my practice, and he no doubt in the course of time was able to continue his journey to Afghanistan.

'Well, as I told you last night, I had a bad fire in my house at Bombay. Half of it was burned down, and, among other things, my pathological collection was largely destroyed. What you see are the poor remains of it. The hand of the hillman went with the rest, but I gave the matter no particular thought at the time. That was six years ago.

'Four years ago – two years after the fire – I was awakened one night by a furious tugging at my sleeve. I sat up under the impression that my favourite mastiff was trying to arouse me. Instead of this, I saw my Indian patient of long ago, dressed in the long grey gown which was the badge of his people. He was holding up his stump and looking reproachfully at me. He then went over to my bottles, which at that time I kept in my room, and he examined them carefully, after which he gave a gesture of anger and vanished. I realised that he had just died, and that he had come to claim my promise that I should keep his limb in safety for him.

'Well, there you have it all, Dr Hardacre. Every night at the same hour for four years this performance has been repeated. It is a simple thing in itself, but it has worn me out like water dropping on a stone. It has brought a vile insomnia with it, for I cannot sleep now for the expectation of his coming. It has poisoned my old age and that of my wife, who has been the sharer in this great trouble. But there is the breakfast gong, and she will be waiting impatiently to know how it fared with you last night. We are both much indebted to you for your gallantry, for it takes something from the weight of our misfortune when we share it, even for a single night, with a friend, and it reassures us as to our sanity, which we are sometimes driven to question.'

This was the curious narrative which Sir Dominick confided to me – a story which to many would have appeared to be a grotesque impossibility, but which, after my experience of the night before, and my previous knowledge of such things, I was prepared to accept as an absolute fact. I thought deeply over the matter, and brought the whole range of my reading and experience to bear upon it. After breakfast, I surprised my host and hostess by announcing that I was returning to London by the next train.

'My dear doctor,' cried Sir Dominick in great distress, 'you make me feel that I have been guilty of a gross breach of hospitality in intruding this unfortunate matter upon you. I should have borne my own burden.'

'It is, indeed, that matter which is taking me to London,' I answered; 'but you are mistaken, I assure you, if you think that my experience of last night was an unpleasant one to me. On the contrary, I am about to ask your permission to return in the evening and spend one more night in your laboratory. I am very eager to see this visitor once again.'

My uncle was exceedingly anxious to know what I was about to do, but my fears of raising false hopes prevented me from telling him. I was back in my own consulting-room a little after luncheon, and was confirming my memory of a passage in a recent book upon occultism which had arrested my attention when I had read it.

'In the case of earth-bound spirits,' said my authority, 'some one dominant idea obsessing them at the hour of death is sufficient to hold them in this material world. They are the amphibia of this life and of the next, capable of passing from one to the other as the turtle passes from land to water. The causes which may bind a soul so strongly to a life which its body has abandoned are any violent emotion. Avarice, revenge, anxiety, love, and pity have all been known to have this effect. As a rule it springs from some unfulfilled wish, and when the wish has been fulfilled the material bond relaxes. There are many cases upon record which show the singular persistence of these visitors, and also their disappearance when their wishes have been fulfilled, or in some cases when a reasonable compromise has been effected.'

'A reasonable compromise effected' – those were the words which I had brooded over all the morning, and which I now verified in the original. No actual atonement could be made here – but

a reasonable compromise! I made my way as fast as a train could take me to the Shadwell Seamen's Hospital, where my old friend Jack Hewett was house-surgeon. Without explaining the situation I made him understand what it was that I wanted.

'A brown man's hand!' said he, in amazement. 'What in the world do you want that for?'

'Never mind. I'll tell you some day. I know that your wards are full of Indians.'

'I should think so. But a hand –' He thought a little and then struck a bell.

'Travers,' said he to a student-dresser, 'what became of the hands of the Lascar which we took off yesterday? I mean the fellow from the East India Dock who got caught in the steam winch.'

'They are in the *post-mortem* room, sir.'

'Just pack one of them in antiseptics and give it to Dr Hardacre.'

And so I found myself back at Rodenhurst before dinner with this curious outcome of my day in town. I still said nothing to Sir Dominick, but I slept that night in the laboratory, and I placed the Lascar's hand in one of the glass jars at the end of my couch.

So interested was I in the result of my experiment that sleep was out of the question. I sat with a shaded lamp beside me and waited patiently for my visitor. This time I saw him clearly from the first. He appeared beside the door, nebulous for an instant, and then hardening into as distinct an outline as any living man. The slippers beneath his grey gown were red and heelless, which accounted for the low, shuffling sound which he made as he walked. As on the previous night he passed slowly along the line of bottles until he paused before that which contained the hand. He reached up to it, his whole figure quivering with expectation, took it down, examined it eagerly, and then, with a face which was convulsed with disappointment, he hurled it down on the floor. There was a crash which resounded through the house, and when I looked up the mutilated Indian had disappeared. A moment later my door flew open and Sir Dominick rushed in.

'You are not hurt?' he cried.

'No – but deeply disappointed.'

He looked in astonishment at the splinters of glass, and the brown hand lying upon the floor.

'Good God!' he cried. 'What is this?'

I told him my idea and its wretched sequel. He listened intently, but shook his head.

'It was well thought of,' said he, 'but I fear that there is no such easy end to my sufferings. But one thing I now insist upon. It is that you shall never again upon any pretext occupy this room. My fears that something might have happened to you – when I heard that crash – have been the most acute of all the agonies which I have undergone. I will not expose myself to a repetition of it.'

He allowed me, however, to spend the remainder of the night where I was, and I lay there worrying over the problem and lamenting my own failure. With the first light of morning there was the Lascar's hand still lying upon the floor to remind me of my fiasco. I lay looking at it – and as I lay suddenly an idea flew like a bullet through my head and brought me quivering with excitement out of my couch. I raised the grim relic from where it had fallen. Yes, it was indeed so. The hand was the *left* hand of the Lascar.

By the first train I was on my way to town, and hurried at once to the Seamen's Hospital. I remembered that both hands of the Lascar had been amputated, but I was terrified lest the precious organ which I was in search of might have been already consumed in the crematory. My suspense was soon ended. It had still been preserved in the *post-mortem* room. And so I returned to Rodenhurst in the evening with my mission accomplished and the material for a fresh experiment.

But Sir Dominick Holden would not hear of my occupying the laboratory again. To all my entreaties he turned a deaf ear. It offended his sense of hospitality, and he could no longer permit it. I left the hand, therefore, as I had done its fellow the night before, and I occupied a comfortable bedroom in another portion of the house, some distance from the scene of my adventures.

But in spite of that my sleep was not destined to be uninterrupted. In the dead of night my host burst into my room, a lamp in his hand. His huge gaunt figure was enveloped in a loose dressing-gown, and his whole appearance might certainly have seemed more formidable to a weak-nerved man than that of the Indian of the night before. But it was not his entrance so much as his expression which amazed me. He had turned suddenly younger by twenty years at the least. His eyes were shining, his features radiant, and he waved one hand in triumph over his head. I sat up astounded, staring sleepily at this extraordinary visitor. But his words soon drove the sleep from my eyes.

'We have done it! We have succeeded!' he shouted. 'My dear Hardacre, how can I ever in this world repay you?'

'You don't mean to say that it is all right?'

'Indeed I do. I was sure that you would not mind being awakened to hear such blessed news.'

'Mind! I should think not indeed. But is it really certain?'

'I have no doubt whatever upon the point. I owe you such a debt, my dear nephew, as I have never owed a man before, and never expected to. What can I possibly do for you that is commensurate? Providence must have sent you to my rescue. You have saved both my reason and my life, for another six months of this must have seen me either in a cell or a coffin. And my wife – it was wearing her out before my eyes. Never could I have believed that any human being could have lifted this burden off me.' He seized my hand and wrung it in his bony grip.

'It was only an experiment – a forlorn hope – but I am delighted from my heart that it has succeeded. But how do you know that it is all right? Have you seen something?'

He seated himself at the foot of my bed.

'I have seen enough,' said he. 'It satisfies me that I shall be troubled no more. What has passed is easily told. You know that at a certain hour this creature always comes to me. To-night he arrived at the usual time, and aroused me with even more violence than is his custom. I can only surmise that his disappointment of last night increased the bitterness of his anger against me. He looked angrily at me, and then went on his usual round. But in a few minutes I saw him, for the first time since this persecution began, return to my chamber. He was smiling. I saw the gleam of his white teeth through the dim light. He stood facing me at the end of my bed, and three times he made the low Eastern salaam which is their solemn leave-taking. And the third time that he bowed he raised his arms over his head, and I saw his *two* hands outstretched in the air. So he vanished, and, as I believe, for ever.'

★ ★ ★ ★ ★

So that is the curious experience which won me the affection and the gratitude of my celebrated uncle, the famous Indian surgeon. His anticipations were realised, and never again was he disturbed by the visits of the restless hillman in search of his lost member. Sir Dominick and Lady Holden spent a very happy old age, unclouded, so far as I know, by any trouble, and they finally died during the great influenza epidemic within a few weeks of each other. In his lifetime he always turned to me for advice in everything which concerned that English life of which he knew so little; and I aided him also in the purchase and development of his estates. It was no great surprise to me, therefore, that I found myself eventually promoted over the heads of five exasperated cousins, and changed in a single day from a hard-working country doctor into the head of an important Wiltshire family. I at least have reason to bless the memory of the man with the brown hand, and the day when I was fortunate enough to relieve Rodenhurst of his unwelcome presence.

THE DEAD HAND (1902)

LT Meade (1844–1914) & Robert Eustace (1854–1943)

LT Meade was the pseudonym of Elizabeth Thomasina Meade Smith, an almost impossibly productive writer of the late Victorian and Edwardian eras who made her first appearance in print in the 1870s and went on to publish close to 300 books. At one stage in her career she was writing ten novels a year. In her lifetime she was best-known as the author of stories for girls, often with a school setting, but she also wrote many crime stories, sometimes in collaboration with other writers. One of her most regular collaborators was Robert Eustace (real name Eustace Robert Barton), a doctor and part-time writer. With Eustace she created a number of series characters for late Victorian and Edwardian magazines including a remarkable femme fatale and supervillain called Madame Sara, and John Bell, a professional ghost-hunter. Eustace outlived Meade by several decades and continued to write fiction in the crime and mystery genre. He also continued to collaborate with other writers, including Dorothy L Sayers with whom he wrote The Documents in the Case, *first published in 1930. Meade and Eustace's palmist-cum-detective Diana Marburg appeared in several stories published in* Pearson's Magazine *in 1902 and collected two years later, together with other fiction, in a volume entitled* The Oracle of Maddox Street. *'The Dead Hand' has its faults as a story but it does include what is one of the most outlandish methods of murder in the crime fiction of the period. For that, if nothing else, it remains worth reading.*

My name is Diana Marburg. I am a palmist by profession. Occult phenomena, spiritualism, clairvoyance, and many other strange mysteries of the unseen world, have, from my earliest years, excited my keen interest.

Being blessed with abundant means, I attended in my youth

many foreign schools of thought. I was a pupil of Lewis, Darling, Braid and others. I studied Reichenbach and Mesmer, and, finally, started my career as a thought reader and palmist in Maddox Street.

Now I live with a brother, five years my senior. My brother Rupert is an athletic Englishman, and also a barrister, with a rapidly growing practice. He loves and pities me – he casts over me the respectability of his presence, and wonders at what he calls my lapses from sanity. He is patient, however, and when he saw that in spite of all expostulation I meant to go my own way, he ceased to try to persuade me against my inclinations.

Gradually the success of my reading of the lines of the human hand brought me fame – my prophecies turned out correct, my intuition led me to right conclusions, and I was sought after very largely by that fashionable world which always follows anything new. I became a favourite in society, and was accounted both curious and bizarre.

On a certain evening in late July, I attended Lady Fortescue's reception in Curzon Street. I was ushered into a small anteroom which was furnished with the view of adding to the weird effect of my own appearance and words. I wore an Oriental costume, rich in colour and bespangled with sparkling gems. On my head I had twisted a Spanish scarf, my arms were bare to the elbows, and my dress open at the throat. Being tall, dark, and, I believe, graceful, my quaint dress suited me well.

Lady Fortescue saw me for a moment on my arrival, and inquired if I had everything I was likely to want. As she stood by the door she turned.

'I expect, Miss Marburg, that you will have a few strange clients to-night. My guests come from a varied and ever widening circle, and to-night all sorts and conditions of men will be present at my reception.'

She left me, and soon afterwards those who wished to inquire of Fate appeared before me one by one.

Towards the close of the evening a tall, dark man was ushered into my presence. The room was shadowy, and I do not think he could see me at once, although I observed him quite distinctly. To the ordinary observer he doubtless appeared as a well set up man of the world, but to me he wore quite a different appearance. I read fear in his eyes, and irresolution, and at the same time cruelty round his lips. He glanced at me as if he meant to defy any message I might have for him, and yet at the same time was obliged to yield to an overpowering curiosity. I asked him his name, which he gave me at once.

'Philip Harman,' he said; 'have you ever heard of me before?'

'Never,' I answered.

'I have come here because you are the fashion, Miss Marburg, and because many of Lady Fortescue's guests are flocking to this room to learn something of their future. Of course you cannot expect me to believe in your strange art, nevertheless, I shall be glad if you will look at my hand and tell me what you see there.'

As he spoke he held out his hand. I noticed that it trembled. Before touching it I looked full at him.

'If you have no faith in me, why do you trouble to come here?' I asked.

'Curiosity brings me to you,' he answered. 'Will you grant my request or not?'

'I will look at your hand first if I may.' I took it in mine. It was a long, thin hand, with a certain hardness about it. I turned the palm upward and examined it through a powerful lens. As I did so I felt my heart beat wildly and something of the fear in Philip Harman's eyes was communicated to me. I dropped the hand, shuddering inwardly as I did so.

'Well,' he asked in astonishment, 'what is the matter, what is my fate? Tell me at once. Why do you hesitate?'

'I would rather not tell you, Mr Harman. You don't believe in me, go away and forget all about me.'

'I cannot do that now. Your look says that you have seen something which you are afraid to speak about. Is that so?'

I nodded my head. I placed my hand on the little round table, which contained a shaded lamp, to steady myself.

'Come,' he said rudely, 'out with this horror – I am quite prepared.'

'I have no good news for you,' I answered. 'I saw something very terrible in your hand.'

'Speak.'

'You are a ruined man,' I said, taking his hand again in mine, and examining it carefully.

'Yes, the marks are unmistakable. You will perpetrate a crime which will be discovered. You are about to commit a murder, and will suffer a shameful death on the scaffold!'

He snatched his hand away with a violent movement and started back. His whole face was quivering with passion.

'How dare you say such infamous things!' he cried. 'You go very far in your efforts to amuse, Miss Marburg.'

'You asked me to tell you,' was my reply.

He gave a harsh laugh, bowed low and went out of the room. I noticed his face as he did so; it was white as death.

I rang my little hand-bell to summon the next guest, and a tall and very beautiful woman between forty and fifty years of age entered. Her dress was ablaze with diamonds, and she wore a diamond star of peculiar brilliancy just above her forehead. Her hair white as snow, and the glistening diamond star in the midst of the white hair, gave to her whole appearance a curious effect.

'My name is Mrs Kenyon,' she said; 'you have just interviewed my nephew, Philip Harman. But what is the matter, my dear,' she said suddenly, 'you look ill.'

'I have had a shock,' was my vague reply, then I pulled myself together.

'What can I do for you?' I asked.

'I want you to tell me my future.'

'Will you show me your hand?'

Mrs Kenyon held it out, I took it in mine. The moment I glanced at it a feeling of relief passed over me. It was full of good qualities – the Mount of Jupiter well developed, the heart-line clear and unchained, a deep, long life-line, and a fate-line ascending clear upon the Mount of Saturn. I began to speak easily and rapidly, and with that fluency which often made me feel that my words were prompted by an unseen presence.

'What you tell me sounds very pleasant,' said Mrs Kenyon, 'and I only hope my character is as good as you paint it. I fear it is not so, however; your words are too flattering, and you think too well of me. But you have not yet touched upon the most important point of all – the future. What is in store for me?'

I looked again very earnestly at the hand. My heart sank a trifle as I did so.

'I am sorry,' I said, 'I have to tell you bad news – I did not notice this at first but I see it plainly now. You are about to undergo a severe shock, a very great grief.'

'Strange,' answered Mrs Kenyon. She paused for a moment, then she said suddenly: 'You gave my nephew a bad report, did you not?'

I was silent. It was one of my invariable rules never to speak of one client to another.

'You need not speak,' she continued, 'I saw it in his face.'

'I hope he will take the warning,' I could not help murmuring faintly. Mrs Kenyon overheard the words.

'And now you tell me that I am to undergo severe trouble. Will it come soon?'

'Yes,' was my answer. 'You will need all your strength to withstand it,' and then, as if prompted by some strange impulse, I added, 'I cannot tell you what that trouble may be, but I like you. If in the time of your trouble I can help you I will gladly do so.'

'Thank you,' answered Mrs Kenyon, 'you are kind. I do not profess to believe in you; that you should be able to foretell the future is, of course, impossible, but I also like you. I hope some day we may meet again.' She held out her hand; I clasped it. A moment later she had passed outside the thick curtain which shut away the anteroom from the gay throng in the drawing-rooms.

I went home late that night. Rupert was in and waiting for me.

'Why, what is the matter, Diana?' he said the moment I appeared. 'You look shockingly ill; this terrible life will kill you.'

'I have seen strange things to-night,' was my answer. I flung myself on the sofa, and for just a moment covered my tired eyes with my hand.

'Have some supper,' said Rupert gently. He led me to the table, and helped me to wine and food.

'I have had a tiring and exciting evening at Lady Fortescue's,' I said. 'I shall be better when I have eaten. But where have you been this evening?'

'At the Apollo – there was plenty of gossip circulating there – two society scandals, and Philip Harman's crash. That is a big affair and likely to keep things pretty lively. But, my dear Di, what is the matter?'

I had half risen from my seat; I was gazing at my brother with fear in my eyes, my heart once again beat wildly.

'Did you say Philip Harman?' I asked.

'Yes, why? Do you know him?'

'Tell me about him at once, Rupert, I must know. What do you mean by his crash?'

'Oh, he is one of the plungers, you know. He has run through the Harman property and cannot touch the Kenyon.'

'The Kenyon!' I exclaimed.

'Yes. His uncle, Walter Kenyon, was a very rich man, and has left all his estates to his young grandson, a lad of about thirteen. That boy stands between Harman and a quarter of a million. But why do you want to know?'

'Only that I saw Philip Harman to-night,' was my answer.

'You did? That is curious. He asked you to prophesy with regard to his fate?'

'He did, Rupert.'

'And you told him?'

'What I cannot tell you. You know I never divulge what I see in my clients' hands.'

'Of course you cannot tell me, but it is easy to guess that you gave him bad news. They say he wants to marry the heiress and beauty of the season, Lady Maud Greville. If he succeeds in this he will be on his feet once more, but I doubt if she will have anything to say to him. He is an attractive man in some ways and good-looking, but the Countess of Cheddsleigh keeps a sharp look out on the future of her only daughter.'

'Philip Harman must on no account marry an innocent girl,' was my next impulsive remark. 'Rupert, your news troubles me very much, it confirms –' I could not finish the sentence. I was overcome by what Rupert chose to consider intense nervousness.

'You must have your quinine and go to bed,' he said; 'come, I insist, I won't listen to another word.'

A moment later I had left him, but try as hard as I would I could not sleep that night. I felt that I myself was on the brink of a great catastrophe, that I personally, was mixed up in this affair. In all my experience I had never seen a hand like Philip Harman's before. There was no redeeming trait in it. The lines which denoted crime and disaster were too indelibly marked to be soon forgotten. When at last I did drop asleep that hand accompanied me into the world of dreams.

The London season came to an end. I heard nothing more about Philip Harman and his affairs, and in the excitement and interest of leaving town, was beginning more or less to forget him, when on the 25th of July, nearly a month after Lady Fortescue's party, a servant entered my consulting-room with a card. The man told me that a lady was waiting to see me, she begged for an interview at once on most urgent business. I glanced at the card. It bore the name of Mrs Kenyon.

The moment I saw it that nervousness which had troubled me on the night when I saw Philip Harman and read his future in the ghastly lines of his hand returned. I could not speak at all for a moment; then I said, turning to the man who stood motionless waiting for my answer:

'Show the lady up immediately.'

Mrs Kenyon entered. She came hurriedly forward. When last I saw her she was a beautiful woman with great dignity of bearing and a kindly, sunshiny face. Now as she came into the room she was so changed that I should scarcely have known her. Her dress bore marks of disorder and hasty arrangement, her eyes were red with weeping.

'Pardon my coming so early, Miss Marburg,' she said at once; then, without waiting for me to speak, she dropped into a chair.

'I am overcome,' she gasped, 'but you promised, if necessary, to help me. Do you remember my showing you my hand at Lady Fortescue's party?'

'I remember you perfectly, Mrs Kenyon. What can I do for you?'

'You told me then that something terrible was about to happen. I did not believe it. I visited you out of curiosity and had no faith in you, but your predictions have come true, horribly true. I have come to you now for the help which you promised to give me if I needed it, for I believe it lies in your power to tell me something I wish to discover.'

'I remember everything,' I replied gravely. 'What is it you wish me to do?'

'I want you to read a hand for me and to tell me what you see in it.'

'Certainly, but will you make an appointment?'

'Can you come with me immediately to Godalming? My nephew Philip Harman has a place there.'

'Philip Harman!' I muttered.

'Yes,' she answered, scarcely noticing my words, 'my only son and I have been staying with him. I want to take you there; can you come immediately?'

'You have not mentioned the name of the person whose hand you want me to read?'

'I would rather not do so – not yet, I mean.'

'But can you not bring him or her here? I am very busy just now.'

'That is impossible,' replied Mrs Kenyon. 'I am afraid I must ask you to postpone all your other engagements, this thing is most imperative. I cannot bring the person whose hand I want you to read here, nor can there be any delay. You must see him if possible to-day. I implore you to come. I will give you any fee you like to demand.'

'It is not a question of money,' I replied, 'I am interested in you. I will do what you require.' I rose as I spoke. 'By the way,' I added, 'I presume that the person whose hand you wish me to see has no objection to my doing so, otherwise my journey may be thrown away.'

'There is no question about that,' replied Mrs Kenyon. 'I thank you more than I can say for agreeing to come.'

A few moments later we were on our way to the railway station. We caught our train, and between twelve and one o'clock arrived at Godalming. A carriage was waiting for us at the station, we drove for nearly two miles and presently found ourselves in a place with large shady grounds. We drew up beside a heavy portico; a manservant came gravely forward to help us to alight and we entered a large hall.

I noticed a curious hush about the place, and I observed that the man who admitted us did not speak, but glanced inquiringly at Mrs Kenyon, as if for directions.

'Show Miss Marburg into the library,' was her order. 'I will be back again in a moment or two,' she added, glancing at me.

I was ushered into a well-furnished library; there was a writing-table at one end of it on which papers of different sorts were scattered. I went forward mechanically and took up an envelope. It was addressed to Philip Harman, Esq., The Priory, Godalming. I dropped it as though I could not bear to touch it. Once again that queer nervousness seized me, and I was obliged to sit down weak and trembling. The next moment the room door was opened.

'Will you please come now, Miss Marburg?' said Mrs Kenyon. 'I will not keep you long.'

We went upstairs together, and paused before a door on the first landing.

'We must enter softly,' said the lady turning to me. There was something in her words and the look on her face which seemed to prepare me, but for what I could not tell. We found ourselves in a large room luxuriously furnished – the window blinds were all down, but the windows themselves were open and the blinds were gently moving to and fro in the soft summer air. In the centre of the room and drawn quite away from the wall was a small iron bedstead. I glanced towards it and a sudden irrepressible cry burst from my lips. On the bed lay a figure covered with a sheet beneath which its outline was indistinctly defined.

'What do you mean by bringing me here?' I said, turning to the elder woman and grasping her by the arm.

'You must not be frightened,' she said gently, 'come up to the bed. Hush, try to restrain yourself. Think of my most terrible grief; this is the hand I want you to read.' As she spoke she drew aside the sheet and I found myself gazing down at the beautiful dead face of a child, a boy of about thirteen years of age.

'Dead! my only son!' said Mrs Kenyon. 'He was drowned this morning. Here is his hand; yesterday it was warm and full of life, now it is cold as marble. Will you take it, will you look at the lines? I want you to tell me if he met his death by accident or by design?'

'You say that you are living in Philip Harman's house?' I said.

'He asked us here on a visit.'

'And this boy, this dead boy stood between him and the Kenyon property?' was my next inquiry.

'How can you tell? How do you know?'

'But answer me, is it true?'

'It is true.' I now went on my knees and took one of the child's small white hands in mine. I began to examine it.

'It is very strange,' I said slowly, 'this child has died a violent death, and it was caused by design.'

'It was?' cried the mother. 'Can you swear it?' She clutched me by the arm.

'I see it, but I cannot quite understand it,' I answered. 'There is a strong indication here that the child was murdered, and yet had I seen this hand in life I should have warned the boy against lightning, but a death by lightning would be accidental. Tell me how did the boy die?'

'By drowning. Early this morning he was bathing in the pool which adjoins a wide stream in the grounds. He did not return. We hastened to seek for him and found his body floating on the surface of the water. He was quite dead.'

'Was the pool deep?'

'In one part it was ten feet deep, the rest of the pool was shallow. The doctor has been, and said that the child must have had a severe attack of cramp, but even then the pool is small, and he was a good swimmer for his age.'

'Was no one with him?'

'No. His cousin, Philip Harman, often accompanied him, but he bathed alone this morning.'

'Where was Mr Harman this morning?'

'He went to town by an early train, and does not know yet. You say you think it was murder. How do you account for it?'

'The boy may have been drowned by accident, but I see something more in his hand than mere drowning, something that baffles me, yet it is plain – lightning. Is there no mark on the body?'

'Yes, there is a small blue mark just below the inner ankle of the right foot, but I think that was a bruise he must have got yesterday. The doctor said it must have been done previously and not in the pool as it would not have turned blue so quickly.'

'May I see it?'

Mrs Kenyon raised the end of the sheet and showed the mark. I looked at it long and earnestly.

'You are sure there was no thunder-storm this morning?' I asked.

'No, it was quite fine.'

I rose slowly to my feet. 'I have looked at the boy's hand as you asked me,' I said. 'I must repeat my words – there are indications that he came by his death not by accident but design.'

Mrs Kenyon's face underwent a queer change as I spoke. She came suddenly forward, seized me by the arms and cried:

'I believe you, I believe you. I believe that my boy has been murdered in some fiendish and inexplicable way. The police have been here already, and of course there will be an inquest, but no one is suspected. Who are we to suspect?'

'Philip Harman,' I could not help answering.

'Why? Why do you say that?'

'I am not at liberty to tell you. I make the suggestion.'

'But it cannot be the case. The boy went to bathe alone in perfect health. Philip went to town by an earlier train than usual. I saw him off myself, I walked with him as far as the end of the avenue. It was soon afterwards that I missed my little Paul, and began to wonder why he had not returned to the house. I went with a servant to the pool and I saw, oh, I saw that which will haunt me to my dying day. He was my only son, Miss Marburg, my one great treasure. What you have suggested, what I myself, alas, believe, drives me nearly mad. But you must tell me why you suspect Philip Harman.'

'Under the circumstances it may not be wrong to tell you,' I said slowly. 'The night I read your hand I also as you know read his. I saw in his hand that he was about to be a murderer. I told him so in as many words.'

'You saw that! You told him! Oh, this is too awful! Philip has wanted money of late and has been in the strangest state. He has always been somewhat wild and given to speculation, and lately I know lost heavily with different ventures. He proposed to a young girl, a great friend of mine last week, but she would have nothing to do with him. Yes, it all seems possible. My little Paul stood between him and a great property. But how did he do it? There is not a particle of evidence against him. Your word goes for nothing, law and justice would only scout you. But we must act, Miss Marburg, and you must help me to prove the murder of my boy, to discover the murderer. I shall never rest until I have avenged him.'

'Yes, I will help you,' I answered.

As I descended the stairs accompanied by Mrs Kenyon a strange thought struck me.

'I have promised to help you, and we must act at once,' I said. 'Will you leave this matter for the present in my hands, and will you let me send a telegram immediately to my brother? I shall need his assistance. He is a barrister and has chambers in town, but he will come to me at once. He is very clever and practical.'

'Is he entirely in your confidence?'

'Absolutely. But pray tell me when do you expect Mr Harman back?'

'He does not know anything at present, as he was going into the country for the day; he will be back as usual to-night.'

'That is so much the better. May I send for my brother?'

'Do anything you please. You will find some telegraph forms in the hall and the groom can take your message at once.'

I crossed the hall, found the telegraph forms on a table, sat down and filled one in as follows:

'Come at once – I need your help most urgently. Diana.'

I handed the telegram to a servant, who took it away at once.

'And now,' I said turning to Mrs Kenyon, 'will you show me the pool? I shall go there and stay till my brother arrives.'

'You will stay there, why?'

'I have my own reasons for wishing to do so. I cannot say more now. Please show me the way.'

We went across the garden and into a meadow beyond. At the bottom of this meadow ran a swift-flowing stream. In the middle of the stream was the pool evidently made artificially. Beside it on the bank stood a small tent for dressing. The pool itself was a deep basin in the rock about seven yards across, surrounded by drooping willows which hung over it. At the upper end the stream fell into it in a miniature cascade – at the lower end a wire fence crossed it. This was doubtless done in order to prevent the cattle stirring the water.

I walked slowly round the pool, looking down into its silent depths without speaking. When I came back to where Mrs Kenyon was standing I said slowly:

'I shall remain here until my brother comes. Will you send me down a few sandwiches, and bring him or send him to me directly he arrives?'

'But he cannot be with you for some hours,' said Mrs Kenyon. 'I fail to understand your reason.'

'I scarcely know that yet myself,' was my reply, 'but I am certain I am acting wisely. Will you leave me here? I wish to be alone in order to think out a problem.'

Mrs Kenyon slowly turned and went back to the house.

'I must unravel this mystery,' I said to myself. 'I must sift from the apparent facts of the case the awful truth which lies beneath. That sixth sense which has helped me up to the present shall help me to the end. Beyond doubt foul play has taken place. The boy met his death in this pool, but how? Beyond doubt this is the only spot where a solution can be found. I will stay here and think the matter through. If anything dangerous or fatal was put into the pool the murderer shall not remove his awful weapon without my knowledge.'

So I thought and the moments flew. My head ached with the intensity of my thought, and as the afternoon advanced I was no nearer a solution than ever.

It was between four and five o'clock when to my infinite relief I saw Rupert hurrying across the meadow.

'What is the meaning of this, Diana?' he said. 'Have you lost your senses? When I got your extraordinary wire I thought you must be ill.'

I stood up, clasped his hands and looked into his face.

'Listen,' I said. 'A child has been murdered, and I want to discover the murderer. You must help me.'

'Are you mad?' was his remark.

'No, I am sane,' I answered. 'Little Paul Kenyon has been murdered. Do you remember telling me that he stood between Philip Harman and the Kenyon property? He was drowned this morning in this pool, the supposition being that the death occurred through accident. Now listen, Rupert, we have got to discover how the boy really met his death. The child was in perfect health when he entered the pool, his dead body was found floating on the water half-an-hour afterwards. The doctor said he died from drowning due to cramp. What caused such sudden and awful cramp as would drown a boy of his age within a few paces of the bank?'

'But what do you expect to find here?' said Rupert. He looked inclined to laugh at me when first he arrived, but his face was grave now, and even pale.

'Come here,' I said suddenly, 'I have already noticed one strange thing; it is this. Look!'

As I spoke I took his hand and approached the wire fence which protected the water from the cattle. Leaning over I said:

'Look down. Whoever designed this pool, for it was, of course, made artificially, took more precaution than is usual to prevent the water being contaminated. Do you see that fine wire netting which goes down to the bottom of the pool? That wire has been put there for some other reason than to keep cattle out. Rupert, do you think by any possibility it has been placed there to keep something in the pool?'

Rupert bent down and examined the wire carefully.

'It is curious,' he said. 'I see what you mean.' A frown had settled on his face. Suddenly he turned to me.

'Your suggestion is too horrible. Diana. What can be in the pool? Do you mean something alive, something –' he stopped speaking, his eyes were fixed on my face with a dawning horror.

'Were there any marks on the boy?' was his next question.

'One small blue mark on the ankle. Ah! look, what is that?' At the further end and in the deep part of the pool I suddenly saw the surface move and a slight eddying swirl appear on the water. It increased into ever widening circles and vanished. Rupert's bronzed face was now almost as white as mine.

'We must drag the pool immediately,' he said. 'Harman cannot

134

prevent us; we have seen enough to warrant what we do; I cannot let this pass. Stay here, Diana, and watch. I will bring Mrs Kenyon with me and get her consent.'

Rupert hurriedly left me and went back to the house across the meadow. It was fully an hour before he returned. The water was once more perfectly still. There was not the faintest movement of any living thing beneath its surface. At the end of the hour I saw Mrs Kenyon, my brother, a gardener, and another man coming across the meadow. One of the men was dragging a large net, one side of which was loaded with leaden sinkers – the other held an old-fashioned single-barrelled gun.

Rupert was now all activity. Mrs Kenyon came and stood by my side without speaking. Rupert gave quick orders to the men. Under his directions one of them waded through the shallows just below the pool, and reaching the opposite bank, threw the net across, then the bottom of the net with the sinkers was let down into the pool.

When this was done Rupert possessed himself of the gun and stood at the upper end of the pool beside the little waterfall. He then gave the word to the men to begin to drag. Slowly and gradually they advanced, drawing the net forward, while all our eyes were fixed upon the water. Not a word was spoken; the men had not taken many steps when again was seen the swirl in the water, and a few little eddies were sucked down. A sharp cry broke from Mrs Kenyon's lips. Rupert kept the gun in readiness.

'What is it?' cried Mrs Kenyon, but the words had scarcely died on her lips before a dark body lashed the surface of the water and disappeared. What it was we none of us had the slightest idea; we all watched spell-bound.

Still the net moved slowly on, and now the agitation of the water became great. The creature, whatever it was, lashed and lunged to and fro, now breaking back against the net, and now attempting to spring up the smooth rock and so escape into the stream.

The next instant Rupert raised the gun, and fired.

As we caught a glimpse and yet another glimpse of the long coiling body I wondered if there was a snake in the pool.

'Come on, quicker now,' shouted Rupert to the men, and they pressed forward, holding the creature in the net, and, drawing it every moment nearer the rock. The next instant Rupert raised the gun, and leaning over the water, fired down. There was a burst of spray, and as the smoke cleared we saw that the water was stained with red blood.

Seizing the lower end of the net and exercising all their strength the men now drew the net up. In its meshes, struggling in death agony, was an enormous eel. The next moment it was on the grass coiling to and fro. The men quickly dispatched it with a stick, and then we all bent over it. It was an extraordinary looking creature, six feet in length, yet it had none of the ordinary appearance of the eel. I had never seen anything like it before. Rupert went down on his knees to examine it carefully. He suddenly looked up. A terrible truth had struck him – his face was white. 'What is it?' gasped poor Mrs Kenyon.

'You were right, Diana,' said Rupert. 'Look, Mrs Kenyon. My sister was absolutely right. Call her power what you will, she was guided by something too wonderful for explanation. This is an electric eel, no native of these waters--it was put here by someone. This is murder. One stroke from the tail of such an eel would give a child such a dreadful shock that he would be paralysed, and would drown to a certainty.'

'Then that explains the mark by lightning on the dead child's hand,' I said.

'Yes,' answered my brother. 'The police must take the matter up.'

Before that evening Mr Harman was arrested. The sensational case which followed was in all the papers. Against my will, I was forced to attend the trial in order to give the necessary evidence. It was all too damning and conclusive. The crime was brought home to the murderer, who suffered the full penalty of the law.

THE GATEWAY OF THE MONSTER (1910)

William Hope Hodgson (1877–1918)

Renowned for pioneering horror novels such as The House on the Borderland *and* The Ghost Pirates, *William Hope Hodgson was born in Essex, the son of a clergyman. He had worked as a merchant seaman, as the owner of a School of Physical Culture and as a public lecturer before his first short story appeared in* The Royal Magazine *in 1904. He published dozens of other stories in a variety of genres, as well as several novels, over the next fourteen years. Hope Hodgson served in the Royal Artillery in the First World War and he was killed in action in April 1918. The first six Carnacki stories appeared in* The Idler *and* The New Magazine *in the years between 1910 and 1912 and were collected in book form in* Carnacki, the Ghost-Finder *in 1913. Nearly thirty years after Hodgson's death, three more stories were included in an expanded volume of the same title, published by Arkham House in America. Carnacki is a Holmes-like figure who lives in bachelor rooms in Cheyne Walk, Chelsea and relates his strange experiences to a group of friends who gather there. Although he is, in some ways, a curiously colourless character, Carnacki has become probably the best known of all the early occult detectives. He has reappeared in a number of new adventures, written by contemporary authors, and he was a member of 'The League of Extraordinary Gentlemen' in Alan Moore's series of graphic novels of that name.*

In response to Carnacki's usual card of invitation to have dinner and listen to a story, I arrived promptly at 427, Cheyne Walk, to find the three others who were always invited to these happy little times, there before me. Five minutes later, Carnacki, Arkright,

Jessop, Taylor, and I were all engaged in the 'pleasant occupation' of dining.

'You've not been long away, this time,' I remarked, as I finished my soup; forgetting momentarily Carnacki's dislike of being asked even to skirt the borders of his story until such time as he was ready. Then he would not stint words.

'That's all,' he replied, with brevity; and I changed the subject, remarking that I had been buying a new gun, to which piece of news he gave an intelligent nod, and a smile which I think showed a genuinely good-humoured appreciation of my intentional changing of the conversation.

Later, when dinner was finished, Carnacki snugged himself comfortably down in his big chair, along with his pipe, and began his story, with very little circumlocution: –

'As Dodgson was remarking just now, I've only been away a short time, and for a very good reason too – I've only been away a short distance. The exact locality I am afraid I must not tell you; but it is less than twenty miles from here; though, except for changing a name, that won't spoil the story. And it *is* a story too! One of the most extraordinary things ever I have run against.

'I received a letter a fortnight ago from a man I must call Anderson, asking for an appointment. I arranged a time, and when he came, I found that he wished me to investigate, and see whether I could not clear up a long-standing and well – too well – authenticated case of what he termed "haunting". He gave me very full particulars, and, finally, as the case seemed to present something unique, I decided to take it up.

'Two days later, I drove to the house, late in the afternoon. I found it a very old place, standing quite alone in its own grounds. Anderson had left a letter with the butler, I found, pleading excuses for his absence, and leaving the whole house at my disposal for my investigations. The butler evidently knew the object of my visit, and I questioned him pretty thoroughly during dinner, which I had in rather lonely state. He is an old and privileged servant, and had the history of the Grey Room exact in detail. From him I learned more particulars regarding two things that Anderson had mentioned in but a casual manner. The first was that the door of the Grey Room would be heard in the dead of night to open, and slam heavily, and this even though the butler knew it was locked, and the key on the bunch in his pantry. The second was that the bedclothes would always be found torn off the bed, and hurled in a heap into a corner.

'But it was the door slamming that chiefly bothered the old butler. Many and many a time, he told me, had he lain awake and just got shivering with fright, listening; for sometimes the door would be slammed time after time – thud! thud! thud! – so that sleep was impossible.

'From Anderson, I knew already that the room had a history extending back over a hundred and fifty years. Three people had been strangled in it – an ancestor of his and his wife and child. This is authentic, as I had taken very great pains to discover; so that you can imagine it was with a feeling I had a striking case to investigate, that I went upstairs after dinner to have a look at the Grey Room.

'Peter, the old butler, was in rather a state about my going, and assured me with much solemnity that in all the twenty years of his service, no one had ever entered that room after nightfall. He begged me, in quite a fatherly way, to wait till the morning, when there would be no danger, and then he could accompany me himself.

'Of course, I smiled a little at him, and told him not to bother. I explained that I should do no more than look round a bit, and, perhaps, affix a few seals. He need not fear; I was used to that sort of thing. But he shook his head, when I said that.

'"There isn't many ghosts like oürs, sir," he assured me, with mournful pride. And, by Jove! he was right, as you will see.

'I took a couple of candles, and Peter followed, with his bunch of keys. He unlocked the door; but would not come inside with me. He was evidently in a fright, and he renewed his request, that I would put off my examination, until daylight. Of course,

I laughed at him again, and told him he could stand sentry at the door, and catch anything that came out.

'"It never comes outside, sir," he said, in his funny, old, solemn manner. Somehow, he managed to make me feel as if I were going to have the "creeps" right away. Anyway, it was one to him, you know.

'I left him there, and examined the room. It is a big apartment, and well furnished in the grand style, with a huge four-poster, which stands with its head to the end wall. There were two candles on the mantelpiece, and two on each of the three tables that were in the room. I lit the lot, and after that, the room felt a little less inhumanly dreary; though, mind you, it was quite fresh, and well kept in every way.

'After I had taken a good look round, I sealed lengths of baby ribbon across the windows, along the walls, over the pictures, and over the fireplace and the wall-closets. All the time, as I worked, the butler stood just without the door, and I could not persuade him to enter; though I jested him a little, as I stretched the ribbons, and went here and there about my work. Every now and again, he would say: – "You'll excuse me, I'm sure, sir; but I do wish you would come out, sir. I'm fair in a quake for you."

'I told him he need not wait; but he was loyal enough in his way to what he considered his duty. He said he could not go away and leave me all alone there. He apologised; but made it very clear that I did not realise the danger of the room; and I could see, generally, that he was in a pretty frightened state. All the same, I had to make the room so that I should know if anything material entered it; so I asked him not to bother me, unless he really heard or saw something. He was beginning to get on my nerves, and the "feel" of the room was bad enough, without making it any nastier.

'For a time further, I worked, stretching ribbons across the floor, and sealing them, so that the merest touch would have broken them, were anyone to venture into the room in the dark with the intention of playing the fool. All this had taken me far longer than I had anticipated; and, suddenly, I heard a clock strike eleven. I had taken off my coat soon after commencing work; now, however, as I had practically made an end of all that I intended to do, I walked across to the settee, and picked it up. I was in the act of getting into it, when the old butler's voice (he had not said a word for the last hour) came sharp and frightened: – "Come out, sir, quick! There's something going to happen!" Jove! but I jumped, and then, in the same moment, one of the candles on the table to the left went out. Now whether it was the wind, or what, I do not know; but, just for a moment, I was enough startled to make a run for the door; though I am glad to say that I pulled up, before I reached it. I simply could not bunk out, with the butler standing there, after having, as it were, read him a sort of lesson on "bein' brave, y'know." So I just turned right round, picked up the two candles off the mantelpiece, and walked across to the table near the bed. Well, I saw nothing. I blew out the candle that was still alight; then I went to those on the two tables, and blew them out. Then, outside of the door, the old man called again: – "Oh! sir, do be told! Do be told!"

"'All right, Peter," I said, and by Jove, my voice was not as steady as I should have liked! I made for the door, and had a bit of work, not to start running. I took some thundering long strides, as you can imagine. Near the door, I had a sudden feeling that there was a cold wind in the room. It was almost as if the window had been suddenly opened a little. I got to the door, and the old butler gave back a step, in a sort of instinctive way. "Collar the candles, Peter!" I said, pretty sharply, and shoved them into his hands. I turned, and caught the handle, and slammed the door shut, with a crash. Somehow, do you know, as I did so, I thought I felt something pull back on it; but it must have been only fancy. I turned the key in the lock, and then again, double-locking the door. I felt easier then, and set-to and sealed the door. In addition, I put my card over the keyhole, and sealed it there; after which I pocketed the key, and went downstairs – with Peter, who was nervous and silent, leading the way. Poor old beggar! It had not struck me until that moment that he had been enduring a considerable strain during the last two or three hours.

'About midnight, I went to bed. My room lay at the end of the corridor upon which opens the door of the Grey Room. I counted the doors between it and mine, and found that five rooms lay between. And I am sure you can understand that I was not sorry. Then, just as I was beginning to undress, an idea came to me, and I took my candle and sealing wax, and sealed the doors of all five rooms. If any door slammed in the night, I should know just which one.

'I returned to my room, locked the door, and went to bed. I was waked suddenly from a deep sleep by a loud crash somewhere out in the passage. I sat up in bed, and listened, but heard nothing. Then I lit my candle. I was in the very act of lighting it when there came the bang of a door being violently slammed, along the corridor. I jumped out of bed, and got my revolver. I unlocked the door, and went out into the passage, holding my candle high, and keeping the pistol ready. Then a queer thing happened. I could not go a step towards the Grey Room. You all know I am not really a cowardly chap. I've gone into too many cases connected with ghostly things, to be accused of that; but I tell you I funked it; simply funked it, just like any blessed kid. There was something precious unholy in the air that night. I ran back into my bedroom, and shut and locked the door. Then I sat on the bed all night, and listened to the dismal thudding of a door up the corridor. The sound seemed to echo through all the house.

'Daylight came at last, and I washed and dressed. The door had not slammed for about an hour, and I was getting back my nerve again. I felt ashamed of myself; though, in some ways it was silly; for when you're meddling with that sort of thing, your nerve is bound to go, sometimes. And you just have to sit quiet and call yourself a coward until daylight. Sometimes it is more than just cowardice, I fancy. I believe at times it is something warning you, and fighting *for* you. But, all the same, I always feel mean and miserable, after a time like that.

'When the day came properly, I opened my door, and, keeping my revolver handy, went quietly along the passage. I had to pass the head of the stairs, along the way, and who should I see coming up, but the old butler, carrying a cup of coffee. He had merely tucked his nightshirt into his trousers, and he had an old pair of carpet slippers on.

'"Hullo, Peter!" I said, feeling suddenly cheerful; for I was as glad as any lost child to have a live human being close to me. "Where are you off to with the refreshments?"

'The old man gave a start, and slopped some of the coffee. He stared up at me, and I could see that he looked white and done-up. He came on up the stairs, and held out the little tray to me. "I'm very thankful indeed, sir, to see you safe and well," he said. "I feared, one time, you might risk going into the Grey Room, sir. I've lain awake all night, with the sound of the Door. And when it came light, I thought I'd make you a cup of coffee. I knew you would want to look at the seals, and somehow it seems safer if there's two, sir."

'"Peter," I said, "you're a brick. This is very thoughtful of you." And I drank the coffee. "Come along," I told him, and handed him back the tray. "I'm going to have a look at what the Brutes have been up to. I simply hadn't the pluck to in the night."

'"I'm very thankful, sir," he replied. "Flesh and blood can do nothing, sir, against devils; and that's what's in the Grey Room after dark."

'I examined the seals on all the doors, as I went along, and found them right; but when I got to the Grey Room, the seal was broken; though the card, over the keyhole, was untouched. I ripped it off, and unlocked the door, and went in, rather cautiously, as you can imagine; but the whole room was empty of anything to frighten one, and there was heaps of light. I examined all my seals, and not a single one was disturbed. The old butler had followed me in, and, suddenly, he called out: – "The bedclothes, sir!"

'I ran up to the bed, and looked over; and, surely, they were lying in the corner to the left of the bed. Jove! you can imagine how queer I felt. Something *had* been in the room. I stared for a while, from the bed, to the clothes on the floor. I had a feeling that I did not want to touch either. Old Peter, though, did not seem to be affected that way. He went over to the bed-coverings, and was going to pick them up, as, doubtless, he had done every day these twenty years back; but I stopped him. I wanted nothing touched, until I had finished my examination. This, I must have spent a full hour over, and then I let Peter straighten up the bed; after which we went out, and I locked the door; for the room was getting on my nerves.

'I had a short walk, and then breakfast; after which I felt more my own man, and so returned to the Grey Room, and, with Peter's help, and one of the maids, I had everything taken out of the room, except the bed – even the very pictures. I examined the walls, floor and ceiling then, with probe, hammer and magnifying glass; but found nothing suspicious. And I can assure you, I began to realise, in very truth, that some incredible thing had been loose in the room during the past night. I sealed up everything again, and went out, locking and sealing the door, as before.

'After dinner, Peter and I unpacked some of my stuff, and I fixed up my camera and flashlight opposite to the door of the Grey Room, with a string from the trigger of the flashlight to the door. Then, you see, if the door were really opened, the flashlight would blare out, and there would be, possibly, a very queer picture to examine in the morning. The last thing I did, before leaving, was to uncap the lens; and after that I went off to my bedroom, and to bed; for I intended to be up at midnight; and to ensure this, I set my little alarm to call me; also I left my candle burning.

'The clock woke me at twelve, and I got up and into my dressing-gown and slippers. I shoved my revolver into my right side-pocket, and opened my door. Then, I lit my dark-room lamp, and withdrew the slide, so that it would give a clear light.

144

I carried it up the corridor, about thirty feet, and put it down on the floor, with the open side away from me, so that it would show me anything that might approach along the dark passage. Then I went back, and sat in the doorway of my room, with my revolver handy, staring up the passage towards the place where I knew my camera stood outside the door of the Grey Room.

'I should think I had watched for about an hour and a half, when, suddenly, I heard a faint noise, away up the corridor. I was immediately conscious of a queer prickling sensation about the back of my head, and my hands began to sweat a little. The following instant, the whole end of the passage flicked into sight in the abrupt glare of the flashlight. There came the succeeding darkness, and I peered nervously up the corridor, listening tensely, and trying to find what lay beyond the faint glow of my dark-lamp, which now seemed ridiculously dim by contrast with the tremendous blaze of the flash-power... And then, as I stooped forward, staring and listening, there came the crashing thud of the door of the Grey Room. The sound seemed to fill the whole of the large corridor, and go echoing hollowly through the house. I tell you, I felt horrible – as if my bones were water. Simply beastly. Jove! how I did stare, and how I listened. And then it came again – thud, thud, thud, and then a silence that was almost worse than the noise of the door; for I kept fancying that some awful thing was stealing upon me along the corridor. And then, suddenly, my lamp was put out, and I could not see a yard before me. I realised all at once that I was doing a very silly thing, sitting there, and I jumped up. Even as I did so, I *thought* I heard a sound in the passage, and quite *near* me. I made one backward spring into my room, and slammed and locked the door. I sat on my bed, and stared at the door. I had my revolver in my hand; but it seemed an abominably useless thing. I felt that there was something the other side of that door. For some unknown reason I *knew* it was pressed up against the door, and it was soft. That was just what I thought. Most extraordinary thing to think.

'Presently I got hold of myself a bit, and marked out a Pentacle hurriedly with chalk on the polished floor; and there I sat in it almost until dawn. And all the time, away up the corridor, the door of the Grey Room thudded at solemn and horrid intervals. It was a miserable, brutal night.

'When the day began to break, the thudding of the door came gradually to an end, and, at last, I got hold of my courage, and went along the corridor, in the half light, to cap the lens of my camera. I can tell you, it took some doing; but if I had not done so my photograph would have been spoilt, and I was tremendously keen to save it. I got back to my room, and then set–to and rubbed out the five–pointed star in which I had been sitting.

'Half an hour later there was a tap at my door. It was Peter with my coffee. When I had drunk it, we both went along to the Grey Room. As we went, I had a look at the seals on the other doors; but they were untouched. The seal on the door of the Grey Room was broken, as also was the string from the trigger of the flashlight; but the card over the keyhole was still there. I ripped it off, and opened the door. Nothing unusual was to be seen until we came to the bed; then I saw that, as on the previous day, the bedclothes had been torn off, and hurled into the left–hand corner, exactly where I had seen them before. I felt very queer; but I did not forget to look at all the seals, only to find that not one had been broken.

'Then I turned and looked at old Peter, and he looked at me, nodding his head.

'"Let's get out of here!" I said. "It's no place for any living human to enter, without proper protection."

'We went out then, and I locked and sealed the door, again.

'After breakfast, I developed the negative; but it showed only the door of the Grey Room, half opened. Then I left the house, as I wanted to get certain matters and implements that might be necessary to life; perhaps to the spirit; for I intended to spend the coming night in the Grey Room.

'I got back in a cab, about half–past five, with my apparatus, and this, Peter and I carried up to the Grey Room, where I piled it carefully in the centre of the floor. When everything was in the room, including a cat which I had brought, I locked and sealed the door, and went towards the bedroom, telling Peter I should not be down for dinner. He said, "Yes, sir," and went downstairs, thinking that I was going to turn in, which was what I wanted him to believe, as I knew he would have worried both me and himself, if he had known what I intended.

'But I merely got my camera and flashlight from my bedroom, and hurried back to the Grey Room. I locked and sealed myself in, and set to work, for I had a lot to do before it got dark.

'First, I cleared away all the ribbons across the floor; then I carried the cat – still fastened in its basket – over towards the far wall, and left it. I returned then to the centre of the room, and measured out a space twenty-one feet in diameter, which I swept with a "broom of hyssop". About this, I drew a circle of chalk, taking care never to step over the circle. Beyond this I smudged, with a bunch of garlic, a broad belt right around the chalked circle, and when this was complete, I took from among my stores in the centre a small jar of a certain water. I broke away the parchment, and withdrew the stopper. Then, dipping my left forefinger in the little jar, I went round the circle again, making upon the floor, just within the line of chalk, the Second Sign of the Saaamaaa Ritual, and joining each Sign most carefully with the left-handed crescent. I can tell you, I felt easier when this was done, and the "water circle" complete. Then, I unpacked some more of the stuff that I had brought, and placed a lighted candle in the "valley" of each Crescent. After that, I drew a Pentacle, so that each of the five points of the defensive star touched the chalk circle. In the five points of the star I placed five portions of the bread, each wrapped in linen, and in the five "vales", five opened jars of the water I had used to make the "water circle". And now I had my first protective barrier complete.

'Now, anyone, except you who know something of my methods of investigation, might consider all this a piece of useless

147

and foolish superstition; but you all remember the Black Veil case, in which I believe my life was saved by a very similar form of protection, whilst Aster, who sneered at it, and would not come inside, died. I got the idea from the Sigsand MS, written, so far as I can make out, in the fourteenth century. At first, naturally, I imagined it was just an expression of the superstition of his time; and it was not until a year later that it occurred to me to test his "Defense", which I did, as I've just said, in that horrible Black Veil business. You know how *that* turned out. Later, I used it several times, and always I came through safe, until that Moving Fur case. It was only a partial "Defense" therefore, and I nearly died in the Pentacle. After that I came across Professor Garder's "Experiments with a Medium". When they surrounded the Medium with a current, in vacuum, he lost his power – almost as if it cut him off from the Immaterial. That made me think a lot; and that is how I came to make the Electric Pentacle, which is a most marvellous "Defense" against certain manifestations. I used the shape of the defensive star for this protection, because I have, personally, no doubt at all but that there is some extraordinary virtue in the old magic figure. Curious thing for a Twentieth Century man to admit, is it not? But, then, as you all know, I never did, and never will, allow myself to be blinded by the little cheap laughter. I ask questions, and keep my eyes open.

'In this last case I had little doubt that I had run up against a supernatural monster, and I meant to take every possible care; for the danger is abominable.

'I turned – to now to fit the Electric Pentacle, setting it so that each of its "points" and "vales" coincided exactly with the "points" and "vales" of the drawn pentagram upon the floor. Then I connected up the battery, and the next instant the pale blue glare from the intertwining vacuum tubes shone out.

'I glanced about me then, with something of a sigh of relief, and realised suddenly that the dusk was upon me, for the window was grey and unfriendly. Then round at the big, empty room, over the double barrier of electric and candle light. I had an abrupt, extraordinary sense of weirdness thrust upon me – in the air, you know; as it were, a sense of something inhuman impending. The room was full of the stench of bruised garlic, a smell I hate.

'I turned now to the camera, and saw that it and the flashlight were in order. Then I tested my revolver, carefully; though I had little thought that it would be needed. Yet, to what extent materialisation of an ab-natural creature is possible, given favourable conditions, no one can say; and I had no idea what horrible thing I was going to see, or feel the presence of. I might, in the end, have to fight with a materialised monster. I did not know, and could only be prepared. You see, I never forgot that three other people had been strangled in the bed close to me, and the fierce slamming of the door I had heard myself. I had no doubt that I was investigating a dangerous and ugly case.

'By this time, the night had come; though the room was very light with the burning candles; and I found myself glancing behind me, constantly, and then all round the room. It was nervy work waiting for that thing to come. Then, suddenly, I was aware of a little, cold wind sweeping over me, coming from behind. I gave one great nerve-thrill, and a prickly feeling went all over the back of my head. Then I hove myself round with a sort of stiff jerk, and stared straight against that queer wind. It seemed to come from the corner of the room to the left of the bed – the place where both times I had found the heap of tossed bedclothes. Yet, I could see nothing unusual; no opening – nothing!....

'Abruptly, I was aware that the candles were all a-flicker in that unnatural wind... I believe I just squatted there and stared in a horribly frightened, wooden way for some minutes. I shall never be able to let you know how disgustingly horrible it was sitting in that vile, cold wind! And then, flick! flick! flick! all the candles round the outer barrier went out; and there was I, locked and sealed in that room, and with no light beyond the weakish blue glare of the Electric Pentacle.

'A time of abominable tenseness passed, and still that wind blew upon me; and then, suddenly, I knew that something stirred in the corner to the left of the bed. I was made conscious of it, rather by some inward, unused sense than by either sight or sound; for the pale, short-radius glare of the Pentacle gave but a very poor light for seeing by. Yet, as I stared, something began slowly to grow upon my sight – a moving shadow, a little darker than the surrounding shadows. I lost the thing amid the vagueness, and for a moment or two I glanced swiftly from side to side, with a fresh, new sense of impending danger. Then my attention was directed to the bed. All the coverings were being drawn steadily off, with a hateful, stealthy sort of motion. I heard the slow, dragging slither of the clothes; but I could see nothing of the thing that pulled. I was aware in a funny, subconscious, introspective fashion that the "creep" had come upon me; yet that I was cooler mentally than I had been for some minutes; sufficiently so to feel that my hands were sweating coldly, and to shift my revolver, half-consciously, whilst I rubbed my right hand dry upon my knee; though never, for an instant, taking my gaze or my attention from those moving clothes.

'The faint noises from the bed ceased once, and there was a most intense silence, with only the sound of the blood beating in my head. Yet, immediately afterwards, I heard again the slurring of the bedclothes being dragged off the bed. In the midst of my nervous tension I remembered the camera, and reached round for it; but without looking away from the bed. And then, you know, all in a moment, the whole of the bed coverings were torn off with extraordinary violence, and I heard the flump they made as they were hurled into the corner.

'There was a time of absolute quietness then for perhaps a couple of minutes; and you can imagine how horrible I felt. The bedclothes had been thrown with such savageness! And, then again, the brutal unnaturalness of the thing that had just been done before me!

'Abruptly, over by the door, I heard a faint noise – a sort of crickling sound, and then a pitter or two upon the floor. A great nervous thrill swept over me, seeming to run up my spine and over the back of my head; for the seal that secured the door had just been broken. Something was there. I could not see the door; at least, I mean to say that it was impossible to say how much I actually saw, and how much my imagination supplied. I made it out, only as a continuation of the grey walls... And then it seemed to me that something dark and indistinct moved and wavered there among the shadows.

'Abruptly, I was aware that the door was opening, and with an effort I reached again for my camera; but before I could aim it the door was slammed with a terrific crash that filled the whole room with a sort of hollow thunder. I jumped, like a frightened child. There seemed such a power behind the noise; as though a vast, wanton Force were "out". Can you understand?

'The door was not touched again; but, directly afterwards, I heard the basket, in which the cat lay, creak. I tell you, I fairly pringled all along my back. I knew that I was going to learn definitely whether whatever was abroad was dangerous to Life. From the cat there rose suddenly a hideous caterwaul, that ceased abruptly; and then – too late – I snapped off the flashlight. In the great glare, I saw that the basket had been overturned, and the lid was wrenched open, with the cat lying half in, and half out upon the floor. I saw nothing else, but I was full of the knowledge that I was in the presence of some Being or Thing that had power to destroy.

'During the next two or three minutes, there was an odd, noticeable quietness in the room, and you must remember I was half-blinded, for the time, because of the flashlight; so that the whole place seemed to be pitchy dark just beyond the shine of the Pentacle. I tell you it was most horrible. I just knelt there in the star, and whirled round, trying to see whether anything was coming at me.

'My power of sight came gradually, and I got a little hold of myself; and abruptly I saw the thing I was looking for, close to the "water circle". It was big and indistinct, and wavered curiously, as though the shadow of a vast spider hung suspended in the air, just beyond the barrier. It passed swiftly round the circle, and seemed to probe ever towards me; but only to draw back with extraordinary jerky movements, as might a living person if they touched the hot bar of a grate.

'Round and round it moved, and round and round I turned. Then, just opposite to one of the "vales" in the Pentacles, it seemed to pause, as though preliminary to a tremendous effort. It retired almost beyond the glow of the vacuum light, and then came straight towards me, appearing to gather form and solidity as it came. There seemed a vast, malign determination behind the movement, that must succeed. I was on my knees, and I jerked back, falling on to my left hand and hip, in a wild endeavour to get back from the advancing thing. With my right hand I was grabbing madly for my revolver, which I had let slip. The brutal thing came with one great sweep straight over the garlic and the "water circle", almost to the vale of the Pentacle. I believe I yelled. Then, just as suddenly as it had swept over, it seemed to be hurled back by some mighty, invisible force.

'It must have been some moments before I realised that I was safe; and then I got myself together in the middle of the Pentacles, feeling horribly gone and shaken, and glancing round and round the barrier; but the thing had vanished. Yet, I had learnt something, for I knew now that the Grey Room was haunted by a monstrous Hand.

'Suddenly, as I crouched there, I saw what had so nearly given the monster an opening through the barrier. In my movements within the Pentacle I must have touched one of the jars of water; for just where the thing had made its attack the jar that guarded the "deep" of the "vale" had been moved to one side, and this had left one of the "five doorways" unguarded. I put it back, quickly, and felt almost safe again, for I had found the cause, and the "defense" was still good. And I began to hope again that I should see the morning come in. When I saw that thing so nearly succeed, I had an awful, weak, overwhelming feeling that the "barriers" could never bring me safe through the night against such a Force. You can understand?

'For a long time I could not see the Hand; but, presently, I thought I saw, once or twice, an odd wavering, over among the shadows near the door. A little later, as though in a sudden fit of malignant rage, the dead body of the cat was picked up, and beaten with dull, sickening blows against the solid floor. That made me feel rather queer.

'A minute afterwards, the door was opened and slammed twice with tremendous force. The next instant the thing made one swift, vicious dart at me, from out of the shadows. Instinctively, I started sideways from it, and so plucked my hand from upon the Electric Pentacle, where – for a wickedly careless moment – I had placed it. The monster was hurled off from the neighbourhood of the Pentacles; though – owing to my inconceivable foolishness – it had been enabled for a second time to pass the outer barriers. I can tell you, I shook for a time, with sheer funk. I moved right to the centre of the Pentacles again, and knelt there, making myself as small and compact as possible.

'As I knelt, there came to me presently, a vague wonder at the two "accidents" which had so nearly allowed the brute to get at me. Was I being *influenced* to unconscious voluntary actions that endangered me? The thought took hold of me, and I watched my every movement. Abruptly, I stretched a tired leg, and knocked over one of the jars of water. Some was spilled; but, because of my suspicious watchfulness, I had it upright and back within the vale while yet some of the water remained. Even as I did so, the vast, black, half-materialised Hand beat up at me out of the shadows, and seemed to leap almost into my face, so nearly did it approach; but for the third time it was thrown back by some altogether enormous, over-mastering force. Yet, apart from the dazed fright in which it left me, I had for a moment that feeling of spiritual sickness, as if some delicate, beautiful, inward grace had suffered, which is felt only upon the too near approach of the ab-human, and is more dreadful, in a strange way, than any physical pain that can be suffered. I knew by this more of the extent and closeness of the danger; and for a long time I was simply cowed by the butt-headed brutality of that Force upon my spirit. I can put it no other way.

'I knelt again in the centre of the Pentacles, watching myself with more fear, almost, than the monster; for I knew now that, unless I guarded myself from every sudden impulse that came to me, I might simply work my own destruction. Do you see how horrible it all was?

'I spent the rest of the night in a haze of sick fright, and so tense that I could not make a single movement naturally. I was in such fear that any desire for action that came to me might be prompted by the Influence that I knew was at work on me. And outside of the barrier that ghastly thing went round and round, grabbing and grabbing in the air at me. Twice more was the body of the dead cat molested. The second time, I heard every bone in its body scrunch and crack. And all the time the horrible wind was blowing upon me from the corner of the room to the left of the bed.

'Then, just as the first touch of dawn came into the sky, that unnatural wind ceased, in a single moment; and I could see no sign of the Hand. The dawn came slowly, and presently the wan light filled all the room, and made the pale glare of the Electric Pentacle look more unearthly. Yet, it was not until the day had fully come, that I made any attempt to leave the barrier, for I did not know but that there was some method abroad, in the sudden stopping of that wind, to entice me from the Pentacles.

'At last, when the dawn was strong and bright, I took one last look round, and ran for the door. I got it unlocked, in a nervous and clumsy fashion, then locked it hurriedly, and went to my bedroom, where I lay on the bed, and tried to steady my nerves. Peter came, presently, with the coffee, and when I had drunk it, I told him I meant to have a sleep, as I had been up all night. He took the tray, and went out quietly; and after I had locked my door I turned in properly, and at last got to sleep.

'I woke about midday, and after some lunch, went up to the Grey Room. I switched off the current from the Pentacle, which

I had left on in my hurry; also, I removed the body of the cat. You can understand I did not want anyone to see the poor brute. After that, I made a very careful search of the corner where the bedclothes had been thrown. I made several holes, and probed, and found nothing. Then it occurred to me to try with my instrument under the skirting. I did so, and heard my wire ring on metal. I turned the hook end that way, and fished for the thing. At the second go, I got it. It was a small object, and I took it to the window. I found it to be a curious ring, made of some greying material. The curious thing about it was that it was made in the form of a pentagon; that is, the same shape as the inside of the magic Pentacle, but without the "mounts", which form the points of the defensive star. It was free from all chasing or engraving.

'You will understand that I was excited, when I tell you that I felt sure I held in my hand the famous Luck Ring of the Anderson family; which, indeed, was of all things the one most intimately connected with the history of the haunting. This ring was handed on from father to son through generations, and always – in obedience to some ancient family tradition – each son had to promise never to wear the ring. The ring, I may say, was brought home by one of the Crusaders, under very peculiar circumstances; but the story is too long to go into here.

'It appears that young Sir Hulbert, an ancestor of Anderson's, made a bet, in drink, you know, that he would wear the ring that night. He did so, and in the morning his wife and child were found strangled in the bed, in the very room in which I stood. Many people, it would seem, thought young Sir Hulbert was guilty of having done the thing in drunken anger; and he, in an attempt to prove his innocence, slept a second night in the room. He also was strangled. Since then, as you may imagine, no one has ever spent a night in the Grey Room, until I did so. The ring had been lost so long, that it had become almost a myth; and it was most extraordinary to stand there, with the actual thing in my hand, as you can understand.

'It was whilst I stood there, looking at the ring, that I got an idea. Supposing that it were, in a way, a doorway – you see what I mean? A sort of gap in the world-hedge. It was a queer idea, I know, and probably was not my own, but came to me from the Outside. You see, the wind had come from that part of the room where the ring lay. I thought a lot about it. Then the shape – the inside of a Pentacle. It had no "mounts", and without mounts, as the Sigsand MS has it: – "Thee mownts wych are thee Five Hills of safetie. To lack is to gyve pow'r to thee daemon; and surelie to fayvor the Evill Thynge." You see, the very shape of the ring was significant; and I determined to test it.

'I unmade the Pentacle, for it must be made afresh *and around* the one to be protected. Then I went out and locked the door; after which I left the house, to get certain matters, for neither "yarbs nor fyre nor water" must be used a second time. I returned about seven-thirty, and as soon as the things I had brought had been carried up to the Grey Room, I dismissed Peter for the night, just as I had done the evening before. When he had gone downstairs, I let myself into the room, and locked and sealed the door. I went to the place in the centre of the room where all the stuff had been packed, and set to work with all my speed to construct a barrier about me and the ring.

'I do not remember whether I explained it to you. But I had reasoned that, if the ring were in any way a "medium of admission", and it were enclosed with me in the Electric Pentacle, it would be, to express it loosely, insulated. Do you see? The Force, which had visible expression as a Hand, would have to stay beyond the Barrier which separates the Ab from the Normal; for the "gateway" would be removed from accessibility.

'As I was saying, I worked with all my speed to get the barrier completed about me and the ring, for it was already later than I cared to be in that room "unprotected". Also, I had a feeling that there would be a vast effort made that night to regain the use of the ring. For I had the strongest conviction that the ring was a necessity to materialisation. You will see whether I was right.

'I completed the barriers in about an hour, and you can imagine something of the relief I felt when I felt the pale glare of the Electric Pentacle once more all about me. From then, onwards, for about two hours, I sat quietly, facing the corner from which the wind came. About eleven o'clock a queer knowledge came that something was near to me; yet nothing happened for a whole hour after that. Then, suddenly, I felt the cold, queer wind begin to blow upon me. To my astonishment, it seemed now to come from behind me, and I whipped round, with a hideous quake of fear. The wind met me in the face. It was blowing up from the floor close to me. I stared down, in a sickening maze of new frights. What on earth had I done now! The ring was there, close beside me, where I had put it. Suddenly, as I stared, bewildered, I was aware that there was something queer about the ring – funny shadowy movements and convolutions. I looked at them, stupidly. And then, abruptly, I knew that the wind was blowing up at me from the ring. A queer indistinct smoke became visible to me, seeming to pour upwards through the ring, and mix with the moving shadows. Suddenly, I realised that I was in more than any mortal danger; for the convoluting shadows about the ring were taking shape, and the death-hand was forming *within* the Pentacle. My Goodness! do you realise it! I had brought the "gateway" into the Pentacles, and the brute was coming through – pouring into the material world, as gas might pour out from the mouth of a pipe.

'I should think that I knelt for a moment in a sort of stunned fright. Then, with a mad, awkward movement, I snatched at the ring, intending to hurl it out of the Pentacle. Yet it eluded me, as though some invisible, living thing jerked it hither and thither. At last, I gripped it; yet, in the same instant, it was torn from my grasp with incredible and brutal force. A great, black shadow covered it, and rose into the air, and came at me. I saw that it was the Hand, vast and nearly perfect in form. I gave one crazy yell, and jumped over the Pentacle and the ring of burning candles, and ran despairingly for the door. I fumbled idiotically and ineffectually with the key, and all the time I stared, with a fear that was like insanity, towards the Barriers. The Hand was plunging towards me; yet, even as it had been unable to pass into the Pentacle when the ring was without, so, now that the ring was within, it had no power to pass out. The monster was chained, as surely as any beast would be, were chains riveted upon it.

'Even then, I got a flash of this knowledge; but I was too utterly shaken with fright, to reason; and the instant I managed to get the key turned, I sprang into the passage, and slammed the door with a crash. I locked it, and got to my room somehow; for I was trembling so that I could hardly stand, as you can imagine. I locked myself in, and managed to get the candle lit; then I lay down on my bed, and kept quiet for an hour or two, and so I got steadied.

'I got a little sleep, later; but woke when Peter brought my coffee. When I had drunk it I felt altogether better, and took the old man along with me whilst I had a look into the Grey Room. I opened the door, and peeped in. The candles were still burning, wan against the daylight; and behind them was the pale, glowing star of the Electric Pentacle. And there, in the middle, was the ring... the gateway of the monster, lying demure and ordinary.

'Nothing in the room was touched, and I knew that the brute had never managed to cross the Pentacles. Then I went out, and locked the door.

'After a sleep of some hours, I left the house. I returned in the afternoon in a cab. I had with me an oxy-hydrogen jet, and two cylinders, containing the gases. I carried the things into the Grey Room, and there, in the centre of the Electric Pentacle, I erected the little furnace. Five minutes later the Luck Ring, once the "luck", but now the "bane", of the Anderson family, was no more than a little solid splash of hot metal.'

Carnacki felt in his pocket, and pulled out something wrapped in tissue paper. He passed it to me. I opened it, and found a small circle of greyish metal, something like lead, only harder and rather brighter.

'Well?' I asked, at length, after examining it and handing it round to the others. 'Did that stop the haunting?'

Carnacki nodded. 'Yes,' he said. 'I slept three nights in the Grey Room, before I left. Old Peter nearly fainted when he knew that I meant to; but by the third night he seemed to realise that the house was just safe and ordinary. And, you know, I believe, in his heart, he hardly approved.'

Carnacki stood up and began to shake hands. 'Out you go!' he said, genially. And, presently, we went, pondering, to our various homes.

THE BOY OF BLACKSTOCK (1914)

Alice Askew (1874–1917) and Claude Askew (1865–1917)

The son of a clergyman, Claude Askew was at school at Eton and then travelled on the Continent as a young man. He married Alice Leake, the daughter of an army colonel, in 1900 and they were soon earning their living with their pens. Their first successes were with newspaper serials but they rapidly moved on to hardcover fiction. The Askews were astonishingly prolific and published nearly ninety books in a dozen years (nine novels appeared under their names in 1913 alone) but almost all of them have been forgotten and are long out of print. Their one venture into the realm of the supernatural consisted of eight stories which appeared in an obscure magazine named The Weekly Tale-Teller *in 1914. These featured an intrepid psychic detective named Aylmer Vance and his Watson-like sidekick Dexter. Dexter and Vance meet while they are both on holiday and discover a common interest in the supernatural. The first few stories consist of Vance's earlier experiences which he relates to Dexter in the inn where they are staying; in later ones, such as 'The Boy of Blackstock' the two work together. During the First World War, both Askews travelled to Serbia to work with a field hospital attached to the Serbian army and to write about the country which was one of Britain's allies in the war. In 1917, they both died when the Italian steamer on which they were making their way to Corfu to join Serbian soldiers in exile was torpedoed by a German submarine and sank.*

HAVE INTERESTING CASE ON HAND. IF NOTHING BETTER TO DO, JOIN ME TOMORROW, HEDSTONE, ESSEX.

Such was the wording of a telegram which I received (at the little French watering-place where I happened to be staying) from

160

Aylmer Vance, whom I imagined to be somewhere in Syria, busy with the exploration of certain ancient ruins.

It was autumn, and I, for my part, was getting tired of a rather purposeless Continental ramble, so I hailed Vance's telegram with joy. I cabled back that I was coming at once, caught a night boat from Dieppe, spent an hour or two in London, and arrived at Hedstone Grange, my friend's house in Essex, in time for lunch.

He would not say a word about the 'case', however, until we had disposed of that meal and were lazily indulging in dessert. For himself he ate very little but fruit and vegetables at any time.

'Syria will keep till later on,' he observed then. 'I had decided to go, and ran down to Hedstone to get a few things together. And then I received a visit from a certain gentleman, and – well, it promised to be interesting, so I sent you that cable.'

He interrupted my expression of pleasure that he had done so by asking a question. 'Do you know the meaning of the term "Poultergeist", Dexter?' he inquired.

I had heard the expression. 'Isn't it a German word that expresses a sort of mischievous ghost?' I replied. 'An elemental spirit that pulls furniture about, rings bells, smashes crockery, and makes itself generally obnoxious? Is that the kind of thing that we've to deal with this time?'

Aylmer smiled. 'Perhaps,' he responded with his usual caution. 'But there are circumstances about this "Poultergeist" – if the term is at all relevant – that lifts it above the common. The ghost of Blackstock Priory – where we are invited to go tomorrow – is really a family spectre, and it bears a name that is traditional – the Mischievous Boy of Blackstock – you may have heard of it, for the old legend is well-known. It belongs to the Rystone family. Lord Rystone owns Blackstock Priory to this day, though the possession was once very bitterly disputed.'

'I've an idea that I've heard the story,' I put in here, 'but I should like you to refresh my memory.'

'The tradition goes back to the Stuart times,' resumed Vance, 'and, of course, there is a tragedy connected with it. The Lord

Rystone of that day happened to have a very beautiful young wife of whom he was immensely proud, and at the same time, inordinately jealous – probably with good reason, for she appears to have been as frivolous as she was beautiful. Anyhow, the story goes that one day he surprised his wife, under compromising conditions, in the company of a certain handsome young fellow named Gregory Laidlaw, who was the son of the very man who disputed Lord Rystone's title to the property of Blackstock. Well, the husband's jealousy and wrath got the better of him, and he murdered them both upon the spot – murdered them in cold blood just where he had found them, in a certain room at Blackstock Priory which, at that time, was his wife's boudoir. He then reported what he had done, and, in the result, was acquitted – or received no punishment worth speaking about.

'But he wasn't let off so easily by his victim, Gregory Laidlaw. Lord Rystone continued to live at Blackstock, which, by the way, is in Essex, and at no great distance from here, but his life was made a burden for him. The "Mischievous Boy" soon began his pranks. I take it that the term "Boy" has been applied to Gregory Laidlaw, or, rather, to Gregory Laidlaw's ghost, more on account of the monkey-tricks that he perpetrated than because of his actual age – according to the story he must have been at least twenty-three or twenty-four when he was murdered. Anyway, he gave Lord Rystone no peace, never making himself actually visible, but playing the most ridiculous pranks at inopportune times – throwing open doors, wailing and laughing about the corridors, pealing the bells, and often frightening people out of their wits by touching them with his cold, clammy hands.

'Well, this went on for months and months, until one day Lord Rystone did actually see his enemy. Something – heaven knows what – took him to the room where the tragedy had been enacted – he said he obeyed an impulse that he couldn't resist – and there he saw both his victims, and Gregory, his hand upon his heart and a derisive smile upon his lips, bowed to him three times. A few days later Lord Rystone died.

'After that, Master Gregory played no more pranks unless his room – the scene of his murder – was interfered with – which it was by several subsequent Lord Rystones. People who were given that room to sleep in were frightened out of their wits – their bedclothes were pulled off them or they were jerked about in the most uncomfortable fashion – but the Boy himself was not seen. He appeared only once to each Lord Rystone in succession – and that was as a foreteller of death.

'At last the Rystones became sick of their ancestral ghosts, and let the Priory on a ninety-nine years' lease to the then representative of the Laidlaw family – which was really as it should be, for the Laidlaws were the first owners of the property which they had been unfairly jostled out of. They were Essex people, which the Rystones were not, and had always been popular in the country. As soon as Mr Laidlaw came into possession he had the haunted room shut up, and from that day on nothing whatever was heard of the "Mischievous Boy".'

Aylmer Vance paused and carefully peeled the skin from an apple to which he had just helped himself. Having consumed the fruit, he resumed: 'The lease granted to the Laidlaws has now expired, and the present Lord Rystone, who appears to be a man of obstinate and cantankerous temper, has refused to renew it. He has, in fact, elected to go and live at Blackstock himself.'

'And the "Mischievous Boy" has broken out again,' I hazarded, 'and is giving him a warm time of it?'

'That is so,' Aylmer smiled his slow smile. 'Lord Rystone refused, however, to believe that there is any truth in the old tradition, and maintains that he is being made the victim of a conspiracy. He suspects some agent of his late tenants to be at the bottom of the whole thing – for the Laidlaws want to get back to Blackstock, and the people of the neighbourhood want nothing so much as to see them reinstated. In spite of this belief, he has come to me, which proves that there is some latent superstition about him, though he won't admit it.'

'Or, of course,' I ventured, 'there may be some other natural cause for what is going on. I know that this sort of thing is usually associated with a human subject – some hysterical individual affected, perhaps, by the old tradition. Doesn't the "Poultergeist" usually act through a human medium? You have told me of such cases. There was Halton Manor, for instance. Do you know anything of Lord Rystone's family?'

Vance nodded appreciatively. He liked me to show an intelligent interest in his cases.

'I know very little further at present,' he responded. 'Lord Rystone was not very communicative. It appears that he has been in residence at Blackstock for about a month, and I imagine that there is no-one in the family except himself, his wife, his two boys, and their tutor. The boys are his sons by his first wife, for you may remember that it is only a couple of years since he married for the second time. His wife is ever so much younger than himself, and she was, I believe, the daughter of a clergyman, quite a poor man, who is now the vicar of Blackstock. These things I know from hearsay – local gossip. I've met the vicar – his name is Gaynor – the Revd Alison Gaynor – at some county function. An able man, from all accounts, and one who is ambitious for higher things. Of course, he obtained his present living through the influence of his son-in-law. But, for the moment, all this is outside the question. The point we have to solve is whether the manifestations at Blackstock are of human or superhuman origin – and we'll get to work tomorrow. I mentioned that I propose to bring a friend with me, so you are expected.'

The next day, accordingly, we proceeded by car to Blackstock Priory, which is situated to the north-east of the county, a lonely and rather uninviting spot not far away from the sea.

We arrived in the course of the afternoon, and we found the whole household, together with one or two visitors, in the garden, partaking of tea under a huge oak tree that was still leafy in spite of its great age.

Lord Rystone came forward to receive us, and I was formally introduced.

The man's appearance did not impress me favourably. I could readily understand why Vance had described him as an obstinate, pigheaded man. He had a square jaw and an ugly mouth that had a way of twisting sarcastically when he spoke. One could imagine him capable of saying most unpleasant things upon the slightest provocation. He had black hair and black bushy eyebrows which came close together over the bridge of his nose. I put him down as being about fifty years of age, perhaps a little more.

His voice was loud and raucous.

'Glad to know you, Mr Dexter,' he said, 'and I hope you and Mr Vance will find means to put an end to this infernal nuisance that I've got to submit to in this house. Of course, I don't believe for a moment that it's anything to do with spooks, and the story of the Mischievous Boy is nothing but a silly superstition. No, sir, I don't believe in spooks, and I can tell you straight away that I suspect my servants. There are people about the place who have a spite against me and who want nothing better than to turn me out. They think they can frighten me away, but that's where they are mistaken. I'm not the kind of man to give in when I've made up my mind about a thing.'

It wasn't the time to argue the point, so I merely made some commonplace observation, after which I was introduced to the rest of the company.

Naturally, my interest at that moment was centred upon Lady Rystone.

She was charmingly pretty after a delicate Dresden china sort of style. She could not have been much over twenty, very fair and with tiny little hands and feet. She had eyes and lips that seemed made for love and laughter, and pretty dimples in her cheeks, but looking at her closely, one felt painfully that all these charming attributes were gradually fading, and that it would not be long before the piquante little face became pinched and fretful.

It was obvious, even to the casual observer, that she was not happy.

What on earth had induced her to marry Lord Rystone? That

was the first thought that shot into my brain on seeing her. Then I remembered that she was the daughter of a poor clergyman, and that probably family interests had been the chief factor in the case.

I felt sorry for her, for certainly she must be paying heavily for her sacrifice.

Lord Rystone's two sons, boys of twelve and fourteen years of age, were present with their tutor, whose name was James Felton. The boys were dark-haired, heavy-jowled young cubs, who had never been to school in their lives, and whose manners were atrocious.

Nor did I like the appearance of the tutor. He, too, seemed to have absorbed some of the prevailing gloom. He was a good-looking young man, but he had a discontented mouth and eyes that seemed to me shifty and untrustworthy.

The rest of the party consisted of the vicar, Lady Rystone's father, who seemed pleased to renew his acquaintance with Vance. He was a handsome man with intelligent, well-cut features, but somehow looked no happier than the rest, and I fancied that he often glanced uneasily at his daughter. Besides him there were a couple of callers, a dull man and his even duller wife; they left soon after we arrived.

After their departure, conversation turned on the supposed haunting, and Lord Rystone repeated the story of the 'Mischievous Boy', the story with which I was already acquainted.

'There's never been a hint of a ghost at the Priory for the last hundred years,' he said. 'And looking up the records, the last allusion I can find to the "Boy's" appearance is when he appeared to my great grandfather some time in the nineteenth century, just before he died. That, of course, was years before the Priory was leased to the Laidlaws. The superstition is, you must understand, that the "Boy" only shows himself when one of our family is going to die – otherwise he is never visible, nor does he get up to his tricks unless the room in which he and his lady love were murdered is interfered with. That's the yarn they tell.'

'And you have opened up that room?' inquired Vance, who had settled himself comfortably in a deck chair.

'Yes, and why not, I should like to know?' retorted Lord Rystone with some asperity. 'It's one of the finest rooms in the house, and situated in a part of the building where it can't be easily dispensed with. It's ridiculous that it should be shut up for ever on account of an old wives' tale. I'm furnishing it as a bedroom, and eventually I shall sleep there myself.'

He spoke the last words defiantly.

'You have the courage of your opinions,' replied Vance quietly. 'But if you desire peace, might it not be just as well to try the effect of closing the room again – as an experiment?'

'No,' was the abrupt and rather surly response. 'I've told you that I don't believe there's anything supernormal in the whole business. It's all a got-up job by someone who wants me to leave the place altogether. If you can prove to me the contrary, Mr Vance, then I'll shut up the room – but not until then.'

While this conversation was in progress, a conversation in which I took no part, I was watching the faces of the rest of the company, and I could not help imagining that the tutor, Mr Felton, kept his dark eyes fixed upon the face of Lady Rystone, and that she was uncomfortably aware of the fact. And I imagined that there was something malignant in his regard – almost a threat – and that he wished to convey the fact to her.

The moment, however, that he noticed that I was looking at him, he turned his attention to his pupils, to whom he made some half-laughing remark.

As for the two boys, they seemed to take the whole thing in the light of a joke, and I could see them giggling together, although they were evidently in some awe of their father.

They were ill-conditioned and badly brought up youngsters, and it naturally occurred to me that they might have something to do with the manifestations – if these really had a human origin.

Anyway, I decided to keep my eyes upon them.

'May I ask,' inquired Vance, addressing our host, 'if you opened up the haunted room as soon as you came into residence at the Priory?'

Lord Rystone shook his head.

'No,' he replied, 'it wasn't till a fortnight later.'

'And did you have any trouble during the first fortnight?'

The answer, rather grudgingly delivered, was again in the negative.

'But it was only after I'd been here a fortnight,' added his lordship, 'that the neighbourhood began to show me that I wasn't wanted. I'd taken on some of the old servants, keepers and others, who had been in the employ of my predecessors. They were a lazy lot, and I told them so – the Laidlaws have always been notorious fools in their treatment of their people – and I suppose the fellows didn't like the new administration. Anyway, they all gave notice in a body, and it was after that the trouble began.'

'I see.'

Aylmer sat back in his chair pensively, and for a little while after that took no part in the general conversation.

One of the boys – the eldest – was recounting how he had been told that morning that one of the servants, happening to pass the door of the haunted room rather late the night before, had heard curious sounds from within, and being braver than most of his fellows, had ventured very gingerly to open the door.

It was not quite dark within, because the moon was shining, and the room, as yet only half-furnished, had not been provided with curtains, and the man declared that he caught sight of what he imagined to be two dim figures standing in the moonlight apparently clasped in each other's arms.

He was not, however, able to swear positively to anything, because before he had had time to open the door wide, it was torn from his hand and then slammed violently in his face.

Lord Rystone frowned heavily. Incredulous though he professed to be, he was palpably worried at this suggestion of the actual appearance of the 'Boy' – an appearance reputed to bode ill.

'Who told you this absurd story, Paul?' he asked gruffly.

'It was Lomax, the under-footman,' responded the boy readily.

'Very well, go and tell Lomax that I want to speak to him at once. We may as well question him here in your presence, Mr Vance.'

Lord Rystone addressed the last words to my friend, who quietly nodded his acquiescence.

And so Paul ran off, evidently delighted with his mission, and a few minutes later returned with the under-footman who, in our presence, confirmed in every respect the story which we had just heard, adding one or two details of his own.

He had imagined that he heard voices in the room, low whisperings, and it was that which had at first attracted his attention, knowing, as he did, that the room was not yet in use, and that, in any case, nobody was likely to be there at that hour of the night.

He told his story gravely, palpably convinced of the truth of every word he said. He seemed to me a well-spoken, dependable sort of young man, and I felt genuinely sorry for him when Lord Rystone, unable to shake his story in any particular, lost his temper, addressed him roughly, and told him that he was a coward and a fool.

'Why on earth didn't you open the door again after it had been slammed in your face?' shouted the angry earl. 'I suppose you were too frightened to do so, eh?'

'I did try,' responded the young man, flushing to his hair, 'but it was no use. The door was locked.'

'Well, that's a proof that you are telling a lie,' was the fierce retort, 'for there's been no key fitted to the lock yet.' He turned to Vance and myself. 'The room had been walled up,' he explained, 'and after I had it opened up, we found an unlocked door without a key; and as I haven't got a new one yet, how was it possible that the door could be locked? The fellow's a palpable liar.'

The natural consequence of this repeated assertion was that the footman gave notice upon the spot – and I may say that I thoroughly sympathised with him under the circumstances.

Lord Rystone fumed with rage. He swore violently without

the smallest regard to the presence of his wife and children.

'It's a conspiracy,' he declared, 'and they are all in it; but I'll get even with them yet.'

Soon after this we went into the house, and Vance and I were left to ourselves till dinner time.

During this interview I took the opportunity of mentioning to him the curious expression which I had seen upon the tutor's face and the significant glance which he had cast at Lady Rystone.

'I don't like the look of that fellow,' I said, 'but, of course, it may only have been my imagination. Have you formed any opinion so far?'

'It's much too early yet to form any opinion,' was my friend's reply. He smiled a little. 'You ought to know by now, Dexter,' he said, 'that I never jump to conclusions.'

At dinner that evening we were introduced to yet another member of the household – Mrs Mellish, who acted as companion to the young countess. She was an elderly and austere woman who did not in the least add to the gaiety of the company.

And it was while we were at dinner that we were treated to our first manifestation of the mischievous influence that was at work in the house.

There came a tremendous crash all of a sudden in the hall without, and on running to the door we discovered the butler standing in the midst of a debris of broken plates and dishes and other paraphernalia that he had been carrying to the dining-room upon a tray.

He was white and trembling, and he had cut his hand a little.

Lord Rystone's cheeks grew florid with rage, and he began to bluster. He had never known such gross carelessness in his life, he declared. What on earth had the man done to drop the tray?

The butler stooped and picked up something from the floor, where it lay among the fragments of broken china.

'That's what did it, your lordship,' he said nervously, holding up for our inspection a heavy flint stone. 'It fell down from overhead right into the middle of my tray. I couldn't help dropping the things, no-one could have.'

The hall was large and square, and a gallery ran round three sides of it. It would have been quite easy, I reflected, for anyone concealed up there to drop the stone as the butler passed below. But the incident made one thing practically certain: if anyone of the house party was responsible for the trouble, there must undoubtedly be a confederate as well.

For we had all, including the two boys, been assembled at the dinner table.

The boys rushed off upstairs, and for the next few minutes, while their father blustered, we could hear them careering up and down the gallery and opening every available door in their pursuit of the ghost. But their efforts were quite futile, and presently they returned, excited and looking upon the whole thing as excellent sport.

I was soon to find out that they behaved in exactly the same way after every manifestation of which they were witness.

The butler was still quaking, partly from fear and partly with wrath at the way his explanation had been received.

'I can't stand it any longer,' he muttered, staunching the blood from a small cut upon his hand. He looked almost as if he were about to faint. 'I'm sorry, my lord, but I should like to leave – tomorrow, if you will allow me.'

'Yes, go and the devil take you,' roared his lordship furiously, after which we all returned to the dining-room and continued our interrupted meal as best we could.

Nothing further occurred till about an hour later, when we were assembled in the drawing-room, except the two boys, who had been sent off to bed.

The first intimation we had of the return of the poltergeist – if poltergeist it was – was the sudden opening of the drawing-room door. It was flung violently back, so violently as nearly to throw it off its hinges, and at the same moment I distinctly heard the sound of a chuckling laugh.

Yet, once again, when we rushed out into the hall, it was to find no trace of any living soul.

Almost immediately afterwards, however, and while we were still standing there literally gaping at each other, a series of bells began to ring, apparently from somewhere in the servants' quarters.

Poor Lady Rystone was nearly in tears — to all appearance terribly afraid.

'Oh, Kelsey,' she entreated her husband, 'what's the use of going on like this? Why won't you shut up the haunted room again, or, better still, why won't you leave this horrid place altogether?'

'I dare say you'd like me to take you away, wouldn't you?' he retorted in a tone that to me sounded quite unnecessarily brutal. 'But I've had enough of London, and so have you, for some time to come. And as for shutting up the haunted room, I am damned if I do. I'll get to the bottom of this infernal conspiracy first.'

There was something terrifying in the frown he bestowed upon his wife, and Lady Rystone seemed to shrink under it – her lips quivered pitifully, and she shook in every limb. I felt more sorry for her than ever, and deeply incensed against the man for his sheer brutality. I was puzzled too, for at the same moment I was again conscious of that queer, menacing look in the tutor's eyes as he watched the scene. There was something horribly exultant about it – I think that is the word that most nearly expresses my meaning.

Well, we had no more alarms that night, and the next day Vance and I set about making a thorough exploration of the Priory, which, I don't think I have mentioned, was a low-built, rambling edifice with walls of considerable thickness.

I suspected secret chambers and passages, and, indeed, several of these were known and pointed out to us by Lord Rystone. For the most part, however, they had been blocked up so efficiently as to render them impossible as hiding-places.

We examined the haunted room.

It was a large, low apartment upon the first floor. After its use as a boudoir by the murdered Lady Rystone, it had been used as a bedroom, and then dismantled because of the hauntings. It was at present unfurnished save for a few old-fashioned chairs and a sofa. It had a painted ceiling, and its walls were hung with faded tapestry. There were one or two curtained recesses which added to the eerie aspect of the room.

'With your permission, Lord Rystone,' said Vance, 'I will pass the night in this room. You need not worry about the bed. I shall be quite comfortable in one of the chairs.'

Permission was granted, and then, very naturally, I asked Vance to allow me to share his vigil. But to my surprise, and a little to my mortification, he refused.

He laid his hand in a friendly manner upon my shoulder.

'Don't be vexed, Dexter,' he said. 'I have my reasons. Believe me, it is for the best.'

He would not give his reasons, and I knew him well enough by now to appreciate that argument was useless, so I was forced to accept the inevitable.

Well, I had thought out all manner of plans for trapping the 'ghost', if the 'ghost' should prove to be human — thread entanglements over the bell-wires, and that sort of thing — but Vance would have none of them.

'Wait till tomorrow,' he said. 'I shall know better then how to act.'

I could not induce him to tell me his suspicions, yet I knew they were already forming in his mind.

At dinner that night there was another unpleasant scene — not due this time to ghostly phenomena.

Lord Rystone came in palpably in a bad temper. He attacked his wife almost before a particle of food had passed his lips.

'Your father's been to see me privately this afternoon, Elsa. Do you know why?'

It was his tone rather than what he said that implied wrath.

She looked up — eagerly, I thought.

'No, Kelsey, what was it?'

'He's giving up his living – the living he begged me for and which I gave him. He's quite independent of me now, if you please. They want him in a large London parish, and I suppose we shall hear of him being made a bishop next. And not a word of gratitude. A wretched penniless curate whom I set on his feet because I happened to take a fancy to his daughter! He fawned about my neck as long as there was anything to be got out of me, but now I may go hang.'

He muttered other things which were only half audible, luckily.

I watched Lady Rystone and wondered at the joy which I read in her eyes – joy which her disconcerted air at this public outbreak could not quite conceal.

She made no retort, carefully avoiding to say a word which might still further incense her husband, and as soon as possible turned the conversation into a safer channel. But I think that Vance, like myself, noticed her flushed cheeks and eager expression.

We had very little in the way of phenomena that evening, and at ten o'clock we parted for the night. Vance went to the haunted room, and I saw him no more till the morning.

He came to me quite early – before I was up – and sat on the edge of my bed.

'Dexter,' he said gravely, 'we have got to give up this job; it isn't in our line. I wish we could leave today, but there are people asked to meet us at dinner. However, tomorrow –'

I sat up in bed in my surprise.

'Vance,' I exclaimed, 'have you solved the mystery?'

He inclined his head. His face was more than usually serious.

'Yes', he said.

'Won't you tell me?'

'When we get home – not now. There's still some work that I must do – and it is no pleasant task. But this I want to ask you – don't trouble me with questions till we are clear of Blackstock Priory.'

I promised that I would not; but, needless to say, I was puzzled

174

to a degree. However, as fate would have it, the day did not pass without my making a discovery on my own account.

It happened in the course of the afternoon.

Vance had gone out on some errand with which he had not acquainted me, and I was amusing myself with a book in the garden. It was a hot day, and I had found a comfortable nook, screened by trees, close to a little glade, where there was a marble seat – probably a trophy carried off from some ancient Italian palace.

I must have dropped off to sleep, for I can only remember starting up at the sound of voices in the glade – from which I was completely hidden.

A woman was speaking – I recognised the voice of Lady Rystone.

'You are an unutterable blackguard' – that is what I heard her say – 'a loathsome blackmailer! But you daren't do what you threaten.'

'Why not?'

The answer came in the suave, displeasing voice of Felton, the tutor.

'Because, however much you might hurt me, my husband would thrash you as you deserve.'

'That may be.' The man gave an ugly laugh. 'Nevertheless, my lady, I refuse to abate one jot of my demand. A thousand pounds – and I know that you've got the money – that you've been saving up for contingencies – pawning your jewels. You could give me that sum without hurting yourself. Come, be sensible.' His voice had a persuasive note in it now. 'I don't want to hurt you, but I'm hard up – desperate. Like yourself, I want to get away from this accursed place, and from those two unlicked cubs I'm supposed to look after. And I can only do it by putting pressure upon you – now that I've found you out. Think of the scandal, my lady, if it became known that the "Mischievous Boy of Blackstock"' – he laughed again – 'is no other than your lover, in order to avoid whom your husband took you away from London, because he had begun to have his suspicions? Supposing Lord Rystone knew – as I know – that this man can get in and out of the Priory as he pleases by means of a secret passage opening into the so-called haunted room? That as long as the haunted room was shut off, you were both quite happy, since you, my lady, had secret access to it as well, but when it was opened up, your trysting place was no longer safe, so you had to have recourse to the old superstition in order to frighten his lordship into walling it off again – or, better still, to compel him to leave the Priory altogether. Supposing all this were known, what then?'

My horror at hearing this cold-blooded revelation may be imagined. I hated to think that, all unwittingly, I had been an eavesdropper; but from the first it was impossible for me to reveal myself – it might only have made matters worse – and I could not steal away without betraying my presence.

So this was the pitiful explanation of the mystery – this was what Vance, too, had found out and refused to tell me!

I could understand his reluctance now.

It was all I could do to restrain myself from springing out of my hiding-place and laying violent hands upon the vile blackmailer – every nerve in my body tingled with the desire to pay him in different coin to what he demanded – but I kept myself in control.

And of the rest of that abominable interview I need record no more than this: Felton accorded his victim a period of twenty-four hours in which to make up her mind. Unless he received his pound of flesh upon the following day, he would unfailingly betray Lady Rystone to her husband.

I waited impatiently for Vance's return, and when, late that afternoon, we met, I told him everything.

He was deeply concerned, for of this trouble threatening Lady Rystone he was quite unaware.

'Twenty-four hours' grace,' he muttered. 'This is serious, Dexter, very serious. For I can foresee what will happen. Lady Rystone and her lover – for it's true about the lover, unfortunately true – will act at once – tonight, instead of waiting till tomorrow, as they proposed.'

He told me of his experiences the night before.

'I had my suspicions,' he said. 'You see, I had had a chat with Gaynor in the garden the day we arrived. The vicar confided to me that his daughter was unhappy – that she was being treated like a prisoner – always watched except when she was in the house – that unpleasant woman, Mrs Mellish, you know. She was too fond of gaiety, and there was a man who was fond of her – a man named Frank Prescot. Anyway, Lord Rystone became jealous and carried her off to Blackstock. And Mr Gaynor blamed himself bitterly. You see, it was on his account that his daughter married – in order that he might get the living and the benefits.

'Well, these things made me suspicious – and I formed my own conclusions, too, by studying Lady Rystone's face. I arranged to spend a night in the haunted room. I found a secret passage – as I had expected to. It leads to a ruined chapel just outside the big wall, and it communicates with another room in the house – an empty one – as well as with the haunted room. So, you see, while the latter was shut up, two people could meet there practically with impunity. It was less safe afterwards, as we know from the experience of Lomax, the under-footman. It is evident, in that case, that the lovers had secured the key, and were able to save themselves by using it.

'And later that night I saw them. Yes, Dexter, the lovers met and never dreamed that they were watched from behind one of those curtained recesses. No-one knew I was spending a night in the haunted room, so they had no suspicions.

'They were only together for a few minutes, and it was to plan an elopement – not for tonight, because there were preparations to be made, but for tomorrow. Lady Rystone considered herself free at last. She had borne all the indignities that her husband heaped upon her because her father had been dependent upon Lord Rystone, but now – you noticed her hardly-concealed joy at dinner when she heard that Gaynor had secured his independence? – she was free to do as she liked, so she declared, and her husband had long ago forfeited, by his brutality, all right to her love. It appears he had struck her over and over again.

'And so everything was settled between them. Tomorrow night they would fly together, and brave the world. But now, Dexter, I foresee that they will change their plans – they will go tonight.'

I admitted the force of this reasoning.

'What is to be done?' I asked.

'I saw Gaynor this afternoon,' resumed Vance, 'and told him everything. His sympathies are wholly with his daughter, but he naturally wishes to save her from taking a false step. We had arranged that he should come tomorrow morning and take her away. Rystone cannot keep her in the Priory by force. And now – well, there is nothing for it but for me to return to the vicarage and warn Gaynor of what has happened. He must act at once, dinner-party or no dinner-party. He must come to the Priory this very evening, see Lady Rystone, and persuade her to go away with him. That is the only practical course.'

And this was the plan upon which we decided. Vance set off at once, and he did not return till near the dinner hour. But he had failed in his mission, for the vicar was away from home, and all efforts to find him had proved unavailing.

That hateful dinner party – how well I remember it! The whole company seemed to be on tenterhooks, and when about ten o'clock Lady Rystone pleaded a bad headache, Vance and I glanced meaningly but helplessly at each other.

Luckily, the guests departed soon after that, and we men – with the exception of the tutor, who had pleaded some excuse – retired to Lord Rystone's study to smoke.

Half an hour later there came a horrible interruption. The door flung open, and Felton, excited and dishevelled, rushed in.

'I've come to warn you, my lord,' he cried. He gazed at us defiantly. 'I consider it my duty to do so. Your wife has introduced her lover into your house. It is he who is the author of the disturbances – which have only been contrived in order that they may continue a guilty intrigue without interruption. They are now –'

I was boiling over with rage.

'This man is a vile blackmailer,' I began, but Lord Rystone silenced me with a gesture. He had risen, and his face was congested with rage.

'Go on, Felton,' he said hoarsely. 'Where are they now?'

'In the haunted room – if you hurry you will find them there together. They are eloping – tonight.' He gnashed his teeth with the wrath of a blackmailer foiled. Lord Rystone did not speak another word. He jerked open a door of his desk, extracted something which he held under his hand, and then, without a glance at any of us, made for the door.

He was across the hall and mounting the stairs before we had time to realise the full horror of the situation.

'Quick – he's got a revolver!' cried Vance.

He set off in pursuit, followed by myself and then by the tutor, who had turned deathly white and staggered as he went.

But Lord Rystone was fleeter than any of us. He had thrown open the door of the haunted room before any of us could come up with him. I heard him mutter a hoarse cry – then he lifted his hand and fired – the shot echoed horribly down the corridor.

The next moment Lord Rystone repeated his cry – but this time it was a scream of fear. He fired again wildly, and then, throwing up his arms, staggered back. Vance caught him as he fell.

And I – for a brief moment I was able to see through the open door into the haunted room. And I was dimly conscious of a figure – that of a young man clad in garments of a bygone day, who stood smiling and bowing towards Lord Rystone, his hand upon his heart.

The 'Mischievous Boy of Blackstock' had fulfilled his destiny.

Lord Rystone died a few days later – of a stroke of apoplexy, so the doctors declared.

And it was not many weeks later that Lady Rystone was quietly married.

THE GOVERNESS'S STORY (1921)

Amyas Northcote (1864–1923)

The son of a Tory politician who had been Chancellor of the Exchequer in Disraeli's government in the 1880s, Amyas Northcote left England for America in his twenties and worked as a businessman in Chicago. He returned to his native country in 1900 and settled in Buckinghamshire where he became a landowner and magistrate. His ghost stories were collected in a volume entitled In Ghostly Company, *his only published work, which appeared two years before his death. Northcote was not a particularly original writer. Many of his stories are reminiscent of those by better known contemporaries such as MR James and EF Benson. However, they remain worth investigating. 'Brickett Bottom', which has appeared in a number of anthologies over the years, is an eerie tale of a house which swallows up an unfortunate young woman who visits it. 'Mr Mortimer's Diary' is the story of a man haunted to madness and destruction by the spirit of a fellow scholar whose work he had stolen. Although it carries faint but definite echoes of Henry James's famous novella* The Turn of the Screw *which was first published in 1898, 'The Governess's Story' has its own atmosphere and effect. The haunting which Miss Hosmer, the governess of the title, investigates is low key and undramatic, and yet, for that very reason, curiously melancholic and memorable.*

We were sitting, a large group of us, round the blazing fire in the old hall one Christmas Eve and the conversation, guided by both hour and place, drifted on to things supernatural.

Among those present was old Miss Hosmer, a lady well-known and popular, who, after an early life of struggle and poverty, was now spending her declining years in comfort on a modest fortune, derived from the bequest of a distant relative. In her youth Miss Hosmer had earned her livelihood as a governess and in the course of her scholastic career she had lived in various families and had undergone various experiences, some grave, some, but, alas, fewer, gay; she had seen the skeletons kept in more than one cupboard and had been the confidante of more than one curious story.

As a rule she was chary of recounting her experiences, since she rightly held that the histories of others, however discovered, should be kept confidential, and that more mischief is the result of idle gossip than comes from malicious tale-bearing. In person, she was small, grey-haired, old-fashioned, with a keen sense of humour twinkling in her blue eyes and a warm corner in her heart for those in difficulty or distress. During the early part of our talk, she had remained silent, listening with a queer expression of detachment to the various stories that circulated round the circle, and contributing nothing to them till directly appealed to by Mrs Leveson, one of her former and well-loved pupils.

In a pause of the conversation, Mrs Leveson turned abruptly to Miss Hosmer and said:

'Can't you tell us a story, Miss Hosmer? I know you have told me more than once that when you were quite a young woman you saw a ghost.'

'No, my dear,' answered Miss Hosmer, 'I never told you that. I never saw a ghost in all my life.'

'But surely you had some queer experience of that nature, didn't you?' returned Mrs Leveson.

'Well,' said the other, 'I did once have an adventure of the sort you mention. I don't often speak of it nowadays, and I try to think of it as little as I can.'

'Why?' I interrupted, 'Is it anything so very dreadful?'

'No,' said Miss Hosmer slowly. 'It was not really dreadful, but it was very, very sad, and I feel, perhaps, that I should be doing harm and causing pain to perfectly innocent people by repeating it.'

'But not if you conceal the names and places,' answered Mr

Davies, the barrister, 'and, now you have roused our curiosity so much, surely you will gratify it and tell us the story.'

Miss Hosmer hesitated for a few minutes, and then replied:

'Well, perhaps you are right and, in any case, I hope and believe that I can so conceal identities that none of you will know of whom I am speaking. But I beg,' she went on, 'that if any of you do guess, you will keep your guesses to yourselves. Two of the people implicated are alive today, and I would not for the world that either of them should have the slightest inkling of what happened in their family when they were little children.'

We promised as she desired, and Miss Hosmer began.

'What I am going to tell you is an experience that I actually underwent many years ago, when I was quite a girl, and had only recently taken up governessing as a means of earning my daily bread. I had been out of a situation for some little time, and was beginning to grow anxious as to my future; so that it was with a feeling of real happiness that one morning I opened a letter from Miss Butler, at whose agency I was registered, in which she asked me to come round to her office as soon as possible. It was not long before I was with her, when she told me that she had just had an application from Lady K, the widow of the late Sir Arthur K, GCMG, for a young lady to come to her in the country to educate her two children, a boy of nine and a little girl of seven, and to give especial attention to preparing the boy for school. Up to the present, so far as I could gather, Lady K had had entire charge of the education of the children since her husband's death, but she did not feel herself capable of instructing the boy sufficiently to prepare him for school, and she also desired a resident governess to continue the girl's education after the boy had left home.

'Miss Butler gave me Lady K's letter to read, and I gleaned from it that the family resided always at the family seat Wyke Hall, near the town of Dellingham, in one of the Midland Counties. The work appeared to be exactly what I wanted and felt capable of undertaking; the terms offered were quite satisfactory, and the quietness of the life was by no means distasteful to me, since I have always been a lover of the country. It was accordingly arranged that I should write to Lady K and seek an interview with her to go further into the matter. I returned to my rooms without delay and, having written and posted my letter, I hunted up an old book of reference that had belonged to my father to see what mention it made of the K family. I quickly found what I sought and learned that Sir Arthur K had died in 1887, leaving three children. He had been twice married, once to a Miss C. in 1874, by whom he had had one son, Edward, born in 1877, and again in 1883 to a Miss Constance G. by whom he had had two children, Arthur, born in 1884, and Eleanor, born in 1886. As the year of which I am speaking was 1893, this would make the ages of the three children sixteen, nine, and seven respectively. Except that the family residence was Wyke Hall, which I knew already, this was all the information my rather out-of-date reference book contained about the K family.

'In course of post I received a reply from Lady K stating that she would be at a certain hotel in London, on a certain not distant date, and asking me to call and see her there. I complied with her request, and one fine morning late in August, 1893, beheld me ushered in a rather nervous condition into the presence of Lady K. On entering the private sitting-room where she was awaiting me, as she rose from her chair to greet me, I saw before me a tall, stately, handsome woman of about thirty-five years of age. She was a blonde with aquiline features, a handsome, well-preserved figure, dressed in handsome though rather old-fashioned clothes. Her voice was gentle, low and cold, with a curiously monotonous intonation. Her manners were dignified and reserved, though perfectly courteous. She was in half-mourning, and wore no jewellery.

'In short, a first glance displayed a rather fine, if cold-looking woman of the world; a closer inspection revealed something else. Beneath all her perfect manners and frigid exterior there seethed a medley of strong passions; and among these, lurking in the depths and only occasionally peeping forth, was fear. I have always been something of a physiognomist, and I felt sure I was not deceived. Of what she was in fear, and of what was concealed beneath that calm exterior, I could not even hazard a guess; but that Lady K possessed a secret, and a painful if not a terrible one, I was not an instant in doubt. After our formal greetings we stood looking at each other, and in that brief moment I formed the conviction that I did not and never could like Lady K. However, it is not for a hard-up governess to pick and choose. If Lady K liked me, I felt I was bound to accept her situation; it would have been impossible for me to go back to Miss Butler and tell her that I had refused an excellent position with a family of standing, simply because I did not like an indescribable something in my would-be employer's face.

'Well, I need not go into the details of my interview with Lady K except to say that she made most particular and minute inquiries into my capabilities, qualities, failings, good points, family and, in fact, every conceivable thing about me. My sense of dislike to her was not intensified by this inquisition; in fact it rather raised her in my opinion as being evidence that she was a careful and conscientious woman. I noticed also that the mention of her children was the sole thing that brought a gleam of light and happiness into that cold, hard face.

Evidently she adored her little Arthur, her little Eleanor. After a long interview we parted, I going out with the assurance of Lady K that, if the references with which I had supplied her were as satisfactory as our conversation, I might consider myself engaged to come to Wyke Hall after the holidays were over – in about a month's time.

'The references proved satisfactory, and one evening in late September saw me arriving at Dellingham Station. It was a fine evening, but the journey from town had been long and tedious and it was growing dark by the time I left the station. Outside, I found awaiting me a well-appointed, single-horse brougham, driven by a neatly liveried and respectful groom.

Into this I mounted and my luggage having been bestowed on the carriage rack we started off for Wyke Hall. So far as I could see, after we had disengaged ourselves from the streets of the little town of Dellingham, we drove through a typical English midland county landscape; gentle rolling hills, green pasture and well-kept arable land were intermingled, and our road seemed to follow generally the course of the little river Dell. We passed smiling farmhouses, and pleasant cottages during the drive: our lines lay in peaceful and homelike places. About five miles from Dellingham, so far as I could judge, the brougham turned up an elm-shaded avenue, and in a few minutes more stopped before the door of Wyke Hall. It was now almost dark, and I could see but little of the house, except that it appeared to be of fair size and to be surrounded by a broad, stone-flagged terrace.

'The front door was opened by a neat-looking footman in livery, behind whom loomed the more dignified form of a middle-aged butler, and I entered the hall, which was of considerable size. Opposite the front door was another, which led into Lady K's private sitting and business room. Close to this second door, the main staircase of the house commenced; this led up to a wide gallery on the first floor. Out of this gallery on the left-hand side opened a swing-door which gave access to the upper passage of the wing. The butler, having relieved me of my handbag and umbrella, led the way across the hall and ushered me into Lady K's room.

'Lady K greeted me with as much cordiality as she appeared capable of assuming, seated me by the fire, ordered me up a belated, but much welcome tea, inquired about my journey and generally did her best to give me a polite welcome. I still, however, could not get over that faint sense of dislike towards her, which I had felt from the first, and it was with relief that I heard her say as I put down my tea cup: "Well, now I suppose you would like to meet the children. I will send for them to come down."

'And in a few minutes down they came, and at once I fell in love with both of them. It has been my lot to teach and to love many young people, but, assuredly, I can say that in all my experience I never met two to whom I took so quick and warm a fancy, and from whom I received so soon such affectionate devotion. Of the two, perhaps my favourite was the boy, Arthur; he was fair like his mother, but instead of her cold expression he was bubbling over with life and good spirits. He was the leader of the two, and ruled his little sister with a vigour, which, if it had not been loving, would have been merciless. She reciprocated his devotion, and was never so happy as when trotting after him and carrying out his instructions. She was dark – I presume she took after her father – and intelligent, but Arthur was an unusually brilliant child.

'We spent a little time in making acquaintance, and I became confirmed in my original opinion that the one really soft spot in Lady K was her passionate adoration of her children.

'After about half an hour thus spent, Lady K rose and said she was sure I would wish to see my own quarters, and we accordingly all of us proceeded upstairs. On reaching the swing-door on the upper floor Lady K pushed it open, and descending a couple of steps we entered the wing of the house, which was traversed by a wide but not lengthy passage terminating in a large window. Lady K threw open the first door on the right hand of this passage and disclosed a large, cheerful-looking room, the schoolroom and general living room, in which the children spent the bulk of their waking hours. Having duly inspected this apartment, we proceeded down the passage to the door of a second room which formed the end room of the house.

'This was my bedroom, and I confess to a feeling of surprise and pleasure at seeing the bright and pretty room, a cheerful fire blazing in the grate, a vase of autumn flowers on the dressing-table, and books and knick-knacks scattered round.

'After a brief pause we returned to the main part of the house, Lady K explaining that the room opposite mine was an unused spare bedroom, whilst the space opposite the schoolroom was occupied by a bath-room, housemaids' closet and similar small offices. On entering the main hall, Lady K pointed out her bedroom, which adjoined the schoolroom, and was situated above the room downstairs into which I had first been shown. In this, she explained, Eleanor slept with her, whilst Arthur's bedroom was the adjoining one, and had formerly been her husband's dressing-room. Beyond these rooms I could see the vista of the main passage through the body of the mansion, but my story does not concern itself with any other than the part of the house I have described, save that I should mention that shortly beyond Arthur's room I saw the bottom of the staircase leading up to the servants' attics overhead.

'Our inspection of the house concluded, Lady K suggested that I should probably wish to retire to my room to unpack and rest, and departed downstairs, taking the children with her.

'I went back to my bedroom, where my luggage, unstrapped and prepared for unpacking, stood neatly ranged, and sat down to think over the events of the last hour. My thoughts should have been pleasant. Here I was welcomed with the utmost courtesy, my future pupils appeared charming and lovable, my surroundings were most comfortable and my convenience had been thoughtfully studied. I should mention that before the children had come down Lady K had outlined her ideas as to hours of study and recreation, subject to my approval, and had arranged that I should breakfast and have tea with the children in the schoolroom, lunch with her and them downstairs, and that after they had retired for the night I should be served with my evening meal upstairs, so that I might have my entire evenings free and to myself. These plans suited me perfectly; all seemed rose coloured, and yet I could not dispel a lurking feeling of ill-ease for which I could not account. On the whole I felt that it centred round the personality of Lady K. Nothing could be more civil than her manner, nothing could excel her apparent kindness, but – I could not complete my thought, and

187

whilst I was still dreaming there came a tap at the door and an old woman, evidently a confidential upper servant, entered. She at once introduced herself as Mason, whom I had heard mentioned as Lady K's personal maid and hitherto the attendant on the children as well. She was a quiet, self-effaced woman, grey haired, blue eyed, and with a sad but not unpleasing face. She explained that she had ventured to come to see if I needed any help, but I suspected that her real motive was to get an early inspection of me, her supplanter with the children. However, I had no wish not to be friendly, and begged her to sit down. She took a chair, and we very quickly found ourselves in friendly talk; she was eloquent on the subject of both the children, but especially of Arthur, and I gleaned a good deal of information from her about their ways and characters. All I heard was satisfactory, but I observed that once or twice when I endeavoured to turn the conversation in the direction of Lady K. Mason immediately became uncommunicative, and swung the talk back on to the merits of the young people. Our chat lasted perhaps half an hour, when Mason departed to assist Lady K at her evening toilet, and shortly after a neat, smiling maidservant, who informed me that she was the schoolroom-maid, knocked at my door with the intelligence that my evening meal was ready in the schoolroom.

'Supper finished, I sat awhile still trying to analyse my thoughts and, not succeeding, I returned to my bedroom where I busied myself with my unpacking until feeling rather tired I desisted and went to bed.

'It was not long, I think, before I fell asleep and slept soundly till I was gradually awakened at what I afterwards ascertained was about half-past eleven by the sound of someone walking about in the room above mine. At first the footsteps seemed to mingle with my dreams, but as my senses became clearer the sounds also became more distinct. They were the footsteps of someone walking hastily and irregularly: at times they fell slowly or stopped, at others they hurried almost into a run. They moved all about the room, not confining themselves to any single path or beat, and, though clear and distinct, were not heavy. I remember wondering at the sex of the walker: the steps sounded too light for those of a man and too long for those of a woman. A slight sense of annoyance passed over me; surely it was very late for a servant to be up, and very improper for one of the apparently highly trained domestics of Wyke Hall to be indulging in such antics. Suddenly I heard a window in the room above thrown wide open with a crash and then followed absolute silence. The steps had ceased, and in a little while I fell asleep to wake the next morning to pouring rain.

'The day was a hopeless one and going out was not to be thought of. Accordingly, after we had finished our first morning's schoolroom work, at which I was delighted with the manners and attitude of both my pupils, Lady K, who had come in more than once to watch our progress, suggested a game in the billiard-room. This room proved to be in the space below the schoolroom and my bedroom, and the game was a great treat to the children, since they explained they were never allowed to play about on the billiard table by themselves, and that Lady K hardly ever used to indulge them by rushing about after the balls. The rest of the day passed without incident, and I retired to rest feeling myself gradually becoming at home and inclined to laugh at my uncomfortable feelings of the evening before.

'I suppose it was the lack of exercise, but I did not fall asleep as promptly as is my usual custom and, as I lay wakeful, all at once I heard the footsteps in the room above. They began absolutely without warning, and as on the previous night moved irregularly about the room, now fast, now slow. I looked at my watch: it was a little after half-past eleven. As on the previous night, I heard the window thrown violently open, and then came silence. I slept after a while undisturbed and woke in the morning with one of my trying sick headaches.

'It was a prostrating one, but I had my duty to attend to, and I got through the morning somehow, but when Lady K came into the schoolroom, towards the end of the lesson I saw her eye me sharply and, I thought, uneasily.

"'Are you not well, Miss Hosmer?" she said.

"'I have only got a tiresome headache," I replied. "I am afraid I am rather subject to them, and I expect it was not getting out yesterday, and sleeping badly brought it on, but it will soon pass off."

"'Did you not sleep well?" queried Lady K with, I thought, a trace of excitement and anxiety in her voice. She hesitated an instant and went on, "I hope nothing disturbed you."

'Yes, there was no doubt – there was anxiety in that last sentence. At the moment the thought of the steps had faded from my mind: as a matter of fact, they had not really disturbed me the night before, or been the cause of my headache.

"'I did not sleep well," I replied, "but it was my headache coming on; my room and bed are most comfortable."

'Lady K looked relieved.

"'Well, you must be quiet now," she said. "I will take the children out and you must rest and get your head better."

'I followed her instructions, lay down, and my headache was so far recovered that I was able to come down to luncheon and go on with the day's programme in the afternoon. This involved an out-of-door excursion, in the shape of a walk; the children lamented the rule, as they wanted to take me round the gardens and stables to exhibit their various treasures, but Lady K had laid down a strict rule. "A walk in the afternoon, playing in the garden in the morning," and Lady K was not one to disobey. So we explored the surrounding Park, and got various views of the house, which showed itself as a finer and larger place than my first nocturnal glimpse had led me to believe. That night the exhaustion following my headache soon put me to sleep, and if the restless domestic walked above me my ears were closed to his or her footsteps.

'The next day broke quiet and uneventful. I felt quite settled down now, my affection for the children grew steadily, and I think they reciprocated it; the servants including Mason were civil and accommodating, and even my subconscious feeling about Lady K was beginning to diminish. But my peace of mind was to receive a shock that day, and that shock came through the innocent instrumentality of my pupils. We had been rambling about the gardens and stables and farmyard, and I had made the acquaintance of "Galloper" and "Queenie", the two ponies, of the carriage horses, of the big Newfoundland "Steady", and of the stable terrier "Spot". I had duly admired the two little plots dignified by the names of Master Arthur's and Miss Eleanor's gardens. I had looked at the pigs and at the poultry, and had gazed from afar upon those more formidable creatures, the cows, and we were now returning home rather hastily, for the lunch hour was close upon us, when an argument arose between the two children, as to the proper allocation of the windows in the façade of the house, Eleanor maintaining and Arthur stoutly disputing as to which exactly were the windows of the schoolroom. Finally I was called upon to umpire the question, and, glancing at the windows in question, I was easily able to give my decision. But as I looked at the house, and at my windows adjoining those in dispute, I had a curious feeling of something being wrong. For a moment I was at a loss, and then it suddenly flashed across me: there were attics over the main body of the house, but the schoolroom and my bedroom were in the wing, and there were no attics above them. Where, then, could be the room above mine in which someone walked at night, and opened the window? A queer uncanny sensation passed over me, but I had no time to think the matter out, for we had reached the house and the luncheon bell was ringing.

'At luncheon Lady K proposed that the afternoon should be devoted to driving into Dellingham to endeavour to acquire certain books, which I had asked for as necessary for my pupils, and I had accordingly no further opportunity to investigate the problem of the footsteps. That evening, though I was rather tired, I must confess that, after the schoolroom maid had removed my supper things and left me alone in the wing of the house, I felt just a trifle nervous and wakeful. However, I got resolutely to bed, and, leaving my candle alight, waited. The expected happened. Just after half-past eleven, without the slightest warning, the steps recommenced their restless pacing. I had nerved myself as to what to do, and I instantly got out of bed and, slipping on my dressing-gown, went out into the passage and closed my door. As soon as I had done so the sound of the footsteps diminished greatly; I went on into the schoolroom and here I could no longer hear them at all. I returned to the passage and, bracing up my courage, opened the door of the spare room. In this room, also, the steps were inaudible; I went back to my bedroom and again they rang out clear and distinct, and in a few minutes more I heard the window thrown up and all became silent. It was clear, therefore, that whatever caused the sound must be directly over my head. I lay awake that night for some time, absorbed in the problem; so far I was puzzled, and slightly nervous, but not exactly frightened. I did not believe in spiritual manifestations, and was convinced that some physical cause was the explanation of the mysterious sounds. At the same time I was sufficiently disturbed in mind to feel that I must discover this cause, or else that I should fall a prey to my nervous imagination. Ultimately I decided on taking the opportunity of the upper part of the house being empty during the servants' dinner hour, and of the children's half an hour with Lady K after our luncheon, to make an exploration of the top story of the mansion. So resolving, I fell asleep.

'The following day I ran briskly upstairs as soon as lunch was finished; the upper floors were deserted as I anticipated, and I made my way undisturbed to the attics. Here, I found the same long passage as below, save for the notable difference that in place of the swing-door opening into the wing there was a closed archway which appeared as if a door had existed there at one time and had been closed up, and instead there was a window in this archway, which gave light to that end of the passage. I approached the window, and opening it looked out. Beneath me, there was nothing except two low gables with a gutter between them which stretched away towards the end of the wing. One of these gables was clearly over my room and the schoolroom, the other over the rooms on the opposite side of the wing passage. A moment's inspection showed clearly enough that it was absolutely impossible for any room to exist within these gables, which could not have been above four feet high at their topmost point. I leaned out of the window for closer inspection, and suddenly noticed with something of a shock that both the roof and the end wall of the house appeared new, not above a few years old at most. Greatly puzzled, I drew back and tried the door of the attic above Lady K's room. It opened easily, and disclosed a room littered with boxes, disused furniture and other lumber. The room was so filled that it would have been impossible for anyone to have paced about it in the fashion I have described; the window also showed no signs of having been opened for a considerable time. Opposite this room was the empty space of the main hall, which extended clear up through the house. I was now greatly puzzled, and, I think, beginning to grow frightened. Who was the walker by night, and where did he walk?

'I had no further time to consider the question as I was compelled to return to my charges, but I decided to take Mason into my confidence and see if she could throw light upon the problem. That afternoon we sallied forth on our usual walk, and this time the children who were my eager guides led me in a new direction. The path which we traversed led us near Wyke churchyard, and we wandered into it to get a nearer view of the quaint old church. As we walked round the outside of the church, Arthur suddenly pulled my arm gently and pointing to a vault a few yards away said:

'"That's where Papa is buried, and poor Brother Edward too."

'The words gave me a start. I knew, of course, that Sir Arthur was dead, and probably buried in the neighbourhood of Wyke, but it had never occurred to me to think that his eldest son should be lying beside him. It is true that I had never up to this moment heard his name mentioned, but I had scarcely thought of him at all; I had supposed him away at school; I had never conceived the possibility of his being dead.

'It has always been my fixed rule never to try and obtain information as to their family affairs from my pupils, but in this instance I could not restrain myself from the question:

"'I did not know your brother was dead. When did it happen?"

"'Oh, a long time ago," said Arthur. "Eleanor cannot even remember him, but I can."

"'I remember him too," said Eleanor.

"'Yes, but you were too little to play with him like I did," said her brother.

'I did not like to press the discussion and the conversation came to an end; but I was more determined than ever to have a talk with old Mason. That evening I was doomed to disappointment, however, for on asking the schoolroom maid if Mason was in her room I was told that she had gone to stay the night with her brother, a tradesman in Dellingham.

'That night I lay awake and listened for the coming of the steps with a haunting sense of fear. There seemed to be no human agency accountable for them; was there some superhuman cause? Had I felt more at my ease with Lady K I think I should have spoken to her, but there seemed to be some bar between us, which forbade any but formal intercourse. And in some way which I cannot define it was borne in upon me that she understood those steps, that in her hands lay the key of the mystery.

'The evening hours passed on, and at the appointed time the steps overhead once more sounded. My nerves had reached such a pitch of excitement that I felt I could have faced anything rather than remain in ignorance of their meaning. Had it been possible for me to have transported myself bodily to whatever place the walker moved in, I verily believe I should have rushed thither to face the unknown, to discover the secret. But it was impossible. I felt that night too terrified to leave my bed for the quiet of the schoolroom and, paradoxical as it seems, though I would have faced a ghost or an evil spirit in the unseen, unknown room above me, I could not face the well-known, quiet passage outside my door. The sounds above me ran their usual course, the steps ceased, the window was flung open, silence ensued and I finally forgot myself in an uneasy sleep.

'I woke the next morning nervous and unrefreshed; at lunch-time my state of nervousness was increased by my becoming painfully conscious of the fact that Lady K was watching me covertly, gloomily, and withal with a certain indefinable expression as of one who expects and awaits a disaster. She talked nothing but commonplaces as usual, and I began to feel more and more confident that in her hands lay the key of the mystery of the night walker. Towards the end of luncheon Lady K observed that as it was Saturday she thought the children might enjoy a ride. This suggestion was eagerly embraced by both of them, and I found myself with the whole afternoon free before me.

'In due course after luncheon, the ponies were announced to be ready, and having seen my charges safely started off in the highest spirits, under the care of a fatherly-looking old coachman, I mounted the stairs, and went directly to Mason's room, which was a small one in the main body of the house not far removed from Lady K's. own bedroom.

'When I entered Mason's room in answer to her "Come in", I fancied that for a moment she looked slightly discomposed, and as if my visit was not over welcome. However, she greeted me civilly, begged me to be seated, and, taking up her needle, resumed her sewing. For a moment there was silence, and then she began to ask questions about the children and their lessons in a vague and preoccupied way, as if solely for the purpose of making conversation and avoiding a disagreeable topic. I answered her as briefly as in courtesy I could do, and then plunged at once into my subject:

'"Mason, who is it that walks about every night over my head?"
'I paused and looked at her. She slowly laid down her work

and, paling steadily till she grew a deathly white, sat staring at me in silence.

"'I cannot understand it," I went on. "What does it mean?"

'She seemed to find her voice with an effort.

"'I don't know what you are talking about, miss," she said. "There is nobody walks about this house at night."

"'I did not say that," I answered. "But there is someone who walks about over my head every night about half-past eleven and then throws open a window loud enough for anyone in the house to hear him."

"'Throws open the window," whispered Mason to herself. "Oh, my God! my God!" Then in a louder tone she went on, "You must be mistaken, miss, there is no room above yours."

"'That makes it all the stranger," I answered. "I know there is no room there, and yet I know the steps are there and nowhere else. What is it, oh, tell me what it is!"

'The strangeness of the episode, the old woman's obvious fear were telling on me; I felt I was losing my self-control, was giving way to panic. By a great effort, I regained my composure, and looking steadily at her said:

"'Mason, there is a story, a dreadful story connected with what I have heard at night. You know it, and you must tell it to me, or I shall go straight to Lady K and ask her to tell me."

"'For the love of God do not do that, miss," cried Mason.

"'Very well then, tell me the story," I answered.

'There was a pause, then Mason said in a low voice:

"'Have you ever heard of Master Edward?"

'I nodded.

"'And that he is dead?" she went on.

"'Yes," I replied, "I have seen his grave."

"'Who told you about him?" said the old woman. "Did anyone tell you he killed himself?"

"'Killed himself!" I exclaimed. "Oh no, oh no. Why, he must have been only a child."

"'I don't know," said Mason. "I don't know," she went on with increasing agitation. "I have always felt sure it was an accident. The jury said it was, but why does he walk? If, poor lamb, he fell out by accident, he would be at rest in heaven, and yet he walks. You, who are a stranger to us all, have heard him. Oh, my lady, my lady, why did you drive him to it?"

'Her agitation was pitiable, and absorbed in that I seemed to forget my own fear. But, as Mason grew calmer, I determined to reach the bottom of the mystery, and at last after much persuasion and many questions I elicited from her the following story:

'Sir Arthur K had been deeply in love with his second wife, and she had apparently returned his affection. At the time of the marriage in 1883, when Mason first came into contact with him, Edward, the child of the first wife, was six years old. He was a pretty, affectionate, spirited boy, a little inclined to be unduly sensitive, but on the whole a perfectly normal, healthy boy. Sir Arthur was much attached to him, and his stepmother treated him with the greatest kindness. This treatment continued after the births of her own two children, all three were treated as her own, and Mason declared that she as well as Sir Arthur believed Lady K really felt an almost equal devotion to them all.

'A change came soon after the death of Sir Arthur in 1887. The bulk of Sir Arthur's estate consisted of the Wyke property, and, at the date of the first marriage, this estate had been settled on the first wife and her children. There was, therefore, little that Sir Arthur could do for the children of his second marriage, save economise and thus form a fund for their benefit, but his brief tenure of life after his second marriage precluded him from accomplishing much in that respect. It is true that he made a will bequeathing any contingent benefit in his estate to his second wife and her children, but this was all. Lady K herself had no fortune to speak of.

'On his papers being opened after his death it was found that Sir Arthur had left his wife and an elderly clergyman, a Mr Cameron who had been an early friend of his, joint guardians of the children. Practically, this amounted to Lady K becoming sole guardian, since Mr Cameron lived in a remote part of England, was in poor health and really took no interest whatever in his wards.

'Mason was most emphatic that at no time was actual cruelty shown the boy, but she admitted that he was neglected. He was neglected in everything, education, manners, health, companions: all that Lady K had was lavished on her own children whilst Edward was stinted in every direction. It speaks volumes for the natural goodness of the boy that he did not grow to hate his little half-brother and -sister, but to the last he was always affectionate and gentle with them, and loved their society. With his stepmother it was different. Violent disputes took place between them, battles in which the impetuous, warm-hearted, neglected child dashed himself in vain against the cold-blooded, heartless woman. Into further details we need not go. Suffice it to say that one evening there was an unusually violent outburst, which ended in Edward rushing, sobbing and distracted, up to his little attic in the wing, for to this remote corner was the future owner of Wyke Hall now exiled. In the morning a gardener found the boy lying on the stone-flagged terrace beneath his window – dead.

'There was an inquest of course, but in deference to the position of the family the inquiry made was as formal as possible. The usual verdict was returned: death by misadventure; and Lady K found herself in the position of own mother to the future lord of Wyke.

'But her demeanour did not change, the coldness and hardness, only melted by her children's embraces, which had been growing on her now for the past few years remained, and she shut herself off deliberately from the neighbours to live solitary with her children.

'After a while rumours began to spread: something had happened at Wyke Hall, the house was haunted. All was very vague, but servants began to leave and it became difficult to replace them. At last Lady K called her household together in the hall and boldly broached the subject to them. Presently she challenged the assembled party.

"'Well, you say that the room my poor Edward lived in is haunted. Will you admit that you are wrong if I pass to-night alone and in peace and quiet there?"

'There was a murmur of assent.

'Lady K was as good as her word. She passed that night alone in the attic; she left it next morning as calm and composed as ever, but, as the servants noticed, a deathly white. And in a week's time workmen came and the attics over the wing were pulled down.

'Since that date, the wing, except for the schoolroom, had not been used; I was the first person to spend a night in it since Lady K had done so three years before.

'This was all Mason could tell me. When she had finished, she sat looking at me.

"'And now you know," she said.

'I was shaking with a mixture of fear and anger.

"'I will stay no longer than I must in this house," I answered as quietly as I could, "and I will never pass another night in that bedroom."

"'I knew you would say that," said Mason. "I will have your things moved at once to the room next to mine."

"'Thank you," I said, and left her.

'All was done as Mason had promised, and that evening saw me installed in my new room. I have never known what the servants thought of the sudden change. I said nothing to the maid, nor she to me. Nor did Lady K make a single comment. At luncheon the next day she was calm and composed as ever; I caught her more than once eyeing me covertly, but she said nothing of note. That evening, having fully made up my mind, I handed her a note informing her that I desired to leave at the end of the term. I gave no reasons. She read my note in my presence, and in a perfectly unmoved voice said:

"'I shall be sorry to lose you, Miss Hosmer."

'Nothing further of the slightest interest transpired during the remainder of my stay at Wyke Hall. I was careful always to leave the schoolroom early in the evening and retire to my new room, and I heard the footsteps no more. My relations with Lady K remained on the same cool and polite footing as ever. Occasionally I thought I saw a look of malice and fear in her eyes, but outwardly we were at peace. To the children I became really attached, and my sole regret at leaving that charming, that dreadful house, was my being parted from them. In fact, as my acquaintance with them grew, I began seriously to regret the approaching close of my relationship with them. I feared I had acted too hastily in resigning my engagement, but it was now too late to draw back. I knew Lady K's secret, and she knew that I knew it; to part was the only alternative.

'Many years have passed since then,' said Miss Hosmer, winding up her story, 'and I have never seen or heard of the family again. I have a vague impression that Lady K is dead, and I pray nightly even now that the wandering spirit of that dead child whom she hunted to his grave has also found eternal rest.'

THE VOICE IN THE NIGHT (1921)

WJ Wintle (1861–1934)

William James Wintle wrote extensively for both newspapers and magazines in the late Victorian and early Edwardian periods. Wide-ranging in his interests, he produced books on subjects as diverse as Prince Albert, Florence Nightingale, and old English songs. He was also an amateur natural historian who published books on shells and microscopy, and was a fellow of the London Zoological Society. A religious man, Wintle later became a lay brother at the Abbey on Caldey Island off the Welsh coast. Ghost Gleams, *published in 1921, was a collection of fifteen tales of the uncanny which he had first invented to entertain the boys who attended the Abbey school. (In his introduction, Wintle noted that 'the gruesome ones met with the best reception.') Although they were first aimed at a juvenile audience, and their oral origins as tales told around a fireside are sometimes a little too evident, Wintle's stories remain well worth reading. He had a lively imagination and* Ghost Gleams *includes a variety of supernatural phenomena from the ghost of a woolly mammoth to giant, bloodsucking spiders. John Barron, the protagonist of 'The Voice in the Night', is not an occult detective like Carnacki or Aylmer Vance but an ordinary squire and landowner who is drawn into investigating a number of strange occurrences on his estate and stumbles upon the terrible truth behind them.*

John Barron was frankly puzzled. He could not make it out at all. He had lived in the place all his life – save for the few years spent at Rugby and Oxford – and nothing of the sort had happened to him before. His people had occupied the estate for generations past; and there was neither record nor tradition of anything of the kind. He did not like it at all. It seemed like an intrusion upon the respectability of his family. And John Barron had a very good opinion of his family.

Certainly he was entitled to have a good opinion of it. He came from a good stock: his ancestry was one to be proud of: his coat of arms had quarterings that few could display: and his immediate forbears had kept up the reputation of their ancestors. He himself could boast a career without reproach: the short time he had spent at the bar was marked by considerable success and still more promise – a promise cut short by the death of his father and his recall to Bannerton to take up the duties of squire, magistrate and county magnate.

In the eyes of his friends and of people generally, he was a man to be envied. He had an ample fortune, a delightful house and estate, hosts of friends, and the best of health. What could a man wish for more? The ladies of the neighbourhood said that he lacked only one thing, and that was a wife. But it may be that they were not entirely unprejudiced judges – the unmarried ones, at any rate. But up till the time of our story John Barron had shown no sign of marrying. He used to boast that he was neither married, nor engaged, nor courting, nor had he his eye on anyone.

And now this annoyance had come to trouble and puzzle him!

What had he done to deserve it? True, he might take the comfort to his soul that it was no immediate concern of his. The affair had not happened to any member of his family or household. Why then should he not mind his own business? But he felt that it was his business. It had happened within the bounds of his manor and almost within sight of his windows. If anything tangible could be connected with it, he was the magistrate whose duty it would be to investigate the matter. But up till the present there was nothing tangible for him to deal with.

The whole business was a mystery: and John Barron disapproved of mysteries. Mysteries savoured of detectives and the police court. When unravelled they usually proved to be sordid and undesirable; and when not unravelled they brought with them a vague sense of discomfort and of danger. As a lawyer he held that mysteries had no right to exist. That they should continue to exist was a sort of reflection on the profession, as well as upon the public intelligence.

And yet here was the parish of Bannerton in the hands of a mystery of the first water. As a magistrate, John Barron had officially looked into the matter; and, as a lawyer, he had spent some hours in carefully considering it; but entirely without any practical result. The mystery was not merely unsolved: it had even thickened!

This was the history with which he was faced. A fortnight before, the occupants of a cottage on the outskirts of the village – a gardener and his wife – had left their little daughter of three years old in the house while they went on an errand. The child was soundly asleep in its cot; and they locked the door as they went out. They were absent about twenty minutes; and were nearing the house when they heard the screams of a child. The father rushed forward, unlocked the door, and the two parents entered together.

The child's cot was in the living room into which the front door opened. As they went in, the screams ceased and a terrible gasping sound took their place. Then they saw that the cot was hidden by some dark body that seemed to be lying on it. This they hardly saw, though they were quite clear that it was there, for it seemed to melt away like a mist when they rushed into the room. Certainly it was nothing solid, for it completely disappeared without a sound. It could not have dashed out through the door, for the parents were hardly clear of the door when it vanished.

They had returned only just in time to save the life of the child. At first it was doubtful if they were in time, for the doctor held out little hope. But after a day or two, the child took a turn for the better, and was now out of danger. It had evidently been attacked by some kind of savage animal, which had torn at its throat and had only just failed to sever the arteries of the neck. In the opinion of the doctor and of John Barron himself, the wounds suggested that the assailant had been a very large dog. But it was strange that a dog of such size had not done far worse damage. One might have expected that it would have killed the child with a single bite.

But was it a dog? If so, how did it enter the house? The door in front was locked, as we have seen; that at the back was bolted; and all the windows were shut and fastened. There was no apparent way by which it could possibly have got into the house. And we have already seen that its way of going was equally mysterious.

The most careful examination of the room and of the premises generally failed to yield the smallest clue. Nothing had been disturbed or damaged, and there were no footprints. The only thing at all unusual was the presence of an earthy or mouldy odour which was noticed by the doctor when he entered the room and also by some other persons who were on the scene soon afterwards. John Barron had the same impression when he went to the cottage some hours later, but the odour was then so faint that he could not be at all sure about its existence.

By way of embroidery to the story came two or three items of local gossip of the usual sort. An old woman nearby said that she was looking out of her window to see the state of the weather a little earlier in the evening, when she saw a huge black dog run across the lane and go in the direction of the cottage. According to her tale, the dog limped as if lame or very much tired.

Three people said they had been disturbed for two or three nights previous by the howling of a dog in the distance; and a farmer in the parish complained that his sheep had apparently been chased about the field during the night by some wandering dog.

He loudly vowed vengeance on dogs in general; but, as none of the sheep had been worried, nobody took much notice. All these tales came to the ears of John Barron; but to a man accustomed to weigh evidence they were negligible.

But he attached much more importance to another piece of evidence, if such it might be called. As the injured child began to get better, and was able to talk, an attempt was made to find out if it could give any information about the attack. As it had been asleep when attacked, it did not see the arrival of its assailant; and the only thing it could tell was:

'Nasty, ugly lady bit me!'

This seemed absurd; but, when asked about the dog, it persisted in saying, 'No dog. Nasty ugly lady!'

The parents were inclined to laugh at what they thought a mere childish fancy; but the trained lawyer was considerably impressed by it. To him there were three facts available. The wounds seemed to have been caused by a large dog: the child said she had been bitten by an ugly lady: and the parents had actually seen the form of the assailant. Unfortunately it had disappeared before they could make out any details; but they said it was about the size of a very large dog, and was dark in colour.

The local gossip was of small importance and was such as might be expected under the circumstances. But, for what it was worth, it all pointed to a dog or dog-like animal. But how could it have entered the closed house; how did it get away; and why did the child persist in her story of an ugly lady? The only theory that would at all fit the case was that supplied by the old Norse legends of the werewolf. But who believes such stories now?

So it was not to be wondered at that John Barron was puzzled. He was rather annoyed too. Bannerton had its average amount of crime; but it was in a small way and could generally be disposed of at the petty sessions. It was not often that a case had to be sent to the assizes, and the newspapers seldom got any sensational copy from the quiet little place.

He reflected with some small satisfaction that it was lucky the child had not died; for in that case there must have been an inquest and the inevitable publicity. If his suspicions were well founded, the case would have yielded something far more sensational than generally falls to the lot of the local reporter.

But a day or two later he had more to ponder over. Things had developed – and in a way that he did not like. The farmer had again complained that his sheep had been chased about the field during the night; and this time more damage had been done.

Two of the sheep had died; but the strange thing was that they had hardly been bitten at all. Their wounds were so slight that their death could only be attributed to fright and exhaustion. It was very curious that the dog – if dog it was – had not mauled them worse and made a meal of them. The suggestion that it was some very small dog was negatived by the fact that what wounds there were must have been made by a large animal. It really looked as if the animal had not sufficient strength to finish its evil work.

But John Barron had another item of evidence which he was keeping to himself for the present. During each of the two past nights he had woken up without any apparent reason soon after midnight. And each time he had heard the Cry in the Night. It was a voice borne on the night air which he never expected to hear in England; and least of all in Bannerton.

The voice came from the moor that stood above the little hamlet; and it rose and fell on the silence like the cry of a spirit in distress. It began with a low wail of unspeakable sadness; then rose and fell in lamentable ululations; and then died away into sobs and silence.

The voice came at intervals for more than an hour: and the second night it was stronger and seemed nearer than the first. John Barron had no difficulty in recognising that long-drawn cry. He had heard it before when travelling in the wilder parts of Russia. It was the howling of a wolf!

But there are no wolves in England. True, it might have been an escaped animal from some travelling menagerie; but such an animal would have made worse havoc of the sheep. And if this was the assailant of the little child, how did it get in; how did it get away; and why did the child still persist in saying that it was not a dog but a lady who bit her?

The next few days saw the plot thicken. Other people heard the voice in the night, and put it down to a stray dog out on the moor. Another farmer's sheep were worried, and this time one of them was partly eaten. So a chase was arranged, and all the local farmers and many other people banded together to hunt the sheep-killer. For two days the moor was scoured, and the adjacent woods thoroughly beaten, but without coming across any signs of the miscreant.

But John Barron heard a story from one of the farmers that set him thinking. He noticed that this man seemed to avoid a little thicket beside the moor, suggesting that there was a better path at some distance from it; and after some pressing he explained the real reason for this. But he was careful to add that of course he was not himself superstitious, but his wife had queer notions and had begged him to avoid the place.

It seemed that not long before, some wandering gipsies who from time to time camped on the moor, had secretly buried an old woman in the thicket and had never returned to the moor since. Of course there were the inevitable additions to a tale of this sort. The old lady was alleged to have been the queen of the gipsy tribe; and she was also said to have been a witch of the most malignant kind; and these were supposed to have been the reasons for her secret burial in this lonely spot. It did not seem to occur to the farmer that the gipsies thus saved the expense of a regular funeral. Very few people knew the story, and they thought it well to hold their peace. It was not worthwhile to make enemies of the gipsies, who could so easily have their revenge by robbing hen-roosts or even by driving cattle; to say nothing of the more mysterious doings with which they were credited.

John Barron began to put things together. The whole business had a distinct resemblance to the tales of the werewolf in the Scandinavian literature of the Middle Ages. Here we had a woman of suspicious reputation buried in a lonely place without Christian rites; and soon afterwards a mysterious wolf roams the district in search of blood – just like the werewolf.

But who believes such stories now, except a few ghost-ridden cranks with shattered nerves and unbalanced minds? The whole thing is absurd.

Still, the mystery had to be cleared up; for John Barron had not the slightest intention of letting it simply slide into the refuse heap of unsolved problems. He kept his own counsel; but he meant to get to the bottom of it. Perhaps if he had realised the horror that lay at the bottom of it, he would have let it alone.

In the meantime the farmers had taken their own steps to deal with the sheep-worrying nuisance. Tempting morsels, judiciously seasoned with poison, were laid about; but with the sole result of causing the untimely death of a valued sheep-dog. Night after night the younger men, armed with guns, sat up and watched; but without success. Nothing happened, the sheep were undisturbed, and it really seemed as if the invader had left the neighbourhood. But John Barron knew that once a dog has taken to worrying sheep, it can never be cured. If the mysterious visitor was a dog, he would most certainly return if still alive and able to travel: if it was not a dog – well, anything might happen. So he continued to watch even after the general hunt for the dog had ceased.

Soon he had his reward. One very dark and stormy night, he again heard the distant voice in the night. It came very faintly rising and falling on the air, for the breeze was strong and the sound had to travel against the wind. Then he left the house, carrying his gun, and took up his post on rising ground that commanded the road that led from the moor.

Presently the cry came nearer, and then nearer still, till it was evident that the wolf had left the moor and was approaching the farms. Several dogs barked; but they were not the barks of challenge and defiance, but rather the timid yelps of fear. Then the howling came from a turn in the road so close at hand that John Barron, who was by no means a timid or nervous man, could hardly resist a shudder.

He silently cocked his gun, crept softly from behind the hedge into the road, and waited.

Then a small, shrivelled old woman came into sight, walking with the aid of a stick. She hobbled along with surprising briskness for so old a woman until a turn in the road brought her suddenly face to face with him. And then something happened.

He was not a man addicted to fancies; nor was he at all lacking in powers of description as a rule; but he could never state quite clearly what it was that really happened. Probably it was because he did not quite know. He could only speak of an impression rather than of certain experience. According to him, the old woman gave him one glance of unspeakable malignancy; and then he seemed to become dazed or semi-conscious for a moment. It could have been only a matter of a second or two: but during that short space of time the old woman vanished. John Barron pulled himself together just in time to see a large wolf disappear round the turn of the road.

Naturally enough, he was somewhat confused by his startling experience. But there was no doubt about the presence of the wolf. He only just saw it; but he saw it quite clearly for about a second of time. Whether the wolf accompanied the old woman, or the old woman turned into a wolf, he neither saw nor could know. But each supposition was open to many obvious objections.

John Barron spent some time next day in thinking the thing out; and then it suddenly occurred to him to visit the thicket by the moorside and see the grave of the gipsy. He did not expect that there would be anything to see; but still it might be worthwhile to take a look at the place.

So he strolled in that direction early in the afternoon. The thicket occupied a kind of little dell lying under the edge of the moor and was densely filled with small trees and undergrowth. But a scarcely visible path led into it; and, pushing his way through, he found that there was a small open space in the middle. Evidently this was the site of the gipsy grave. And there he found it: but he found more than he expected.

Not only was the grave there, but it lay open! The loose earth was heaped up on either side, and had the appearance of having been scraped out by some animal. And, sure enough, the footprints of a very large dog or wolf were to be seen in several places.

John Barron was simply horrified to find that the grave had

been thus desecrated – and apparently in a manner that suggested an even worse horror. But, after a moment of hesitation, he stepped to the edge of the grave and looked in. What he saw was less appalling than he feared. There lay the coffin, exposed to view; but there was no sign that it had been opened or tampered with in any way.

There was evidently only one thing to be done, and that was to cover up the coffin decently and fill in the grave again. He would borrow a spade at the nearest cottage on some pretence and get the job done. He turned away to do this; but as he went through the thicket he could have sworn that he heard a sound like muffled laughter! And he could not get away from the notion that the laughter had some quality closely resembling the howling of a wolf. He called himself a fool for thinking such a thing – but he thought it all the same.

He borrowed the spade and filled the grave, beating the earth down as hard as he could; and again, as he turned away after completing the task, he heard that muffled laugh. But this time it was even less distinct than before, and somehow it sounded underground. He was rather glad to get away.

It may well be imagined that he had plenty to occupy his thoughts for the rest of the day; and even when he sought to sleep he could not. He lay tossing uneasily, thinking all the time of the mysterious grave and the events that certainly seemed now to be connected with it.

Then, soon after midnight, he heard the voice in the night again. The wolf howled a long way off at first; then came a long interval of silence; and then the voice sounded so close to the house that Barron started up in alarm and he heard his dog give a cry of fear. Then the silence fell again; and sometime later the howling was again heard in the distance.

Next morning he found his favourite dog lying dead beside his kennel; and it was only too evident how he had met his end. His neck was almost severed by one fearful bite; but the strange thing was that there was very little blood to be seen. A closer examination showed that the dog had bled to death; but where was the blood? Natural wolves tear their prey and devour it. They do not suck its blood. What kind of a wolf could this be?

John Barron found the answer next day. He was walking in the direction of the moor late in the afternoon, as it grew towards dusk, when he heard shrieks of terror coming from a little side lane.

He ran to the rescue, and there he saw a little child of the village lying on the ground, with a huge wolf in the act of tearing at its throat.

Fortunately he had his gun with him; and, as the wolf sprang off its victim when he shouted, he fired. The range was a short one, and the beast got the full force of the charge.

It bounded into the air and fell in a heap. But it got up again, and went off in a limping gallop in the way that wolves will often do even when mortally wounded. It made for the moor.

John Barron saw that it had received its death wound, and so gave it no further attention for the moment. Some men came running up at his shouts, and with their assistance he took the wounded child to the local doctor. Happily he had been in time to save its life.

Then he reloaded his gun, took a man with him, and followed the track of the wolf. It was not difficult to follow, for blood-stains on the road at frequent intervals showed plainly enough that it was severely wounded. As Barron expected, the track led straight to the thicket and entered it.

The two men followed cautiously; but they found no wolf. In the midst of the thicket lay the grave once more uncovered. And there beside it lay the body of a little old woman, drenched with blood. She was quite dead, and the terrible gunshot wound in her side told its own story. And the two men noticed that her canine teeth projected slightly beyond her lips on each side – like those of a snarling wolf – and they were blood-stained.

THE DEATH HOUND (1922)

Dion Fortune (1890–1946)

Violet Mary Firth was born in Llandudno into a wealthy English family which had made its money in the Sheffield steel industry. As a young woman she studied psychology and psychoanalysis but soon began to gravitate towards the wilder shores of occultism and white magic. Immersing herself first in the ideas of the Theosophists and then in the work of the Alpha et Omega, an offshoot of the Order of the Golden Dawn, she eventually founded her own magical society, the Fraternity of the Inner Light, in 1924. Claiming contact with a group of exalted souls known as the 'Ascended Masters' (their number included Jesus and Socrates), she published The Cosmic Doctrine, *a text she said had been dictated to her by these friends from another world. Under the pen-name of Dion Fortune, she continued to publish works about occultism, magic and esoteric philosophy for the rest of her life. She also published a good deal of fiction, including fantasy novels with titles like* The Goat-Foot God *and* The Demon Lover, *and a series of short stories about a psychic detective and healer named Dr Taverner (reportedly based on her mentor in magic, an Irish magus named Theodore Moriarty) which first appeared in* Royal Magazine *in 1922 and were then published in book form four years later as* The Secrets of Doctor Taverner. *Intended to reflect Dion Fortune's own decidedly odd ideas about this world and the next, the Taverner stories are nonetheless surprisingly good fun to read.*

'Well?' said my patient when I had finished stethoscoping him, 'have I got to go softly all the days of my life?'

'Your heart is not all it might be,' I replied, 'but with care it ought to last as long as you want it. You must avoid all undue exertion, however.'

The man made a curious grimace. 'Supposing exertion seeks me out?' he asked.

'You must so regulate your life as to reduce the possibility to a minimum.'

Taverner's voice came from the other side of the room. 'If you have finished with his body, Rhodes, I will make a start on his mind.'

'I have a notion,' said our patient, 'that the two are rather intimately connected. You say I must keep my body quiet,' – he looked at me – 'but what am I to do if my mind deliberately gives it shocks?' and he turned to my colleague.

'That is where I come in,' said Taverner. 'My friend has told you what to do; now I will show you how to do it. Come and tell me your symptoms.'

'Delusions,' said the stranger as he buttoned his shirt. 'A black dog of ferocious aspect who pops out of dark corners and chivvies me, or tries to. I haven't done him the honour to run away from him yet; I daren't, my heart's too dickey, but one of these days I am afraid I may, and then I shall probably drop dead.'

Taverner raised his eyes to me in a silent question. I nodded; it was quite a likely thing to happen if the man ran far or fast.

'What sort of a beast is your dog?' enquired my colleague.

'No particular breed at all. Just a plain dog, with four legs and a tail, about the size of a mastiff, but not of the mastiff build.'

'How does he make his appearance?'

'Difficult to say; he does not seem to follow any fixed rule, but usually after dusk. If I am out after sundown, I may look over my shoulder and see him padding along behind me, or if I am sitting in my room between daylight fading and lamp lighting, I may see him crouching behind the furniture watching his opportunity.'

'His opportunity for what?'

'To spring at my throat.'

'Why does he not take you unawares?'

'This is what I cannot make out. He seems to miss so many

chances, for he always waits to attack until I am aware of his presence.'

'What does he do then?'

'As soon as I turn and face him, he begins to close in on me! If I am out walking, he quickens his pace so as to overtake me, and if I am indoors he sets to work to stalk me round the furniture. I tell you, he may only be a product of my imagination, but he is an uncanny sight to watch.'

The speaker paused and wiped away the sweat that had gathered on his forehead during this recital.

Such a haunting is not a pleasant form of obsession for any man to be afflicted with, but for one with a heart like our patient's it was peculiarly dangerous.

'What defence do you offer to this creature?' asked Taverner.

'I keep on saying to it "You're not real, you know, you are only a beastly nightmare, and I'm not going to let myself be taken in by you."'

'As good a defence as any,' said Taverner. 'But I notice you talk to it as if it were real.'

'By Jove, so I do!' said our visitor thoughtfully; 'that is something new. I never used to do that. I took it for granted that the beast wasn't real, was only a phantom of my own brain, but recently a doubt has begun to creep in. Supposing the thing is real after all? Supposing it really has power to attack me? I have an underlying suspicion that my hound may not be altogether harmless after all.'

'He will certainly be exceedingly dangerous to you if you lose your nerve and run away from him. So long as you keep your head, I do not think he will do you any harm.'

'Precisely. But there is a point beyond which one may not keep one's head. Supposing, night after night, just as you were going off to sleep, you wake up knowing the creature is in the room, you see his snout coming round the corner of the curtain, and you pull yourself together and get rid of him and settle down again. Then just as you are getting drowsy, you take a last look round to make sure that all is safe, and you see something dark moving between you and the dying glow of the fire. You daren't go to sleep, and you can't keep awake. You may know perfectly well that it is all imagination, but that sort of thing wears you down if it is kept up night after night.'

'You get it regularly every night?'

'Pretty nearly. Its habits are not absolutely regular, however, except that, now you come to mention it, it always gives me Friday night off; if it weren't for that, I should have gone under long ago. When Friday comes I say to it: "Now, you brute, this is your beastly Sabbath," and go to bed at eight and sleep the clock round.'

'If you care to come down to my nursing home at Hindhead, we can probably keep the creature out of your room and ensure you a decent night's sleep,' said Taverner. 'But what we really want to know is –' he paused almost imperceptibly, 'why your imagination should haunt you with dogs, and not, shall we say, with scarlet snakes in the time-honoured fashion.'

'I wish it would,' said our patient. 'If it was snakes I could "put more water with it" and drown them, but this slinking black beast –' he shrugged his shoulders and followed the butler out of the room.

'Well, Rhodes, what do you make of it?' asked my colleague after the door closed.

'On the face of it,' I said, 'it looks like an ordinary example of delusions, but I have seen enough of your queer cases not to limit myself to the internal mechanism of the mind alone. Do you consider it possible that we have another case of thought transference?'

'You are coming along,' said Taverner, nodding his head at me approvingly. 'When you first enjoined me, you would unhesitatingly have recommended bromide for all the ills the mind is heir to; now you recognise that there are more things in heaven and earth than were taught you in the medical schools.

'So you think we have a case of thought transference? I am

inclined to think so too. When a patient tells you his delusions, he stands up for them, and often explains to you that they are psychic phenomena, but when a patient recounts psychic phenomena, he generally apologises for them, and explains that they are delusions. But why doesn't the creature attack and be done with it, and why does it take its regular half-holiday as if it were under the Shop Hours Act?'

He suddenly slapped his hand down on the desk.

'Friday is the day the Black Lodges meet. We must be on their trail again; they will get to know me before we have finished. Someone who got his occult training in a Black Lodge is responsible for that ghost hound. The reason that Martin gets to sleep in peace on Friday night is that his would-be murderer sits in Lodge that evening and cannot attend to his private affairs.'

'His would-be-murderer?' I questioned.

'Precisely. Anyone who sends a haunting like that to a man with a heart like Martin's knows that it means his death sooner or later. Supposing Martin got into a panic and took to his heels when he found the dog behind him in a lonely place?'

'He might last for half-a-mile,' I said, 'but I doubt if he would get any further.'

'This is a clear case of mental assassination. Someone who is a trained occultist has created a thought-form of a black hound, and he is sufficiently in touch with Martin to be able to convey it to his mind by means of thought transference, and Martin sees, or thinks he sees, the image that the other man is visualising.

'The actual thought-form itself is harmless except for the fear it inspires, but should Martin lose his head and resort to vigorous physical means of defence, the effort would precipitate a heart attack, and he would drop dead without the slightest evidence to show who caused his death. One of these days we will raid those Black Lodges, Rhodes; they know too much. Ring up Martin at the Hotel Cecil and tell him we will drive him back with us tonight.'

'How do you propose to handle the case?' I asked.

'The house is covered by a psychic bell jar, so the thing cannot get at him while he is under its protection. We will then find out who is the sender, and see if we can deal with him and stop it once and for all. It is no good disintegrating the creature, its master would only manufacture another; it is the man behind the dog that we must get at.

'We shall have to be careful, however, not to let Martin think we suspect he is in any danger, or he will lose his one defence against the creature, a belief in its unreality. That adds to our difficulties, because we daren't question him much, lest we rouse his suspicions. We shall have to get at the facts of the case obliquely.'

On the drive down to Hindhead, Taverner did a thing I had never heard him do before, talk to a patient about his occult theories. Sometimes, at the conclusion of a case, he would explain the laws underlying the phenomena in order to rid the unknown of its terrors and enable his patient to cope with them, but at the outset, never.

I listened in astonishment, and then I saw what Taverner was fishing for. He wanted to find out whether Martin had any knowledge of occultism himself, and used his own interest to waken the other's – if he had one.

My colleague's diplomacy bore instant fruit. Martin was also interested in these subjects, though his actual knowledge was nil – even I could see that.

'I wish you and Mortimer could meet,' he said. 'He is an awfully interesting chap. We used to sit up half the night talking of these things at one time.'

'I should be delighted to meet your friend,' said Taverner. 'Do you think he could be persuaded to run down one Sunday and see us? I am always on the lookout for anyone I can learn something from.'

'I – I am afraid I could not get hold of him now,' said our companion, and lapsed into a preoccupied silence from which all Taverner's conversational efforts failed to rouse him. We had evidently struck some painful subject, and I saw my colleague make a mental note of the fact.

As soon as we got in, Taverner went straight to his study, opened the safe, and took out a card index file.

'Maffeo, Montague, Mortimer,' he muttered, as he turned the cards over. 'Anthony William Mortimer. Initiated into the Order of the Cowled Brethren, October, 1912; took office as Armed Guard, May, 1915. Arrested on suspicion of espionage, March, 1916. Prosecuted for exerting undue influence in the making of his mother's will. (Everybody seems to go for him, and no one seems to be able to catch him.) Became Grand Master of the Lodge of Set the Destroyer. Knocks, two, three, two, password, "Jackal".'

'So much for Mr Mortimer. A good man to steer clear of, I should imagine. Now I wonder what Martin has done to upset him.'

As we dared not question Martin, we observed him, and I very soon noticed that he watched the incoming posts with the greatest anxiety. He was always hanging about the hall when they arrived, and seized his scanty mail with eagerness, only to lapse immediately into despondency. Whatever letter it was that he was looking for never came. He did not express any surprise at this, however, and I concluded that he was rather hoping against hope than expecting something that might happen.

Then one day he could stand it no longer, and as for the twentieth time I unlocked the mailbag and informed him that there was nothing for him, he blurted out: 'Do you believe that "absence makes the heart grow fonder", Dr Rhodes?'

'It depends on the nature,' I said. 'But I have usually observed if you have fallen out with someone, you are more ready to overlook his shortcomings when you have been away from him for a time.'

'But if you are fond of someone?' he continued, half-anxiously, half-shamefacedly.

'It is my belief that love cools if it is not fed,' I said. 'The human mind has great powers of adaptation, and one gets used, sooner or later, to being without one's nearest and dearest.'

'I think so, too,' said Martin, and I saw him go off to seek consolation from his pipe in a lonely corner.

'So there is a woman in the case,' said Taverner when I reported the incident. 'I should rather like to have a look at her. I think I shall set up as a rival to Mortimer; if he sends black thought forms, let me see what I can do with a white one.'

I guessed that Taverner meant to make use of the method of silent suggestion, of which he was a past master.

Apparently Taverner's magic was not long in working, for a couple of days later I handed Martin a letter which caused his face to light up with pleasure, and sent him off to his room to read it in private. Half an hour later he came to me in the office and said:

'Dr Rhodes, would it be convenient if I had a couple of guests to lunch tomorrow?'

I assured him that this would be the case, and noted the change wrought in his appearance by the arrival of the long wished-for letter. He would have faced a pack of black dogs at that moment.

Next day I caught sight of Martin showing two ladies round the grounds, and when they came into the dining-room he introduced them as Mrs and Miss Hallam. There seemed to be something wrong with the girl, I thought; she was so curiously distrait and absent-minded. Martin, however, was in the seventh heaven; the man's transparent pleasure was almost amusing to witness. I was watching the little comedy with a covert smile, when suddenly it changed to tragedy.

As the girl stripped her gloves off she revealed a ring upon the third finger of her left hand. It was undoubtedly an engagement ring. I raised my eyes to Martin's face, and saw that his were fixed upon it. In the space of a few seconds the man crumpled; the happy little luncheon party was over. He strove to play his part as host, but the effort was pitiful to watch, and I was thankful when the close of the meal permitted me to withdraw.

I was not allowed to escape, however. Taverner caught my arm as I was leaving the room and drew me out on the terrace.

'Come along,' he said. 'I want to make friends with the Hallam family; they may be able to throw some light on our problem.'

We found that Martin had paired off with the mother, so we had no difficulty in strolling round the garden with the girl between us. She seemed to welcome the arrangement, and we had not been together many minutes before the reason was made evident.

'Dr Taverner,' she said, 'may I talk to you about myself?'

'I shall be delighted, Miss Hallam,' he replied. 'What is it you want to ask me about?'

'I am so very puzzled about something. Is it possible to be in love with a person you don't like?'

'Quite possible,' said Taverner, 'but not likely to be very satisfactory.'

'I am engaged to a man,' she said, sliding her engagement ring on and off her finger, 'whom I am madly, desperately in love with when he is not there, and as soon as he is present I feel a sense of horror and repulsion for him. When I am away, I long to be with him, and when I am with him, I feel as if everything were wrong and horrible. I cannot make myself clear, but do you grasp what I mean?'

'How did you come to get engaged to him?' asked Taverner.

'In the ordinary way. I have known him nearly as long as I have Billy,' indicating Martin, who was just ahead of us, walking with the mother.

'No undue influence was used?' said Taverner.

'No, I don't think so. He just asked me to marry him, and I said I would.'

'How long before that had you known that you would accept him if he proposed to you?'

'I don't know. I hadn't thought of it; in fact the engagement was as much a surprise to me as to everyone else. I had never thought of him in that way till about three weeks ago, and then I suddenly realised that he was the man I wanted to marry. It was a sudden impulse, but so strong and clear that I knew it was the thing for me to do.'

'And you do not regret it?'

'I did not until today, but as I was sitting in the dining room I suddenly felt how thankful I should be if I had not got to go back to Tony.'

Taverner looked at me. 'The psychic isolation of this house has its uses,' he said. Then he turned to the girl again. 'You don't suppose that it was Mr Mortimer's forceful personality that influenced your decision?'

I was secretly amused at Taverner's shot in the dark, and the way the girl walked blissfully into his trap.

'Oh, no,' she said, 'I often get those impulses; it was on just such a one that I came down here.'

'Then,' said Taverner, 'it may well be on just such another that you got engaged to Mortimer, so I may as well tell you that it was I who was responsible for that impulse.'

The girl stared at him in amazement.

'As soon as I knew of your existence I wanted to see you. There is a soul over there that is in my care at present, and I think you play a part in his welfare.'

'I know I do,' said the girl, gazing at the broad shoulders of the unconscious Martin with so much wistfulness and yearning that she clearly betrayed where her real feelings lay.

'Some people send telegrams when they wish to communicate, but I don't; I send thoughts, because I am certain they will be obeyed. A person may disregard a telegram, but he will act on a thought, because he believes it to be his own; though, of course, it is necessary that he should not suspect he is receiving suggestion, or he would probably turn round and do the exact opposite.'

Miss Hallam stared at him in astonishment.

'Is such a thing possible?' she exclaimed. 'I can hardly believe it.'

'You see that vase of scarlet geraniums to the left of the path? I will make your mother turn aside and pick one. Now watch.'

We both gazed at the unconscious woman as Taverner concentrated his attention upon her, and sure enough, as they drew abreast of the vase, she turned aside and picked a scarlet blossom.

'What are you doing to our geraniums?' Taverner called to her.

'I am so sorry,' she called back, 'I am afraid I yielded to a sudden impulse.'

'All thoughts are not generated within the mind that thinks them,' said Taverner. 'We are constantly giving each other unconscious suggestions, and influencing minds without knowing it, and if a man who understands the power of thought deliberately trains his mind in its use, there are few things he cannot do.'

We had regained the terrace in the course of our walk, and Taverner took his farewell and retired to the office. I followed him, and found him with the safe open and his card index upon the table.

'Well, Rhodes, what do you make of it all?' he greeted me.

'Martin and Mortimer after the same girl,' said I. 'And Mortimer uses for his private ends the same methods you use on your patients.'

'Precisely, 'said Taverner. 'An excellent object lesson in the ways of black and white occultism. We both study the human mind – we both study the hidden forces of nature; I use my knowledge for healing and Mortimer uses his for destruction.'

'Taverner,' I said, facing him, 'what is to prevent you also from using your great knowledge for personal ends?'

'Several things, my friend,' he replied. 'In the first place, those who are taught as I am taught are (though I say it who shouldn't) picked men, carefully tested. Secondly, I am a member of an organisation which would assuredly exact retribution for the abuse of its training; and, thirdly, knowing what I do, I dare not abuse the powers that have been entrusted to me. There is no such thing as a straight line in the universe; everything works in curves; therefore it is only a matter of time before that which you send out from your mind returns to it. Sooner or later Martin's dog will come home to its master.'

Martin was absent from the evening meal, and Taverner immediately enquired his whereabouts.

'He walked over with his friends to the crossroads to put them on the bus for Haslemere,' someone volunteered, and Taverner, who did not seem too well satisfied, looked at his watch.

'It will be light for a couple of hours yet,' he said. 'If he is not in by dusk, Rhodes, let me know.'

It was a grey evening, threatening storm, and darkness set in early. Soon after eight I sought Taverner in his study and said: 'Martin isn't in yet, doctor.'

'Then we had better go and look for him,' said my colleague.

We went out by the window to avoid observation on the part of our other patients, and, making our way through the shrubberies, were soon out upon the moor.

'I wish we knew which way he would come,' said Taverner. 'There is a profusion of paths to choose from. We had better get on to high ground and watch for him with the field-glasses.'

We made our way to a bluff topped with wind-torn Scotch firs, and Taverner swept the heather paths with his binoculars. A mile away he picked out a figure moving in our direction, but it was too far off for identification.

'Probably Martin,' said my companion, 'but we can't be sure yet. We had better stop up here and await events; if we drop down into the hollow we shall lose sight of him. You take the glasses; your eyes are better than mine. How infernally early it is getting dark tonight. We ought to have had another half-hour of daylight.'

A cold wind had sprung up, making us shiver in our thin clothes, for we were both in evening dress and hatless. Heavy grey clouds were banking up in the west, and the trees moaned uneasily. The man out on the moor was moving at a good pace, looking neither to right nor left. Except for his solitary figure the great grey waste was empty.

All of a sudden the swinging stride was interrupted; he looked over his shoulder, paused, and then quickened his pace. Then he looked over his shoulder again and broke into a half trot. After a few yards of this he dropped to a walk again, and held steadily on his way, refusing to turn his head.

I handed the glasses to Taverner.

'It's Martin right enough,' he said; 'and he has seen the dog.'

We could make out now the path he was following, and, descending from the hill, set out at a rapid pace to meet him. We had gone about a quarter of a mile when a sound arose in the darkness ahead of us; the piercing, inarticulate shriek of a creature being hunted to death.

Taverner let out such a halloo as I did not think human lungs were capable of. We tore along the path to the crest of a rise, and as we raced down the opposite slope, we made out a figure struggling across the heather. Our white shirt fronts showed up plainly in the gathering dusk, and he headed towards us. It was Martin running for his life from the death hound.

I rapidly outdistanced Taverner, and caught the hunted man in my arms as we literally cannoned into each other in the narrow path. I could feel the played-out heart knocking like a badly-running engine against his side. I laid him flat on the ground, and Taverner coming up with his pocket medicine case, we did what we could.

We were only just in time. A few more yards and the man would have dropped. As I straightened my back and looked round into the darkness, I thanked God that I had not that horrible power of vision which would have enabled me to see what it was that had slunk off over the heather at our approach. That something went I had no doubt, for half a dozen sheep, grazing a few hundred yards away, scattered to give it passage.

We got Martin back to the house and sat up with him. It was touch-and-go with that ill-used heart, and we had to drug the racked nerves into oblivion.

Shortly after midnight Taverner went to the window and looked out.

'Come here, Rhodes,' he said. 'Do you see anything?'

I declared that I did not.

'It would be a very good thing for you if you did,' declared Taverner. 'You are much too fond of treating the thought-forms that a sick mind breeds as if, because they have no objective existence, they were innocuous. Now come along and see things from the viewpoint of the patient.'

He commenced to beat a tattoo upon my forehead, using a peculiar syncopated rhythm. In a few moments I became conscious of a feeling as if a suppressed sneeze were working its way from my nose up into my skull. Then I noticed a faint luminosity appear in the darkness without, and I saw that a greyish-white film extended outside the window. Beyond that I saw the Death Hound!

A shadowy form gathered itself out of the darkness, took a run towards the window, and leapt up, only to drive its head against the grey film and fall back. Again it gathered itself together, and again it leapt, only to fall back baffled. A soundless baying seemed to come from the open jaws, and in the eyes gleamed a light that was not of this world. It was not the green luminosity of an animal, but a purplish grey reflected from some cold planet beyond the range of our senses.

'That is what Martin sees nightly,' said Taverner, 'only in his case the thing is actually in the room. Shall I open a way through the psychic bell jar it is hitting its nose against, and let it in?'

I shook my head and turned away from that nightmare vision. Taverner passed his hand rapidly across my forehead with a peculiar snatching movement.

'You are spared a good deal,' he said, 'but never forget that the delusions of a lunatic are just as real to him as that hound was to you.'

We were working in the office next afternoon when I was summoned to interview a lady who was waiting in the hall. It was Miss Hallam, and I wondered what had brought her back so quickly.

'The butler tells me that Mr Martin is ill and I cannot see him, but I wonder if Dr Taverner could spare me a few minutes?'

I took her into the office, where my colleague expressed no surprise at her appearance.

'So you have sent back the ring?' he observed.

'Yes,' she said. 'How do you know? What magic are you working this time?'

'No magic, my dear Miss Hallam, only common sense. Something has frightened you. People are not often frightened to any great extent in ordinary civilised society, so I conclude that something extraordinary must have happened. I know you to be connected with a dangerous man, so I look in his direction. What are you likely to have done that could have roused his enmity? You have just been down here, away from his influence, and in the company of the man you used to care for; possibly you have undergone a revulsion of feeling. I want to find out, so I express my guess as a statement; you, thinking I know everything, make no attempt at denial, and therefore furnish me with the information I want.'

'But, Dr Taverner,' said the bewildered girl, 'why do you trouble to do all this when I would have answered your question if you had asked me?'

'Because I want you to see for yourself the way in which it is possible to handle an unsuspecting person,' said he. 'Now tell me what brought you here.'

'When I got back last night, I knew I could not marry Tony Mortimer,' she said, 'and in the morning I wrote to him and told him so. He came straight round to the house and asked to see me. I refused, for I knew that if I saw him I should be right back in his power again. He then sent up a message to say that he would not leave until he had spoken to me, and I got in a panic. I was afraid he would force his way upstairs, so I slipped out of the back door and took the train down here, for somehow I felt that you understood what was being done to me, and would be able to help. Of course, I know that he cannot put a pistol to my head and force me to marry him, but he has so much influence over me that I am afraid he may make me do it in spite of myself.'

'I think,' said Taverner, 'that we shall have to deal drastically with Master Anthony Mortimer.'

Taverner took her upstairs, and allowed her and Martin to look at each other for exactly one minute without speaking, and then handed her over to the care of the matron.

Towards the end of dinner that evening I was told that a gentleman desired to see the secretary, and went out to the hall to discover who our visitor might be. A tall, dark man with very peculiar eyes greeted me.

'I have called for Miss Hallam,' he said.

'Miss Hallam?' I repeated as if mystified.

'Why, yes,' he said, somewhat taken aback. 'Isn't she here?'

'I will enquire of the matron,' I answered.

I slipped back into the dining-room, and whispered to Taverner, 'Mortimer is here.'

He raised his eyebrows. 'I will see him in the office,' he said.

Thither we repaired, but before admitting our visitor, Taverner arranged the reading lamp on his desk in such a way that his own features were in deep shadow and practically invisible.

Then Mortimer was shown in. He assumed an authoritative manner. 'I have come on behalf of her mother to fetch Miss Hallam home,' said he. 'I should be glad if you would inform her I am here.'

'Miss Hallam will not be returning tonight, and has wired her mother to that effect.'

'I did not ask you what Miss Hallam's plans were; I asked you to let her know I was here and wished to see her. I presume you are not going to offer any objection?'

'But I am,' said Taverner. 'I object strongly.'

'Has Miss Hallam refused to see me?'

'I have not inquired.'

'Then by what right do you take up this outrageous position?'

'By this right,' said Taverner, and made a peculiar sign with his left hand. On the forefinger was a ring of most unusual workmanship that I had never seen before.

Mortimer jumped as if Taverner had put a pistol to his head; he leant across the desk and tried to distinguish the shadowed features, then his gaze fell upon the ring.

'The Senior of Seven,' he gasped, and dropped back a pace. Then he turned and slunk towards the door, flinging over his shoulder such a glance of hate and fear as I had never seen before. I swear he bared his teeth and snarled.

'Brother Mortimer,' said Taverner, 'the dog returns to its kennel tonight.'

'Let us go to one of the upstairs windows and see that he really takes himself off,' went on Taverner.

From our vantage point we could see our late visitor making his way along the sandy road that led to Thursley. To my surprise, however, instead of keeping straight on, he turned and looked back.

'Is he going to return?' I said in surprise.

'I don't think so,' said Taverner. 'Now watch; something is going to happen.'

Again Mortimer stopped and looked around, as if in surprise. Then he began to fight. Whatever it was that attacked him evidently leapt up, for he beat it away from his chest; then it circled round him, for he turned slowly so as to face it. Yard by yard he worked his way down the road, and was swallowed up in the gathering dusk.

'The hound is following its master home,' said Taverner.

We heard next morning that the body of a strange man had been found near Bramshott. It was thought he had died of heart failure, for there were no marks of violence on his body.

'Six miles !' said Taverner. 'He ran well!'

THE SHUNNED HOUSE (1924)

HP Lovecraft (1890–1937)

Lovecraft was born in Providence, Rhode Island and, apart from a short period in which he married and moved to New York, he spent his life there. During his lifetime, his fiction was published only in the amateur press and in pulp magazines, most notably Weird Tales. *His work was known only to readers of such publications and to a small circle of admirers which included fellow authors like Robert. E. Howard (creator of Conan the Barbarian), August Derleth and a young Robert Bloch, later the author of* Psycho. *After his death, at the age of only 46, Lovecraft's stories were promoted by Derleth, who published collections of them under his Arkham House imprint, and by other enthusiasts. His reputation began to grow. Today he is considered probably the most influential horror writer of the first half of the twentieth century. Novellas like* At the Mountains of Madness *and stories such as 'The Dunwich Horror' are classics of the genre and the Cthulhu Mythos, the fictional universe which he created, lives on in his own writings and in those of dozens of other authors who have been inspired to add to it. 'The Shunned House', in which an unnamed narrator and his uncle Elihu Whipple investigate the terrible history of an old building in Providence, was written in 1924. It was prepared for publication by a private press in 1928 but was not released. It was only finally published after Lovecraft's death in the October 1937 issue of* Weird Tales.

I.

From even the greatest of horrors irony is seldom absent. Sometimes it enters directly into the composition of the events, while sometimes it relates only to their fortuitous position among persons and places. The latter sort is splendidly exemplified by a case in the ancient city of Providence, where in the late forties Edgar Allan Poe used to sojourn often during his unsuccessful wooing of the gifted poetess, Mrs Whitman. Poe generally stopped at the Mansion House in Benefit Street – the renamed Golden Ball Inn whose roof has sheltered Washington, Jefferson, and Lafayette – and his favourite walk led northward along the same street to Mrs Whitman's home and the neighbouring hillside churchyard of St. John's, whose hidden expanse of eighteenth-century gravestones had for him a peculiar fascination.

Now the irony is this. In this walk, so many times repeated, the world's greatest master of the terrible and the bizarre was obliged to pass a particular house on the eastern side of the street; a dingy, antiquated structure perched on the abruptly rising side-hill, with a great unkempt yard dating from a time when the region was partly open country. It does not appear that he ever wrote or spoke of it, nor is there any evidence that he even noticed it. And yet that house, to the two persons in possession of certain information, equals or outranks in horror the wildest phantasy of the genius who so often passed it unknowingly, and stands starkly leering as a symbol of all that is unutterably hideous.

The house was – and for that matter still is – of a kind to attract the attention of the curious. Originally a farm or semi-farm building, it followed the average New England colonial lines of the middle eighteenth century – the prosperous peaked-roof sort, with two stories and dormerless attic, and with the Georgian doorway and interior panelling dictated by the progress of taste at that time. It faced south, with one gable end buried to the lower windows in the eastward rising hill, and the other exposed to the foundations toward the street. Its construction, over a century and a half ago, had followed the grading and straightening of the road in that especial vicinity; for Benefit Street – at first called Back Street – was laid out as a lane winding amongst the graveyards of the first settlers, and straightened only when the removal of the bodies to the North Burial Ground made it decently possible to cut through the old family plots.

At the start, the western wall had lain some twenty feet up a precipitous lawn from the roadway; but a widening of the street at about the time of the Revolution sheared off most of the intervening space, exposing the foundations so that a brick basement wall had to be made, giving the deep cellar a street frontage with door and two windows above ground, close to the new line of public travel. When the sidewalk was laid out a century ago the last of the intervening space was removed; and Poe in his walks must have seen only a sheer ascent of dull grey brick flush with the sidewalk and surmounted at a height of ten feet by the antique shingled bulk of the house proper.

The farm-like grounds extended back very deeply up the hill, almost to Wheaton Street. The space south of the house, abutting on Benefit Street, was of course greatly above the existing sidewalk level, forming a terrace bounded by a high bank wall of damp, mossy stone pierced by a steep flight of narrow steps which led inward between canyon-like surfaces to the upper region of mangy lawn, rheumy brick walls, and neglected gardens whose dismantled cement urns, rusted kettles fallen from tripods of knotty sticks, and similar paraphernalia set off the weather-beaten front door with its broken fanlight, rotting Ionic pilasters, and wormy triangular pediment.

What I heard in my youth about the shunned house was merely that people died there in alarmingly great numbers. That, I was told, was why the original owners had moved out some twenty years after building the place. It was plainly unhealthy, perhaps because of the dampness and fungous growth in the cellar, the general sickish smell, the draughts of the hallways, or the quality of the well and pump water. These things were bad enough, and these were all that gained belief among the persons whom I knew. Only the notebooks of my antiquarian uncle, Dr Elihu Whipple, revealed to me at length the darker, vaguer surmises which formed an undercurrent of folklore among old-time servants and humble folk; surmises which never travelled far, and which were largely forgotten when Providence grew to be a metropolis with a shifting modern population.

The general fact is, that the house was never regarded by the solid part of the community as in any real sense 'haunted'. There were no widespread tales of rattling chains, cold currents of air, extinguished lights, or faces at the window. Extremists sometimes said the house was 'unlucky', but that is as far as even they went. What was really beyond dispute is that a frightful proportion of persons died there; or more accurately, *had* died there, since after some peculiar happenings over sixty years ago the building had become deserted through the sheer impossibility of renting it. These persons were not all cut off suddenly by any one cause; rather did it seem that their vitality was insidiously sapped, so that each one died the sooner from whatever tendency to weakness he may have naturally had. And those who did not die displayed in varying degree a type of anaemia or consumption, and sometimes a decline of the mental faculties, which spoke ill for the salubriousness of the building. Neighbouring houses, it must be added, seemed entirely free from the noxious quality.

This much I knew before my insistent questioning led my uncle to shew me the notes which finally embarked us both on our hideous investigation. In my childhood the shunned house was vacant, with barren, gnarled, and terrible old trees, long, queerly pale grass, and nightmarishly misshapen weeds in the high terraced yard where birds never lingered. We boys used to overrun the place, and I can still recall my youthful terror not only at the morbid strangeness of this sinister vegetation, but at the eldritch atmosphere and odour of the dilapidated house, whose unlocked front door was often entered in quest of shudders. The small-paned windows were largely broken, and a nameless air of desolation hung round the precarious panelling, shaky interior shutters, peeling wall-paper, falling plaster, rickety staircases, and such fragments of battered furniture as still remained. The dust and cobwebs added their touch of the fearful; and brave indeed was the boy who would voluntarily ascend the ladder to the attic, a vast raftered length lighted only by small blinking windows in the gable ends, and filled with a massed wreckage of chests, chairs, and spinning-wheels which infinite years of deposit had shrouded and festooned into monstrous and hellish shapes.

But after all, the attic was not the most terrible part of the house. It was the dank, humid cellar which somehow exerted the strongest repulsion on us, even though it was wholly above ground on the street side, with only a thin door and window-pierced brick wall to separate it from the busy sidewalk. We scarcely knew whether to haunt it in spectral fascination, or to shun it for the sake of our souls and our sanity. For one thing, the bad odour of the house was strongest there; and for another thing, we did not like the white fungous growths which occasionally sprang up in rainy summer weather from the hard earth floor. Those fungi, grotesquely like the vegetation in the yard outside, were truly horrible in their outlines; detestable parodies of toadstools and Indian pipes, whose like we had never seen in any other situation. They rotted quickly, and at one stage became slightly phosphorescent; so that nocturnal passers-by sometimes spoke of witch-fires glowing behind the broken panes of the foetor-spreading windows.

We never – even in our wildest Hallowe'en moods – visited this cellar by night, but in some of our daytime visits could detect the phosphorescence, especially when the day was dark and wet. There was also a subtler thing we often thought we detected – a very strange thing which was, however, merely suggestive at most. I refer to a sort of cloudy whitish pattern on the dirt floor – a vague, shifting deposit of mould or nitre which we sometimes thought we could trace amidst the sparse fungous growths near the huge fireplace of the basement kitchen. Once in a while it struck us that this patch bore an uncanny resemblance to a doubled-up human figure, though generally no such kinship existed, and often there was no whitish deposit whatever. On a certain rainy afternoon when this illusion seemed phenomenally strong, and when, in addition, I had fancied I glimpsed a kind of thin, yellowish, shimmering exhalation rising

233

from the nitrous pattern toward the yawning fireplace, I spoke to my uncle about the matter. He smiled at this odd conceit, but it seemed that his smile was tinged with reminiscence. Later I heard that a similar notion entered into some of the wild ancient tales of the common folk – a notion likewise alluding to ghoulish, wolfish shapes taken by smoke from the great chimney, and queer contours assumed by certain of the sinuous tree-roots that thrust their way into the cellar through the loose foundation-stones.

II.

Not till my adult years did my uncle set before me the notes and data which he had collected concerning the shunned house. Dr Whipple was a sane, conservative physician of the old school, and for all his interest in the place was not eager to encourage young thoughts toward the abnormal. His own view, postulating simply a building and location of markedly unsanitary qualities, had nothing to do with abnormality; but he realised that the very picturesqueness which aroused his own interest would in a boy's fanciful mind take on all manner of gruesome imaginative associations.

The doctor was a bachelor; a white-haired, clean-shaven, old-fashioned gentleman, and a local historian of note, who had often broken a lance with such controversial guardians of tradition as Sidney S. Rider and Thomas W. Bicknell. He lived with one manservant in a Georgian homestead with knocker and iron-railed steps, balanced eerily on a steep ascent of North Court Street beside the ancient brick court and colony house where his grandfather – a cousin of that celebrated privateersman, Capt. Whipple, who burnt His Majesty's armed schooner *Gaspee* in 1772 – had voted in the legislature on May 4, 1776, for the independence of the Rhode Island Colony. Around him in the damp, low-ceiled library with the musty white panelling, heavy carved overmantel, and small-paned, vine-shaded windows, were the relics and records of his ancient family, among which were

234

many dubious allusions to the shunned house in Benefit Street. That pest spot lies not far distant – for Benefit runs ledgewise just above the court-house along the precipitous hill up which the first settlement climbed.

When, in the end, my insistent pestering and maturing years evoked from my uncle the hoarded lore I sought, there lay before me a strange enough chronicle. Long-winded, statistical, and drearily genealogical as some of the matter was, there ran through it a continuous thread of brooding, tenacious horror and preternatural malevolence which impressed me even more than it had impressed the good doctor. Separate events fitted together uncannily, and seemingly irrelevant details held mines of hideous possibilities. A new and burning curiosity grew in me, compared to which my boyish curiosity was feeble and inchoate. The first revelation led to an exhaustive research, and finally to that shuddering quest which proved so disastrous to myself and mine. For at last my uncle insisted on joining the search I had commenced, and after a certain night in that house he did not come away with me. I am lonely without that gentle soul whose long years were filled only with honour, virtue, good taste, benevolence, and learning. I have reared a marble urn to his memory in St. John's churchyard – the place that Poe loved – the hidden grove of giant willows on the hill, where tombs and headstones huddle quietly between the hoary bulk of the church and the houses and bank walls of Benefit Street.

The history of the house, opening amidst a maze of dates, revealed no trace of the sinister either about its construction or about the prosperous and honourable family who built it. Yet from the first a taint of calamity, soon increased to boding significance, was apparent. My uncle's carefully compiled record began with the building of the structure in 1763, and followed the theme with an unusual amount of detail. The shunned house, it seems, was first inhabited by William Harris and his wife Rhoby Dexter, with their children, Elkanah, born in 1755, Abigail, born in 1757, William, Jr., born in 1759, and Ruth, born in 1761. Harris was a substantial merchant and seaman in the West India trade, connected with the firm of Obadiah Brown and his nephews. After Brown's death in 1761, the new firm of Nicholas Brown & Co. made him master of the brig *Prudence,* Providence-built, of 120 tons, thus enabling him to erect the new homestead he had desired ever since his marriage.

The site he had chosen – a recently straightened part of the new and fashionable Back Street, which ran along the side of the hill above crowded Cheapside – was all that could be wished, and the building did justice to the location. It was the best that moderate means could afford, and Harris hastened to move in before the birth of a fifth child which the family expected. That child, a boy, came in December; but was still-born. Nor was any child to be born alive in that house for a century and a half.

The next April sickness occurred among the children, and Abigail and Ruth died before the month was over. Dr Job Ives diagnosed the trouble as some infantile fever, though others declared it was more of a mere wasting-away or decline. It seemed, in any event, to be contagious; for Hannah Bowen, one of the two servants, died of it in the following June. Eli Liddeason, the other servant, constantly complained of weakness; and would have returned to his father's farm in Rehoboth but for a sudden attachment for Mehitabel Pierce, who was hired to succeed Hannah. He died the next year – a sad year indeed, since it marked the death of William Harris himself, enfeebled as he was by the climate of Martinique, where his occupation had kept him for considerable periods during the preceding decade.

The widowed Rhoby Harris never recovered from the shock of her husband's death, and the passing of her first-born Elkanah two years later was the final blow to her reason. In 1768 she fell victim to a mild form of insanity, and was thereafter confined to the upper part of the house; her elder maiden sister, Mercy Dexter, having moved in to take charge of the family. Mercy was a plain, raw-boned woman of great strength; but her health visibly declined from the time of her advent. She was greatly devoted to her unfortunate sister, and had an especial affection for her only surviving nephew William, who from a sturdy infant had become a sickly, spindling lad. In this year the servant Mehitabel died, and the other servant, Preserved Smith, left without coherent explanation – or at least, with only some wild tales and a complaint that he disliked the smell of the place. For a time Mercy could secure no more help, since the seven deaths and case of madness, all occurring within five years' space, had begun to set in motion the body of fireside rumour which later became so bizarre. Ultimately, however, she obtained new servants from out of town; Ann White, a morose woman from that part of North Kingstown now set off as the township of Exeter, and a capable Boston man named Zenas Low.

It was Ann White who first gave definite shape to the sinister idle talk. Mercy should have known better than to hire anyone from the Nooseneck Hill country, for that remote bit of backwoods was then, as now, a seat of the most uncomfortable superstitions. As lately as 1892 an Exeter community exhumed a dead body and ceremoniously burnt its heart in order to prevent certain alleged visitations injurious to the public health and peace, and one may imagine the point of view of the same section in 1768. Ann's tongue was perniciously active, and within a few months Mercy discharged her, filling her place with a faithful and amiable Amazon from Newport, Maria Robbins.

Meanwhile poor Rhoby Harris, in her madness, gave voice to dreams and imaginings of the most hideous sort. At times her screams became insupportable, and for long periods she would utter shrieking horrors which necessitated her son's temporary residence with his cousin, Peleg Harris, in Presbyterian Lane near the new college building. The boy would seem to improve after these visits, and had Mercy been as wise as she was well-meaning, she would have let him live permanently with Peleg. Just what Mrs Harris cried out in her fits of violence, tradition hesitates to say; or rather, presents such extravagant accounts that they nullify themselves through sheer absurdity. Certainly it sounds absurd to hear that a woman educated only in the rudiments of French often shouted for hours in a coarse and idiomatic form of that language, or that the same person, alone and guarded, complained wildly of a staring thing which bit and chewed at her. In 1772 the servant Zenas died, and when Mrs Harris heard of it she laughed with a shocking delight utterly foreign to her. The next year she herself died, and was laid to rest in the North Burial Ground beside her husband.

Upon the outbreak of trouble with Great Britain in 1775, William Harris, despite his scant sixteen years and feeble constitution, managed to enlist in the Army of Observation under General Greene; and from that time on enjoyed a steady rise in health and prestige. In 1780, as a Captain in Rhode Island forces in New Jersey under Colonel Angell, he met and married Phebe Hetfield of Elizabethtown, whom he brought to Providence upon his honourable discharge in the following year.

The young soldier's return was not a thing of unmitigated happiness. The house, it is true, was still in good condition; and the street had been widened and changed in name from Back Street to Benefit Street. But Mercy Dexter's once robust frame had undergone a sad and curious decay, so that she was now a stooped and pathetic figure with hollow voice and disconcerting pallor – qualities shared to a singular degree by the one remaining servant Maria. In the autumn of 1782 Phebe Harris gave birth to a still-born daughter, and on the fifteenth of the next May Mercy Dexter took leave of a useful, austere, and virtuous life.

William Harris, at last thoroughly convinced of the radically unhealthful nature of his abode, now took steps toward quitting it and closing it forever. Securing temporary quarters for himself and his wife at the newly opened Golden Ball Inn, he arranged for the building of a new and finer house in Westminster Street, in the growing part of the town across the Great Bridge. There, in 1785, his son Dutee was born; and there the family dwelt till the encroachments of commerce drove them back across the river and over the hill to Angell Street, in the newer East Side residence district, where the late Archer Harris built his sumptuous but hideous French-roofed mansion in 1876. William and Phebe both succumbed to the yellow fever epidemic of 1797, but Dutee was brought up by his cousin Rathbone Harris, Peleg's son.

Rathbone was a practical man, and rented the Benefit Street house despite William's wish to keep it vacant. He considered it an obligation to his ward to make the most of all the boy's property, nor did he concern himself with the deaths and illnesses which caused so many changes of tenants, or the steadily growing aversion with which the house was generally regarded. It is likely that he felt only vexation when, in 1804, the town council ordered him to fumigate the place with sulphur, tar, and gum camphor on account of the much-discussed deaths of four persons, presumably caused by the then diminishing fever epidemic. They said the place had a febrile smell.

Dutee himself thought little of the house, for he grew up to be a privateersman, and served with distinction on the *Vigilant* under Capt. Cahoone in the War of 1812. He returned unharmed, married in 1814, and became a father on that memorable night of September 23, 1815, when a great gale drove the waters of the bay over half the town, and floated a tall sloop well up Westminster Street so that its masts almost tapped the Harris windows in symbolic affirmation that the new boy, Welcome, was a seaman's son.

Welcome did not survive his father, but lived to perish gloriously at Fredericksburg in 1862. Neither he nor his son Archer knew of the shunned house as other than a nuisance almost impossible to rent – perhaps on account of the mustiness and sickly odour of unkempt old age. Indeed, it never was rented after a series of deaths culminating in 1861, which the excitement of the war tended to throw into obscurity. Carrington Harris, last of the male line, knew it only as a deserted and somewhat picturesque centre of legend until I told him my experience. He had meant to tear it down and build an apartment house on the site, but after my account decided to let it stand, install plumbing, and rent it. Nor has he yet had any difficulty in obtaining tenants. The horror has gone.

III.

It may well be imagined how powerfully I was affected by the annals of the Harrises. In this continuous record there seemed to me to brood a persistent evil beyond anything in Nature as I had known it; an evil clearly connected with the house and not with the family. This impression was confirmed by my uncle's less systematic array of miscellaneous data – legends transcribed from servant gossip, cuttings from the papers, copies of death-certificates by fellow-physicians, and the like. All of this material I cannot hope to give, for my uncle was a tireless antiquarian and very deeply interested in the shunned house; but I may refer to several dominant points which earn notice by their recurrence through many reports from diverse sources. For example, the servant gossip was practically unanimous in attributing to the fungous and malodorous *cellar* of the house a vast supremacy in evil influence. There had been servants – Ann White especially – who would not use the cellar kitchen, and at least three well-defined legends bore upon the queer quasi-human or diabolic outlines assumed by tree-roots and patches of mould in that region. These latter narratives interested me profoundly, on account of what I had seen in my boyhood, but I felt that most of the significance had in each case been largely obscured by additions from the common stock of local ghost lore.

Ann White, with her Exeter superstition, had promulgated the most extravagant and at the same time most consistent tale; alleging that there must lie buried beneath the house one of those vampires – the dead who retain their bodily form and live on the blood or breath of the living – whose hideous legions send their preying shapes or spirits abroad by night. To destroy a vampire one must, the grandmothers say, exhume it and burn its heart, or at least drive a stake through that organ; and Ann's dogged insistence on a search under the cellar had been prominent in bringing about her discharge.

Her tales, however, commanded a wide audience, and were the more readily accepted because the house indeed stood on land once used for burial purposes. To me their interest depended less on this circumstance than on the peculiarly appropriate way in which they dovetailed with certain other things – the complaint of the departing servant Preserved Smith, who had preceded Ann and never heard of her, that something 'sucked his breath' at night; the death-certificates of fever victims of 1804, issued by Dr Chad Hopkins, and shewing the four deceased persons all unaccountably lacking in blood; and the obscure passages of poor Rhoby Harris's ravings, where she complained of the sharp teeth of a glassy-eyed, half-visible presence.

Free from unwarranted superstition though I am, these things produced in me an odd sensation, which was intensified by a pair of widely separated newspaper cuttings relating to deaths in the shunned house – one from the *Providence Gazette and Country-Journal* of April 12, 1815, and the other from the *Daily Transcript and Chronicle* of October 27, 1845 – each of which detailed an appallingly grisly circumstance whose duplication was remarkable. It seems that in both instances the dying person, in 1815 a gentle old lady named Stafford and in 1845 a schoolteacher of middle age named Eleazar Durfee, became transfigured in a horrible way; glaring glassily and attempting to bite the throat of the attending physician. Even more puzzling, though, was the final case which put an end to the renting of the house – a series of anaemia deaths preceded by progressive madnesses wherein the patient would craftily attempt the lives of his relatives by incisions in the neck or wrist.

This was in 1860 and 1861, when my uncle had just begun his medical practice; and before leaving for the front he heard much of it from his elder professional colleagues. The really inexplicable thing was the way in which the victims – ignorant people, for the ill-smelling and widely shunned house could now be rented to no others – would babble maledictions in French, a language they could not possibly have studied to any extent. It made one think of poor Rhoby Harris nearly a century before, and so moved my uncle that he commenced collecting historical data on the house after listening, some time subsequent to his return from the war, to the first-hand account of Drs. Chase and Whitmarsh. Indeed, I could see that my uncle had thought deeply on the subject, and that he was glad of my own interest – an open-minded and sympathetic interest which enabled him to discuss with me matters at which others would merely have laughed. His fancy had not gone so far as mine, but he felt that the place was rare in its imaginative potentialities, and worthy of note as an inspiration in the field of the grotesque and macabre.

For my part, I was disposed to take the whole subject with profound seriousness, and began at once not only to review the evidence, but to accumulate as much more as I could. I talked with the elderly Archer Harris, then owner of the house, many times before his death in 1916; and obtained from him and his still surviving maiden sister Alice an authentic corroboration of all the family data my uncle had collected. When, however, I asked them what connexion with France or its language the house could have, they confessed themselves as frankly baffled and ignorant as I. Archer knew nothing, and all that Miss Harris could say was that an old allusion her grandfather, Dutee Harris, had heard of might have shed a little light. The old seaman, who had survived his son Welcome's death in battle by two years, had not himself known the legend; but recalled that his earliest nurse, the ancient Maria Robbins, seemed darkly aware of something that might have lent a weird significance to the French ravings of Rhoby Harris, which she had so often heard during the last days of that hapless woman. Maria had been at the shunned house from 1769 till the removal of the family in 1783, and had seen Mercy Dexter die. Once she hinted to the child Dutee of a somewhat peculiar circumstance in Mercy's last moments, but he had soon forgotten all about it save that it was something peculiar. The granddaughter, moreover, recalled even this much with difficulty. She and her brother were not so much interested in the house as was Archer's son Carrington, the present owner, with whom I talked after my experience.

Having exhausted the Harris family of all the information it could furnish, I turned my attention to early town records and deeds with a zeal more penetrating than that which my uncle had occasionally shewn in the same work. What I wished was a comprehensive history of the site from its very settlement in 1636 – or even before, if any Narragansett Indian legend could be unearthed to supply the data. I found, at the start, that the land had been part of the long strip of home lot granted originally to John Throckmorton; one of many similar strips beginning at the Town Street beside the river and extending up over the hill to a line roughly corresponding with the modern Hope Street. The Throckmorton lot had later, of course, been much subdivided; and I became very assiduous in tracing that section through which Back or Benefit Street was later run. It had, a rumour indeed said, been the Throckmorton graveyard; but as I examined the records more carefully, I found that the graves had all been transferred at an early date to the North Burial Ground on the Pawtucket West Road.

Then suddenly I came – by a rare piece of chance, since it was not in the main body of records and might easily have been missed – upon something which aroused my keenest eagerness, fitting in as it did with several of the queerest phases of the affair. It was the record of a lease, in 1697, of a small tract of ground to an Etienne Roulet and wife. At last the French element had appeared – that, and another deeper element of horror which the name conjured up from the darkest recesses of my weird and heterogeneous reading – and I feverishly studied the platting of the locality as it had been before the cutting through and partial straightening of Back Street between 1747 and 1758. I found what I had half expected, that where the shunned house now stood the Roulets had laid out their graveyard behind a one-story and attic cottage, and that no record of any transfer of graves existed. The document, indeed, ended in much confusion; and I was forced to ransack both the Rhode Island Historical Society and Shepley Library before I could find a local door which the name Etienne Roulet would unlock. In the end I did find something; something of such vague but monstrous import that I set about at once to examine the cellar of the shunned house itself with a new and excited minuteness.

The Roulets, it seemed, had come in 1696 from East Greenwich, down the west shore of Narragansett Bay. They were Huguenots from Caude, and had encountered much opposition before the Providence selectmen allowed them to settle in the town. Unpopularity had dogged them in East Greenwich, whither they had come in 1686, after the revocation of the Edict of Nantes, and rumour said that the cause of dislike extended beyond mere racial and national prejudice, or the land disputes which involved other French settlers with the English in rivalries which not even Governor Andros could quell. But their ardent Protestantism – too ardent, some whispered – and their evident distress when virtually driven from the village down the bay, had moved the sympathy of the town fathers. Here the strangers had been granted a haven; and the swarthy Etienne Roulet, less apt at agriculture than at reading queer books and drawing queer diagrams, was given a clerical post in the warehouse at Pardon Tillinghast's wharf, far south in Town Street. There had, however, been a riot of some sort later on – perhaps forty years later, after old Roulet's death – and no one seemed to hear of the family after that.

For a century and more, it appeared, the Roulets had been well remembered and frequently discussed as vivid incidents in the quiet life of a New England seaport. Etienne's son Paul, a surly fellow whose erratic conduct had probably provoked the riot which wiped out the family, was particularly a source of speculation; and though Providence never shared the witchcraft panics of her Puritan neighbours, it was freely intimated by old wives that his prayers were neither uttered at the proper time nor directed toward the proper object. All this had undoubtedly formed the basis of the legend known by old Maria Robbins. What relation it had to the French ravings of Rhoby Harris and other inhabitants of the shunned house, imagination or future discovery alone could determine. I wondered how many of those who had known the legends realised that additional link with the terrible which my wide reading had given me; that ominous item in the annals of morbid horror which tells of the creature *Jacques Roulet, of Caude,* who in 1598 was condemned to death as a daemoniac but afterward saved from the stake by the Paris parliament and shut in a madhouse. He had been found covered with blood and shreds of flesh in a wood, shortly after the killing and rending of a boy by a pair of wolves. One wolf was seen to lope away unhurt. Surely a pretty hearthside tale, with a queer significance as to name and place; but I decided that the Providence gossips could not have generally known of it. Had they known, the coincidence of names would have brought some drastic and frightened action – indeed, might not its limited whispering have precipitated the final riot which erased the Roulets from the town?

I now visited the accursed place with increased frequency; studying the unwholesome vegetation of the garden, examining all the walls of the building, and poring over every inch of the earthen cellar floor. Finally, with Carrington Harris's permission, I fitted a key to the disused door opening from the cellar directly upon Benefit Street, preferring to have a more immediate access to the outside world than the dark stairs, ground floor hall, and front door could give. There, where morbidity lurked most thickly, I searched and poked during long afternoons when the sunlight filtered in through the cobwebbed above-ground windows, and a sense of security glowed from the unlocked door which placed me only a few feet from the placid sidewalk outside. Nothing new rewarded my efforts – only the same depressing mustiness and faint suggestions of noxious odours and nitrous outlines on the floor – and I fancy that many pedestrians must have watched me curiously through the broken panes.

At length, upon a suggestion of my uncle's, I decided to try the spot nocturnally; and one stormy midnight ran the beams of an electric torch over the mouldy floor with its uncanny shapes and distorted, half-phosphorescent fungi. The place had dispirited me curiously that evening, and I was almost prepared when I saw – or thought I saw – amidst the whitish deposits a particularly sharp definition of the 'huddled form' I had suspected from boyhood. Its clearness was astonishing and unprecedented – and as I watched I seemed to see again the thin, yellowish, shimmering exhalation which had startled me on that rainy afternoon so many years before.

Above the anthropomorphic patch of mould by the fireplace it rose; a subtle, sickish, almost luminous vapour which as it hung trembling in the dampness seemed to develop vague and shocking suggestions of form, gradually trailing off into nebulous decay and passing up into the blackness of the great chimney with a foetor in its wake. It was truly horrible, and the more so to me because of what I knew of the spot. Refusing to flee, I watched it fade – and as I watched I felt that it was in turn watching me greedily with eyes more imaginable than visible. When I told my uncle about it he was greatly aroused; and after a tense hour of reflection, arrived at a definite and drastic decision. Weighing in his mind the importance of the matter, and the significance of our relation to it, he insisted that we both test – and if possible destroy – the horror of the house by a joint night or nights of aggressive vigil in that musty and fungus-cursed cellar.

IV.

On Wednesday, June 25, 1919, after a proper notification of Carrington Harris which did not include surmises as to what we expected to find, my uncle and I conveyed to the shunned house two camp chairs and a folding camp cot, together with some scientific mechanism of greater weight and intricacy. These we placed in the cellar during the day, screening the windows with paper and planning to return in the evening for our first vigil. We had locked the door from the cellar to the ground floor; and having a key to the outside cellar door, we were prepared to leave our expensive and delicate apparatus – which we had obtained secretly and at great cost – as many days as our vigils might need to be protracted. It was our design to sit up together till very late, and then watch singly till dawn in two-hour stretches, myself first and then my companion; the inactive member resting on the cot.

The natural leadership with which my uncle procured the instruments from the laboratories of Brown University and the Cranston Street Armoury, and instinctively assumed direction of our venture, was a marvellous commentary on the potential vitality and resilience of a man of eighty-one. Elihu Whipple had lived according to the hygienic laws he had preached as a physician, and but for what happened later would be here in full vigour today. Only two persons suspect what did happen – Carrington Harris and myself. I had to tell Harris because he owned the house and deserved to know what had gone out of it. Then too, we had spoken to him in advance of our quest; and I felt after my uncle's going that he would understand and assist me in some vitally necessary public explanations. He turned very pale, but agreed to help me, and decided that it would now be safe to rent the house.

To declare that we were not nervous on that rainy night of watching would be an exaggeration both gross and ridiculous. We were not, as I have said, in any sense childishly superstitious, but scientific study and reflection had taught us that the known universe of three dimensions embraces the merest fraction of the whole cosmos of substance and energy. In this case an overwhelming preponderance of evidence from numerous authentic sources pointed to the tenacious existence of certain forces of great power and, so far as the human point of view is concerned, exceptional malignancy. To say that we actually believed in vampires or werewolves would be a carelessly inclusive statement. Rather must it be said that we were not prepared to deny the possibility of certain unfamiliar and unclassified modifications of vital force and attenuated matter; existing very infrequently in three-dimensional space because of its more intimate connexion with other spatial units, yet close enough to the boundary of our own to furnish us occasional manifestations which we, for lack of a proper vantage-point, may never hope to understand.

In short, it seemed to my uncle and me that an incontrovertible array of facts pointed to some lingering influence in the shunned house; traceable to one or another of the ill-favoured French settlers of two centuries before, and still operative through rare and unknown laws of atomic and electronic motion. That the family of Roulet had possessed an abnormal affinity for outer circles of entity – dark spheres which for normal folk hold only repulsion and terror – their recorded history seemed to prove. Had not, then, the riots of those bygone seventeen-thirties set moving certain kinetic patterns in the morbid brain of one or more of them – notably the sinister Paul Roulet – which obscurely survived the bodies murdered and buried by the mob, and continued to function in some multiple-dimensioned space along the original lines of force determined by a frantic hatred of the encroaching community?

Such a thing was surely not a physical or biochemical impossibility in the light of a newer science which includes the theories of relativity and intra-atomic action. One might easily imagine an alien nucleus of substance or energy, formless or otherwise, kept alive by imperceptible or immaterial subtractions from the life-force or bodily tissues and fluids of other and more palpably living things into which it penetrates and with whose fabric it sometimes completely merges itself. It might be actively hostile, or it might be dictated merely by blind motives of self-preservation. In any case such a monster must of necessity be in our scheme of things an anomaly and an intruder, whose extirpation forms a primary duty with every man not an enemy to the world's life, health, and sanity.

What baffled us was our utter ignorance of the aspect in which we might encounter the thing. No sane person had even seen it, and few had ever felt it definitely. It might be pure energy – a form ethereal and outside the realm of substance – or it might be partly material; some unknown and equivocal mass of plasticity, capable of changing at will to nebulous approximations of the solid, liquid, gaseous, or tenuously unparticled states. The anthropomorphic patch of mould on the floor, the form of the yellowish vapour, and the curvature of the tree-roots in some of the old tales, all argued at least a remote and reminiscent connexion with the human shape; but how representative or permanent that similarity might be, none could say with any kind of certainty.

We had devised two weapons to fight it; a large and specially fitted Crookes tube operated by powerful storage batteries and provided with peculiar screens and reflectors, in case it proved intangible and opposable only by vigorously destructive ether radiations, and a pair of military flame-throwers of the sort used in the World War, in case it proved partly material and susceptible of mechanical destruction – for like the superstitious Exeter rustics, we were prepared to burn the thing's heart out if heart existed to burn. All this aggressive mechanism we set in the cellar in positions carefully arranged with reference to the cot and chairs, and to the spot before the fireplace where the mould had taken strange shapes. That suggestive patch, by the way, was only faintly visible when we placed our furniture and instruments, and when we returned that evening for the actual vigil. For a moment I half doubted that I had ever seen it in the more definitely limned form – but then I thought of the legends.

Our cellar vigil began at 10 pm, daylight saving time, and as it continued we found no promise of pertinent developments. A weak, filtered glow from the rain-harassed street-lamps outside, and a feeble phosphorescence from the detestable fungi within, shewed the dripping stone of the walls, from which all traces of whitewash had vanished; the dank, foetid, and mildew-tainted hard earth floor with its obscene fungi; the rotting remains of what had been stools, chairs, and tables, and other more shapeless furniture; the heavy planks and massive beams of the ground floor overhead; the decrepit plank door leading to bins and chambers beneath other parts of the house; the crumbling stone staircase with ruined wooden hand-rail; and the crude and cavernous fireplace of blackened brick where rusted iron fragments revealed the past presence of hooks, andirons, spit, crane, and a door to the Dutch oven – these things, and our austere cot and camp chairs, and the heavy and intricate destructive machinery we had brought.

We had, as in my own former explorations, left the door to the street unlocked; so that a direct and practical path of escape might lie open in case of manifestations beyond our power to deal with. It was our idea that our continued nocturnal presence would call forth whatever malign entity lurked there; and that being prepared, we could dispose of the thing with one or the other of our provided means as soon as we had recognised and observed it sufficiently. How long it might require to evoke and extinguish the thing, we had no notion. It occurred to us, too, that our venture was far from safe; for in what strength the thing might appear no one could tell. But we deemed the game worth the hazard, and embarked on it alone and unhesitatingly; conscious that the seeking of outside aid would only expose us to ridicule and perhaps defeat our entire purpose. Such was our frame of mind as we talked – far into the night, till my uncle's growing drowsiness made me remind him to lie down for his two-hour sleep.

Something like fear chilled me as I sat there in the small hours alone – I say alone, for one who sits by a sleeper is indeed alone; perhaps more alone than he can realise. My uncle breathed heavily, his deep inhalations and exhalations accompanied by the rain outside, and punctuated by another nerve-racking sound of distant dripping water within – for the house was repulsively damp even in dry weather, and in this storm positively swamp-like. I studied the loose, antique masonry of the walls in the fungus-light and the feeble rays which stole in from the street through the screened windows; and once, when the noisome atmosphere of the place seemed about to sicken me, I opened the door and looked up and down the street, feasting my eyes on familiar sights and my nostrils on the wholesome air. Still nothing occurred to reward my watching; and I yawned repeatedly, fatigue getting the better of apprehension.

Then the stirring of my uncle in his sleep attracted my notice. He had turned restlessly on the cot several times during the latter half of the first hour, but now he was breathing with unusual irregularity, occasionally heaving a sigh which held more than a few of the qualities of a choking moan. I turned my electric flashlight on him and found his face averted, so rising and crossing to the other side of the cot, I again flashed the light to see if he seemed in any pain. What I saw unnerved me most surprisingly, considering its relative triviality. It must have been merely the association of any odd circumstance with the sinister nature of our location and mission, for surely the circumstance was not in itself frightful or unnatural. It was merely that my uncle's facial expression, disturbed no doubt by the strange dreams which our situation prompted, betrayed considerable agitation, and seemed not at all characteristic of him. His habitual expression was one of kindly and well-bred calm, whereas now a variety of emotions seemed struggling within him. I think, on the whole, that it was this *variety* which chiefly disturbed me. My uncle, as he gasped and tossed in increasing perturbation and with eyes that had now started open, seemed not one but many men, and suggested a curious quality of alienage from himself.

All at once he commenced to mutter, and I did not like the look of his mouth and teeth as he spoke. The words were at first indistinguishable, and then – with a tremendous start – I recognised something about them which filled me with icy fear till I recalled the breadth of my uncle's education and the interminable translations he had made from anthropological and antiquarian articles in the *Revue des Deux Mondes*. For the venerable Elihu Whipple was muttering *in French,* and the few phrases I could distinguish seemed connected with the darkest myths he had ever adapted from the famous Paris magazine.

Suddenly a perspiration broke out on the sleeper's forehead, and he leaped abruptly up, half awake. The jumble of French changed to a cry in English, and the hoarse voice shouted excitedly, 'My breath, my breath!' Then the awakening became complete, and with a subsidence of facial expression to the normal state my uncle seized my hand and began to relate a dream whose nucleus of significance I could only surmise with a kind of awe.

He had, he said, floated off from a very ordinary series of dream-pictures into a scene whose strangeness was related to nothing he had ever read. It was of this world, and yet not of it – a shadowy geometrical confusion in which could be seen elements of familiar things in most unfamiliar and perturbing combinations. There was a suggestion of queerly disordered pictures superimposed one upon another; an arrangement in which the essentials of time as well as of space seemed dissolved and mixed in the most illogical fashion. In this kaleidoscopic vortex of phantasmal images were occasional snapshots, if one might use the term, of singular clearness but unaccountable heterogeneity.

Once my uncle thought he lay in a carelessly dug open pit, with a crowd of angry faces framed by straggling locks and three-cornered hats frowning down on him. Again he seemed to be in the interior of a house – an old house, apparently – but the details and inhabitants were constantly changing, and he could never be certain of the faces or the furniture, or even of the room itself, since doors and windows seemed in just as great a state of flux as the more presumably mobile objects. It was queer – damnably queer – and my uncle spoke almost sheepishly, as if half expecting not to be believed, when he declared that of the strange faces many had unmistakably borne the features of the Harris family. And all the while there was a personal sensation of choking, as if some pervasive presence had spread itself through his body and sought to possess itself of his vital processes. I shuddered at the thought of those vital processes, worn as they were by eighty-one years of continuous functioning, in conflict with unknown forces of which the youngest and strongest system might well be afraid; but in another moment reflected that dreams are only dreams, and that these uncomfortable visions could be, at most, no more than my uncle's reaction to the investigations and expectations which had lately filled our minds to the exclusion of all else.

Conversation, also, soon tended to dispel my sense of strangeness; and in time I yielded to my yawns and took my turn at slumber. My uncle seemed now very wakeful, and welcomed his period of watching even though the nightmare had aroused him far ahead of his allotted two hours. Sleep seized me quickly, and I was at once haunted with dreams of the most disturbing kind. I felt, in my visions, a cosmic and abysmal loneness; with hostility surging from all sides upon some prison where I lay confined. I seemed bound and gagged, and taunted by the echoing yells of distant multitudes who thirsted for my blood. My uncle's face came to me with less pleasant associations than in waking hours, and I recall many futile struggles and attempts to scream. It was not a pleasant sleep, and for a second I was not sorry for the echoing shriek which clove through the barriers of dream and flung me to a sharp and startled awakeness in which every actual object before my eyes stood out with more than natural clearness and reality.

V.

I had been lying with my face away from my uncle's chair, so that in this sudden flash of awakening I saw only the door to the street, the more northerly window, and the wall and floor and ceiling toward the north of the room, all photographed with morbid vividness on my brain in a light brighter than the glow of the fungi or the rays from the street outside. It was not a strong or even a fairly strong light; certainly not nearly strong enough to read an average book by. But it cast a shadow of myself and the cot on the floor, and had a yellowish, penetrating force that hinted at things more potent than luminosity. This I perceived with unhealthy sharpness despite the fact that two of my other senses were violently assailed. For on my ears rang the reverberations of that shocking scream, while my nostrils revolted at the stench which filled the place. My mind, as alert as my senses, recognised the gravely unusual; and almost automatically I leaped up and turned about to grasp the destructive instruments which we had left trained on the mouldy spot before the fireplace. As I turned, I dreaded what I was to see; for the scream had been in my uncle's voice, and I knew not against what menace I should have to defend him and myself.

Yet after all, the sight was worse than I had dreaded. There are horrors beyond horrors, and this was one of those nuclei of all dreamable hideousness which the cosmos saves to blast an accursed and unhappy few. Out of the fungus-ridden earth steamed up a vaporous corpse-light, yellow and diseased, which bubbled and lapped to a gigantic height in vague outlines half-human and half-monstrous, through which I could see the chimney and fireplace beyond. It was all eyes – wolfish and mocking – and the rugose insect-like head dissolved at the top to a thin stream of mist which curled putridly about and finally vanished up the chimney. I say that I saw this thing, but it is only in conscious retrospection that I ever definitely traced its damnable approach to form. At the time it was to me only a seething, dimly phosphorescent cloud of fungous loathsomeness, enveloping and dissolving to an abhorrent plasticity the one object to which all my attention was focussed. That object was my uncle – the venerable Elihu Whipple – who with blackening and decaying features leered and gibbered at me, and reached out dripping claws to rend me in the fury which this horror had brought.

It was a sense of routine which kept me from going mad. I had drilled myself in preparation for the crucial moment, and blind training saved me. Recognising the bubbling evil as no substance reachable by matter or material chemistry, and therefore ignoring the flame-thrower which loomed on my left, I threw on the current of the Crookes tube apparatus, and focussed toward that scene of immortal blasphemousness the strongest ether radiations which man's art can arouse from the spaces and fluids of Nature. There was a bluish haze and a frenzied sputtering, and the yellowish phosphorescence grew dimmer to my eyes. But I saw the dimness was only that of contrast, and that the waves from the machine had no effect whatever.

Then, in the midst of that daemoniac spectacle, I saw a fresh horror which brought cries to my lips and sent me fumbling and staggering toward that unlocked door to the quiet street, careless of what abnormal terrors I loosed upon the world, or what thoughts or judgments of men I brought down upon my head. In that dim blend of blue and yellow the form of my uncle had commenced a nauseous liquefaction whose essence eludes all description, and in which there played across his vanishing face such changes of identity as only madness can conceive. He was at once a devil and a multitude, a charnel-house and a pageant. Lit by the mixed and uncertain beams, that gelatinous face assumed a dozen – a score – a hundred – aspects; grinning, as it sank to the ground on a body that melted like tallow, in the caricatured likeness of legions strange and yet not strange.

I saw the features of the Harris line, masculine and feminine, adult and infantile, and other features old and young, coarse and refined, familiar and unfamiliar. For a second there flashed a degraded counterfeit of a miniature of poor mad Rhoby Harris that I had seen in the School of Design Museum, and another time I thought I caught the raw-boned image of Mercy Dexter as I recalled her from a painting in Carrington Harris's house. It was frightful beyond conception; toward the last, when a curious blend of servant and baby visages flickered close to the fungous floor where a pool of greenish grease was spreading, it seemed as though the shifting features fought against themselves, and strove to form contours like those of my uncle's kindly face. I like to think that he existed at that moment, and that he tried to bid me farewell. It seems to me I hiccoughed a farewell from my own parched throat as I lurched out into the street; a thin stream of grease following me through the door to the rain-drenched sidewalk.

The rest is shadowy and monstrous. There was no one in the soaking street, and in all the world there was no one I dared tell. I walked aimlessly south past College Hill and the Athenaeum, down Hopkins Street, and over the bridge to the business section where tall buildings seemed to guard me as modern material things guard the world from ancient and unwholesome wonder. Then grey dawn unfolded wetly from the east, silhouetting the archaic hill and its venerable steeples, and beckoning me to the place where my terrible work was still unfinished. And in the end I went, wet, hatless, and dazed in the morning light, and entered that awful door in Benefit Street which I had left ajar, and which still swung cryptically in full sight of the early householders to whom I dared not speak.

The grease was gone, for the mouldy floor was porous. And in front of the fireplace was no vestige of the giant doubled-up form in nitre. I looked at the cot, the chairs, the instruments, my neglected hat, and the yellowed straw hat of my uncle. Dazedness was uppermost, and I could scarcely recall what was dream and what was reality. Then thought trickled back, and I knew that I had witnessed things more horrible than I had dreamed. Sitting down, I tried to conjecture as nearly as sanity would let me just what had happened, and how I might end the horror, if indeed it had been real. Matter it seemed not to be, nor ether, nor anything else conceivable by mortal mind. What, then, but some exotic *emanation;* some vampirish vapour such as Exeter rustics tell of as lurking over certain churchyards? This I felt was the clue, and again I looked at the floor before the fireplace where the mould and nitre had taken strange forms. In ten minutes my mind was made up, and taking my hat I set out for home, where I bathed, ate, and gave by telephone an order for a pickaxe, a spade, a military gas-mask, and six carboys of sulphuric acid, all to be delivered the next morning at the cellar door of the shunned house in Benefit Street. After that I tried to sleep; and failing, passed the hours in reading and in the composition of inane verses to counteract my mood.

At 11 am the next day I commenced digging. It was sunny weather, and I was glad of that. I was still alone, for as much as I feared the unknown horror I sought, there was more fear in the thought of telling anybody. Later I told Harris only through sheer necessity, and because he had heard odd tales from old people which disposed him ever so little toward belief. As I turned up the stinking black earth in front of the fireplace, my spade causing a viscous yellow ichor to ooze from the white fungi which it severed, I trembled at the dubious thoughts of what I might uncover. Some secrets of inner earth are not good for mankind, and this seemed to me one of them.

My hand shook perceptibly, but still I delved; after a while standing in the large hole I had made. With the deepening of the hole, which was about six feet square, the evil smell increased; and I lost all doubt of my imminent contact with the hellish thing whose emanations had cursed the house for over a century and a half. I wondered what it would look like – what its form and substance would be, and how big it might have waxed through long ages of life-sucking. At length I climbed out of the hole and dispersed the heaped-up dirt, then arranging the great carboys of acid around and near two sides, so that when necessary I might empty them all down the aperture in quick succession. After that I dumped earth only along the other two sides; working more slowly and donning my gas-mask as the smell grew. I was nearly unnerved at my proximity to a nameless thing at the bottom of a pit.

Suddenly my spade struck something softer than earth. I

shuddered, and made a motion as if to climb out of the hole, which was now as deep as my neck. Then courage returned, and I scraped away more dirt in the light of the electric torch I had provided. The surface I uncovered was fishy and glassy – a kind of semi-putrid congealed jelly with suggestions of translucency. I scraped further, and saw that it had form. There was a rift where a part of the substance was folded over. The exposed area was huge and roughly cylindrical; like a mammoth soft blue-white stovepipe doubled in two, its largest part some two feet in diameter. Still more I scraped, and then abruptly I leaped out of the hole and away from the filthy thing; frantically unstopping and tilting the heavy carboys, and precipitating their corrosive contents one after another down that charnel gulf and upon the unthinkable abnormality whose titan *elbow* I had seen.

The blinding maelstrom of greenish-yellow vapour which surged tempestuously up from that hole as the floods of acid descended, will never leave my memory. All along the hill people tell of the yellow day, when virulent and horrible fumes arose from the factory waste dumped in the Providence River, but I know how mistaken they are as to the source. They tell, too, of the hideous roar which at the same time came from some disordered water-pipe or gas main underground – but again I could correct them if I dared. It was unspeakably shocking, and I do not see how I lived through it. I did faint after emptying the fourth carboy, which I had to handle after the fumes had begun to penetrate my mask; but when I recovered I saw that the hole was emitting no fresh vapours.

The two remaining carboys I emptied down without particular result, and after a time I felt it safe to shovel the earth back into the pit. It was twilight before I was done, but fear had gone out of the place. The dampness was less foetid, and all the strange fungi had withered to a kind of harmless greyish powder which blew ash-like along the floor. One of earth's nethermost terrors had perished forever; and if there be a hell, it had received at last the daemon soul of an unhallowed thing. And as I patted down the last spadeful of mould, I shed the first of the many tears with which I have paid unaffected tribute to my beloved uncle's memory.

The next spring no more pale grass and strange weeds came up in the shunned house's terraced garden, and shortly afterward Carrington Harris rented the place. It is still spectral, but its strangeness fascinates me, and I shall find mixed with my relief a queer regret when it is torn down to make way for a tawdry shop or vulgar apartment building. The barren old trees in the yard have begun to bear small, sweet apples, and last year the birds nested in their gnarled boughs.

THE SHUT ROOM (1930)

Henry S Whitehead (1882–1932)

Born in New Jersey, Whitehead was educated at Harvard where he was a classmate of future President Franklin D. Roosevelt. His career was in the Episcopal Church and he was archdeacon of the Virgin Islands in the 1920s before becoming rector of a church in Florida. A regular correspondent of HP Lovecraft, who much admired his work and collaborated with him on a story called 'The Trap', Whitehead published his fiction in Weird Tales *and other pulp magazines of the period. Many of his stories drew on his experiences of living in the West Indies and these ones remain his best-known writings. The most recent collection of his fiction, published in 2012, was entitled* Voodoo Tales. *Several of Whitehead's stories, including ones set in the West Indies, can be classified as occult detective fiction. In 'Black Tancrède', for instance, his regular narrator and obvious alter ego Gerald Canevin investigates the haunting of a hotel on the island of St. Thomas by the vengeful spirit of a black slave, cruelly punished for his role in a nineteenth-century uprising. In 'The Shut Room', we find Canevin in England where he joins forces with the nobleman Lord Carruth to look into a puzzling case which begins with the mysterious disappearances of boots and shoes from an old coaching inn on the Brighton road and ends in an encounter with a long-dead highwayman.*

It was Sunday morning and I was coming out of All Saints' Church, Margaret Street, along with other members of the hushed and reverent congregation when, near the entrance doors, a hand fell lightly on my shoulder. Turning, I perceived it was the Earl of Carruth. I nodded, without speaking, for there is that in the atmosphere of this great church, especially after one of its magnificent services and heart-searching sermons, which precludes anything like the hum of conversation which one meets with in many places of worship.

In these worldly and 'scientific' days, it is unusual to meet with a person of Lord Carruth's intellectual and scientific attainments who troubles very much about religion. As for me, Gerald Canevin, I have always been a church-going fellow.

Carruth accompanied me in silence through the entrance doors and out into Margaret Street. Then, linking his arm in mine, he guided me, still in silence, to where his Rolls-Royce car stood at the curbstone.

'Have you any luncheon engagement, Mr Canevin?' he inquired, when we were just beside the car, the footman holding the door open.

'None whatever,' I replied.

'Then do me the pleasure of lunching with me,' invited Carruth.

'I was planning on driving from church to your rooms,' he explained, as soon as we were seated and the car whirling us noiselessly toward his town house in Mayfair. 'A rather extraordinary matter has come up, and Sir John has asked me to look into it. Should you care to hear about it?'

'Delighted,' I acquiesced, and settled myself to listen.

To my surprise, Lord Carruth began reciting a portion of the Nicene Creed, to which, sung very beautifully by the All Saints' choir, we had recently been listening.

'Maker of Heaven and earth,' quoted Carruth musingly, 'and of all things – visible and *invisible*.' I started forward in my seat. He had given a peculiar emphasis to the last word, 'invisible'.

'A fact,' I ejaculated, 'constantly forgotten by the critics of religion! The Church has always recognised the existence of the invisible creation.'

'Right, Mr Canevin. And – this invisible creation; it doesn't mean merely angels?'

'No one who has lived in the West Indies can doubt that,' I replied.

'Nor in India,' countered Carruth. 'The fact – that the Creed attributes to God the authorship of an invisible creation – is an interesting commentary on the much-quoted remark of Hamlet to Horatio: "There are more things in Heaven and earth, Horatio, than are dreamed of in your philosophy." Apparently, Horatio's philosophy, like that of the present day, took little account of the spiritual side of affairs; left out God *and what He had made*. Perhaps Horatio had recited the creed a thousand times, and never realized what that clause implies!'

'I have thought of it often, myself,' said I. 'And now – I am all curiosity – what, please, is the application?'

'It is an occurrence in one of the old coaching inns,' began Carruth, 'on the Brighton Road; a very curious matter. It appears that the proprietor – a gentleman, by the way, Mr William Snow, purchased the inn for an investment just after the Armistice – has been having a rather unpleasant time of it. It has to do with shoes.'

'Shoes?' I inquired, 'shoes!' It seemed an abrupt transition from the Nicene Creed to shoes!

'Yes,' replied Carruth, 'and not only shoes but all sorts of leather affairs. In fact, the last and chief difficulty was about the disappearance of a commercial traveller's leather sample-case. But I perceive we are arriving home. We can continue the account at luncheon.'

During lunch he gave me a rather full account, with details, of what had happened at The Coach and Horses Inn on the Brighton Road, an account which I will briefly summarise as follows.

Snow, the proprietor, had bought the old inn partly for business reasons and partly for sentimental. It had been a portion, up to about a century before, of his family's landed property. He had repaired and enlarged it, modernised it in some ways, and in general restored a much run-down institution, making The Coach and Horses into a paying investment. He had retained, so far as possible, the antique architectural features of the old coaching inn, and before very long had built up a motor clientele of large proportions by sound and careful management.

Everything, in fact, had prospered with the gentleman-innkeeper's affairs until there began, some four months back, a series of unaccountable disappearances. The objects which had, as it were, vanished into thin air were all – and this seemed to me the most curious and bizarre feature of Carruth's recital – leather articles. Pair after pair of shoes or boots, left outside the bedroom doors at night, would be gone the next morning. Naturally the 'boots' was suspected of theft. But the 'boots' had been able to prove his innocence easily enough. He was, it seemed, a rather intelligent broken-down jockey, of a keen wit. He had assured Mr Snow of his surprise, as well as of his innocence, and suggested that he take a week's holiday to visit his aged mother in Kent and that a substitute 'boots', chosen by the proprietor, should take his place. Snow had acquiesced, and the disappearance of the guests' footwear had continued, to the consternation of the substitute, a total stranger, obtained from a London agency.

That exonerated Billings, the jockey, who came back to his duties at the end of his holiday with his character as an honest servant intact. Moreover, the disappearances had not been confined to boots and shoes. Pocket books, leather baggage, bags, cigarette cases – all sorts of leather articles went the way of the earlier boots and shoes, and beside the expense and annoyance of replacing these, Mr Snow began to be seriously concerned about the reputation of his house. An inn in which one's leather belongings are known to be unsafe would not be a very strong financial asset. The matter had come to a head through the disappearance of the commercial traveller's sample-case, as noted by Carruth in his first brief account of this mystery. The main difficulty in this affair was that the traveller had been a salesman of jewellery, and Snow had been confronted with the bill for several hundred pounds, which he had felt constrained to pay. After that he had laid the mysterious matter before Sir John Scott, head of Scotland Yard, and Scott had called in Carruth because he had recognised in Snow's story certain elements which caused him to believe that this was no case for mere criminal investigation.

After lunch Carruth ordered the car again, and, after stopping at my rooms for some additional clothing and other necessities for an over-night visit, we started along the Brighton road for the scene of the difficulty.

We arrived about four that Sunday afternoon, and immediately went into conference with the proprietor.

Mr William Snow was a youngish middle-aged gentleman, very well dressed, and obviously a person of intelligence and natural attainments. He gave us all the information possible, repeating, with many details, the matter which I have already summarised, while we listened in silence. When he had finished: 'I should like to ask some questions,' said Carruth.

'I am prepared to answer anything you wish to enquire about,' Mr Snow assured us.

'Well, then, about the sentimental element in your purchase of the inn, Mr Snow – tell us, if you please, what you may know of the most ancient history of this old hostelry. I have no doubt there is history connected with it, situated where it is. Undoubtedly, in the coaching days of the Four Georges, it must have been the scene of many notable gatherings.'

'You are right, Lord Carruth. As you know, it was a portion of the property of my family. All the old registers are intact, and are at your disposal. It is an inn of very ancient foundation. It was, indeed, old in those days of the Four Georges, to whom you refer. The records go back well into the sixteenth century, in fact; and there was an inn here even before registers were kept. They are of comparatively modern origin, you know. Your ancient landlord kept, I imagine, only his "reckoning"; he was not concerned with records; even licenses are comparatively modern, you know.'

The registers were produced, a set of bulky, dry-smelling, calf-bound volumes. There were eight of them. Carruth and I looked at each other with a mutual shrug.

'I suggest,' said I, after a slight pause, 'that perhaps you, Mr

Snow, may already be familiar with the contents of these. I should imagine it might require a week or two of pretty steady application even to go through them cursorily.'

Mr William Snow smiled. 'I was about to offer to mention the high points,' said he. 'I have made a careful study of these old volumes. And I can undoubtedly save you both a great deal of reading. The difficulty is – what shall I tell you? If only I knew what to put my finger upon – but I do not, you see!'

'Perhaps we can manage that,' threw in Carruth, 'but first, may we not have Billings in and question him?'

The former jockey, now the boots at The Coach and Horses, was summoned and proved to be a wizened, copper-faced individual, with a keen eye and a deferential manner. Carruth invited him to a seat and he sat, gingerly, on the very edge of a chair while we talked with him. I will make no attempt to reproduce his accent, which is quite beyond me. His account was somewhat as follows, omitting the questions asked him both by Carruth and myself.

'At first it was only boots and shoes. Then other things began to go. The things always disappeared at night. Nothing ever disappeared before midnight, because I've sat up and watched many's the time. Yes, we tried everything: even tying up leather things, traps! Yes, sir – steel traps baited with a boot! Twice we did that. Both times the boot was gone in the morning, the trap not even sprung! No, sir – no one possibly among the servants. Yet, an "inside" job; it couldn't possibly have been otherwise. From all over the house, yes. My old riding boots – two pairs – gone completely; not a trace; right out of my room. That was when I was down in Kent as Mr Snow's told you, gentlemen. The man who took my place slept in my room, left the door open one night – boots gone in the morning, right under his nose.

'Seen anything? Well, sir, in a manner, yes – in a manner, no! To be precise, no. I can't say I ever saw anything, that is, anybody; no, nor any apparatus as you might say, in a manner of speaking – no hooks, no strings, nothing used to take hold of the things – but –'

Here Billings hesitated, glanced at his employer, looked down at his feet, and his coppery face turned a shade redder.

'Gentlemen,' said he, as though coming to a resolution. 'I can only tell you God's truth about it. You may think me barmy – shouldn't blame you if you did! But I'm as much interested in this 'ere thing myself as Mr Snow 'imself, barring that I 'aven't had to pay the score – make up the value of the things I mean, as 'e 'as. I'll tell you, so 'elp me Gawd, gentlemen, it's a fact – I *'ave* seen something, absurd as it'll seem to you. I've seen –'

Billings hesitated once more, dropped his eyes, looked distressed, glanced at all of us in the most shamefaced, deprecating manner imaginable, twiddled his hands together, looked, in short, as though he were about to own up to it that he was, after all, responsible for the mysterious disappearances; then finally said, 'I've seen things disappear – through the air! Now – it's hout! But it's a fact, gentlemen all – so 'elp me, it's the truth. Through the air, just as if someone were carrying them away – someone invisible I mean, in a manner of speaking – bloomin' pair of boots, swingin' along through the bloomin' air – enough to make a man say 'is prayers, for a fact!'

It took considerable assuring on the part of Carruth and myself to convince the man Billings that neither of us regarded him as demented, or, as he pithily expressed it, 'barmy'. We assured him while our host sat looking at him with a slightly puzzled frown, that, on the contrary, we believed him implicitly, and furthermore we regarded his statement as distinctly helpful. Mr Snow, obviously convinced that something in his diminutive servitor's mental works was unhinged, almost demurred to our request that we go, forthwith, and examine the place in the hotel where Billings alleged his marvel to have occurred.

We were conducted up two flights of winding steps to the storey which had, in the inn's older days, plainly been an attic. There, Billings indicated, was the scene of the disappearance of the 'bloomin' boot swingin' along – unaccompanied through the bloomin' air'.

It was a sunny corridor, lighted by the spring sunlight through several quaint, old-fashioned, mullioned windows. Billings showed us where he had sat, on a stool in the corridor, watching; indicated the location of the boots, outside a doorway of one of the less expensive guest-rooms; traced for us the route taken by the disappearing boots.

This route led us around a corner of the corridor, a corner which, the honest 'boots' assured us, he had been 'too frightened' to negotiate on the dark night of the alleged marvel.

But we went around it, and there, in a small right-angled hallway, it became at once apparent to us that the boots on that occasion must have gone through one of two doorways, opposite each other at either side, or else vanished into thin air.

Mr Snow, in answer to our remarks on this subject, threw open the door at the right. It led to a small, but sunny and very comfortable-looking bed-chamber, shining with honest cleanliness and decorated tastefully with chintz curtains with valances, and containing several articles of pleasant, antique furniture. This room, as the repository of air-travelling boots, seemed unpromising. We looked in in silence.

'And what is on the other side of this short corridor?' I enquired.

'The "shut room",' replied Mr William Snow.

Carruth and I looked at each other.

'Explain, please,' said Carruth.

'It is merely a room which has been kept shut, except for an occasional cleaning,' replied our host readily, 'for more than a century. There was, as a matter of fact, a murder committed in it in the year 1818 and it was, thereafter, disused. When I purchased the inn, I kept it shut, partly, I dare say, for sentimental reasons; partly, perhaps, because it seemed to me a kind of asset for an ancient hostelry. It has been known as "the shut room" for over a hundred years. There was, otherwise, no reason why I should not have put the room in use. I am not in the least superstitious.'

'When was the room last opened?' I enquired.

'It was cleaned about ten days ago, I believe,' answered Mr Snow.

'May we examine it?' asked Carruth.

'Certainly,' agreed Snow, and forthwith sent Billings after the key.

'And may we hear the story – if you know the details – of the murder to which you referred?' Carruth asked.

'Certainly,' said Snow, again. 'But it is a long and rather complicated story. Perhaps it would be better during dinner.'

In this decision, we acquiesced, and, Billings returning with the key, Snow unlocked the door and we looked into 'the shut room'. It was quite empty, and the blinds were drawn down over two windows. Carruth raised these, letting in a flood of sunlight. The room was utterly characterless to all appearance, but – I confess to a certain 'sensitivity' in such matters – I 'felt' something like a faint, ominous chill. It was not, as the word I have used suggests, anything like physical cold. It was, so to express it, mentally cold. I despair of expressing what I mean more clearly. We looked over the entire room, an easy task as there was absolutely nothing to attract the eye. Both the windows were in the wall at our right hand as we entered, and, save for the entrance door through which we had just come, the other three walls were quite blank.

Carruth stepped half-way out through the doorway and looked at the width of the wall in which the door was set. It was, perhaps, ten inches thick. He came back into the room, measured with his glance the distance from the window-wall to the blank wall opposite the windows, again stepped outside, into the passageway this time, and along it until he came to the place where the short passage turned into the longer corridor from which we had entered it. He turned to his right this time, I following him curiously, that is, in the direction opposite that from which we had walked along the corridor, and tapped lightly on the wall there.

'About the same thickness, what?' he enquired of Snow.

'I believe so,' came the answer. 'We can easily measure it.'

'No, it will not be necessary, I think. We know that it is approximately the same.' Carruth ceased speaking and we followed him back into the room once more. He walked straight across it, rapped on the wall opposite the doorway.

'And how thick is this wall?' he enquired.

'It is impossible to say,' replied Snow, looking slightly mystified. 'You see, there are no rooms on that side, only the outer wall, and no window through which we could easily estimate the thickness. I suppose it is the same as the others, about ten inches I'd imagine.'

Carruth nodded, and led the way out into the hallway once more. Snow looked enquiringly at Carruth, then at me.

'It may as well be locked again,' offered Carruth, 'but – I'd be grateful if you'd allow me to keep the key until tomorrow.'

Snow handed him the key without comment, but a slight look of puzzlement was on his face as he did so. Carruth offered no comment, and I thought it wise to defer the question that was on my lips until later when we were alone. We started down the long corridor towards the staircase, Billings touching his forehead and stepping on ahead of us and disappearing rapidly down the stairs, doubtless to his interrupted duties in the scullery.

'It is time to think of which rooms you would prefer,' suggested our pleasant-voiced host as we neared the stairs. 'Suppose I show you some which are not occupied, and you may, of course, choose which suit you best.'

'On this floor, if you please,' said Carruth, positively.

'As you wish, of course,' agreed Snow, 'but, the better rooms are on the floor below. Would you not, perhaps, prefer –'

'Thank you, no,' answered Carruth. 'We shall prefer to be up here if we may, and – if convenient – a large room with two beds.'

'That can be managed very easily,' agreed Snow. He stepped a few paces along the corridor, and opened a door. A handsome, large room, very comfortably and well furnished, came to our view. Its excellence spoke well for the management of The Coach and Horses. The 'better' rooms must indeed be palatial if this were a fair sample of those somewhat less desirable.

'This will answer admirably,' said Carruth, directing an eyebrow at me. I nodded hastily. I was eager to acquiesce to anything he might have in mind.

'Then we shall call it settled,' remarked Snow. 'I will have your things brought up at once. Perhaps you would like to remain here now?'

'Thank you,' said Carruth. 'What time do we dine?'

'At seven, if you please, or later, if you prefer. I am having a private room for the three of us.'

'That will answer splendidly,' agreed Carruth, and I added a word of agreement. Mr Snow hurried off to attend to the sending up of our small luggage, and Carruth drew me at once into the room.

'I am more than a little anxious,' he began, 'to hear that tale of the murder. It is an extraordinary step forward – do you not agree with me? – that Billings's account of the disappearing boots – "through the air" – should fit so neatly and unexpectedly into their going around that corner of the corridor where "the shut room" is. It sets us forward, I imagine. What is your impression, Mr Canevin?'

'I agree with you heartily,' said I. 'The only point on which I am not clear is the matter of the thickness of the walls. Is there anything in that?'

'If you will allow me, I'll defer the explanation of that until we have had the account of the murder at dinner,' said Carruth, and, our things arriving at that moment, we set about preparing for dinner.

Dinner, in a small and beautifully furnished private room, did more, if anything more were needed, to convince me that Mr Snow's reputation as a successful modern inn-keeper had been well earned. It was a thoroughly delightful meal in all respects, but that, in a general way, is really all that I remember about it because my attention was wholly occupied in taking in every detail of the strange story which our host unfolded to us beginning with the fish course – I think it was fried sole – and which ended only when we were sipping the best coffee I had tasted in England since my arrival from our United States.

'In the year 1818,' said Mr Snow, 'near the end of the long reign of King George III – the king, you will remember, Mr Canevin, who gave you Americans your Fourth of July – this house was kept by one James Titmarsh. Titmarsh was a very old man. It was his boast that he had taken over the landlordship in the year that His Most Gracious Majesty, George III, had come to the throne, and that he would last as long as the king reigned! That was in the year 1760, and George III had been reigning for fifty-eight years. Old Titmarsh, you see, must have been somewhere in the neighbourhood of eighty, himself.

'Titmarsh was something of a "character". For some years the actual management of the inn had devolved upon his nephew, Oliver Titmarsh, who was middle-aged, and none too respectable, though, apparently, an able taverner. Old Titmarsh, if tradition is to be believed, had many a row with his deputy, but, being himself childless, he was more or less dependent on Oliver, who consorted with low company for choice, and did not bear the best of reputations in the community. Old Titmarsh's chief bugbear, in connection with Oliver, was the latter's friendship with Simon Forrester. Forrester lacked only a bard to be immortal. But – there was no Cowper to his John Gilpin, so to speak. No writer of the period, or indeed since, has chosen to set forth Forrester's exploits. Forrester was the very king-pin of the highwaymen, operating with extraordinary success and daring along the much-travelled Brighton Road.

'Probably Old Titmarsh was philosopher enough to ignore his nephew's associations and acts, as long as he attended to the business of the inn. The difficulty, in connection with Forrester, was that Forrester, an extraordinarily bold fellow, whose long immunity from the gallows had caused him to believe himself possessed of a kind of charmed life, constantly resorted to The Coach and Horses, which, partly because of its convenient location, and partly because of its good cheer, he made his house-of-call.

'During the evening of the first of June, in the year 1818, a Royal Courier paused at The Coach and Horses for some refreshment and a fresh mount. This gentleman carried one of the old king's peremptory messages to the Prince of Wales, then sojourning at Brighton, and who, under his sobriquet of "First Gentleman of Europe", was addicted to a life which sadly irked his royal parent at Whitehall. It was an open secret that only Prince George's importance to the realm as heir apparent to the throne prevented some very drastic action being taken against him for his innumerable follies and extravagances, on the part of king and parliament. This, you will recall, was two years before the old king died and "The First Gentleman" came to the throne as George IV.

'The Royal Messenger, Sir William Greaves, arriving about nine in the evening after a hard ride, went into the coffee room, to save the time which the engagement and preparation of a private room would involve, and when he paid his score, showed a purse full of broad gold pieces. He did not know that Simon Forrester, sitting behind him over a great mug of mulled port, took careful note of this unconscious display of wealth in ready money. Sir William delayed no longer than was necessary to eat a chop and drink a pot of "Six Ale". Then, his spurs clanking, he took his departure.

'He was barely out of the room, when Forrester, his wits, perhaps, affected by the potations which he had been imbibing, called for his own mount, Black Bess, and rose, slightly stumbling, to his feet, to speed the pot-boy on his way to the stables.

'"Ye'll not be harrying a Royal Messenger a-gad's sake, Simon," protested his companion, who was no less a person than Oliver Titmarsh, seizing his crony by his ruffled sleeve of laced satin.

'"Unhand me!" thundered Forrester; then, boastfully, "There's no power in England'll stay Sim Forrester when he chooses to take the road!"

'Somewhat unsteadily he strode to the door, and roared his commands to the stable-boy, who was not leading Black Bess rapidly enough to suit his drunken humour. Once in the saddle, the fumes of the wine he had drunk seemed to evaporate. Without a word Simon Forrester set out, sitting his good mare like a statue, in the wake of Sir William Greaves towards Brighton.

'The coffee-room – as Oliver Titmarsh turned back to it from the doorway whither he had accompanied Forrester – seethed into an uproar. Freed from the dominating presence of the truculent ruffian who would as soon slit a man's throat as look him in the eye along the sights of his horse-pistol behind the black mask, the numerous guests, silent before, had found their tongues. Oliver Titmarsh sought to drown out their clamour of protest, but before he could succeed, Old Titmarsh, attracted by the unwonted noise, had hobbled down the short flight of steps from his private cubbyhole and entered the room.

'It required only a moment, despite Oliver's frantic efforts to stem the tide of comment, before the old man had grasped the purport of what was toward. Oliver secured comparative silence, then urged his aged uncle to retire. The old man did so, muttering helplessly, internally cursing his age and feebleness which made it out of the question for him to regulate this scandal which had originated at his inn. A King's Messenger, then as now, was sacred in the eyes of all decent citizens. A King's Messenger – to be called on to "stand and deliver" by the villainous Forrester! It was too much. Muttering and grumbling, the old man left the room, but, instead of going back to his easy-chair and his pipe and glass, he stepped out through the kitchens, and, without so much as a lantern to light his path, groped his way to the stables.

'A few minutes later the sound of horse's hoofs in the cobbled stable-yard brought a pause in the clamour which had once more broken out and now raged in the coffee-room. Listening, those in the coffee-room heard the animal trot out through the gate, and the diminishing sound of its galloping as it took the road toward Brighton. Oliver Titmarsh rushed to the door, but the horse and its rider were already out of sight. He ran up to his ancient uncle's room, only to find the crafty old man apparently dozing in his chair. He hastened to the stables. One of the grooms was gone, and the best saddle-horse. From the others, duly warned by Old Titmarsh, he could elicit nothing. He returned to the coffee-room in a towering rage and forthwith cleared it, driving his guests out before him in a protesting herd.

'Then he sat down alone, a fresh bottle before him, to await developments.

'It was more than an hour later when he heard the distant beat of a galloping horse's hoofs through the quiet June night, and a few minutes later Simon Forrester rode into the stable-yard and cried out for an hostler for his Bess.

'He strode into the coffee-room a minute later, a smirk of satisfaction on his ugly, scarred face. Seeing his crony, Oliver, alone, he drew up a chair opposite to him, removed his coat, hung it over the back of his chair, and placed over its back where the coat hung the elaborate leather harness consisting of crossed straps and holsters which he always wore. From the holsters protruded the grips of "Jem and Jack", as Forrester humorously named his twin horse-pistols, huge weapons, splendidly kept, each of which threw an ounce ball. Then, drawing back the chair, he sprawled in it at his ease, fixing on Oliver Titmarsh an evil grin and bellowing loudly for wine.

'"For," he protested, "my throat is full of the dust of the road, Oliver, and, lad, there's enough to settle the score, never doubt me!" and out upon the table he cast the bulging purse which Sir William Greaves had momentarily displayed when he paid his score an hour and half back.

'Oliver Titmarsh, horrified at this evidence that his crony had actually dared to molest a King's Messenger, glanced hastily and fearfully about him, but the room, empty and silent save for their own presence, held no prying inimical informer. He began to urge upon Forrester the desirability of retiring. It was approaching eleven o'clock, and while the coffee-room was, fortunately, empty, no one knew who might enter from the road or come down from one of the guest-rooms at any moment. He shoved the bulging purse, heavy with its broad gold-pieces, across the table to his crony, beseeching him to pocket it, but Forrester, drunk with the pride of his exploit, which was unique among the depredations of the road's gentry, boasted loudly and tossed off glass after glass of the heavy port wine a trembling pot-boy had fetched him.

'Then Oliver's entreaties were supplemented from an unexpected source. Old Titmarsh, entering through a door in the rear wall of the room, came silently and leaned over the back of the ruffian's chair, and added a persuasive voice to his nephew's entreaties.

'"Best go up to bed now, Simon, my lad," croaked the old man, wheedlingly, patting the bulky shoulders of the hulking ruffian with his palsied old hands.

'Forrester, surprised, turned his head and goggled at the grey-beard. Then, with a great laugh, and tossing off a final bumper, he rose unsteadily to his feet, and thrust his arms into the sleeves of the fine coat which old Titmarsh, having detached from the back of the chair, held out to him

'"I'll go, I'll go, old Gaffer," he kept repeating, as he struggled into his coat, with mock jocularity, "seeing you're so careful of me! Gad's hooks! I might as well! There be no more purses to rook this night, it seems!"

'And with this, pocketing the purse, and taking over his arm the pistol-harness which the old man thrust at him, the villain lumbered up the stairs to his accustomed room.

'"Do thou go after him, Oliver," urged the old man. "I'll bide here and lock the doors. There'll likely be no further custom this night."

Oliver Titmarsh, sobered, perhaps, by his fears, followed Forrester up the stairs, and the old man, crouched in one of the chairs, waited and listened, his ancient ears cocked against a certain sound he was expecting to hear.

'It came within a quarter of an hour – the distant beat of the hoofs of horses, many horses. It was, indeed, as though a considerable company approached The Coach and Horses along the Brighton Road. Old Titmarsh smiled to himself and crept toward the inn doorway. He laboriously opened the great oaken door and peered into the night. The sound of many hoofbeats was now clearer, plainer.

'Then, abruptly, the hoofbeats died on the calm June air. Old Titmarsh, somewhat puzzled, listened, tremblingly. Then he smiled in his beard once more. Strategy, this! Someone with a head on his shoulders was in command of that troop! They had stopped, at some distance, lest the hoofbeats should alarm their quarry.

'A few minutes later the old man heard the muffled sound of careful footfalls, and, within another minute, a King's Officer had crept up beside him.

'"He's within," whispered old Titmarsh, "and well gone by now in his damned drunkard's slumber. Summon the troopers, sir. I'll lead to where the villain sleeps. He hath the purse of His Majesty's Messenger upon him. What need ye of better evidence?"

'"Nay," replied the train-band captain in a similar whisper, "that evidence, even, is not required. We have but now taken up the dead body of Sir William Greaves beside the high road, an ounce ball through his honest heart. 'Tis a case, this, of drawing and quartering, Titmarsh; thanks to your good offices in sending your boy for me."

'The troopers gradually assembled. When eight had arrived, the captain, preceded by old Titmarsh and followed in turn by his trusty eight, mounted the steps to where Forrester slept. It was, as you guessed, the empty room you examined this afternoon, "the shut room" of this house.

'At the foot of the upper stairs the captain addressed his men

in a whisper: "A desperate man, this, lads. 'Ware bullets! Yet –
he must needs be taken alive, for the assizes, and much credit to
them that take him. He hath been a pest of the road as well ye
know these many years agone. Upon him, then, ere he rises from
his drunken sleep! He hath partaken heavily. Pounce upon him
ere he rises."

'A mutter of acquiescence came from the troopers. They
tightened their belts, and stepped alertly, silently, after their
leader, preceded by their ancient guide carrying a pair of candles.

'Arrived at the door of the room the captain disposed his men
and crying out "in the King's name!" four of these stout fellows
threw themselves against the door. It gave at once under that
massed impact, and the men rushed into the room, dimly lighted
by old Titmarsh's candles.

'Forrester, his eyes blinking evilly in the candle-light, was
half-way out of bed when they got into the room. He slept, he
was accustomed to boast, "with one eye open, drunk or sober!"
Throwing off the coverlid, the highwayman leaped for the chair
over the back of which hung his fine laced coat, the holsters
uppermost. He plunged his hands into the holsters, and stood, for
an instant, the very picture of baffled amazement.

'The holsters were empty!

'Then, as four stalwart troopers flung themselves upon him to
bear him to the floor, there was heard old Titmarsh's harsh senile
cackle.

'"'Twas I that robbed ye, ye villain – took your pretty boys,
your "Jem" and your "Jack" out the holsters whiles ye were
strugglin' into your fine coat! Ye'll not abide in a decent house
beyond this night, I'm thinking; and 'twas the old man that did
for ye, murdering wretch that ye are!"

'A terrific struggled ensued. With or without his Pretty Boys
Simon Forrester was a thoroughly tough customer, versed in every
sleight of hand-to-hand fighting. He bit and kicked; he elbowed
and gouged. He succeeded in hurling one of the troopers bodily
against the blank wall, and the man sank there and lay still, a

motionless heap. After a terrific struggle, the other three who had cast themselves upon him, the remaining troopers and their captain standing aside because there was not room to get at him in the mêlée, he succeeded in getting the forefinger of one of the troopers, who had reached for a face-hold upon him, between his teeth, and bit through it at the joint.

'Frantic with pain and rage this trooper, disengaging himself, and before he could be stopped, seized a heavy oaken bench and, swinging it through the air, brought it down on Simon Forrester's skull. No human bones, even Forrester's, could sustain that murderous assault. The tough wood crunched through his skull, and thereafter he lay quiet. Simon Forrester would never be drawn and quartered, not even hanged. Simon Forrester, ignobly, as he had lived was dead; it remained for the troopers only to carry out the body and for their captain to indite his report.

'Thereafter the room was stripped and closed by Old Titmarsh himself, who lived on for two more years, making good his frequent boast that his reign over The Coach and Horses would equal that of King George III over his realm. The old king died in 1820, and Old Titmarsh did not long survive him. Oliver, now a changed man, because of this occurrence, succeeded to the lease of the inn, and during his landlordship the room remained closed. It has been closed, out of use, ever since.'

Mr Snow brought his story, and his truly excellent dinner, to a close simultaneously. It was I who broke the little silence which followed his concluding words.

'I congratulate you, sir, upon the excellence of your narrative gift. I hope that if I come to record this affair, as I have already done with respect to certain odd happenings which have come under my view, I shall be able, as nearly as possible, to reproduce your words.' I bowed to our host over my coffee cup.

'Excellent, excellent indeed!' added Carruth, nodding and smiling pleasantly in Mr Snow's direction. 'And now – for the questions, if you don't mind. There are several which have occurred to me; doubtless also to Mr Canevin.'

Snow acquiesced affably. 'Anything you care to ask, of course.'

'Well, then,' it was Carruth, to whom I had indicated precedence in the questioning, 'tell us, if you please, Mr Snow – you seem to have every particular at your very fingers' ends – the purse with the gold? That, I suppose was confiscated by the train-band captain and eventually found its way back to Sir William Greaves' heirs. That is the high probability, but – do you happen to know as a matter of fact?'

'The purse went back to Lady Greaves.'

'Ah! And Forrester's effects – I understand he used the room from time to time. Did he have anything, any personal property in it? If so, what became of it?'

'It was destroyed, burned. No one claimed his effects. Perhaps he had no relatives. Possibly no one dared to come forward. Everything in his possession was stolen, or, what is the same, the fruit of his thefts.'

'And – the pistols, "Jem and Jack"? Those names rather intrigued me. What disposition was made of them, if you happen to know? Old Titmarsh had them, of course, concealed somewhere, probably in that "cubby-hole" of his which you mentioned.'

'Ah,' said Mr Snow, rising, 'there I can really give you some evidence. The pistols are in my office – in the Chubbs' safe, along with the holster-apparatus, the harness which Forrester wore under his laced coat. I will bring them in.'

'Have you the connection, Mr Canevin?' Lord Carruth enquired of me as soon as Snow had left the dining-room.

'Yes,' said I, 'the connection is clear enough; clear as a pikestaff, to use one of your time-honoured British expressions, although I confess never to have seen a pikestaff in my life! But, apart from the fact that the holsters are made of leather; the well-known background of the unfulfilled desire persisting after death, and the obvious connection between the point of disappearance of those "walking boots" of Billings, with "the shut room", I must confess myself at a loss. The veriest tyro at this sort of thing

279

would connect these points, I imagine. There it is, laid out for us, directly before our mental eyes so to speak. But – what I fail to understand is not so much who takes them – that by a long stretch of the imagination might very well be the persistent "shade", "Ka", "projected embodiment" of Simon Forrester. No – what gets me is – *where does the carrier of boots and satchels and jewellers' sample-cases put them?* That room is utterly, absolutely, physically empty, and boots and shoes are material affairs, Lord Carruth.'

Carruth nodded gravely. 'You have put your finger on the main difficulty, Mr Canevin. I am not at all sure I can explain it, or even that we shall be able to solve the mystery after all. My experience in India does not help. But – there is one very vague case, right here in England, which may be a parallel one. I suspect, not to put too fine a point on the matter, that the abstracted things may very well be behind that rear-most wall, the wall opposite the doorway in "the shut room".'

'But,' I interjected, 'that is impossible, is it not? The wall is material – brick and stone and plaster. It is not subject to the strange laws of personality. How – ?'

The return of the gentleman-landlord of The Coach and Horses at this moment put an end to this conversation, but not to my wonder. I imagined that the 'case' alluded to by my companion would be that one of the tortured 'ghost' of the jester which, with a revenge-motive, haunted a room in an ancient house and even managed to equip the room itself with some of its revengeful properties or motives. The case had been recorded by Mr Hodgson, and later Carruth told me that this was the one he had in mind. This, it seemed to me, was a very different matter. However –

Mr Snow laid the elaborate and beautifully made 'harness' of leather straps out on the table beside the after-dinner coffee service. The grips of 'Jem and Jack' peeped out of their holsters. The device was not unlike those used by our own American desperadoes, men like the famous Earp brothers and 'Doc' Holliday whose 'six-guns' were carried handily in slung holsters in front of the body. We examined these antique weapons, murderous-looking pistols of the 'bulldog' type, built for business, and Carruth ascertained that neither 'Jem' nor 'Jack' was loaded.

'Is there anyone on that top floor?' enquired Carruth.

'No one save yourselves, excepting some of the servants, who are at the other end of the house,' returned Snow.

'I am going to request you to let us take these pistols and the "harness" upstairs when we retire,' said Carruth, and again the obliging Snow agreed. 'Everything I have is at your disposal, gentlemen,' said he, 'in the hope that you will be able to end this annoyance for me. It is too early in the season at present for the inn to have many guests. Do precisely as you wish, in all ways.'

Shortly after nine o'clock, we took leave of our pleasant host, and, carrying the 'harness' and pistols divided between us, we mounted to our commodious bed-chamber. A second bed had been moved into it, and the fire in the grate took off the slight chill of the spring evening. We began our preparations by carrying the high-powered electric torches we had obtained from Snow along the corridor and around the corner to 'the shut room'. We unlocked the door and ascertained that the two torches would be quite sufficient to work by. Then we closed but did not lock the door, and returned to our room.

Between us, we moved a solidly built oak table to a point diagonally across the corridor from our open bedroom door, and on this we placed the 'harness' and pistols. Then, well provided with smoke-materials, we sat down to wait in such positions that both of us could command the view of our trap. It was during the conversation which followed that Carruth informed me that the case to which he had alluded was the one recorded by the occult writer, Hodgson. It was familiar to both of us. I will not cite it. It may be read by anybody who has the curiosity to examine it; it is in the collection entitled *Carnacki the Ghost-Finder* by William Hope Hodgson. In that account it is the floor of the 'haunted' room which became adapted to the revenge-motive of the persistent 'shade' of the malignant court jester, tortured to death many years before his 'manifestation' by his fiendish lord and master.

We realised that, according to the man Billings's testimony, we need not be on the alert before midnight. Carruth therefore read from a small book which he had brought with him, and I busied myself in making the careful notes which I have consulted in recording Mr Snow's narrative of Simon Forrester, while that narrative was fresh in my memory. It was a quarter before midnight when I had finished. I took a turn about the room to refresh my somewhat cramped muscles, and returned to my comfortable chair.

Midnight struck from the French clock on our mantelpiece, and Carruth and I both, at that signal, began to give our entire attention to the articles on the table in the hallway out there.

It occurred to me that this joint watching, as intently as the circumstances seemed to warrant to both of us, might prove very wearing, and I suggested that we watch alternately, for about fifteen minutes each. We did so, I taking the first turn. Nothing occurred – not a sound, not the smallest indication that there might be anything untoward going on out there in the corridor.

At twelve-fifteen, Carruth began to watch the table, and it was, I should imagine, about five minutes later that his hand fell lightly on my arm, pressing it and arousing me to the keenest attention. I looked intently at the things on the table. The 'harness' was moving toward the left-hand edge of the table. We could both hear, now, the slight scraping sound made by the leather weighted by the twin pistols, and, even as we looked, the whole apparatus lifted itself – or so it appeared to us – from the supporting table, and began, as it were, to float through the air a distance of about four feet from the ground toward the turn which led to 'the shut room'.

We rose, simultaneously, for we had planned carefully on what we were to do, and followed. We were in time to see the articles 'float' around the corner, and increasing our pace – for we had been puzzled about how anything material, like the boots, could get through the locked door – watched, in the rather dim light of that short hallway, what would happen.

What happened was that the 'harness' and pistols reached the door, and then the door opened. They went through, and the door shut behind them, precisely as though someone, invisible to us, were carrying them. We heard distinctly the slight sound which a gently closed door makes as it comes to, and there we were, standing outside in the hallway looking at each other. It is one thing to figure out, beforehand, the science of occult occurrences, even upon the basis of such experience as Carruth and I possessed. It is, distinctly, another, to face the direct operation of something motivated by the Powers beyond the ken of ordinary humanity. I confess to certain 'cold chills', and Carruth's face was *very pale*.

We switched on our electric torches as we had arranged to do, and Carruth, with a firm hand which I admired if I did not, precisely, envy, reached out and turned the knob of the door. We walked into 'the shut room'...

Not all our joint experience had prepared us for what we saw. I could not forbear clutching Carruth's free arm, the one not engaged with the torch, as he stood beside me. And I testify that his arm was as still and firm as a rock. It steadied me to realise such fortitude, for the sight before us was enough to unnerve the most hardened investigator of the unearthly.

Directly in front of us, but facing the blank wall at the far end of the room, stood a half-materialised man. The gleam of my torch threw a faint shadow on the wall in front of him, the rays passing through him as though he were not there, and yet with a certain dimming. The shadow visibly increased in the few brief instants of our utter silence, and then we observed that the figure was struggling with something. Mechanically we concentrated both electric rays on the figure and then we saw clearly. A bulky man, with a bull-neck and close-cropped iron-grey hair, wearing a fine satin coat and what were called in their day, 'small cloths' or tight-fitting knee-trousers with silk stockings and heavy, buckled shoes, was raising and fitting about his waist, over the coat, the 'harness' with the pistols.

Abruptly, the materialisation appearing to be now complete,

he turned upon us, with an audible snarl and baleful, glaring little eyes like a pig's, deep set in a hideous, scarred face, and then he spoke – he spoke, and he had been dead for more than a century!

'Ah-h-h-h!' he snarled, evilly, 'you would come in upon me, eh! I'll teach ye manners…' and he ended this diatribe with a flood of the foulest language imaginable, stepping with little, almost mincing, down-toed steps toward us all the time he poured out his filthy curses and revilings. I was completely at a loss what to do. I realise – these ideas went through my mind with the rapidity of thought – that the pistols were unloaded! I told myself that this was some weird hallucination – that the shade of no dead-and-gone desperado could harm us. Yet – it was a truly terrifying experience, be the man shade or true flesh and blood.

Then Carruth spoke to him, in quiet persuasive tones.

'But – you have your pistols now, Simon Forrester. It was we who put them where you could find them, your pretty boys, "Jem and Jack". That was what you were trying to find, was it not? And now – you have them. There is nothing further for you to do – you have them, they are just under your hands where you can get at them whenever you wish.'

At this the spectre, or materialisation of Simon Forrester, blinked at us, a cunning light in his evil little eyes, and dropped his hands with which he had but now been gesticulating violently on the grips of the pistols. He grinned, evilly, spat in a strange fashion, over his shoulder.

'Ay' he said, more moderately now, 'ay – I have 'em – Jemmy and Jack, my trusties, my pretty boys.' He fondled the butts with his huge hands, hands that could have strangled an ox, and spat over his shoulder.

'There is no necessity for you to remain, then, is there?' said Carruth softly, persuasively.

The simulacrum of Simon Forrester frowned, looked a bit puzzled, then nodded its head several times.

'You can rest now – now that you have Jem and Jack,' suggested Carruth, almost in a whisper, and as he spoke, Forrester turned away and stepped over to the blank wall at the far side of the room, opposite the doorway, and I could hear Carruth draw in his breath softly and feel the iron grip of his fingers on my arm. 'Watch!' he whispered in my ear, 'watch now.'

The solid wall seemed to wave and buckle before Forrester, almost as though it were not a wall but a sheet of white cloth, held and waved by hands as cloth is waved in a theatre to simulate waves. More and more cloth-like the wall became, and, as we gazed at this strange sight, the simulacrum of Simon Forrester seemed to become less opaque, to melt and blend in with the wavering wall, which gradually ceased to move, and then he was gone and the wall was as it had been before…

On Monday morning, at Carruth's urgent solicitation, Snow assembled a force of labourers, and we watched while they broke down the wall of 'the shut room' opposite the doorway. At last, as Carruth had expected, a pick went through, and, the interested workmen, labouring with a will, broke through into a narrow, cell-like room the plaster of which indicated that it had been walled up perhaps two centuries before, or even earlier – a 'priest's hole' in all probability, of the early post-Reformation period near the end of the sixteenth century.

Carruth stopped the work as soon as it was plain what was here, and turned out the workmen, who went protestingly. Then, with only our host working beside us, and the door of the room locked on the inside, we continued the job. At last the aperture was large enough, and Carruth went through. We heard an exclamation from him, and then he began to hand out articles through the rough hole in the masonry – leather articles – boots innumerable, ladies' reticules, hand-luggage, the missing jeweller's sample case with its contents intact – innumerable other articles, and, last of all, the 'harness' with the pistols in the holsters.

Carruth explained the 'jester case' to Snow, who shook his head over it. 'It's quite beyond me, Lord Carruth,' said he, 'but, as you say this annoyance is at an end, I am quite satisfied; and – I'll take your advice and make sure by pulling down the whole room, breaking out the corridor walls, and joining it to the room across the way. I confess I cannot make head or tail of your explanation – the unfulfilled wish, the "materialisation", and the strange fact that this business only began a short time ago. But – I'll do exactly what you have recommended, about the room, that is. The restoration of the jeweller's case will undoubtedly enable me to get back the sum I paid to Messrs. Hopkins and Barth of Liverpool when it disappeared in my house. Can you give me any explanation of why the "shade" of Forrester remained quiet for a century and more and only started up the other day, so to speak?'

'It is because the power to materialise came very slowly,' answered Carruth, 'coupled as it undoubtedly was with the gradual breaking down of the room's material resistance. It is very difficult to realise the extraordinary force of an unfulfilled wish, on the part of a forceful, brutal, wholly selfish personality like Forrester's. It is, really, what we must call spiritual power, even though the "spirituality" was the reverse of what we commonly understand by that term. The wish and force of Forrester's persistent desire, through the century, have been working steadily, and, as you have told us, the room has been out of use for more than a century. There were no common, everyday affairs to counteract that malign influence – no "interruptions", if I make myself clear.'

'Thank you,' said Mr Snow. 'I do not clearly understand. These matters are outside my province. But – I am exceedingly grateful to you both.' Our host bowed courteously. 'Anything I can possibly do, in return –'

'There is nothing – nothing whatever,' said Carruth quietly; 'but, Mr Snow, there is another problem on your hands which perhaps you will have some difficulty in solving, and concerning which, to our regret –' – he looked gravely at me – 'I fear neither Mr Canevin with his experience, nor I with mine, will be able to assist you.'

'And what, pray, is that?' asked Mr Snow, turning slightly pale.

He would, I perceive, be very well satisfied to have his problems behind him.

'The problem is,' said Carruth, even more gravely I imagined, 'it is – what disposal are you to make of fifty-eight pairs of assorted boots and shoes?'

And Snow's relieved laughter was the last of the impressions which I took with me as we rode back to London in Carruth's car, of The Coach and Horses inn on the Brighton Road.

About Us

In addition to No Exit Press, Oldcastle Books has a number of other imprints, including Kamera Books, Creative Essentials, Pulp! The Classics, Pocket Essentials and High Stakes Publishing
> oldcastlebooks.co.uk

For more information about Crime Books > crimetime.co.uk

Check out the kamera film salon for independent, arthouse and world cinema > kamera.co.uk

For more information, media enquiries and review copies please contact marketing > marketing@oldcastlebooks.co.uk